Early Autumn

Early Autumn

Louis Bromfield

MINT EDITIONS

Early Autumn was first published in 1926.

This edition published by Mint Editions 2023.

ISBN 9781513210858 | E-ISBN 9781513209654

Published by Mint Editions®

MINT
EDITIONS
minteditionbooks.com

Publishing Director: Katie Connolly
Design: Ponderosa Pine Design
Production and Project Management: Micaela Clark
Typesetting: Westchester Publishing Services

Contents

Chapter I

I

THERE WAS A BALL IN the old Pentland house because for the first time in nearly forty years there was a young girl in the family to be introduced to the polite world of Boston and to the elect who had been asked to come on from New York and Philadelphia. So the old house was all bedizened with lanterns and bunches of late spring flowers, and in the bare, white-painted, dignified hallway a negro band, hidden discreetly by flowers, sat making noisy, obscene music.

Sybil Pentland was eighteen and lately returned from school in Paris, whither she had been sent against the advice of the conservative members of her own family, which, it might have been said, included in its connections most of Boston. Already her great-aunt, Mrs. Cassandra Struthers, a formidable woman, had gone through the list of eligible young men—the cousins and connections who were presentable and possessed of fortunes worthy of consideration by a family so solidly rich as the Pentlands. It was toward this end that the ball had been launched and the whole countryside invited, young and old, spry and infirm, middle-aged and dowdy—toward this end and with the idea of showing the world that the family had lost none of its prestige for all the lack of young people in its ranks. For this prestige had once been of national proportions, though now it had shrunk until the Pentland name was little known outside New England. Rather, it might have been said that the nation had run away from New England and the Pentland family, leaving it stranded and almost forgotten by the side of the path which marked an unruly, almost barbaric progress away from all that the Pentland family and the old house represented.

Sybil's grandfather had seen to it that there was plenty of champagne; and there were tables piled with salads and cold lobster and sandwiches and hot chicken in chafing-dishes. It was as if a family whose whole history had been marked by thrift and caution had suddenly cast to the winds all semblance of restraint in a heroic gesture toward splendor.

But in some way, the gesture seemed to be failing. The negro music sounded wild and spirited, but also indiscreet and out of place in a house so old and solemn. A few men and one or two women known for their fondness for drink consumed a great deal of champagne, but only dulness came of it, dulness and a kind of dead despair. The rich, the splendorous, the gorgeous, the barbaric, had no place in rooms where the kind Mr. Longfellow and the immortal Messrs. Emerson and Lowell had once sat and talked of life. In a hallway, beneath the gaze of a row of ancestors remarkable for the grimness of their faces, the music appeared to lose its quality of abandon; it did not belong in this genteel world. On the fringes of the party there was some drunkenness among the undergraduates imported from Cambridge, but there was very little gaiety. The champagne fell upon barren ground. The party drooped.

Though the affair was given primarily to place Sybil Pentland upon the matrimonial market of this compact world, it served, too, as an introduction for Thérèse Callendar, who had come to spend the summer at Brook Cottage across the stony meadows on the other side of the river from Pentlands; and as a reintroduction of her mother, a far more vivid and remarkable person. Durham and the countryside thereabouts was familiar enough to her, for she had been born there and passed her childhood within sight of the spire of the Durham town meeting house. And now, after an absence of twenty years, she had come back out of a world which her own people—the people of her childhood— considered strange and ungenteel. Her world was one filled with queer people, a world remote from the quiet old house at Pentlands and the great brownstone houses of Commonwealth Avenue and Beacon Street. Indeed, it was this woman, Sabine Callendar, who seemed to have stolen all the thunder at the ball; beside her, neither of the young girls, her own daughter nor Sybil Pentland, appeared to attract any great interest. It was Sabine whom everyone noticed, acquaintances of her childhood because they were devoured by curiosity concerning those missing twenty years, and strangers because she was the most picturesque and arresting figure at the ball.

It was not that she surrounded herself by adoring young men eager to dance with her. She was, after all, a woman of forty-six, and she had no tolerance for mooning boys whose conversation was limited to bootlegging and college clubs. It was a success of a singular sort, a triumph of indifference.

People like Aunt Cassie Struthers remembered her as a shy and awkward young girl with a plain face, a good figure and brick-red hair which twenty years ago had been spoken of as "Poor Sabine's ugly red hair." She was a girl in those days who suffered miserably at balls and dinners, who shrank from all social life and preferred solitude. And now, here she was—returned—a tall woman of forty-six, with the same splendid figure, the same long nose and green eyes set a trifle too near each other, but a woman so striking in appearance and the confidence of her bearing that she managed somehow to dim the success even of younger, prettier women and virtually to extinguish the embryonic young things in pink-and-white tulle. Moving about indolently from room to room, greeting the people who had known her as a girl, addressing here and there an acquaintance which she had made in the course of the queer, independent, nomadic life she had led since divorcing her husband, there was an arrogance in her very walk that frightened the young and produced in the older members of Durham community (all the cousins and connections and indefinable relatives), a sense of profound irritation. Once she had been one of them, and now she seemed completely independent of them all, a traitress who had flung to the winds all the little rules of life drilled into her by Aunt Cassie and other aunts and cousins in the days when she had been an awkward, homely little girl with shocking red hair. Once she had belonged to this tight little world, and now she had returned—a woman who should have been defeated and a little declassée and somehow, irritatingly, was not. Instead, she was a "figure" much sought after in the world, enveloped by the mysterious cloud of esteem which surrounds such persons—a woman, in short, who was able to pick her friends from the ranks of distinguished and even celebrated people. It was not only because this was true, but because people like Aunt Cassie *knew* it was true, that she aroused interest and even indignation. She had turned her back upon them all and no awful fate had overtaken her; instead, she had taken a firm hold upon life and made of it a fine, even a glittering, success; and this is a thing which is not easily forgiven.

As she moved through the big rooms—complete and perfect from her superbly done, burnished red hair to the tips of her silver slippers—there was about her an assurance and an air of confidence in her own perfection that bordered upon insolence. There was a hard radiance and beauty in the brilliant green dress and the thin chain of diamonds that dimmed all of the others, that made most of the women seem dowdy and put together with pins. Undoubtedly her presence also served to dampen the gaiety. One knew from the look in the disdainful green eyes and the faint mocking smile on the frankly painted red mouth that she was aware of the effect she made and was delighted with her triumph. Wherever she went, always escorted by some man she had chosen with the air of conferring a favor, a little stir preceded her. She was indeed very disagreeable. . .

If she had a rival in all the crowd that filled the echoing old house, it was Olivia Pentland—Sybil's mother—who moved about, alone most of the time, watching her guests, acutely conscious that the ball was not all it should have been. There was about her nothing flamboyant and arresting, nothing which glittered with the worldly hardness of the green dress and the diamonds and burnished red hair of Sabine Callendar; she was, rather, a soft woman, of gentleness and poise, whose dark beauty conquered in a slower, more subtle fashion. You did not notice her at once among all the guests; you became aware of her slowly, as if her presence had the effect of stealing over you with the vagueness of a perfume. Suddenly you marked her from among all the others. . . with a sense of faint excitement. . . a pale white face, framed by smooth black hair drawn back low over the brows in a small knot at the back of her head. You noticed the clear, frank blue eyes, that in some lights seemed almost black, and most of all you noticed when she spoke that her voice was low, warm, and in a way irresistible, a voice with a hundred shades of color. She had a way, too, of laughing, when she was struck by the absurdity of something, that was like a child. One knew her at once for a great lady. It was impossible to believe that she was nearly forty and the mother of Sybil and a boy of fifteen.

Circumstance and a wisdom of her own had made of her a woman who seemed inactive and self-effacing. She had a manner of doing things effortlessly, with a great quietness, and yet, after one came to know her, one felt that she missed little which took place within sight or hearing—not only the obvious things which any stupid person might have noticed, but the subtle, indefinite currents which passed from one person to another. She possessed, it seemed, a marvelous gift for smoothing out troubles. A security, of the sort which often marks those who suffer from a too great awareness, enveloped and preceded her, turning to calm all the troubled world about her. Yet she was disturbing, too, in an odd, indefinable way. There was always a remoteness and a mystery, a sense almost of the *fey*. It was only after one had known her for a long time, enveloped in the quietness of her pleasant presence, that a faint sense of uneasiness was born. It would occur to you, with the surprise almost of a shock, that the woman you saw before you, the woman who was so gentle and serene, was not Olivia Pentland at all, but a kind of lay figure which concealed, far beneath the veneer of charm, a woman you did not know at all, who was remote and sad and perhaps lonely. In the end, she disturbed the person of discernment far more profoundly than the glittering, disagreeable Sabine Callendar.

In the midst of the noise and confusion of the ball, she had been moving about, now in this big room, now in that one, talking quietly to her guests, watching them, seeing that all went well; and, like all the others, she was fascinated at the spectacle of Sabine's rebellion and triumph, perhaps even a little amused at the childishness of such defiance in a woman of forty-six who was clever, independent and even distinguished, who need not have troubled to flaunt her success.

Watching Sabine, whom she knew intimately enough, she had guessed that underneath the shell made so superbly by hairdresser, couturier and jeweler there lay hidden an awkward, red-haired little girl who was having her revenge now, walking roughshod over all the prejudices and traditions of such people as Aunt Cassie and John Pentland and Cousin Struthers Smallwood, D.D., whom Sabine always called "the Apostle to the Genteel." It was almost, thought Olivia, as if Sabine, even after an exile of twenty years, was still afraid of them and that curious, undefeatable power which they represented.

But Sabine, she knew, was observing the party at the same time. She had watched her all the evening in the act of "absorbing" it; she knew that when Sabine walked across from Brook Cottage the next day, she would know everything that had happened at the ball, for she had a passion for inspecting life. Beneath the stony mask of indifference there boiled a perpetual and passionate interest in the intricacies of human affairs. Sabine herself had once described it as "the curse of analysis which took all the zest out of life."

She was fond of Sabine as a creature unique in the realm of her experience, one who was amusing and actually made fetishes of truth and reality. She had a way of turning her intellect (for it was really a great intellect) upon some tangled, hopeless situation to dissolve it somehow into its proper elements and make it appear suddenly clear, uncomplicated and, more often than not, unpleasant; because the truth was not always a sweet and pleasant thing.

II

No one suffered more keenly from Sabine's triumphant return than the invincible Aunt Cassie. In a way, she had always looked upon

Sabine, even in the long years of her voluntary exile from the delights of Durham, as her own property, much as she might have looked upon a dog, if, indeed, the old lady had been able to bear the society of anything so untidy as a dog. Childless herself, she had exercised all her theories of upbringing upon the unfortunate orphaned little daughter of her husband's brother.

At the moment, the old lady sat halfway down the white stairs, her sharp black eyes surveying the ball with a faint air of disapproval. The noisy music made her nervous and uneasy, and the way young girls had of using paint and powder seemed to her cheap and common. "One might as well brush one's teeth at the dinnertable." Secretly, she kept comparing everything with the ball given for herself forty years earlier, an event which had resulted at length in the capture of Mr. Struthers. Dressed economically (for she made it a point of honor to live on the income of her income), and in mourning for a husband dead eight years earlier, she resembled a dignified but slightly uneasy crow perched on a fence.

It was Sabine who observed that Aunt Cassie and her "lady companion," Miss Peavey, sitting on the steps together, resembled a crow and a pouter pigeon. Miss Peavey was not only fat, she was actually bulbous—one of those women inclined by nature toward "flesh," who would have been fat on a diet of sawdust and distilled water; and she had come into the family life nearly thirty years earlier as a companion, a kind of slave, to divert Aunt Cassie during the long period of her invalidism. She had remained there ever since, taking the place of a husband who was dead and children who had never been born.

There was something childlike about Miss Peavey—some people said that she was not quite bright—but she suited Aunt Cassie to a T, for she was as submissive as a child and wholly dependent in a financial sense. Aunt Cassie even gave her enough to make up for the losses she incurred by keeping a small shop in Boston devoted to the sale of "artistic" pottery. Miss Peavey was a lady, and though penniless, was "well connected" in Boston. At sixty she had grown too heavy for her birdlike little feet and so took very little exercise. Tonight she was dressed in a very fancy gown covered with lace and sequins and passementerie, rather in the mode which someone had told her was her style in the far-off days of her girlhood. Her hair was streaked with gray and cut short in a shaggy, uneven fashion; not, however, because short hair was *chic*, but because she had cut it ten years before short hair had been heard of, in a sudden futile gesture of freedom at the terrible moment she made her one feeble attempt to escape Aunt Cassie and lead her own life. She had come back in the end, when her poor savings gave out and bankruptcy faced her, to be received by Aunt Cassie with dignified sighs and flutters as a returned and repentant prodigal. In this role she had lived ever since in a state of complete subjection. She was Aunt Cassie's creature now, to go where Aunt Cassie ordered, to do as she was bid, to be an earpiece when there was at hand no one more worthy of address.

At the sight of Sabine's green dress and red hair moving through the big hall below them, Aunt Cassie said, with a gleam in her eye: "Sabine seems to be worried about her daughter. The poor child doesn't seem to be having a success, but I suppose it's no wonder. The poor thing is very plain. I suppose she got the sallow skin from her father. He was part Greek and French. . . Sabine was never popular as a young girl herself."

And she fell to speculating for the hundredth time on the little-known circumstances of Sabine's unhappy marriage and divorce, turning the morsels over and over again with a variety of speculation and the interjection of much pious phraseology; for in Aunt Cassie's speech God seemed to have a hand in everything. He had a way of delivering trials and blessings indiscriminately, and so in the end became responsible for everything.

Indeed, she grew a bit spiteful about Sabine, for there was in the back of her mind the memory of an encounter, a day or two earlier, when she had been put completely to rout. It was seldom that Aunt Cassie met anyone who was a match for her, and when such an encounter took place the memory of it rankled until she found some means of subduing the offender. With Miss Peavey she was completely frank, for through long service this plump, elderly virgin had come to be a sort of confessor in whose presence Aunt Cassie wore no mask. She was always saying, "Don't mind Miss Peavey. She doesn't matter."

"I find Sabine extremely hard and worldly," she was saying. "I would never know her for the same modest young girl she was on leaving me." She sighed abysmally and continued, "But, then, we mustn't judge. I suppose the poor girl has had a great deal of misery. I pity her to the depths of my heart!"

In Aunt Cassie's speeches, in every phrase, there was always a certain mild theatrical overtone as if she sought constantly to cast a sort of melodramatic haze over all she said. Nothing was ever stated simply.

Everything from the sight of a pot of sour cream to the death of her husband affected her extravagantly, to the depths of her soul.

But this brought no response from Miss Peavey, who seemed lost in the excitement of watching the young people, her round candid eyes shining through her pince-nez with the eagerness of one who has spent her whole life as a "lady companion." At moments like this, Aunt Cassie felt that Miss Peavey was not quite bright, and sometimes said so.

Undiscouraged, she went on. "Olivia looks bad, too, tonight. . . very tired and worn. I don't like those circles under her eyes. . . I've thought for a long time that she was unhappy about something."

But Miss Peavey's volatile nature continued to lose itself completely in the spectacle of young girls who were so different from the girls of her day; and in the fascinating sight of Mr. Hoskins, a fat, sentimental, middle-aged neighbor who had taken a glass too much champagne and was talking archly to the patient Olivia. Miss Peavey had quite forgotten herself in the midst of so much gaiety. She did not even see the glances of Aunt Cassie in her direction—glances which plainly said, "Wait until I get you alone!"

For a long time Aunt Cassie had been brooding over what she called "Olivia's strange behavior." It was a thing which she had noticed for the first time a month or two earlier when Olivia, in the midst of one of Aunt Cassie's morning calls, had begun suddenly, quietly, to weep and had left the room without a word of explanation. It had gone from bad to worse lately; she felt Olivia slipping away from all control directly in opposition to her own benevolent advice. There was the matter of this very ball. Olivia had ignored her counsels of economy and thrift, and now Aunt Cassie was suffering, as if the champagne which flowed so freely were blood drawn from her own veins. Not for a century, since Savina Pentland purchased a parure of pearls and emeralds, had so much Pentland money been expended at one time on mere pleasure.

She disapproved, too, of the youthfulness of Olivia and of Sabine. Women of their ages ought not to look so fresh and young. There was something vulgar, even a little improper, in a woman like Sabine who at forty-six looked thirty-five. At thirty, Aunt Cassie herself had settled down as a middle-aged woman, and since then she had not changed greatly. At sixty-five, "childless and alone in the world" (save, of course, for Miss Peavey), she was much the same as she had been at thirty in the role of wife to the "trying Mr. Struthers." The only change had been her recovery from a state of semi-invalidism, a miracle occurring simultaneously with the passing of Mr. Struthers.

She had never quite forgiven Olivia for being an outsider who had come into the intricate web of life at Pentlands out of (of all places) Chicago. Wisps of mystery and a faint sense of the alien had clung to her ever since. Of course, it wasn't to be expected that Olivia could understand entirely what it meant to marry into a family whose history was so closely woven into that of the Massachusetts Bay Colony and the life of Boston. What could it mean to Olivia that Mr. Longfellow and Mr. Lowell and Dr. Holmes had often spent weeks at Pentlands? That Mr. Emerson himself had come there for weekends? Still (Aunt Cassie admitted to herself), Olivia had done remarkably well. She had been wise enough to watch and wait and not go ahead strewing her path with blunders.

Into the midst of these thoughts the figure of Olivia herself appeared, moving toward the stairway, walking beside Sabine. They were laughing over something, Sabine in the sly, mocking way she had, and Olivia mischievously, with a suspicious twinkle in her eyes. Aunt Cassie was filled with an awful feeling that they were sharing some joke about the people at the ball, perhaps even about herself and Miss Peavey. Since Sabine had returned, she felt that Olivia had grown even more strange and rebellious; nevertheless, she admitted to herself that there was a distinction about them both. She preferred the quiet distinction of Olivia to the violence of the impression made by the glittering Sabine. The old lady sensed the distinction, but, belonging to a generation which lived upon emotion rather than analysis, she did not get to the root of it. She did not see that one felt at once on seeing Olivia, "Here is a lady!"—perhaps, in the true sense of the word, the only lady in the room. There was a gentleness about her and a softness and a proud sort of poise—all qualities of which Aunt Cassie approved; it was the air of mystery which upset the old lady. One never knew quite what Olivia was thinking. She was so gentle and soft-spoken. Sometimes of late, when pressing Olivia too hotly, Aunt Cassie, aware of rousing something indefinably perilous in the nature of the younger woman, drew back in alarm.

Rising stiffly, the old lady groaned a little and, moving down the stairs, said, "I must go, Olivia dear," and, turning, "Miss Peavey will go with me."

Miss Peavey would have stayed, because she was enjoying herself, looking down on all those young people, but she had obeyed the commands of Aunt Cassie for too long, and now she rose, complaining faintly, and made ready to leave.

Olivia urged them to stay, and Sabine, looking at the old lady out of green eyes that held a faint glitter of hatred, said abruptly: "I always thought you stayed until the bitter end, Aunt Cassie."

A sigh answered her. . . a sigh filled with implications regarding Aunt Cassie's position as a lonely, ill, bereft, widowed creature for whom life was finished long ago. "I am not young any longer, Sabine," she said. "And I feel that the old ought to give way to the young. There comes a time. . ."

Sabine gave an unearthly chuckle. "Ah," she said, in her hard voice, "I haven't begun to give up yet. I am still good for years."

"You're not a child anymore, Sabine," the old lady said sharply.

"No, certainly I'm not a child anymore." And the remark silenced Aunt Cassie, for it struck home at the memory of that wretched scene in which she had been put to rout so skilfully.

There was a great bustle about getting the two old ladies under way, a great search for cloaks and scarfs and impedimenta; but at last they went off, Aunt Cassie saying over her thin, high shoulder, "Will you say goodbye to your dear father-in-law, Olivia? I suppose he's playing bridge with Mrs. Soames."

"Yes," replied Olivia from the terrace, "he's playing bridge with Mrs. Soames."

Aunt Cassie merely cleared her throat, forcibly, and with a deep significance. In her look, as in the sound of her voice, she managed to launch a flood of disapproval upon the behavior of old John Pentland and old Mrs. Soames.

Bidding the driver to go very slowly, she climbed into her shabby, antiquated motor, followed respectfully by Miss Peavey, and drove off down the long elm-bordered drive between the lines of waiting motors.

Olivia's "dear father-in-law" was Aunt Cassie's own brother, but she chose always to relate him to Olivia, as if in some way it bound Olivia more closely, more hopelessly, into the fabric of the family.

As the two younger women reentered the house, Olivia asked, "Where's Thérèse? I haven't seen her for more than an hour."

"She's gone home."

"Thérèse. . . gone home. . . from a ball given for her!"

Olivia halted in astonishment and stood leaning against the wall, looking so charming and lovely that Sabine thought, "It's a sin for a woman so beautiful to have such a life."

Aloud Sabine said, "I caught her stealing away. She walked across to the cottage. She said she hated it and was miserable and bored and would rather be in bed." Sabine shrugged her handsome shoulders and added, "So I let her go. What difference does it make?"

"None, I suppose."

"I never force her to do things of this sort. I had too much forcing when I was young; Thérèse is to do exactly as she likes and be independent. The trouble is, she's been spoilt by knowing older men and men who talk intelligently." She laughed and added, "I was wrong about coming back here. I'll never marry her off in this part of the world. The men are all afraid of her."

Olivia kept seeing the absurd figure of Sabine's daughter, small and dark, with large burning eyes and an air of sulky independence, striding off on foot through the dust of the lane that led back to Brook Cottage. She was so different from her own daughter, the quiet, well-mannered Sybil.

"I don't think she's properly impressed by Durham," said Olivia, with a sudden mischievous smile.

"No. . . she's bored by it."

Olivia paused to say goodnight to a little procession of guests. . . the Pingree girls dressed alike in pink tulle; the plump Miss Perkins, who had the finest collection of samplers in New England; Rodney Phillips, whose life was devoted to breeding springers and behaving like a perfect English gentleman; old Mr. Tilney, whose fortune rested on the mills of Durham and Lynn and Salem; and Bishop Smallwood, a cousin of the Pentlands and Sabine (whom Sabine called the Apostle of the Genteel). The Bishop complimented Olivia on the beauty of her daughter and coquetted heavily with Sabine. Motors rushed out from among the lilacs and syringas and bore them away one by one.

When they had gone Sabine said abruptly, "What sort of man is this Higgins. . . I mean your head stableman?"

"A good sort," replied Olivia. "The children are very fond of him. Why?"

"Oh. . . no reason at all. I happened to think of him tonight because I noticed him standing on the terrace just now looking in at the ball."

"He was a jockey once. . . a good one, I believe, until he got too heavy. He's been with us ten years. He's good and reliable and sometimes very funny. Old Mr. Pentland depends on him for everything. . . Only he has a way of getting into scrapes with the girls from the village. He seems irresistible to them. . . and he's an immoral scamp."

Sabine's face lighted up suddenly, as if she had made a great discovery. "I thought so," she observed, and wandered away abruptly to continue the business of "absorbing" the ball.

She had asked about Higgins because the man was stuck there in her brain, set in the midst of a strange, confused impression that disturbed a mind usually marked by precision and clarity. She did not understand why it was that he remained the most vivid of all the kaleidoscopic procession of the ball. He had been an outsider, a servant, looking in upon it, and yet there he was—a man whom she had never noticed before—vivid and clear-cut, dominating the whole evening.

It had happened a little earlier when, standing in the windowed alcove of the old red-paneled writingroom, she had turned her back for a moment on the ball, to look out upon the distant marshes and the sea, across meadows where every stone and tree and hedge was thrown into a brilliant relief by the clarity of the moonlight and the thin New England air. And trapped suddenly by the still and breathless beauty of the meadows and marshes and distant white dunes, lost in memories more than twenty years old, she had found herself thinking: "It was always like this. . . rather beautiful and hard and cold and a little barren, only I never saw it before. It's only now, when I've come back after twenty years, that I see my own country exactly as it is."

And then, standing there quite alone, she had become aware slowly that she was being watched by someone. There was a sudden movement among the lilacs that stood a little way off wrapped in thick black shadows. . . the faintest stirring of the leaves that drew her sharply back to a consciousness of where she was and why she was there; and, focusing all her attention, she was able to make out presently a short, stocky little figure, and a white face peering out from among the branches, watching the dancers who moved about inside the house. The sight produced in her suddenly a sensation of uneasiness and a faint prickling of the skin, which slipped away presently when she recognized the odd, prematurely wrinkled face of Higgins, the Pentland groom. She must have seen him a dozen times before, barely noticing him, but now she saw him with a kind of illuminating clarity, in a way which made his face and figure unforgettable.

He was clad in the eternal riding-breeches and a sleeveless cotton shirt that exposed the short, hairy, muscular arms. Standing there he

LOUIS BROMFIELD

seemed, with his arched, firmly planted legs, like some creature rooted into the soil. . . like the old apple-tree which stood in the moonlight showering the last of its white petals on the black lawn. There was something unpleasant in the sight, as if (she thought afterwards) she had been watched without knowing it by some animal of an uncanny intelligence.

And then abruptly he had slipped away again, shyly, among the branches of the lilacs. . . like a faun.

OLIVIA, LOOKING AFTER SABINE AS she walked away, smiled at the knowledge of where she was bound. Sabine would go into the old writingroom and there, sitting in a corner, would pretend that she was interested in the latest number of the *Mercure de France* or some fashion paper, and all the time she would be watching, listening, while old John Pentland and poor battered old Mrs. Soames sat playing bridge with a pair of contemporaries. Sabine, she knew, wanted to probe the lives of the two old people. She wasn't content like the others at Pentlands to go on pretending that there had never been anything between them. She wanted to get to the root of the story, to know the truth. It was the truth, always the truth, which fascinated Sabine.

And Olivia felt a sudden, swift, almost poignant wave of affection for the abrupt, grim woman, an affection which it was impossible to express because Sabine was too scornful of all sentiment and too shut in ever to receive gracefully a demonstration; yet she fancied that Sabine knew she was fond of her, in the same shy, silent way that old John Pentland knew she was fond of him. It was impossible for either of them ever to speak of such simple things as affection.

Since Sabine had come to Durham, it seemed to Olivia that life was a little less barren and not quite so hopeless. There was in Sabine a curious hard, solid strength which the others, save only the old man, lacked completely. Sabine had made some discovery in life that had set her free. . . of everything but that terrible barrier of false coldness.

In the midst of these thoughts came another procession of retreating guests, and the sadness, slipping away from Olivia's face, gave way to a perfect, artificial sort of gaiety. She smiled, she murmured, "Goodnight, must you go," and, "Goodnight, I'm so glad that you liked the ball." She was arch with silly old men and kind to the shy young ones and repeated the same phrases over and over again monotonously. People went away saying, "What a charming woman Olivia Pentland is!"

Yet immediately afterward she did not remember who had passed by her.

One by one the guests departed, and presently the black musicians packed up their instruments and went away, and at last Sybil appeared, shy and dark, looking a little pale and tired in her clinging gown of pale green. At sight of her daughter a little thrill of pride ran through Olivia. She was the loveliest of all the girls at the ball, not the most flamboyant, but the gentlest and really the most beautiful. She possessed the same slow beauty of her mother, which enveloped one in a kind of mist that lingered long after she herself had gone away. She was neither loud and mannish and vulgar like the "horsey" women nor common like the girls who used too much paint and tried to behave like women of the world. There was already about her the timelessness that envelops a lady no matter the generation in which she appears; there was a mystery, a sophistication and knowledge of life which put to rout all the cheap flashiness of the others. And yet, somehow, that same cool, shy poise and beauty frightened people. Boys who were used to calling young girls "Good old So-and-so" found themselves helpless before the dignity of a young girl who looked in her green gown a little like a cool wood-nymph. It troubled Olivia profoundly, not for herself, but because she wanted the girl to be happy—more than that, to know the depths of happiness which she herself had sensed but never found. It was in a way as if she saw herself again in Sybil, as if looking back now from the pinnacle of her own experience she could guide this younger self, standing on the brink of life, along paths less barren than those trod by her own feet. It was so necessary that Sybil should fall in love with a man who would make her happy. With most girls it would make little difference one way or another, so long as they had money; if they were unhappy or bored they would divorce their husbands and try again because that was the rule in their world. But with Sybil, marriage would be either an immense, incalculable happiness or a profound and hopeless tragedy.

She thought suddenly of what Sabine had said of Thérèse a little while before. "I was wrong about coming back here. I'll never marry her off in this part of the world."

It was true somehow of Sybil. The girl, in some mysterious fashion, knew what it was she wanted; and this was not a life which was safe and assured, running smoothly in a rigid groove fixed by tradition and circumstance. It was not marriage with a man who was like all the other men in his world. It went deeper than all that. She wanted somehow to get far down beneath the surface of that life all about her, deep down where there was a savor to all she did. It was a hunger which Olivia understood well enough.

The girl approached her mother and, slipping her arm about her waist, stood there, looking for all the world like Olivia's sister.

"Have you enjoyed it?" asked Olivia.

"Yes. . . It's been fun."

Olivia smiled. "But not too much?"

"No, not too much." Sybil laughed abruptly, as if some humorous memory had suddenly come to life.

"Thérèse ran away," said her mother.

"I know. . . she told me she was going to."

"She didn't like it."

"No. . . she thought the boys stupid."

"They're very much like all boys of their age. It's not an interesting time."

Sybil frowned a little. "Thérèse doesn't think so. She says all they have to talk about is their clubs and drinking. . . neither subject is of very much interest."

"They might have been, if you'd lived here always. . . like the other girls. You and Thérèse see it from the outside." The girl didn't answer, and Olivia asked: "You don't think I was wrong in sending you to France to school?"

Quickly Sybil looked up. "Oh, no. . . no," she said, and then added with smoldering eagerness, "I wouldn't have changed it for anything in the world."

"I thought you might enjoy life more if you saw a little more than one corner of it. . . I wanted you to be away from here for a little time." (She did not say what she thought—"because I wanted you to escape the blight that touches everything at Pentlands.")

"I'm glad," the girl replied. "I'm glad because it makes everything different. . . I can't explain it. . . Only as if everything had more meaning than it would have otherwise."

Suddenly Olivia kissed her daughter and said: "You're a clever girl; things aren't wasted on you. And now go along to bed. I'll stop in to say goodnight."

She watched the girl as she moved away through the big empty hall past the long procession of Pentland family portraits, thinking all the while that beside them Sybil seemed so fresh and full of warm eager life; and when at last she turned, she encountered her father-in-law and old Mrs. Soames moving along the narrow passage that led from the writingroom. It struck her sharply that the gaunt, handsome old John Pentland seemed really old tonight, in a way he had never been before, old and a little bent, with purplish circles under his bright black eyes.

Old Mrs. Soames, with her funny, intricate, dyed-black coiffure and rouged cheeks and sagging chin supported by a collar of pearls, leaned on his arm—the wreck of a handsome woman who had fallen back upon such silly, obvious tricks as rouge and dye—a vain, tragic old woman who never knew that she was a figure of fun. At sight of her, there rose in Olivia's mind a whole vista of memories—assembly after assembly with Mrs. Soames in stomacher and tiara standing in the reception line bowing and smirking over rites that had survived in a provincial fashion some darker, more barbaric, social age.

And the sight of the old man walking gently and slowly, out of deference to Mrs. Soames' infirmities, filled Olivia with a sudden desire to weep.

John Pentland said, "I'm going to drive over with Mrs. Soames, Olivia dear. You can leave the door open for me." And giving his daughter-in-law a quick look of affection he led Mrs. Soames away across the terrace to his motor.

It was only after they had gone that Olivia discovered Sabine standing in the corridor in her brilliant green dress watching the two old people from the shadow of one of the deep-set windows. For a moment, absorbed in the sight of John Pentland helping Mrs. Soames with a grim courtliness into the motor, neither of them spoke, but as the motor drove away down the long drive under the moon-silvered elms, Sabine sighed and said, "I can remember her as a great beauty. . . a really great beauty. There aren't anymore like her, who make their beauty a profession. I used to see her when I was a little girl. She was beautiful—like Diana in the hunting-field. They've been like that for. . . for how long. . . It must be forty years, I suppose."

"I don't know," said Olivia quietly. "They've been like that ever since I came to Pentlands." (And as she spoke she was overcome by a terrible feeling of sadness, of an abysmal futility. It had come to her more and more often of late, so often that at times it alarmed her lest she was growing morbid.)

Sabine was speaking again in her familiar, precise, metallic voice. "I wonder," she said, "if there has ever been anything. . ."

Olivia, divining the rest of the question, answered it quickly, interrupting the speech. "No. . . I'm sure there's never been anything more than we've seen. . . I know him well enough to know that."

For a long time Sabine remained thoughtful, and at last she said: "No. . . I suppose you're right. There couldn't have been anything. He's the last of the Puritans. . . The others don't count. They go on pretending, but they don't believe anymore. They've no vitality left. They're only hypocrites and shadows. . . He's the last of the royal line."

She picked up her silver cloak and, flinging it about her fine white shoulders, said abruptly: "It's almost morning. I must get some sleep. The time's coming when I have to think about such things. We're not as young as we once were, Olivia."

On the moonlit terrace she turned and asked: "Where was O'Hara? I didn't see him."

"No. . . he was asked. I think he didn't come on account of Anson and Aunt Cassie."

The only reply made by Sabine was a kind of scornful grunt. She turned away and entered her motor. The ball was over now and the last guest gone, and she had missed nothing—Aunt Cassie, nor old John Pentland, nor O'Hara's absence, nor even Higgins watching them all in the moonlight from the shadow of the lilacs.

The night had turned cold as the morning approached and Olivia, standing in the doorway, shivered a little as she watched Sabine enter her motor and drive away. Far across the meadows she saw the lights of John Pentland's motor racing along the lane on the way to the house of old Mrs. Soames; she watched them as they swept out of sight behind the birch thicket and reappeared once more beyond the turnpike, and as she turned away at last it occurred to her that the life at Pentlands had undergone some subtle change since the return of Sabine.

Chapter II

I t was Olivia's habit (and in some way every small action at Pentlands came inevitably to be a habit) to go about the house each night before climbing the paneled stairs, to see that all was in order, and by instinct she made the little tour as usual after Sabine had disappeared, stopping here and there to speak to the servants, bidding them to go to bed and clear away in the morning. On her way she found that the door of the drawing room, which had been open all the evening, was now, for some reason, closed.

It was a big square room belonging to the old part of the house that had been built by the Pentland who made a fortune out of equipping privateers and practising a sort of piracy upon British merchantmen—a room which in the passing of years had come to be a museum filled with the relics and souvenirs of a family which could trace its ancestry back three hundred years to a small dissenting shopkeeper who had stepped ashore on the bleak New England coast very soon after Miles Standish and Priscilla Alden. It was a room much used by all the family and had a worn, pleasant look that compensated for the monstrous and incongruous collection of pictures and furniture. There were two or three Sheraton and Heppelwhite chairs and a handsome old mahogany table, and there were a plush sofa and a vast rocking-chair of uncertain ancestry, and a hideous bronze lamp that had been the gift of Mr. Longfellow to old John Pentland's mother. There were two execrable water-colors—one of the Tiber and the Castle San Angelo and one of an Italian village—made by Miss Maria Pentland during a tour of Italy in 1846, and a stuffed chair with tassels, a gift from old Colonel Higginson, a frigid steel engraving of the Signing of the Declaration which hung over the white mantelpiece, and a complete set of Woodrow Wilson's History of the United States given by Senator Lodge (whom Aunt Cassie always referred to as "dear Mr. Lodge"). In this room were collected mementoes of long visits paid by Mr. Lowell and Mr. Emerson and General Curtis and other good New Englanders, all souvenirs which Olivia had left exactly as she found them when she came to the big house as the bride of Anson Pentland; and to those who knew the room and the family there was nothing unbeautiful or absurd about it. The effect was historical. On entering it one almost expected a guide to step forward and say, "Mr. Longfellow once wrote at this desk," and, "This was Senator Lodge's favorite chair." Olivia knew each tiny thing in the room with a sharp sense of intimacy.

She opened the door softly and found that the lights were still burning and, strangest of all, that her husband was sitting at the old desk surrounded by the musty books and yellowed letters and papers from which he was compiling laboriously a book known as "The Pentland Family and the Massachusetts Bay Colony." The sight of him surprised her, for it was his habit to retire punctually at eleven every night, even on such an occasion as this. He had disappeared hours earlier from the ball, and he still sat here in his dinner coat, though it was long after midnight.

She had entered the room so softly that he did not hear her and for a moment she remained silently looking down at him, as if undetermined whether to speak or to go quietly away. He sat with his back to her so that the sloping shoulders and the thin, ridged neck and partly bald head stood outlined against the white of the paneling. Suddenly, as if conscious of being watched, he turned and looked at her. He was a man of forty-nine who looked older, with a long horseface like Aunt Cassie's—a face that was handsome in a tired, yellow sort of way— and small, round eyes the color of pale-blue porcelain. At the sight of Olivia the face took on a pouting expression of sourness. . . a look which she knew well as one that he wore when he meant to complain of something.

"You are sitting up very late," she observed quietly, with a deliberate air of having noticed nothing unusual.

"I was waiting to speak to you. I want to talk with you. Please sit down for a moment."

There was an odd sense of strangeness in their manner toward each other, as if there had never been, even years before when the children were babies, any great intimacy between them. On his part there was, too, a sort of stiff and nervous formality, rather quaint and Victorian, and touched by an odd air of timidity. He was a man who would always do not perhaps the proper thing, but the thing accepted by his world as "proper."

It was the first time since morning that the conversation between them had emerged from the set pattern which it had followed day after day for so many years. When he said that he wanted to speak to her, it meant usually that there was some complaint to be made against the servants, more often than not against Higgins, whom he disliked with an odd, inexplicable intensity.

Olivia sat down, irritated that he should have chosen this hour when she was tired, to make some petty comment on the workings of the house. Half without thinking and half with a sudden warm knowledge that it would annoy him to see her smoking, she lighted a cigarette; and as she sat there, waiting until he had blotted with scrupulous care the page on which he had been writing, she became conscious slowly of a strange, unaccustomed desire to be disagreeable, to create in some way an excitement that would shatter for a moment the overwhelming sense of monotony and so relieve her nerves. She thought, "What has come over me? Am I one of those women who enjoys working up scenes?"

He rose from his chair and stood, very tall and thin, with drooping shoulders, looking down at her out of the pale eyes. "It's about Sybil," he said. "I understand that she goes riding every morning with this fellow O'Hara."

"That's true," replied Olivia quietly. "They go every morning before breakfast, before the rest of us are out."

He frowned and assumed almost mechanically a manner of severe dignity. "And you mean to say that you have known about it all along?"

"They meet down in the meadows by the old gravel-pit because he doesn't care to come up to the house."

"He knows, perhaps, that he wouldn't be welcome."

Olivia smiled a little ironically. "I'm sure that's the reason. That's why he didn't come tonight, though I asked him. You must know, Anson, that I don't feel as you do about him."

"No, I suppose not. You rarely do."

"There's no need to be unpleasant," she said quietly.

"You seem to know a great deal about it."

"Sybil tells me everything she does. It is much better to have it that way, I think."

Watching him, it gave her a faint, warm sense of satisfaction to see that Anson was annoyed by her calmness, and yet she was a little ashamed, too, for wanting the excitement of a small scene, just a tiny scene, to make life seem a little more exciting. He said, "But you know how Aunt Cassie and my father feel about O'Hara."

Then, for the first time, Olivia began to see light in the darkness. "Your father knows all about it, Anson. He has gone with them himself on the red mare, once or twice."

"Are you sure of that?"

"Why should I make up such a ridiculous lie? Besides, your father and I get on very well. You know that." It was a mild thrust which had its success, for Anson turned away angrily. She had really said to him, "Your father comes to *me* about everything, not to *you*. He is not the one who objects or I should have known." Aloud she said, "Besides, I have seen him with my own eyes."

"Then I will take it on my own responsibility. I don't like it and I want it stopped."

At this speech Olivia's brows arched ever so slightly with a look which might have been interpreted either as one of surprise or one of mockery or perhaps a little of both. For a moment she sat quite still, thinking, and at last she said, "Am I right in supposing that Aunt Cassie is at the bottom of this?" When he made no reply she continued, "Aunt Cassie must have gotten up very early to see them off." Again a silence, and the dark little devil in Olivia urged her to say, "Or perhaps she got her information from the servants. She often does, you know."

Slowly, while she was speaking, her husband's face had grown more and more sour. The very color of the skin seemed to have changed so that it appeared faintly green in the light from the Victorian luster just above his narrow head.

"Olivia, you have no right to speak of my aunt in that way."

"We needn't go into that. I think you know that what I said was the truth." And a slow warmth began to steal over her. She was getting beneath his skin. After all those long years, he was finding that she was not entirely gentle.

He was exasperated now and astonished. In a more gentle voice he said, "Olivia, I don't understand what has come over you lately."

She found herself thinking, wildly, "Perhaps he is going to soften. Perhaps there is still a chance of warmth in him. Perhaps even now, after so long, he is going to be pleasant and kind and perhaps. . . perhaps. . . more."

"You're very queer," he was saying. "I'm not the only one who finds you so."

"No," said Olivia, a little sadly. "Aunt Cassie does, too. She's been telling all the neighborhood that I seem to be unhappy. Perhaps it's because I'm a little tired. I've not had much rest for a long time now. . . from Jack, from Aunt Cassie, from your father. . . and. . . from *her*." At the last word she made a curious little half-gesture in the direction of the dark north wing of the big house.

She watched him, conscious that he was shocked and startled by her mentioning in a single breath so many things which they never discussed at Pentlands, things which they buried in silence and tried to destroy by pretending that they did not exist.

"We ought to speak of those things, sometimes," she continued sadly. "Sometimes when we are entirely alone with no one about to hear, when it doesn't make any difference. We can't pretend forever that they don't exist."

For a time he was silent, groping obviously, in a kind of desperation for something to answer. At last he said feebly, "And yet you sit up all night playing bridge with Sabine and old Mrs. Soames and Father."

"That does me good. You must admit that it is a change at least."

But he only answered, "I don't understand you," and began to pace up and down in agitation while she sat there waiting, actually waiting, for the thing to work itself up to a climax. She had a sudden feeling of victory, of intoxication such as she had not known in years, not since she was a young girl; and at the same time she wanted to laugh, wildly, hysterically, at the sight of Anson, so tall and thin, prancing up and down.

Opposite her he halted abruptly and said, "And I can see no good in inviting Mrs. Soames here so often."

She saw now that the tension, the excitement between them, was greater even than she had imagined, for Anson had spoken of Mrs. Soames and his father, a thing which in the family no one ever mentioned. He had done it quite openly, of his own free will.

"What harm can it do now? What difference can it make?" she asked. "It is the only pleasure left to the poor battered old thing, and one of the few left to your father."

Anson began to mutter in disgust. "It is a silly affair. . . two old. . . old. . ." He did not finish the sentence, for there was only one word that could have finished it and that was a word which no gentleman and certainly no Pentland ever used in referring to his own father.

"Perhaps," said Olivia, "it is a silly affair now. . . I'm not so sure that it always was."

"What do you mean by that? Do you mean. . ." Again he fumbled for words, groping to avoid using the words that clearly came into his mind. It was strange to see him brought face to face with realities, to see him grow so helpless and muddled. "Do you mean," he stammered, "that my father has ever behaved. . ." he choked and then added, "dishonorably."

"Anson. . . I feel strangely like being honest tonight. . . just for once. . . just for once."

"You are succeeding only in being perverse."

"No. . ." and she found herself smiling sadly, "unless you mean that in this house. . . in this room. . ." She made a gesture which swept within the circle of her white arm all that collection of Victorian souvenirs, all the mementoes of a once sturdy and powerful Puritan family, ". . . in this room to be truthful and honest is to be perverse."

He would have interrupted her here, angrily, but she raised her hand and continued, "No, Anson; I shall tell you honestly what I think. . . whether you want to hear it or not. I don't hope that it will do any good. . . I do not know whether, as you put it, your father has behaved dishonorably or not. I hope he has. . . I hope he was Mrs. Soames' lover in the days when love could have meant something to them. . . Yes. . . something fleshly is exactly what I mean. . . I think it would have been better. I think they might have been happy. . . really happy for a little time. . . not just living in a state of enchantment when one day is exactly like the next. . . I think your father, of all men, has deserved that happiness. . ." She sighed and added in a low voice, "There, now you know!"

For a long time he simply stood staring at the floor with the round, silly blue eyes which sometimes filled her with terror because they were so like the eyes of that old woman who never left the dark north wing and was known in the family simply as *she*, as if there was very little that was human left in her. At last he muttered through the drooping mustache, as if speaking to himself, "I can't imagine what has happened to you."

"Nothing," said Olivia. "Nothing. I am the same as I have always been, only tonight I have come to the end of saying 'yes, yes' to everything, of always pretending, so that all of us here may go on living undisturbed in our dream. . . believing always that we are superior to everyone else on the earth, that because we are rich we are powerful and righteous, that because. . . oh, there is no use in talking. . . I am just the same as I have always been, only tonight I have spoken out. We all live in a dream here. . . a dream that some day will turn sharply into a nightmare. And then what will we do? What will you do. . . and Aunt Cassie and all the rest?"

In her excitement her cheeks grew flushed and she stood up, very tall and beautiful, leaning against the mantelpiece; but her husband did not notice her. He appeared to be lost in deep thought, his face contorted with a kind of grim concentration.

"I know what has happened," he said presently. "It is Sabine. She should never have come back here. She was like that always. . . stirring up trouble. . . even as a little girl. She used to break up our games by saying: 'I won't play house. Who can be so foolish as to pretend muddy water is claret! It's a silly game.'"

"Do you mean that she is saying it again now. . . that it's a silly game to pretend muddy water is claret?"

He turned away without answering and began again to pace up and down over the enormous faded roses of the old Victorian carpet. "I don't know what you're driving at. All I know is that Sabine. . . Sabine. . . is an evil woman."

"Do you hate Sabine because she is a friend of mine?"

She had watched him for so many years disliking the people who were her friends, managing somehow to get rid of them, to keep her from seeing them, to force her into those endless dinners at the houses of the safe men he knew, the men who had gone to his college and belonged to his club, the men who would never do anything that was unexpected. And in the end she had always done as he wanted her to do. It was perhaps a manifestation of his resentment toward all those whom he could not understand and even (she thought) feared a little—the attitude of a man who will not allow others to enjoy what he could not take for himself. It was the first time she had ever spoken of this dog-in-the-manger game, but she found herself unable to keep silent. It was as if some power outside her had taken possession of her body. She had a strange sensation of shame at the very moment she spoke, of shame at the sound of her own voice, a little strained and hysterical.

There was something preposterous, too, in the sight of Anson prancing up and down the old room filled with all the souvenirs of that decayed respectability in which he wrapped himself. . . prancing up and down with all his prejudices and superstitions bristling. And now Olivia had dragged the truth uncomfortably into the light.

"What an absurd thing to say!" he said bitterly.

Olivia sighed. "No, I don't think so. . . I think you know exactly what I mean." (She knew the family game of pretending never to understand a truthful, unpleasant statement.)

But this, too, he refused to answer. Instead, he turned to her more savage and excited than she had ever seen him, so moved that he seemed for a second to attain a pale flash of power and dignity. "And I don't like that Fiji Islander of a daughter of hers, who has been dragged all over the world and had her head filled with barbaric ideas."

At the sight of him and the sound of his voice Olivia experienced a sudden blinding flash of intuition that illuminated the whole train of their conversation, indeed, the whole procession of the years she had spent here at Pentlands or in the huge brownstone house in Beacon Street. She knew suddenly what it was that frightened Anson and Aunt Cassie and all that intricate world of family. They were terrified lest the walls, the very foundations, of their existence be swept away leaving them helpless with all their little prides and vanities exposed, stripped of all the laws and prejudices which they had made to protect them. It was why they hated O'Hara, an Irishman and a Roman Catholic. He had menaced their security. To be exposed thus would be a calamity, for in any other world save their own, in a world where they stood unprotected by all that money laid away in solid trust funds, they would have no existence whatever. They would suddenly *be* what they *really* were.

She saw sharply, clearly, for the first time, and she said quietly, "I think you dislike Thérèse for reasons that are not fair to the girl. You distrust her because she is different from all the others. . . from the sort of girls that you were trained to believe perfect. Heaven knows there are enough of them about here. . . girls as like as peas in a pod."

"And what about this boy who is coming to stay with Sabine and her daughter. . . this American boy with a French name who has never seen his own country until now? I suppose he'll be as queer as all the others. Who knows anything about him?"

"Sabine," began Olivia.

"Sabine!" he interrupted. "Sabine! What does she care who he is or where he comes from? She's given up decent people long ago, when she went away from here and married that Levantine blackguard of a husband. Sabine! . . . Sabine would only like to bring trouble to us. . . the people to whom she belongs. She hates us. . . She can barely speak to me in a civil fashion."

Olivia smiled quietly and tossed her cigarette into the ashes beneath the cold steel engraving of the Signing. "You are beginning to talk nonsense, Anson. Let's stick to facts, for once. I've met the boy in Paris. . . Sybil knew him there. He is intelligent and handsome and treats women as if they were something more than stable boys. There are still a few of us left who like to be treated thus. . . as women. . . a few of us even here in Durham. No, I don't imagine you'll care for him.

He won't belong to your club or to your college, and he'll see life in a different way. He won't have had his opinions already made, waiting for him."

"It's my children I'm thinking of. . . I don't want them picking up with anyone, with the first person who comes along."

Olivia did not smile. She turned away now and said softly, "If it's Jack you're worrying about, you needn't fuss any longer. He won't marry Thérèse. I don't think you know how ill he is. . . I don't think, sometimes, that you really know anything about him at all."

"I always talk with the doctors."

"Then you ought to know that they're silly. . . the things you're saying."

"All the same, Sabine ought never to have come back here. . ."

She saw now that the talk was turning back into the inevitable channel of futility where they would go round and round, like squirrels in a cage, arriving nowhere. It had happened this way so many times. Turning with an air of putting an end to the discussion, she walked over to the fireplace. . . pale once more, with faint, mauve circles under her dark eyes. There was a fragility about her, as if this strange spirit which had flamed up so suddenly were too violent for the body.

"Anson," she said in a low voice, "please let's be sensible. I shall look into this affair of Sybil and O'Hara and try to discover whether there is anything serious going on. If necessary, I shall speak directly to both of them. I don't approve, either, but not for the same reason. He is too old for her. You won't have any trouble. You will have to do nothing. . . As to Sabine, I shall continue to see as much of her as I like."

In the midst of the speech she had grown suddenly, perilously, calm in the way which sometimes alarmed her husband and Aunt Cassie. Sighing a little, she continued, "I have been good and gentle, Anson, for years and years, and now, tonight. . . tonight I feel as if I were coming to the end of it. . . I only say this to let you know that it can't go on forever."

Picking up her scarf, she did not wait for him to answer her, but moved away toward the door, still enveloped in the same perilous calm. In the doorway she turned. "I suppose we can call the affair settled for the moment?"

He had been standing there all the while watching her out of the round cold blue eyes with a look of astonishment as if after all those years he had seen his wife for the first time; and then slowly the look of astonishment melted into one of slyness, almost of hatred, as if he thought, "So this is what you really are! So you have been thinking these things all these years and have never belonged to us at all. You have been hating us all the while. You have always been an outsider—a common, vulgar outsider."

His thin, discontented lips had turned faintly gray, and when he spoke it was nervously, with a kind of desperation, like a small animal trapped in a corner. The words came out from the thin lips in a sharp, quick torrent, like the rush of white-hot steel released from a cauldron. . . words spoken in a voice that was cold and shaken with hatred.

"In any case," he said, "in any case. . . I will not have my daughter marry a shanty Irishman. . . There is enough of that in the family."

For a moment Olivia leaned against the doorsill, her dark eyes wide with astonishment, as if she found it impossible to believe what she had heard. And then quietly, with a terrible sadness and serenity in her voice, she murmured almost to herself, "What a rotten thing to say!" And after a little pause, as if still speaking to herself, "So that is what you have been thinking for twenty years!" And again, "There is a terrible answer to that. . . It's so terrible that I shan't say it, but I think you. . . you and Aunt Cassie know well enough what it is."

Closing the door quickly, she left him there, startled and exasperated, among all the Pentland souvenirs, and slowly, in a kind of nightmare, she made her way toward the stairs, past the long procession of Pentland ancestors—the shopkeeping immigrant, the witch-burner, the professional evangelist, the owner of clipper ships, and the tragic, beautiful Savina Pentland—and up the darkened stairway to the room where her husband had not followed her in more than fifteen years.

ONCE IN HER OWN ROOM she closed the door softly and stood in the darkness, listening, listening, listening. . . There was at first no sound save the blurred distant roar of the surf eating its way into the white dunes and the far-off howling of a beagle somewhere in the direction of the kennels, and then, presently, there came to her the faint sound of soft, easy breathing from the adjoining room. It was regular, easy and quiet, almost as if her son had been as strong as O'Hara or Higgins or that vigorous young de Cyon whom she had met once for a little while at Sabine's house in Paris.

The sound filled her with a wild happiness, so that she forgot even what had happened in the drawing room a little while before. As she undressed in the darkness she stopped now and then to listen again in a kind of fierce tension, as if by wishing it she could keep the sound from ever dying away. For more than three years she had never once entered this room free from the terror that there might only be silence to welcome her. And at last, after she had gone to bed and was falling asleep, she was wakened sharply by another sound, quite different, the sound of a wild, almost human cry. . . savage and wicked, and followed by the thud thud of hoofs beating savagely against the walls of a stall, and then the voice of Higgins, the groom, cursing wickedly. She had heard it before—the sound of old John Pentland's evil, beautiful red mare kicking the walls of her stall and screaming wildly. There was an unearthly, implacable hatred between her and the little apelike man. . . and yet a sort of fascination, too.

As she sat up in her bed, listening, and still startled by the wild sound, she heard her son saying:

"Mama, are you there?"

"Yes."

She rose and went into the other room, where, in the dim light from the night-lamp, the boy was sitting up in bed, his pale blond hair all rumpled, his eyes wide open and staring a little.

"You're all right, Jack?" she whispered. "There's nothing the matter?"

"No—nothing. I had a bad dream and then I heard the red mare."

He looked pale and ill, with the blue veins showing on his temples; yet she knew that he was stronger than he had been for months. He was fifteen, and he looked younger than his age, rather like a boy of thirteen or fourteen, but he was old, too, in the timeless fashion of those who have always been ill.

"Is the party over? . . . Have they all gone?" he asked.

"Yes, Jack. . . It's almost daylight. You'd better try to sleep again."

He lay down without answering her, and as she bent to kiss him goodnight, she heard him say softly, "I wish I could have gone to the party."

"You will, Jack, some day—before very long. You're growing stronger everyday."

Again a silence, while Olivia thought bitterly, "He knows that I'm lying. He knows that what I've said is not the truth."

Aloud she said, "You'll go to sleep now—like a good boy."

"I wish you'd tell me about the party."

Olivia sighed. "Then I must close Nannie's door, so we won't waken her." And she closed the door leading to the room where the old nurse slept, and seating herself on the foot of her son's bed, she began a recital of who had been at the ball, and what had happened there, bit by bit, carefully and with all the skill she was able to summon. She wanted to give him, who had so little chance of living, all the sense of life she was able to evoke.

She talked on and on, until presently she noticed that the boy had fallen asleep and that the sky beyond the marshes had begun to turn gray and rose and yellow with the rising day.

Chapter III

I

WHEN OLIVIA FIRST CAME TO the old house as the wife of Anson Pentland, the village of Durham, which lay inland from Pentlands and the sea, had been invisible, lying concealed in a fold of the land which marked the faint beginnings of the New Hampshire mountains. There had been in the view a certain sleepy peacefulness: one knew that in the distant fold of land surmounted by a single white spire there lay a quiet village of white wooden houses built along a single street called High Street that was dappled in summer with the shadows of old elm-trees. In those days it had been a country village, half asleep, with empty shuttered houses here and there falling into slow decay—a village with fewer people in it than there had been a hundred years before. It had stayed thus sleeping for nearly seventy-five years, since the day when a great migration of citizens had robbed it of its sturdiest young people. In the thick grass that surrounded the old meeting house there lay a marble slab recording the event with an inscription which read:

> FROM THIS SPOT ON THE FOURTEENTH DAY OF AUGUST, EIGHTEEN HUNDRED AND EIGHTEEN, THE REVEREND JOSIAH MILFORD, PASTOR OF THIS CHURCH, WITH ONE HUNDRED AND NINETY MEMBERS OF HIS CONGREGATION—MEN, WOMEN AND CHILDREN—SET OUT, SECURE IN THEIR FAITH IN ALMIGHTY GOD, TO ESTABLISH HIS WILL AND POWER IN THE WILDERNESS OF THE WESTERN RESERVE.

Beneath the inscription were cut the names of those families who had made the journey to found a new town which had since surpassed sleepy Durham a hundred times in wealth and prosperity. There was no Pentland name among them, for the Pentlands had been rich even in the year eighteen hundred and eighteen, and lived in winter in Boston and in summer at Durham, on the land claimed from the wilderness by the first of the family.

From that day until the mills came to Durham the village sank slowly into a kind of lethargy, and the church itself, robbed of its strength, died presently and was changed into a dusty museum filled with homely early

American furniture and spinning-wheels—a place seldom visited by anyone and painted grudgingly every five years by the town council because it was popularly considered an historical monument. The Pentland family long ago had filtered away into the cold faith of the Unitarians or the more compromising and easy creeds of the Episcopal church.

But now, nearly twenty years after Olivia had come to Pentlands, the village was alive again, so alive that it had overflowed its little fold in the land and was streaming down the hill on the side next to the sea in straight, plain columns of ugly stucco bungalows, each filled with its little family of Polish millworkers. And in the town, across High Street from the white-spired old meeting house, there stood a new church, built of stucco and green-painted wood and dedicated to the great Church of Rome. In the old wooden houses along High Street there still lingered remnants of the old families. . . old Mrs. Featherstone, who did washing to support four sickly grandchildren who ought never to have been born; Miss Haddon, a queer old woman who wore a black cape and lived on a dole from old John Pentland as a remote cousin of the family; Harry Peckhan, the village carpenter; old Mrs. Malson, living alone in a damp, gaunt and beautiful old house filled with bits of jade and ivory brought back from China by her grandfather's clippers; Miss Murgatroyd, who had long since turned her bullfinch house into a shabby tearoom. They remained here and there, a few worn and shabby-genteel descendants of those first settlers who had come into the country with the Pentlands.

But the mills had changed everything, the mills which poured wealth into the pockets of a dozen rich families who lived in summer within a few miles of Durham.

Even the countryside itself had changed. There were no longer any of the old New Englanders in possession of the land. Sometimes in riding along the lanes one encountered a thin, silly-faced remnant of the race sitting on a stone wall chewing a bit of grass; but that was all: the others had been swallowed up long ago in the mills of Salem and Lynn or died away, from too much inbreeding and too little nourishment. The few farms that remained fell into the hands of Poles and Czechs, solid, square people who were a little pagan in their closeness to the earth and the animals which surrounded them, sturdy people, not too moral, who wrought wonders with the barren, stony earth of New England and stood behind their walls staring wide-eyed while the grand people like the Pentlands rode by in pink coats surrounded by the waving nervous tails of foxhounds. And, one by one, other old farms were being turned back into a wilderness once more so that there would be plenty of room for the horses and hounds to run after foxes and bags of aniseed.

It had all changed enormously. From the upper windows of the big Georgian brick house where the Pentlands lived, one could see the record of all the changes. The windows commanded a wide view of a landscape composed of grubby meadows and stone walls, thickets of pine and white birches, marshes, and a winding sluggish brown river. Sometimes in the late autumn the deer wandered down from the mountains of New Hampshire to spoil the fox hunting by leading the hounds astray after game that was far too fleet for them.

And nearer at hand, nestled within a turn of the river, lay the land where Sabine Callender had been born and had lived until she was a grown woman—the land which she had sold carelessly to O'Hara, an Irish politician and a Roman Catholic, come up from nowhere to take possession of it, to clip its hedges, repair its sagging walls, paint its old buildings and put up gates and fences that were too shiny and new. Indeed, he had done it so thoroughly and so well that the whole place had a little the air of a suburban real estate development. And now Sabine had returned to spend the summer in one of his houses and to be very friendly with him in the face of Aunt Cassie and Anson Pentland, and a score of others like them.

Olivia knew this wide and somberly beautiful landscape, every stick and stone of it, from the perilous gravel-pit, half-hidden by its fringe of elder-bushes, to the black pine copse where Higgins had discovered only a day or two before a new litter of foxes. She knew it on gray days when it was cold and depressing, on those bright, terribly clear New England days when every twig and leaf seemed outlined by light, and on those damp, cold days when a gray fog swept in across the marshes from the sea to envelop all the countryside in gray darkness. It was a hard, uncompromising, stony country that was never too cheerful.

It was a country, too, which gave her an old feeling of loneliness. . . a feeling which, strangely enough, seemed to increase rather than diminish as the years passed. She had never accustomed herself to its occasional dreariness. In the beginning, a long while ago, it had seemed to her green and peaceful and full of quiet, a place where she might find rest and peace. . . but she had come long since to see it as it was, as Sabine had seen it while she stood in the window of the writingroom, frightened by the sudden queer apparition of the little groom—a country beautiful, hard and cold, and a little barren.

II

THERE WERE TIMES WHEN THE memories of Olivia's youth seemed to sharpen suddenly and sweep in upon her, overwhelming all sense of the present, times when she wanted suddenly and fiercely to step back into that far-off past which had seemed then an unhappy thing; and these were the times when she felt most lonely, the times when she knew how completely, with the passing of years, she had drawn into herself; it was a process of protection like a tortoise drawing in its head. And all the while, in spite of the smiles and the politeness and the too facile amiability, she felt that she was really a stranger at Pentlands, that there were certain walls and barriers which she could never break down, past which she could never penetrate, certain faiths in which it was impossible for her to believe.

It was difficult now for her to remember very clearly what had happened before she came to Durham; it all seemed lost, confused, buried beneath the weight of her devotion to the vast family monument of the Pentlands. She had forgotten the names of people and places and confused the days and the years. At times it was difficult for her to remember the endless confusing voyages back and forth across the Atlantic and the vast, impersonal, vacuous hotels which had followed each other in the bleak and unreal procession of her childhood.

She could remember with a certain pitiful clarity two happy years spent at the school in Saint-Cloud, where for months at a time she had lived in a single room which she might call her own, where she had rested, free from the terror of hearing her mother say, "We must pack today. We are leaving tomorrow for St. Petersburg or London or San Remo or Cairo. . ."

She could scarcely remember at all the immense house of chocolate-colored stone fitted with fantastic turrets and balconies that overlooked Lake Michigan. It had been sold and torn down long ago, destroyed like all else that belonged to the far-off past. She could not remember the father who had died when she was three; but of him there remained at least a yellowing photograph of a great, handsome, brawny man with a humorous Scotch-Irish face, who had died at the moment when his name was coming to be known everywhere as a power in Washington.

No, nothing remained of him save the old photograph, and the tenuous, mocking little smile which had come down to her, the way she had of saying, "Yes! Yes!" pleasantly when she meant to act in quite the contrary fashion.

There were times when the memory of her own mother became vague and fantastic, as if she had been no more than a figure out of some absurd photograph of the early nineteen hundreds. . . the figure of a pretty woman, dressed fashionably in clothes that flowed away in both directions, from a wasp waist. It was like a figure out of one of those old photographs which one views with a kind of melancholy amusement. She remembered a vain, rather selfish and pretty woman, fond of flattery, who had been shrewd enough never to marry anyone of those gallant dark gentlemen with high-sounding titles who came to call at the eternal changeless hotel sittingroom, to take her out to garden parties and fêtes and races. And always in the background of the memory there was the figure of a dark little girl, overflowing with spirits and a hunger for friends, who was left behind to amuse herself by walking out with the Swiss governess, to make friends among the children she encountered in the parks or on the beaches and the boulevards of whatever European city her mother was visiting at the moment. . . friends whom she saw today and who were vanished tomorrow never to be seen again. Her mother, she saw now, belonged to the America of the nineties. She saw her now less as a real person than a character out of a novel by Mrs. Wharton.

But she had never remarried; she had remained the rich, pretty Mrs. McConnel of Chicago until that tragic day (the clearest of all Olivia's memories and the most terrible) when she had died of fever abruptly in a remote and squalid Italian village, with only her daughter (a girl of seventeen), a quack doctor and the Russian driver of her motor to care for her.

The procession of confused and not-too-cheerful memories came to a climax in a gloomy, red brick house off Washington Square, where she had gone as an orphan to live with a rigid, bejetted, maternal aunt who had believed that the whole world revolved about Lenox, the Hudson River Valley and Washington Square—an aunt who had never spoken to Olivia's father because she, like Anson and Aunt Cassie, had a prejudice against Irishmen who appeared out of nowhere, engaging, full of life and high spirits.

So at eighteen she had found herself alone in the world save for one bejetted aunt, with no friends save those she had picked up as a child on beaches and promenades, whose names she could no longer even remember. And the only fixed world she knew was the world of the aunt who talked incessantly of the plush, camphor-smelling splendor of a New York which no longer existed.

Olivia saw it all clearly now. She saw why it was that when Anson Pentland came one night to call upon her aunt she had thought him an elegant and fascinating man whose presence at dinner had the power of transforming the solid walnut and mahogany diningroom into a brilliant place. He was what girls called "an older man," and he had flattered her by his politeness and attentions. He had even taken her chaperoned by the aunt, to see a performance of "The City," little knowing that the indecorousness to be unfolded there would force them to leave before the play was over. They had gone on a Thursday evening (she could even remember the very day) and she still smiled at the memory of their belief that a girl who had spent all her life in the corridors of European hotels should not know what the play was about.

And then it had all ended by her being asked to Pentlands for a visit. . . to Pentlands, where she had come upon a world such as she had never known before, a world green and peaceful and secure, where everyone was elaborately kind to her for reasons that she never learned until long afterward. They never even told her the truth about Anson's mother, the old woman who lived in solitude in the north wing. She was, they said, too ill at the moment to see anyone. Pentlands, in that far-off day, had seemed to the tired, friendless girl like some vast, soft green bed where she could fling herself down and rest forever, a world where she could make friends and send down roots that would hold her secure for all time. To a hotel child Pentlands was a paradise; so when Anson Pentland asked her to marry him, she accepted him because she did not find him actually repulsive.

And now, after all those years, it was spring again. . . spring as when she had come to Pentlands for the first time, and she was thirty-nine years old and still young; only everything had changed.

BIT BY BIT, IN THE years that followed the birth of Sybil and then of Jack, the whole picture of the life at Pentlands and in the brownstone house on Beacon Street had come to assume a pattern, to take form out of the first confused and misty impressions, so that, looking back upon it, she was beginning to understand it all with the chill clarity of disillusion.

She saw herself as a shy young girl to whom they had all been elaborately kind because it was so necessary for Anson to have a wife and produce an heir. . . Anson, the last male descendant of such a glorious family. ("The Pentland Family and the Massachusetts Bay Colony.") She saw herself as they must have seen her. . . a pretty young girl, disarmed by their kindness, who was not known in their world but was at least charming and a lady and quite rich. (She knew now how much the money must have counted with Aunt Cassie.) And she saw Anson now, across all the expanse of years, not as a Prince Charming come to rescue her from an ogre aunt, but as he had really been. . . a rather anemic man, past thirty, of an appalling propriety. (There was a bitter humor in the memories of his timid advances toward her, of all the distaste with which he approached the details of marriage. . . a humor which she had come to understand fully only as she grew older and wiser in the ways of the world.) Looking back, she saw him as a man who had tried again and again to marry young women he had known all his life and who had failed because somehow he had gained a mysterious reputation for being a bore. . . a young man who, left to himself, would never have approached any woman, and gone to the grave as virginal as he had been born.

She saw now that he had never been even in the slightest in love with her. He had married her only because he got no peace from all the others, both the living and the dead, who in such a strange fashion seemed also to live at Pentlands. It was Aunt Cassie and even poor silly Miss Peavey and powerful old John Pentland and the cousins and all those dead hanging in neat rows in the hall who had married her. Anson had only been an instrument; and even in the most bitter moments she felt strangely sorry for him, because he, too, had had all his life ruined.

And so, slowly during all those long years, the pretty, shy, unknown Olivia McConnel, whose father was a Democratic politician out of Chicago, had turned into this puzzled, sometimes unhappy woman, the outsider, who had come in some mysterious fashion to be the one upon whom all of them leaned for strength.

She was glad now that she had stood forth boldly at last and faced Anson and all those who stood behind him there in the drawing room, both the living and the dead, peering over his shoulder, urging him on. The unpleasant argument, though it had wounded her, had cleared the air a little. It had laid bare for a second the reality which she had been seeking for so long a time. Anson had been right about Sabine: in the clear bright air of the New England morning she knew that it was the sense of Sabine's nearness which had given her the strength to be unpleasant. Sabine, like herself, had known the great world, and so she was able to see their world here in Durham with a clarity that the others never approached. She was strong, too, in her knowledge that whatever happened she (Olivia) was the one person whom they could not afford to lose, because they had depended on her for too long.

But she was hurt. She kept thinking again and again of what Anson had said. . . *"In any case, I will not have my daughter marry a shanty Irishman. There is enough of that in the family."*

She knew that Anson would suffer from shame for what he had said, but she knew, too, that he would pretend nothing had happened, that he had never made such a speech, because it was unworthy of a gentleman and a Pentland. He would pretend, as he always did, that the scene had never occurred.

When he had made the speech he had meant that she ought to have been thankful that they allowed her to marry into the Pentland family. There was a buried something in them all, a conviction that was a part of their very flesh, which made them believe in such a privilege. And for her who knew so much more than the world knew, who saw so much more than any of them of the truth, there was only one answer, to be wrung from her with a tragic intensity. . . "Oh, my God! . . ."

III

THE DININGROOM WAS LARGE AND square, and having been redecorated in a period later than the rest of the house, was done in heavy mahogany, with a vast shiny table in the center which when reduced to its smallest possible circumference still left those who seated themselves about it formally remote from one another.

It was a well-used table, for since circumstance had kept John Pentland from going into the world, he had brought a part of it into his own home with a hospitality and a warmth that rather upset his sister Cassie. She, herself, like most of the family, had never cared very profoundly for food, looking upon it almost as a necessity. A prune to her palate shared importance as a delicacy with a truffle. In the secrecy of her own house, moved by her passion for economy, she more often than not assuaged her own birdlike appetite with scraps from the cupboard, though at such times the simple but full-blooded Miss Peavey suffered keenly. "A pick-up meal" was a byword with Aunt Cassie, and so she frowned upon the rich food furnished by old John Pentland and his daughter-in-law, Olivia.

Nevertheless, she took a great many meals at the mahogany table and even managed to insinuate within its circle the plump figure of Miss Peavey, whose silly laugh and servile echoes of his sister's opinions the old man detested.

Anson never lunched at home, for he went up to Boston each morning at nine o'clock, like a man of affairs, with much business to care for. He kept an office in Water Street and went to it with a passionate regularity, to spend the day in the petty affairs of club committees and societies for the improvement of this or that; for he was a man who fortified his own soul by arranging the lives of others. He was chairman of a committee which "aired" young girls who had fallen into trouble, and contributed as much as he was able out of his own rather slender income to the activities of the Watch and Ward Society. And a large part of the day was spent in correspondence with genealogists on the subject of "The Pentland Family and the Massachusetts Bay Colony." He did not in a whole year earn enough money to pay the office rent for one month, but he had no patience with the many cases of poverty and destitution which came to his notice. The stocks and bonds of the Pentland estate had been kept carefully out of his reach, by a father who distrusted activities such as Anson's, and even now, when he was nearly fifty. Anson had only a small income left by his grandfather and an allowance, paid him each month by his father, as if he were still a boy in college.

So when Olivia came down to lunch on the day after the ball she was not forced to face Anson and his shame over the scene of the night before. There were only the grandfather and Sybil and Jack—who was well enough to come down.

The old man sat at the head, in the place which he had never relinquished as the dictator, the ruler of all the family. Tall and muscular, he had grown leathery from exposure during the years he had lived in the country, riding day after day in rains and blizzards, in sunlight and in storms, as if there were in him some atavistic hunger for the hardy life led by the first Pentlands to come to Durham. He always rode the vicious and unruly beautiful red mare. . . a grim old man who was a match for her famous bad temper. He was rather like his sister Cassie in appearance—one of the black Pentlands who had appeared mysteriously in the line nearly a hundred years earlier, and he had burning black eyes that looked out from shaggy brows. . . a man as different in appearance and vigor from his son as it was possible to imagine. (For Anson was a typical Pentland—blond, with round blue eyes and an inclination when in health toward ruddiness.) One stood in awe of the old man: there was a grimness about the strong, rough-cut face and contracted lips, and a curious, indefinable air of disapproval which one was never able to pin down or analyze.

He was silent today, in one of the black moods which Olivia knew well meant that he was troubled. She knew that this time it had nothing to do with Jack's illness, for the boy sat there opposite them, looking stronger than he had looked in months. . . blond and pale and thin, with the blue veins showing at his pathetic wrists and on his thin, handsome temples.

Olivia had lived through bad times over Jack and she had lived through them always together with John Pentland, so there had grown up between them—the mother and the grandfather—a sense of understanding which was quite beyond speech. Together they had spent so many nights by the side of the boy, keeping him alive almost by the strength of their united wills, forcing him to live when, gasping for life, he would have slipped away easily into death. Together they had kept him in life, because they both loved him and because he was the last son of the family.

Olivia felt sometimes that Sybil, too, played a part in the never-ending struggle against death. The girl, like her grandfather, never spoke of such things, but one could read them in the troubled depths of her violet eyes. That long, weary struggle was one of the tragedies they never spoke of at Pentlands, leaving it buried in silence. One said, "Jack looks well today," smiling, and, "Perhaps the doctors are wrong." Sybil was watching her brother now, in that quiet, mysterious way she had, watching him cautiously lest he discover that she was watching; for he discovered troubles easily, with the kind of clairvoyance which comes to people who have always been ill.

They barely talked at all during the lunch. Sybil planned to take her brother in the trap to ride over the farm and down to the white dunes.

"Higgins is going with us," she said. "He's going to show us the new litter of foxes in the black thicket."

And Jack said, "It's a funny thing about Higgins. He always discovers such things before anyone else. He knows when it will be a good day for fishing and just when it is going to rain. He's never wrong."

"No. . ." said the grandfather suddenly. "It's a funny thing. He's never wrong. . . not in all the years I've known him."

It was the only time he said anything during the meal, and Olivia, trying to fill in the gaps in the conversation, found it difficult, with the boy sitting opposite her looking so pale and ill. It seemed to her sometimes that he had never really been born, that he had always remained in some way a part of herself. When he was out of her sight, she had no peace because there was always a gnawing terror that she might never see him again. And she knew that deep inside the frail body there was a spirit, a flame, descended from the old man and from herself, which burned passionately with a desire for life, for riding, for swimming, for running across the open meadows. . . a flame that must always be smothered. If only he had been like Anson, his father, who never knew that hunger for life. . .

"Olivia, my dear. . ." The old man was speaking. "Will you have your coffee with me in the library? There is something I want to discuss with you."

She knew it then. She had been right. There *was* something which troubled him. He always said the same thing when he was faced by some problem too heavy for his old shoulders. He always said, "Olivia, my dear. . . Will you come into the library?" He never summoned his own son, or his sister Cassie. . . no one but Olivia. Between them they shared secrets which the others never dreamed of; and when he died, all the troubles would be hers. . . they would be passed on for her to deal with. . . those troubles which existed in a family which the world would have said was rich and respected and quite without troubles.

IV

As SHE LEFT THE ROOM to follow him she stopped for a moment to say to Sybil, "Are you happy, my dear? You're not sorry that you aren't going back to school in Saint-Cloud?"

LOUIS BROMFIELD

"No, Mama; why shouldn't I be happy here? I love it, more than anything in the world."

The girl thrust her hands into the pockets of her riding-coat.

"You don't think I was wrong to send you to France to school. . . away from everyone here?"

Sybil laughed and looked at her mother in the frank, half-mocking way she had when she fancied she had uncovered a plot.

"Are you worrying about marrying me off? I'm only eighteen. I've lots of time."

"I'm worrying because I think you'll be so hard to please."

Again she laughed. "That's true. That's why I'm going to take my time."

"And you're glad to have Thérèse here?"

"Of course. You know I like Thérèse awfully, Mama."

"Very well. . . run along now. I must speak to your grandfather."

And the girl went out onto the terrace where Jack stood waiting in the sun for the trap. He always followed the sun, choosing to sit in it even in midsummer, as if he were never quite warm enough.

She *was* worried over Sybil. She had begun to think that perhaps Aunt Cassie was right when she said that Sybil ought to go to a boarding-school with the girls she had always known, to grow loud and noisy and awkward and play hockey and exchange silly notes with the boys in the boarding-school in the next village. Perhaps it was wrong to have sent Sybil away to a school where she would meet girls from France and England and Russia and South America. . . half the countries of the world; a school where, as Aunt Cassie had said bitterly, she would be forced to associate with the "daughters of dancers and opera singers." She knew now that Sybil hadn't liked the ball anymore than Thérèse, who had run away from it without a word of explanation. Only with Thérèse it didn't matter so much, because the dark stubborn head was filled with all sorts of wild notions about science and painting and weird books on psychology. There was a loneliness about Thérèse and her mother, Sabine Callendar, only with them it didn't matter. They had, too, a hardness, a sense of derision and scorn which protected them. Sybil hadn't any such protections. Perhaps she was even wrong in having made of Sybil a lady—a lady in the old sense of the word—because there seemed to be no place for a lady in the scheme of life as it had existed at the dance the night before. It was perilous, having a lady on one's hands, especially a lady who was certain to take life as passionately as Sybil.

She wanted the girl to be happy, without quite understanding that it was because Sybil seemed the girl she had once been herself, a very part of herself, the part which had never lived at all.

She found her father-in-law seated at his great mahogany desk in the high narrow room walled with books which was kept sacred to him, at the desk from which he managed the farm and watched over a fortune, built up bit by bit shrewdly, thriftily over three hundred years, a fortune which he had never brought himself to trust in the hands of his son. It was, in its gloomy, cold way, a pleasant room, smelling of dogs and apples and wood-smoke, and sometimes of whisky, for it was here that the old man retired when, in a kind of baffled frenzy, he drank himself to insensibility. It was here that he would sometimes sit for a day and a night, even sleeping in his leather chair, refusing to see anyone save Higgins, who watched over him, and Olivia. And so it was Olivia and Higgins who alone knew the spectacle of this solitary drinking. The world and even the family knew very little of it—only the little which sometimes leaked out from the gossip of servants straying at night along the dark lanes and hedges about Durham.

He sat with his coffee and a glass of Courvoisier before him while he smoked, with an air of being lost in some profound worry, for he did not look up at once when she entered, but sat staring before him in an odd, enchanted fashion. It was not until she had taken a cigarette from the silver box and lighted it that he looked up at the sound of the striking match and, focusing the burning black eyes, said to her, "Jack seems very well today."

"Yes, better than he has been in a long time."

"Perhaps, after all, the doctors are wrong."

Olivia sighed and said quietly, "If we had believed the doctors we should have lost him long ago."

"Yes, that's true."

She poured her coffee and he murmured, "It's about Horace Pentland I wanted to speak. He's dead. I got the news this morning. He died in Mentone and now it's a question whether we shall bring him home here to be buried in Durham with the rest of the family."

Olivia was silent for a moment and then, looking up, said "What do you think? How long has it been that he has lived in Mentone?"

"It's nearly thirty years now that I've been sending him money to stay there. He's only a cousin. Still, we had the same grandfather and he'd be the first of the family in three hundred years who isn't buried here."

"There was Savina Pentland. . ."

"Yes. . . But she's buried out there, and she would have been buried here if it had been possible."

And he made a gesture in the direction of the sea, beyond the marshes where the beautiful Savina Pentland, almost a legend now, lay, somewhere deep down in the soft white sand at the bottom of the ocean.

"Would he want to be buried here?" asked Olivia.

"He wrote and asked me. . . a month or two before he died. It seemed to be on his mind. He put it in a strange way. He wrote that he wanted to come home."

Again Olivia was thoughtful for a time. "Strange. . ." she murmured presently, "when people were so cruel to him."

The lips of the old man stiffened a little.

"It was his own fault. . ."

"Still. . . thirty years is a long time."

He knocked the ash from his cigar and looked at her sharply. "You mean that everything may have been forgotten by now?"

Olivia made a little gesture with her white, ringless hands. "Why not?"

"Because people don't forget things like that. . . not in our world, at any rate."

Quietly, far back in her mind, Olivia kept trying to imagine this Horace Pentland whom she had never seen, this shadowy old man, dead now, who had been exiled for thirty years.

"You have no reason for not wanting him here among all the others?"

"No. . . Horace is dead now. . . It can't matter much whether what's left of him is buried here or in France."

"Except, of course, that they may have been kinder to him over there. . . They're not so harsh."

A silence fell over them, as if in some way the spirit of Horace Pentland, the sinner whose name was never spoken in the family save between Olivia and the old man, had returned and stood between them, waiting to hear what was to be done with all that remained of him on this earth. It was one of those silences which, descending upon the old house, sometimes filled Olivia with a vague uneasiness. They had a way of descending upon the household in the long evenings when all the family sat reading in the old drawing room—as if there were figures unseen who stood watching.

"If he wanted to be buried here," said Olivia, "I can see no reason why he should not be."

"Cassie will object to raking up an old scandal that has been forgotten."

"Surely that can't matter now. . . when the poor old man is dead. We can be kind to him now. . . surely we can be kind to him now."

John Pentland sighed abruptly, a curious, heart-breaking sigh that seemed to have escaped even his power of steely control; and presently he said, "I think you are right, Olivia, . . . I will do as you say. . . only we'll keep it a secret between us until the time comes when it's necessary to speak. And then. . . then we'll have a quiet funeral."

She would have left him then save that she knew from his manner that there were other things he wanted to say. He had a way of letting you know his will without speaking. Somehow, in his presence you felt that it was impossible to leave until he had dismissed you. He still treated his own son, who was nearly fifty, as if he were a little boy.

Olivia waited, busying herself by rearranging the late lilacs which stood in a tall silver vase on the polished mahogany desk.

"They smell good," he said abruptly. "They're the last, aren't they?"

"The last until next spring."

"Next spring. . ." he repeated with an air of speaking to himself. "Next spring. . ." And then abruptly, "The other thing was about Sabine. The nurse tells me *she* has discovered that Sabine is here." He made the family gesture toward the old north wing. "She has asked to see Sabine."

"Who told her that Sabine had returned? How could she have discovered it?"

"The nurse doesn't know. She must have heard someone speaking the name under her window. The nurse says that people in her condition have curious ways of discovering such things. . . like a sixth sense."

"Do you want me to ask Sabine? She'd come if I asked her."

"It would be unpleasant. Besides, I think it might do harm in some way."

Olivia was silent for a moment. "How? She probably wouldn't remember Sabine. When she saw her last, Sabine was a young girl."

"She's gotten the idea now that we're all against her, that we're persecuting her in some way." He coughed and blew a cloud of smoke out of his thin-drawn lips. "It's difficult to explain what I mean. . . I mean that Sabine might encourage that feeling. . . quite without meaning to, that Sabine might give her the impression that she was an ally. There's something disturbing about Sabine."

"Anson thinks so, too," said Olivia softly. "He's been talking to me about it."

"She ought never to have come back here. It's difficult. . . what I am trying to say. Only I feel that she's up to some mischief. I think she hates us all."

"Not all of us. . ."

"Not perhaps you. You never belonged here. It's only those of us who have always been here."

"But she's fond of you. . ."

"Her father and I were good friends. He was very like her. . . disagreeable and given to speaking unpleasant truths. . . He wasn't a popular man. Perhaps that's why she's friendly toward me. . . on account of him."

"No, it's more than that. . ."

Slowly Olivia felt herself slipping back into that state of confused enchantment which had overwhelmed her more and more often of late. It seemed that life grew more and more tenuous and complicated, more blurred and indistinct, until at times it became simply a morass of minute problems in which she found herself mired and unable to act. No one spoke directly anymore. It was like living in a world of shadows. And this old man, her father-in-law, was the greatest puzzle of all, because it was impossible ever to know how much he understood of what went on about him, how much he chose to ignore in the belief that by denying its existence it would cease to exist.

Sitting there, puzzled, she began to pull a leaf from the cluster of lilacs into tiny bits.

"Sometimes," she said, "I think Sabine is unhappy. . ."

"No. . . not that. . . She's beyond happiness or unhappiness. There's something hard in her and unrelenting. . . as hard as a cut diamond. She's a clever woman and a queer one. She's one of those strange creatures that are thrown off now and then by people like us. There's nothing else quite like them in the world. They go to strange extremes. Horace was the same. . . in a different, less creditable fashion."

Olivia looked at him suddenly, astonished by the sudden flash of penetration in the old man, one of those sudden, quick gleams which led her to believe that far down, in the depths of his soul, he was far more profound, far more intelligent, unruly and defiant of tradition than he ever allowed the world to suppose. It was always the old question. How much did he know? How much did he not know. . . far back, behind the lined, severe, leathery old face? Or was it a sort of clairvoyance, not of eternal illness, like Jack's, but of old age?

"I shall ask Sabine," she began.

"It's not necessary at the moment. She appears to have forgotten the matter temporarily. But she'll remember it again and then I think it will be best to humor her, whatever comes. She may not think of it again for months. . . until Sabine has gone. . . I only wanted to ask you. . . to consult you, Olivia. I thought you could arrange it."

She rose and, turning to go, she heard him saying, "*She* might like some lilacs in her room." He hesitated and in a flat, dead voice, added, "She used to be very fond of flowers."

Olivia, avoiding the dark eyes, thought, "She used to be very fond of flowers. . . That means forty years ago. . . forty long years. Oh, my God!" But after a second she said simply, "She has taken a dislike to flowers. She fancies they take up the air and stifle her. The sight of them is very bad for her."

"I should have known you'd already thought of it."

For an instant the old man stood facing her with a fixed and searching expression which made her feel shy and led her to turn away from him a little; and then all at once, with an air strangely timid and frightened in a man so grim in appearance, he took her hand and kissing her on the forehead murmured, "You're a good girl, Olivia. They're right in what they say of you. You're a good girl. I don't know how I should have managed without you all these years."

Smiling, she looked at him, and then, touching his hand affectionately, she went out without speaking again, thinking, as she had thought a thousand times, what a terrible thing it must be to have been born so inarticulate and so terrified of feeling as John Pentland. It must be, she thought, like living forever imprisoned in a shell of steel from which one might look out and see friends but never touch or know them.

From the doorway she heard a voice behind her, saying almost joyfully: "The doctors must have been wrong about Jack. You and I together, Olivia, have defeated them."

She said, "Yes," and smiled at him, but when she had turned away again there was in her mind a strange, almost gruesome thought.

"If only Jack lives until his grandfather is dead, the old man will die happy. If only he can be kept alive until then. . ."

She had a strange way of seeing things in the hard light of reality, and an unreal, lonely childhood had fostered the trait. She had been born thus, and now as a woman she found that in a way it was less a curse than a blessing. In a world which survived only by deceiving itself, she found that seeing the truth and knowing it made her strong. Here, perhaps, lay the reason why all of them had come to depend upon her. But there were times, too, when she wanted passionately to be a poor weak feminine creature, a woman who might turn to her husband and find in him someone stronger than herself. She had a curious feeling of envy for Savina Pentland, who was dead before she was born. . . Savina Pentland who had been the beauty of the family, extravagant, reckless, feminine, who bought strings of pearls and was given to weeping and fainting.

But she (Olivia) had only Anson to lean upon.

AFTER SHE HAD GONE AWAY the old man sat for a long time smoking and drinking his brandy, enveloped by a loneliness scarcely more profound than it had been a little while before when he sat talking with Olivia. It was his habit to sit thus sometimes for an hour at a time, unconscious, it seemed, of all the world about him; Olivia had come in more than once at such moments and gone away again, unwilling to shatter the enchantment by so much as a single word.

At last, when the cigar had burned to an end, he crushed out the ember with a short, fierce gesture and, rising, went out of the tall narrow room and along the corridor that led to the dark stairway in the old north wing. These steps he had climbed everyday since it had become necessary to keep *her* in the country the year round. . . everyday, at the same hour, step by step his big heavy-shod boots had trod the same worn stair carpet. It was a journey begun years ago as a kind of pleasure colored by hope, which for a long time now, bereft of all hope, had become merely a monotonous dreary duty. It was like a journey of penance made by some pilgrim on his knees up endless nights of stairs.

For more than twenty years, as far back as Olivia could remember, he had been absent from the house for a night but twice, and then only on occasions of life and death. In all that time he had been twice to New York and never once to the Europe he had not seen since, as a boy, he had made the grand tour on a plan laid out by old General Curtis. . . a time so remote now that it must have seemed part of another life. In all those years he had never once escaped from the world which his family found so perfect and complete and which to him must have seemed always a little cramped and inadequate. Fate and blood and circumstance, one might have said, had worn him down bit by bit until in the end he had come to worship the same gods they worshiped. Now and then he contrived to escape them for a little while by drinking himself into insensibility, but always he awakened again to find that nothing had changed, to discover that his prison was the same. And so, slowly, hope must have died.

But no one knew, even Olivia, whether he was happy or unhappy; and no one would ever really know what had happened to him, deep inside, behind the gray, leathery old face.

The world said, when it thought of him: "There never was such a devoted husband as John Pentland."

Slowly and firmly he walked along the narrow hall to the end and there halted to knock on the white door. He always knocked, for there were times when the sight of him, entering suddenly, affected her so that she became hysterical and beyond all control.

In response to the knock, the door was opened gently and professionally by Miss Egan, an automaton of a nurse—neat, efficient, inhuman and incredibly starched, whose very smile seemed to come and go by some mechanical process, like the sounds made by squeezing a mechanical doll. Only it was impossible to imagine squeezing anything so starched and jagged as the red-faced Miss Egan. It was a smile which sprang into existence upon sight of any member of the family, a smile of false humility which said, "I know very well that you cannot do without me"—the smile of a woman well enough content to be paid three times the wages of an ordinary nurse. In three or four more years she would have enough saved to start a sanatorium of her own.

Fixing her smile, she faced the old man, saying, "She seems quite well today. . . very quiet."

The whole hallway had been flooded at the opening of the door by a thick and complicated odor arising from innumerable medicines that stood row upon row in the obscurity of the dark room. The old man stepped inside, closing the door quickly behind him, for she was affected by too much light. She could not bear to have a door or a window open near her; even on this bright day the drawn shades kept the room in darkness.

She had got the idea somehow that there were people outside who waited to leer at her. . . hundreds of them all pressing their faces against the panes to peep into her bedroom. There were days when she could not be quieted until the window-shades were covered by thick layers of black cloth. She would not rise from her bed until nightfall lest the faces outside might see her standing there in her nightdress.

LOUIS BROMFIELD

It was only when darkness had fallen that the nurse was able by means of trickery and wheedling to air the room, and so it smelled horribly of the medicines she never took, but kept ranged about her, row upon row, like the fetishes of witch-doctors. In this they humored her as they had humored her in shutting out the sunlight, because it was the only way they could keep her quiet and avoid sending her away to some place where she would have been shut behind bars. And this John Pentland would not even consider.

When he entered she was lying in the bed, her thin, frail body barely outlined beneath the bedclothes. . . the mere shadow of a woman who must once have been pretty in a delicate way. But nothing remained now of the beauty save the fine modeling of the chin and nose and brow. She lay there, a queer, unreal old woman, with thin white hair, skin like parchment and a silly, vacant face as unwrinkled as that of a child. As he seated himself beside her, the empty, round blue eyes opened a little and stared at him without any sign of recognition. He took one of the thin, blue-veined hands in his, but it only lay there, lifeless, while he sat, silent and gentle, watching her.

Once he spoke, calling her wistfully by name, "Agnes"; but there was no sign of an answer, not so much as a faint flickering of the white, transparent lids.

And so for an eternity he sat thus in the thick darkness, enveloped by the sickly odor of medicines, until he was roused by a knock at the door and the sudden glare of daylight as it opened and Miss Egan, fixing her flashing and teethy smile, came in and said: "The fifteen minutes is up, Mr. Pentland."

When the door had closed behind him he went away again, slowly, thoughtfully, down the worn stairs and out into the painfully brilliant sunlight of the bright New England spring. Crossing the green terrace, bordered with great clumps of iris and peonies and a few late tulips, he made his way to the stable yard, where Higgins had left the red mare in charge of a Polish boy who did odd tasks about the farm. The mare, as beautiful and delicate as a fine steel spring, stood nervously pawing the gravel and tossing her handsome head. The boy, a great lout with a shock of yellow hair, stood far away from her holding the reins at arm's length. At the sight of the two the old man laughed and said, "You mustn't let her know you're afraid of her, Ignaz."

The boy gave up the reins and retired to a little distance, still watching the mare resentfully. "Well, she tried to bite me!" he said sullenly.

Quickly, with a youthful agility, John Pentland swung himself to her back. . . quickly enough to keep her from sidling away from him. There was a short, fierce struggle between the rider and the horse, and in a shower of stones they sped away down the lane that led across the meadows, past the thicket of black pines and the abandoned gravel-pit, toward the house of Mrs. Soames.

Chapter IV

In the solid corner of the world which surrounded Durham, Aunt Cassie played the role of an unofficial courier who passed from house to house, from piazza to piazza, collecting and passing on the latest bits of news. When one saw a low cloud of dust moving across the brilliant New England sky above the hedges and stone walls of the countryside, one could be certain that it masked the progress of Cassie Struthers on her daily round of calls. She went always on foot, because she detested motors and was terrified of horses; one might see her coming from a great distance, dressed always in dingy black, tottering along very briskly (for a woman of her age and well-advertised infirmities). One came to expect her arrival at a certain hour, for she was, unless there arose in her path some calamity or piece of news of unusual interest, a punctual woman whose life was as carefully ordered as the vast house in which she lived with the queer Aunt Bella.

It was a great box of a dwelling built by the late Mr. Struthers in the days of cupolas and gazebos on land given him by Aunt Cassie's grandfather on the day of her wedding. Inside it was furnished with a great profusion of plush tassels and antimacassars, all kept with the neatness and rigidity of a museum. There were never any cigar ashes on the floor, nor any dust in the corners, for Aunt Cassie followed her servants about with the eye of a fussy old sergeant inspecting his barracks. Poor Miss Peavey, who grew more and more dowdy and careless as old age began to settle over her, led a life of constant peril, and was forced to build a little house near the stables to house her Pomeranians and her Siamese cats. For Aunt Cassie could not abide the thought of "the animals dirtying up the house." Even the "retiring room" of the late Mr. Struthers had been converted since his death into a museum, spotless and purified of tobacco and whisky, where his chair sat before his desk, turned away from it a little, as if his spirit were still seated there. On the desk lay his pipe (as he had left it) and the neat piles of paper (carefully dusted each day but otherwise undisturbed) which he had put there with his own hand on the morning they found him seated on the chair, his head fallen back a little, as if asleep. And in the center of the desk lay two handsomely bound volumes—"Cornices of Old Boston Houses" and "Walks and Talks in New England Churchyards"—which he had written in these last sad years when his life seemed slowly to fade from him. . . the years in which Aunt Cassie seemed rapidly to recover the wiry strength and health for which she had been famous as a girl.

The house, people said, had been built by Mr. Struthers in the expectation of a large family, but it had remained great and silent of children's voices as a tomb since the day it was finished, for Aunt Cassie had never been strong until it was too late for her to bear him heirs.

Sabine Callendar had a whole set of theories about the house and about the married life of Aunt Cassie, but they were theories which she kept, in her way, entirely to herself, waiting and watching until she was certain of them. There was a hatred between the two women that was implacable and difficult to define, an emotion almost of savagery which concealed itself beneath polite phrases and casual observations of an acid character. They encountered each other more frequently than Aunt Cassie would have wished, for Sabine, upon her return to Durham, took up Aunt Cassie's habit of going from house to house on foot in search of news and entertainment. They met in drawing rooms, on piazzas, and sometimes in the very dusty lanes, greeting each other with smiles and vicious looks. They had become rather like two hostile cats watching each other for days at a time, stealthily. Sabine, Aunt Cassie confided in Olivia, made her nervous.

Still, it was Aunt Cassie who had been the first caller at Brook Cottage after the arrival of Sabine. The younger woman had seen her approach, enveloped in a faint cloud of dust, from the windows of Brook Cottage, and the sight filled her with an inexpressible delight. The spare old lady had come along so briskly, almost with impatience, filled with delight (Sabine believed) at having an excuse now to trespass on O'Hara's land and see what he had done to the old cottage. And Sabine believed, too, that she came to discover what life had done to "dear Mr. Struthers' niece, Sabine Callendar." She came as the Official Welcomer of the Community, with hope in her heart that she would find Sabine a returned prodigal, a wrecked woman, ravaged by time and experience, who for twenty years had ignored them all and now returned, a broken and humbled creature, hungry for kindness.

The sight set fire to a whole train of memories in Sabine. . . memories which penetrated deep into her childhood when with her father she had lived in the old house that once stood where O'Hara's new one raised its bright chimneys; memories of days when she had run off by herself to play in the tangled orchard grass among the bleeding-hearts and irises that surrounded this same Brook Cottage where she stood watching the approach of Aunt Cassie. Only, in those days Brook Cottage had been a ruin of a place, with empty windows and sagging doors, ghostly and half-hidden by a shaggy tangle of lilacs and syringas, and now it stood glistening with new paint, the lilacs all neatly clipped and pruned.

There was something in the sight of the old woman's nervous, active figure that struck deep down into a past which Sabine, with the passing of years, had almost succeeded in forgetting; and now it all came back again, sharply and with a kind of stabbing pain, so that she had a sudden odd feeling of having become a little girl again. . . plain, red-haired, freckled and timid, who stood in terror of Aunt Cassie and was always being pulled here and there by a thousand aunts and uncles and cousins because she *would* not be turned into their idea of what a nice little girl ought to be. It was as if the whole past were concentrated in the black figure of the old lady who had been the ring-leader, the viceroy, of all a far-flung tribe, an old woman who had been old even twenty years earlier, lying always on a sofa under a shawl, issuing her edicts, pouring out her ample sympathies, her bitter criticisms. And here she was, approaching briskly, as if the death of Mr. Struthers had somehow released her from bonds which had chafed for too long.

Watching her, one incident after another flashed through the quick, hard brain of Sabine, all recreated with a swift, astounding clarity—the day when she had run off to escape into the world and been found by old John Pentland hiding in the thicket of white birches happily eating blueberries. (She could see his countenance now, stern with its disapproval of such wild behavior, but softening, too, at the sight of the grubby, freckled plain face stained with blueberry juice.) And the return of the captive, when she was surrounded by aunts who dressed her in a clean frock and forced her to sit in the funereal spare bedroom with a New Testament on her knees until she "felt that she could come out and behave like a nice, well-brought-up little girl." She could see the aunts pulling and fussing at her and saying, "What a shame she didn't take after her mother in looks!" and, "She'll have a hard time with such plain, straight red hair."

And there was, too, the memory of that day when Anson Pentland, a timid, spiritless little Lord Fauntleroy of a boy, fell into the river and would have been drowned save for his cousin Sabine, who dragged him out, screaming and drenched, only to receive for herself all the scolding for having led him into mischief. And the times when she had been punished for having asked frank and simple questions which she ought not to have asked.

It was difficult to remember any happiness until the day when her father died and she was sent to New York, a girl of twenty, knowing very little of anything and nothing whatever of such things as love and marriage, to live with an uncle in a tall narrow house on Murray Hill. It was on that day (she saw it now with a devastating clarity as she stood watching the approach of Aunt Cassie) that her life had really begun. Until then her existence had been only a confused and tormented affair in which there was very little happiness. It was only later that reality had come to her, painfully, even tragically, in a whole procession of events which had made her slowly into this hard, worldly, cynical woman who found herself, without quite knowing why, back in a world she hated, standing at the window of Brook Cottage, a woman tormented by an immense and acutely living curiosity about people and the strange tangles which their lives sometimes assumed.

She had been standing by the window thinking back into the past with such a fierce intensity that she quite forgot the approach of Aunt Cassie and started suddenly at the sound of the curious, familiar thin voice, amazingly unchanged, calling from the hallway, "Sabine! Sabine dear! It's your Aunt Cassie! Where are you?" as if she had never left Durham at all, as if nothing had changed in twenty years.

At sight of her, the old lady came forward with little fluttering cries to fling her arms about her late husband's niece. Her manner was that of a shepherd receiving a lost sheep, a manner filled with forgiveness and pity and condescension. The tears welled easily into her eyes and streamed down her face.

Sabine permitted herself, frigidly, to be embraced, and said, "But you don't look a day older, Aunt Cassie. You look stronger than ever." It was a remark which somehow set the whole tone of the relationship between them, a remark which though it sounded sympathetic and even complimentary was a harsh thing to say to a woman who had cherished all her life the tradition of invalidism. It was harsh, too, because it was true. Aunt Cassie at forty-seven had been as shriveled and dried as she was now, twenty years later.

The old woman said, "My dear girl, I am miserable. . . miserable." And drying the tears that streamed down her face she added, "It won't be long now until I go to join dear Mr. Struthers."

Sabine wanted suddenly to laugh, at the picture of Aunt Cassie entering Paradise to rejoin a husband whom she had always called, even in the intimacy of married life, "Mr. Struthers." She kept thinking that Mr. Struthers might not find the reunion so pleasant as his wife anticipated. She had always held a strange belief that Mr. Struthers had chosen death as the best way out.

And she felt a sudden almost warm sense of returning memories, roused by Aunt Cassie's passion for overstatement. Aunt Cassie could never bring herself to say simply, "I'm going to die" which was not at all true. She must say, "I go to join dear Mr. Struthers."

Sabine said, "Oh, no. . . Oh, no. . . Don't say that."

"I don't sleep anymore. I barely close my eyes at night."

She had seated herself now and was looking about her, absorbing everything in the room, the changes made by the dreadful O'Hara, the furniture he had bought for the house. But most of all she was studying Sabine, devouring her with sidelong, furtive glances; and Sabine, knowing her so well, saw that the old woman had been given a violent shock. She had come prepared to find a broken, unhappy Sabine and she had found instead this smooth, rather hard and self-contained woman, superbly dressed and poised, from the burnished red hair (that straight red hair the aunts had once thought so hopeless) to the lizard-skin slippers—a woman who had obviously taken hold of life with a firm hand and subdued it, who was in a way complete.

"Your dear uncle never forgot you for a moment, Sabine, in all the years you were away. He died, leaving me to watch over you." And again the easy tears welled up.

("Oh," thought Sabine, "you don't catch me that way. You won't put me back where I once was. You won't even have a chance to meddle in my life.")

Aloud she said, "It's a pity I've always been so far away."

"But I've thought of you, my dear. . . I've thought of you. Scarcely a night passes when I don't say to myself before going to sleep, 'There is poor Sabine out in the world, turning her back on all of us who love her.'" She sighed abysmally. "I have thought of you, dear. I've prayed for you in the long nights when I have never closed an eye."

And Sabine, talking on half-mechanically, discovered slowly that, in spite of everything, she was no longer afraid of Aunt Cassie. She was no longer a shy, frightened, plain little girl; she even began to sense a challenge, a combat which filled her with a faint sense of warmth. She kept thinking, "She really hasn't changed at all. She still wants to reach out and take possession of me and my life. She's like an octopus reaching out and seizing each member of the family, arranging everything." And she saw Aunt Cassie now, after so many years, in a new light. It seemed to her that there was something glittering and hard and a little sinister beneath all the sighing and tears and easy sympathy. Perhaps she (Sabine) was the only one in all the family who had escaped the reach of those subtle, insinuating tentacles. . . She had run away.

Meanwhile Aunt Cassie had swept from a vivid and detailed description of the passing of Mr. Struthers into a catalogue of neighborhood and family calamities, of deaths, of broken troths, financial disasters, and the appearance on the horizon of the "dreadful O'Hara." She reproached Sabine for having sold her land to such an outsider. And as she talked on and on she grew less and less human and more and more like some disembodied, impersonal force of nature. Sabine, watching her with piercing green eyes, found her a little terrifying. She had sharpened and hardened with age.

She discussed the divorces which had occurred in Boston, and at length, leaning forward and touching Sabine's hand with her thin, nervous one, she said brokenly: "I felt for you in your trouble, Sabine. I never wrote you because it would have been so painful. I see now that I evaded my duty. But I felt for you. . . I tried to put myself in your place. I tried to imagine dear Mr. Struthers being unfaithful to me. . . but, of course, I couldn't. He was a saint." She blew her nose and repeated with passion, as if to herself, "A saint!"

("Yes," thought Sabine, "a saint. . . if ever there was one.") She saw that Aunt Cassie was attacking her now from a new point. She was trying to pity her. By being full of pity the old woman would try to break down her defenses and gain possession of her.

Sabine's green eyes took one hard, glinting look. "Did you ever see my husband?" she asked.

"No," said Aunt Cassie, "but I've heard a great deal of him. I've been told how you suffered."

Sabine looked at her with a queer, mocking expression. "Then you've been told wrongly. He is a fascinating man. I did not suffer. I assure you that I would rather have shared him with fifty other women than have had anyone of the men about here all to myself."

There was a frank immorality in this statement which put Aunt Cassie to rout, bag and baggage. She merely stared, finding nothing to say in reply to such a speech. Clearly, in all her life she had never heard anyone say a thing so bald and so frank, so completely naked of all pretense of gentility.

Sabine went on coldly, pushing her assault to the very end. "I divorced him at last, not because he was unfaithful to me, but because there was another woman who wanted to marry him. . . a woman whom I respect and like. . . a woman who is still my friend. Understand that I loved him passionately. . . in a very fleshly way. One couldn't help it. I wasn't the only woman. . . He was a kind of devil, but a very fascinating one."

The old woman was a little stunned but not by any means defeated. Sabine saw a look come into her eyes, a look which clearly said, "So this is what the world has done to my poor, dear, innocent little Sabine!" At last she said with a sigh, "I find it an amazing world. I don't know what it is coming to."

"Nor I," replied Sabine with an air of complete agreement and sympathy. She understood that the struggle was not yet finished, for Aunt Cassie had a way of putting herself always in an impregnable position, of wrapping herself in layer after layer of sighs and sympathy, of charity and forgiveness, of meekness and tears, so that in the end there was no way of suddenly tearing them aside and saying, "There you are. . . naked at last, a horrible meddling old woman!" And Sabine kept thinking, too, that if Aunt Cassie had lived in the days of her witch-baiting ancestor, Preserved Pentland, she would have been burned for a witch.

And all the while Sabine had been suffering, quietly, deep inside, behind the frankly painted face. . . suffering in a way which no one in the world had ever suspected; for it was like tearing out her heart, to talk thus of Richard Callendar, even to speak his name.

Aloud she said, "And how is Mrs. Pentland. . . I mean Olivia. . . not my cousin. . . I know how *she* is. . . no better."

"No better. . . It is one of those things which I can never understand. . . Why God should have sent such a calamity to a good man like my brother."

"But Olivia. . ." began Sabine, putting an end abruptly to what was clearly the prelude to a pious monologue.

"Oh! . . . Olivia," replied Aunt Cassie, launching into an account of the young Mrs. Pentland. "Olivia is an angel. . . an angel, a blessing of God sent to my poor brother. But she's not been well lately. She's been rather sharp with me. . . even with poor Miss Peavey, who is so sensitive. I can't imagine what has come over her."

It seemed that the strong, handsome Olivia was suffering from nerves. She was, Aunt Cassie said, unhappy about something, although she could not see why Olivia shouldn't be happy. . . a woman with everything in the world.

"Everything?" echoed Sabine. "Has anyone in the world got everything?"

"It is Olivia's fault if she hasn't everything. All the materials are there. She has a good husband. . . a husband who never looks at other women."

"Nor at his own wife either," interrupted Sabine. "I know all about Anson. I grew up with him."

Aunt Cassie saw fit to ignore this. "She's rich," she said, resuming the catalogue of Olivia's blessings.

And again Sabine interrupted, "But what does money mean, Aunt Cassie? In our world one is rich and that's the end of it. One takes it for granted. When one isn't rich any longer, one simply slips out of it. It has very little to do with happiness. . ."

The strain was beginning to show on Aunt Cassie. "You'd find out if you weren't rich," she observed with asperity, "if your father and great-grandfather hadn't taken care of their money." She recovered herself and made a deprecating gesture. "But don't think I'm criticizing dear Olivia. She is the best, the most wonderful woman." She began to wrap herself once more in kindliness and charity and forgiveness. "Only she seems to me to be a little queer lately."

Sabine's artificially crimson mouth took on a slow smile. "It would be too bad if the Pentland family drove two wives insane—one after the other."

Again Aunt Cassie came near to defeat by losing her composure. She snorted, and Sabine helped her out by asking: "And Anson?" ironically. "What is dear Anson doing?"

She told him of Anson's great work, "The Pentland Family and the Massachusetts Bay Colony" and of its immense value as a contribution to the history of the nation; and when she had finished with that, she turned to Jack's wretched health, saying in a low, melancholy voice, "It's only a matter of time, you know. . . At least, so the doctors say. . . With a heart like that it's only a matter of time." The tears came again.

"And yet," Sabine said slowly, "you say that Olivia has everything."

"Well," replied Aunt Cassie, "perhaps not everything."

Before she left she inquired for Sabine's daughter and was told that she had gone over to Pentlands to see Sybil.

"They went to the same school in France," said Sabine. "They were friends there."

"Yes," said Aunt Cassie. "I was against Sybil's going abroad to school. It fills a girl's head with queer ideas. . . especially a school like that where anyone could go. Since she's home, Sybil behaves very queerly. . . I think it'll stand in the way of her success in Boston. The boys don't like girls who are different."

"Perhaps," said Sabine, "she may marry outside of Boston. Men aren't the same everywhere. Even in Boston there must be one or two who don't refer to women as 'Good old So-and-so.' Even in Boston there must be men who like women who are well dressed. . . women who are ladies. . ."

Aunt Cassie began to grow angry again, but Sabine swept over her. "Don't be insulted, Aunt Cassie. I only mean ladies in the old-fashioned, glamorous sense. . . Besides," she continued, "whom could she marry who wouldn't be a cousin or a connection of some sort?"

"She ought to marry here. . . among the people she's always known. There's a Mannering boy who would be a good match, and James Thorne's youngest son."

Sabine smiled. "So you have plans for her already. You've settled it?"

"Of course, nothing is settled. I'm only thinking of it with Sybil's welfare in view. If she married one of those boys she'd know what she was getting. She'd know that she was marrying a gentleman."

"Perhaps. . ." said Sabine. "Perhaps." Somehow a devil had taken possession of her and she added softly, "There was, of course, Horace Pentland. . . One can never be quite sure." (She never forgot anything, Sabine.)

And at the same moment she saw, standing outside the door that opened on the terrace next to the marshes, a solid, dark, heavy figure which she recognized with a sudden feeling of delight as O'Hara. He had been walking across the fields with the wiry little Higgins, who had left him and continued on his way down the lane in the direction of Pentlands. At the sight of him, Aunt Cassie made every sign of an attempt to escape quickly, but Sabine said in a voice ominous with sweetness, "You must meet Mr. O'Hara. I think you've never met him. He's a charming man." And she placed herself in such a position that it was impossible for the old woman to escape without losing every vestige of dignity.

Then Sabine called gently, "Come in, Mr. O'Hara. . . Mrs. Struthers is here and wants so much to meet her new neighbor."

The door opened and O'Hara stepped in, a swarthy, rather solidly built man of perhaps thirty-five, with a shapely head on which the vigorous black hair was cropped close, and with blue eyes that betrayed his Irish origin by the half-hidden sparkle of amusement at this move of Sabine's. He had a strong jaw and full, rather sensual, lips and a curious sense of great physical strength, as if all his clothes were with difficulty modeled to the muscles that lay underneath. He wore no hat, and his skin was a dark tan, touched at the cheekbones by the dull flush of health and good blood.

He was, one would have said at first sight, a common, vulgar man in that narrow-jawed world about Durham, a man, perhaps, who had come by his muscles as a dock-laborer. Sabine had thought him vulgar in the beginning, only to succumb in the end to a crude sort of power which placed him above the realm of such distinctions. And she was a shrewd woman, too, devoted passionately to the business of getting at the essence of people; she knew that vulgarity had nothing to do with a man who had eyes so shrewd and full of mockery.

He came forward quietly and with a charming air of deference in which there was a faint suspicion of nonsense, a curious shadow of vulgarity, only one could not be certain whether he was not being vulgar by deliberation.

"It is a great pleasure," he said. "Of course, I have seen Mrs. Struthers many times. . . at the horse shows. . . the whippet races."

Aunt Cassie was drawn up, stiff as a poker, with an air of having found herself unexpectedly face to face with a rattlesnake.

"I have had the same experience," she said. "And of course I've seen all the improvements you have made here on the farm." The word "improvements" she spoke with a sort of venom in it, as if it had been instead a word like "arson."

"We'll have some tea," observed Sabine. "Sit down, Aunt Cassie."

But Aunt Cassie did not unbend. "I promised Olivia to be back at Pentlands for tea," she said. "And I am late already." Pulling on her black gloves, she made a sudden dip in the direction of O'Hara. "We shall probably see each other again, Mr. O'Hara, since we are neighbors."

"Indeed, I hope so. . ."

Then she kissed Sabine again and murmured, "I hope, my dear, that you will come often to see me, now that you've come back to us. Make my house your own home." She turned to O'Hara, finding a use for him suddenly in her warfare against Sabine. "You know, Mr. O'Hara, she is

LOUIS BROMFIELD

a traitor in her way. She was raised among us and then went away for twenty years. She hasn't any loyalty in her."

She made the speech with a stiff air of playfulness, as if, of course, she were only making a joke and the speech meant nothing at all. Yet the air was filled with a cloud of implications. It was the sort of tactics in which she excelled.

Sabine went with her to the door, and when she returned she discovered O'Hara standing by the window, watching the figure of Aunt Cassie as she moved indignantly down the road in the direction of Pentlands. Sabine stood there for a moment, studying the straight, strong figure outlined against the light, and she got suddenly a curious sense of the enmity between him and the old woman. They stood, the two of them, in a strange way as the symbols of two great forces—the one negative, the other intensely positive; the one the old, the other, the new; the one of decay, the other of vigorous, almost too lush growth. Nothing could ever reconcile them. According to the scheme of things, they would be implacable enemies to the end. But Sabine had no doubts as to the final victor; the same scheme of things showed small respect for all that Aunt Cassie stood for. That was one of the wisdoms Sabine had learned since she had escaped from Durham into the uncompromising realities of the great world.

When she spoke, she said in a noncommittal sort of voice, "Mrs. Struthers is a remarkable woman."

And O'Hara, turning, looked at her with a sudden glint of humor in his blue eyes. "Extraordinary. . . I'm sure of it."

"And a powerful woman," said Sabine. "Wise as a serpent and gentle as a dove. It is never good to underestimate such strength. And now. . . How do you like your tea?"

He took no tea but contented himself with munching a bit of toast and afterward smoking a cigar, clearly pleased with himself in a naïve way in the role of landlord coming to inquire of his tenant whether everything was satisfactory. He had a liking for this hard, clever woman who was now only a tenant of the land—his land—which she had once owned. When he thought of it—that he, Michael O'Hara, had come to own this farm in the midst of the fashionable and dignified world of Durham—there was something incredible in the knowledge, something which never ceased to warm him with a strong sense of satisfaction. By merely turning his head, he could see in the mirror the reflection of the long scar on his temple, marked there by a broken bottle in the midst of a youthful fight along the India Wharf. He, Michael O'Hara, without education save that which he had given himself, without money, without influence, had raised himself to this position before his thirty-sixth birthday. In the autumn he would be a candidate for Congress, certain of election in the back Irish districts. He, Michael O'Hara, was on his way to being one of the great men of New England, a country which had once been the tight little paradise of people like the Pentlands.

Only no one must ever suspect the depth of that great satisfaction.

Yes, he had a liking for this strange woman, who ought to have been his enemy and, oddly enough, was not. He liked the shrewd directness of her mind and the way she had of sitting there opposite him, turning him over and over while he talked, as if he had been a small bug under a microscope. She was finding out all about him; and he understood that, for it was a trick in which he, himself, was well-practised. It was by such methods that he had got ahead in the world. It puzzled him, too, that she should have come out of that Boston-Durham world and yet could be so utterly different from it. He had a feeling that somewhere in the course of her life something had happened to her, something terrible which in the end had given her a great understanding and clarity of mind. He knew, too, almost at once, on the day she had driven up to the door of the cottage, that she had made a discovery about life which he himself had made long since. . . that there is nothing of such force as the power of a person content merely to be himself, nothing so invincible as the power of simple honesty, nothing so successful as the life of one who runs alone. Somewhere she had learned all this. She was like a woman to whom nothing could ever again happen.

They talked for a time, idly and pleasantly, with a sense of understanding unusual in two people who had known each other for so short a time; they spoke of the farm, of Pentlands, of the mills and the Poles in Durham, of the country as it had been in the days when Sabine was a child. And all the while he had that sense of her weighing and watching him, of feeling out the faint echo of a brogue in his speech and the rather hard, nasal quality that remained from those days along India Wharf and the memories of a ne'er-do-well, superstitious Irish father.

He could not have known that she was a woman who included among her friends men and women of a dozen nationalities, who lived a life among the clever, successful people of the world. . . the architects, the painters, the politicians, the scientists. He could not have known the ruthless rule she put up against tolerating any but people who were "complete." He could have known nothing of her other life in Paris, and London, and New York, which had nothing to do with the life in Durham and Boston. And yet he did know. . . He saw that, despite the great difference in their worlds, there was a certain kinship between them, that they had both come to look upon the world as a pie from which any plum might be drawn if one only knew the knack.

And Sabine, on her side, not yet quite certain about casting aside all barriers, was slowly reaching the same understanding. There was no love or sentimentality in the spark that flashed between them. She was more than ten years older than O'Hara and had done with such things long ago. It was merely a recognition of one strong person by another.

It was O'Hara who first took advantage of the bond. In the midst of the conversation, he had turned the talk rather abruptly to Pentlands.

"I've never been there and I know very little of the life," he said, "but I've watched it from a distance and it interests me. It's like something out of a dream, completely dead. . . dead all save for young Mrs. Pentland and Sybil."

Sabine smiled. "You know Sybil, then?"

"We ride together every morning. . . We met one morning by chance along the path by the river and since then we've gone nearly everyday."

"She's a charming girl. . . She went to school in France with my daughter, Thérèse. I saw a great deal of her then."

Far back in her mind the thought occurred to her that there would be something very amusing in the prospect of Sybil married to O'Hara. It would produce such an uproar with Anson and Aunt Cassie and the other relatives. . . A Pentland married to an Irish Roman Catholic politician!

"She is like her mother, isn't she?" asked O'Hara, sitting forward a bit on his chair. He had a way of sitting thus, in the tense, quiet alertness of a cat.

"Very like her mother. . . Her mother is a remarkable woman. . . a charming woman. . . also, I might say, what is the rarest of all things, a really good and generous woman."

"I've thought that. . . I've seen her a half-dozen times. I asked her to help me in planting the garden here at the cottage because I knew she had a passion for gardens. And she didn't refuse. . . though she scarcely knew me. She came over and helped me with it. I saw her then and came to know her. But when that was finished, she went back to Pentlands and I haven't seen her since. It's almost as if she meant to avoid me. Sometimes I feel sorry for her. . . It must be a queer life for a woman like that. . . young and beautiful."

"She has a great deal to occupy her at Pentlands. And it's true that it's not a very fascinating life. Still, I'm sure she couldn't bear being pitied. . . She's the last woman in the world to want pity."

Curiously, O'Hara flushed, the red mounting slowly beneath the dark-tanned skin.

"I thought," he said a little sadly, "that her husband or Mrs. Struthers might have raised objections. . . I know how they feel toward me. There's no use pretending not to know."

"It is quite possible," said Sabine.

There was a sudden embarrassing silence, which gave Sabine time to pull her wits together and organize a thousand sudden thoughts and impressions. She was beginning to understand, bit by bit, the real reasons of their hatred for O'Hara, the reasons which lay deep down underneath, perhaps so deep that none of them ever saw them for what they were.

And then out of the silence she heard the voice of O'Hara saying, in a queer, hushed way, "I mean to ask something of you. . . something that may sound ridiculous. I don't pretend that it isn't, but I mean to ask it anyway."

For a moment he hesitated and then, rising quickly, he stood looking away from her out of the door, toward the distant blue marshes and the open sea. She fancied that he was trembling a little, but she could not be certain. What she did know was that he made an immense and heroic effort, that for a moment he, a man who never did such things, placed himself in a position where he would be defenseless and open to being cruelly hurt; and for the moment all the recklessness seemed to flow out of him and in its place there came a queer sadness, almost as if he felt himself defeated in some way. . .

He said, "What I mean to ask you is this. . . Will you ask me sometimes here to the cottage when she will be here too?" He turned toward her suddenly and added, "It will mean a great deal to me. . . more than you can imagine."

She did not answer him at once, but sat watching him with a poorly concealed intensity; and presently, flicking the cigarette ashes casually from her gown, she asked, "And do you think it would be quite moral of me?"

He shrugged his shoulders and looked at her in astonishment, as if he had expected her, least of all people in the world, to ask such a thing.

"It might," he said, "make us both a great deal happier."

"Perhaps. . . perhaps not. It's not so simple as that. Besides, it isn't happiness that one places first at Pentlands."

"No. . . Still. . ." He made a sudden vigorous gesture, as if to sweep aside all objections.

"You're a queer man. . . I'll see what can be done."

He thanked her and went out shyly without another word, to stride across the meadows, his black head bent thoughtfully, in the direction of his new bright chimneys. At his heels trotted the springer, which had lain waiting for him outside the door. There was something about the robust figure, crossing the old meadow through the blue twilight, that carried a note of lonely sadness. The self-confidence, the assurance, seemed to have melted away in some mysterious fashion. It was almost as if one man had entered the cottage a little while before and another, a quite different man, had left it just now. Only one thing, Sabine saw, could have made the difference, and that was the name of Olivia.

WHEN HE HAD DISAPPEARED SABINE went up to her room overlooking the sea and lay there for a long time thinking. She was by nature an indolent woman, especially at times when her brain worked with a fierce activity. It was working thus now, in a kind of fever, confused and yet tremendously clear; for the visits from Aunt Cassie and O'Hara had ignited her almost morbid passion for vicarious experience. She had a sense of being on the brink of some calamity which, beginning long ago in a hopeless tangle of origins and motives, was ready now to break forth with the accumulated force of years.

It was only now that she began to understand a little what it was that had drawn her back to a place which held memories so unhappy as those haunting the whole countryside of Durham. She saw that it must have been all the while a desire for vindication, a hunger to show them that, in spite of everything, of the straight red hair and the plain face, the silly ideas with which they had filled her head, in spite even of her unhappiness over her husband, she had made of her life a successful, even a brilliant, affair. She had wanted to show them that she stood aloof now and impregnable, quite beyond their power to curb or to injure her. And for a moment she suspected that the half-discerned motive was an even stronger thing, akin perhaps to a desire for vengeance; for she held this world about Durham responsible for the ruin of her happiness. She knew now, as a worldly woman of forty-six, that if she had been brought up knowing life for what it was, she might never have lost the one man who had ever roused a genuine passion in a nature so hard and dry.

It was all confused and tormented and vague, yet the visit of Aunt Cassie, filled with implications and veiled attempts to humble her, had cleared the air enormously.

And behind the closed lids, the green eyes began to see a whole procession of calamities which lay perhaps within her power to create. She began to see how it might even be possible to bring the whole world of Pentlands down about their heads in a collapse which could create only freedom and happiness to Olivia and her daughter. And it was these two alone for whom she had any affection; the others might be damned, gloriously damned, while she stood by without raising a finger.

She began to see where the pieces of the puzzle lay, the wedges which might force open the solid security of the familiar, unchanging world that once more surrounded her.

Lying there in the twilight, she saw the whole thing in the process of being fitted together and she experienced a sudden intoxicating sense of power, of having all the tools at hand, of being the *dea ex machinâ* of the calamity.

She was beginning to see, too, how the force, the power that had lain behind all the family, was coming slowly to an end in a pale, futile weakness. There would always be money to bolster up their world, for the family had never lost its shopkeeping tradition of thrift; but in the end even money could not save them. There came a time when a great fortune might be only a shell without a desiccated rottenness inside.

She was still lying there when Thérèse came in—a short, plain, rather stocky, dark girl with a low straight black bang across her forehead. She was hot and soiled by the mud of the marshes, as the red-haired unhappy little girl had been so many times in that far-off, half-forgotten childhood.

"Where have you been?" she asked indifferently, for there was always a curious sense of strangeness between Sabine and her daughter.

"Catching frogs to dissect," said Thérèse. "They're damned scarce and I slipped into the river."

Sabine, looking at her daughter, knew well enough there was no chance of marrying off a girl so queer, and wilful and untidy, in Durham. She saw that it had been a silly idea from the beginning; but she found satisfaction in the knowledge that she had molded Thérèse's life so that no one could ever hurt her as they had hurt her mother. Out of the queer nomadic life they had led together, meeting all sorts of men and women who were, in Sabine's curious sense of the word, "complete," the girl had pierced her way somehow to the bottom of things. She was building her young life upon a rock, so that she could afford to feel contempt for the very forces which long ago had hurt her mother. She might, like O'Hara, be suddenly humbled by love; but that, Sabine knew, was a glorious thing well worth suffering.

She knew it each time that she looked at her child and saw the clear gray eyes of the girl's father looking out of the dark face with the same proud look of indifferent confidence which had fascinated her twenty years ago. So long as Thérèse was alive, she would never be able wholly to forget him.

"Go wash yourself," she said. "Old Mr. Pentland and Olivia and Mrs. Soames are coming to dine and play bridge."

As she dressed for dinner she no longer asked herself, "Why did I ever imagine Thérèse might find a husband here? What ever induced me to come back here to be bored all summer long?"

She had forgotten all that. She began to see that the summer held prospects of diversion. It might even turn into a fascinating game. She knew that her return had nothing to do with Thérèse's future; she had been drawn back into Durham by some vague but overwhelming desire for mischief.

Chapter V

I

WHEN ANSON PENTLAND CAME DOWN from the city in the evening, Olivia was always there to meet him dutifully and inquire about the day. The answers were always the same: "No there was not much doing in town," and, "It was very hot," or "I made a discovery today that will be of great use to me in the book."

Then after a bath he would appear in tweeds to take his exercise in the garden, pottering about mildly and peering closely with his near-sighted blue eyes at little tags labeled "General Pershing" or "Caroline Testout" or "Poincaré" or "George Washington" which he tied carefully on the new dahlias and roses and smaller shrubs. And, more often than not, the gardener would spend half the next morning removing the tags and placing them on the proper plants, for Anson really had no interest in flowers and knew very little about them. The tagging was only a part of his passion for labeling things; it made the garden at Pentlands seem a more subdued and ordered place. Sometimes it seemed to Olivia that he went through life ticketing and pigeonholing everything that came his way: manners, emotions, thoughts, everything. It was a habit that was growing on him in middle-age.

Dinner was usually late because Anson liked to take advantage of the long summer twilights, and after dinner it was the habit of all the family, save Jack, who went to bed immediately afterward, to sit in the Victorian drawing room, reading and writing letters or sometimes playing patience, with Anson in his corner at Mr. Lowell's desk working over "The Pentland Family and the Massachusetts Bay Colony," and keeping up a prodigious correspondence with librarians and old men and women of a genealogical bent. The routine of the evening rarely changed, for Anson disliked going out and Olivia preferred not to go alone. It was only with the beginning of the summer, when Sybil was grown and had begun to go out occasionally to dinners and balls, and the disturbing Sabine, with her passion for playing bridge, had come into the neighborhood, that the routine was beginning to break up. There were fewer evenings now with Olivia and Sybil playing patience and old John Pentland sitting by the light of Mr. Longfellow's lamp reading or simply staring silently before him, lost in thought.

There were times in those long evenings when Olivia, looking up suddenly and for no reason at all, would discover that Sybil was sitting in the same fashion watching her, and both of them would know that they, like old John Pentland, had been sitting there all the while holding books in their hands without knowing a word of what they had read. It was as if a kind of enchantment descended upon them, as if they were waiting for something. Once or twice the silence had been broken sharply by the unbearable sound of groans coming from the north wing when *she* had been seized suddenly by one of her fits of violence.

Anson's occasional comment and Olivia's visits to Jack's room to see that nothing had happened to him were the only interruptions. They spoke always in low voices when they played double patience in order not to disturb Anson at his work. Sometimes he encountered a bit of information for which he had been searching for a long time and then he would turn and tell them of it.

There was the night when he made his discovery about Savina Pentland. . .

"I was right about Savina Pentland," he said. "She *was* a first cousin and not a second cousin of Toby Cane."

Olivia displayed an interest by saying, "Was that what you wrote to the *Transcript* about?"

"Yes. . . and I was sure that the genealogical editor was wrong. See. . . here it is in one of Jared Pentland's letters at the time she was drowned. . . Jared was her husband. . . He refers to Toby Cane as her only male first cousin."

"That will help you a great deal," said Olivia, "won't it?"

"It will help clear up the chapter about the origins of her family." And then, after a little pause, "I wish that I could get some trace of the correspondence between Savina Pentland and Cane. I'm sure it would be full of things. . . but it seems not to exist. . . only one or two letters which tell nothing."

And then he relapsed again into a complete and passionate silence lost in the rustle of old books and yellowed letters, leaving the legend of Savina Pentland to take possession of the others in the room.

The memory of this woman had a way of stealing in upon the family unaware, quite without their willing it. She was always there in the house, more lively than any of the more sober ancestors, perhaps because of them all she alone had been touched by splendor; she alone had been in her reckless way a great lady. There was a power in her recklessness and extravagance which came, in the end, to obscure all those other plain, solemn-faced, thrifty wives whose portraits adorned the hall of Pentlands, much as a rising sun extinguishes the feeble light of the stars. And about her obscure origin there clung a perpetual aura of romance, since there was no one to know just who her mother was or exactly whence she came. The mother was born perhaps of stock no humbler than the first shopkeeping Pentland to land on the Cape, but there was in her the dark taint of Portuguese blood; some said that she was the daughter of a fisherman. And Savina herself had possessed enough of fascination to lure a cautious Pentland into eloping with her against the scruples that were a very fiber of the Pentland bones and flesh.

The portrait of Savina Pentland stood forth among the others in the white hall, fascinating and beautiful not only because the subject was a dark, handsome woman, but because it had been done by Ingres in Rome during the years when he made portraits of tourists to save himself from starvation. It was the likeness of a small but voluptuous woman with great wanton dark eyes and smooth black hair pulled back from a camellia-white brow and done in a little knot on the nape of the white neck—a woman who looked out of the old picture with the flashing, spirited glance of one who lived boldly and passionately. She wore a gown of peach-colored velvet ornamented with the famous parure of pearls and emeralds given her, to the scandal of a thrifty family, by the infatuated Jared Pentland. Passing the long gallery of portraits in the hallway it was always Savina Pentland whom one noticed. She reigned there as she must have reigned in life, so bold and splendorous as to seem a bit vulgar, especially in a world of such sober folk, yet so beautiful and so spirited that she made all the others seem scarcely worth consideration.

Even in death she had remained an "outsider," for she was the only one of the family who did not rest quietly among the stunted trees at the top of the bald hill where the first Pentlands had laid their dead. All that was left of the warm, soft body lay in the white sand at the bottom of the ocean within sight of Pentlands. It was as if fate had delivered her in death into a grave as tempestuous and violent as she had been in life. And somewhere near her in the restless white sand lay Toby Cane, with whom she had gone sailing one bright summer day when a sudden squall turned a gay excursion into a tragedy.

Even Aunt Cassie, who distrusted any woman with gaze so bold and free as that set down by the brush of Ingres—even Aunt Cassie could

LOUIS BROMFIELD

not annihilate the glamour of Savina's legend. For her there was, too, another, more painful, memory hidden in the knowledge that the parure of pearls and emeralds and all the other jewels which Savina Pentland had wrung from her thrifty husband, lay buried somewhere in the white sand between her bones and those of her cousin. To Aunt Cassie Savina Pentland seemed more than merely a reckless, extravagant creature. She was an enemy of the Pentland fortune and of all the virtues of the family.

The family portraits were of great value to Anson in compiling his book, for they represented the most complete collection of ancestors existing in all America. From the portrait of the emigrating Pentland, painted in a wooden manner by some traveling painter of tavern signs, to the rather handsome one of John Pentland, painted at middle-age in a pink coat by Sargent, and the rather bad and liverish one of Anson, also by Mr. Sargent, the collection was complete save for two—the weak Jared Pentland who had married Savina, and the Pentland between old John's father and the clipper-ship owner, who had died at twenty-three, a disgraceful thing for any Pentland to have done.

The pictures hung in a neat double row in the lofty hall, arranged chronologically and without respect for lighting, so that the good ones like those by Ingres and Sargent's picture of old John Pentland and the unfinished Gilbert Stuart of Ashur Pentland hung in obscure shadows, and the bad ones like the tavern-sign portrait of the first Pentland were exposed in a glare of brilliant light.

This father of all the family had been painted at the great age of eighty-nine and looked out from his wooden background, a grim, hard-mouthed old fellow with white hair and shrewd eyes set very close together. It was a face such as one might find today among the Plymouth Brethren of some remote, half-forgotten Sussex village, the face of a man notable only for the toughness of his body and the rigidity of a mind which dissented from everything. At the age of eighty-four, he had been cast out for dissension from the church which he had come to regard as his own property.

Next to him hung the portrait of a Pentland who had been a mediocrity and left not even a shadowy legend; and then appeared the insolent, disagreeable face of the Pentland who had ducked eccentric old women for witches and cut off the ears of peace-loving Quakers in the colony founded in "freedom to worship God."

The third Pentland had been the greatest evangelist of his time, a man who went through New England holding high the torch, exhorting rude village audiences by the coarsest of language to such a pitch of excitement that old women died of apoplexy and young women gave birth to premature children. The sermons which still existed showed him to be a man uncultivated and at times almost illiterate, yet his vast energy had founded a university and his fame as an exhorter and "the flaming sword of the Lord" had traveled to the ignorant and simple-minded brethren of the English back country.

The next Pentland was the eldest of the exhorter's twenty children (by four wives), a man who clearly had departed from his father's counsels and appeared in his portrait a sensual, fleshly specimen, very fat and almost good-natured, with thick red lips. It was this Pentland who had founded the fortune which gave the family its first step upward in the direction of the gentility which had ended with the figure of Anson bending over "The Pentland Family and the Massachusetts Bay Colony." He had made a large fortune by equipping privateers and practising a near-piracy on British merchantmen; and there was, too, a dark rumor (which Anson intended to overlook) that he had made as much as three hundred percent profit on a single shipload of negroes in the African slave trade.

After him there were portraits of two Pentlands who had taken part in the Revolution and then another hiatus of mediocrity, including the gap represented by the missing Jared; and then appeared the Anthony Pentland who increased the fortune enormously in the clipper trade. It was the portrait of a swarthy, powerful man (the first of the dark Pentlands, who could all be traced directly to Savina's Portuguese blood), painted by a second-rate artist devoted to realism, who had depicted skilfully the warts which marred the distinguished old gentleman. In the picture he stood in the garden before the Pentland house at Durham with marshes in the background and his prize clipper *Semiramis* riding, with all sail up, the distant ocean.

Next to him appeared the portrait of old John Pentland's father—a man of pious expression, dressed all in black, with a high black stock and a wave of luxuriant black hair, the one who had raised the family to really great wealth by contracts for shoes and blankets for the soldiers at Gettysburg and Bull Run and Richmond. After him, gentility had conquered completely, and the Sargent portrait of old John Pentland at middle-age showed a man who was master of hounds and led the life of a country gentleman, a man clearly of power and character, whose strength of feature had turned slowly into the bitter hardness of the old man who sat now in the light of Mr. Longfellow's lamp reading or staring before him into space while his son set down the long history of the family.

The gallery was fascinating to strangers, as the visual record of a family which had never lost any money (save for the extravagance of Savina Pentland's jewels), a family which had been the backbone of a community, a family in which the men married wives for thrift and housewifely virtues rather than for beauty, a family solid and respectable and full of honor. It was a tribe magnificent in its virtue and its strength, even at times in its intolerance and hypocrisy. It stood represented now by old John Pentland and Anson, and the boy who lay above stairs in the room next Olivia's, dying slowly.

AT TEN O'CLOCK EACH NIGHT John Pentland bade them goodnight and went off to bed, and at eleven Anson, after arranging his desk neatly and placing his papers in their respective files, and saying to Olivia, "I wouldn't sit up too late, if I were you, when you are so tired," left them and disappeared. Soon after him, Sybil kissed her mother and climbed the stairs past all the ancestors.

It was only then, after they had all left her, that a kind of peace settled over Olivia. The burdens lifted, and the cares, the worries, the thoughts that were always troubling her, faded into the distance and for a time she sat leaning back in the winged armchair with her eyes closed, listening to the sounds of the night—the faint murmur of the breeze in the faded lilacs outside the window, the creaking that afflicts very old houses in the night, and sometimes the ominous sound of Miss Egan's step traversing distantly the old north wing. And then one night she heard again the distant sound of Higgins' voice swearing at the red mare as he made his round of the stables before going to bed.

And after they had all gone she opened her book and fell to reading. *"Madame de Clèves ne répondit rien, et elle pensoit avec honte qu'elle auroit pris tout ce que l'on disoit du changement de ce prince pour des marques de sa passion, si elle n'avoit point été détrompée. Elle se sentoit quelque aigreur contre Madame la Dauphine. . . ."* This was a world in which she felt somehow strangely at peace, as if she had once lived in it and returned in the silence of the night.

At midnight she closed the book, and making a round of the lower rooms, put out the lights and went up to the long stairway to listen at the doorway of her son's room for the weak, uncertain sound of his breathing.

II

OLIVIA WAS RIGHT IN HER belief that Anson was ashamed of his behavior on the night of the ball. It was not that he made an apology or even mentioned the affair. He simply never spoke of it again. For weeks after the scene he did not mention the name of O'Hara, perhaps because the name brought up inevitably the memory of his sudden, insulting speech; but his sense of shame prevented him from harassing her on the subject. What he never knew was that Olivia, while hating him for the insult aimed at her father, was also pleased in a perverse, feminine way because he had displayed for a moment a sudden fit of genuine anger. For a moment he had come very near to being a husband who might interest his wife.

But in the end he only sank back again into a sea of indifference so profound that even Aunt Cassie's campaign of insinuations and veiled proposals could not stir him into action. The old woman managed to see him alone once or twice, saying to him, "Anson, your father is growing old and can't manage everything much longer. You must begin to take a stand yourself. The family can't rest on the shoulders of a woman. Besides, Olivia is an outsider, really. She's never understood our world." And then, shaking her head sadly, she would murmur, "There'll be trouble, Anson, when your father dies, if you don't show some backbone. You'll have trouble with Sybil; she's very queer and pig-headed in her quiet way, just as Olivia was in the matter of sending her to school in Paris."

And after a pause, "I am the last person in the world to interfere; it's only for your own good and Olivia's and all the family's."

And Anson, to be rid of her, would make promises, facing her with averted eyes in some corner of the garden or the old house where she had skilfully run him to earth beyond the possibility of escape. And he would leave her, troubled and disturbed because the world and this family which had been saddled unwillingly upon him, would permit him no peace to go on with his writing. He really hated Aunt Cassie because she had never given him any peace, never since the days when she had kept him in the velvet trousers and Fauntleroy curls which spurred the jeers of the plain, red-haired little Sabine. She had never ceased to reproach him for "not being a man and standing up for his rights." It seemed to him that Aunt Cassie was always hovering near, like a dark persistent fury, always harassing him; and yet he knew, more by instinct than by any process of reasoning, that she was his ally against the others, even his own wife and father and children. He and Aunt Cassie prayed to the same gods.

So he did nothing, and Olivia, keeping her word, spoke of O'Hara to Sybil one day as they sat alone at breakfast.

The girl had been riding with him that very morning and she sat in her riding-clothes, her face flushed by the early morning exercise, telling her mother of the beauties of the country back of Durham, of the new beagle puppies, and of the death of "Hardhead" Smith, who was the last farmer of old New England blood in the county. His half-witted son, she said, was being taken away to an asylum. O'Hara, she said, was buying his little stony patch of ground.

When she had finished, her mother said, "And O'Hara? You like him, don't you?"

Sybil had a way of looking piercingly at a person, as if her violet eyes tried to bore quite through all pretense and unveil the truth. She had a power of honesty and simplicity that was completely disarming, and she used it now, smiling at her mother, candidly.

"Yes, I like him very much. . . But. . . but. . ." She laughed softly. "Are you worrying about my marrying him, my falling in love—because you needn't. I am fond of him because he's the one person around here who likes the things I like. He loves riding in the early morning when the dew is still on the grass and he likes racing with me across the lower meadow by the gravel-pit, and well—he's an interesting man. When he talks, he makes sense. But don't worry; I shan't marry him."

"I *was* interested," said Olivia, "because you do see him more than anyone about here."

Again Sybil laughed. "But he's old, Mama. He's more than thirty-five. He's middle-aged. I know what sort of man I want to marry. I know exactly. He's going to be my own age."

"One can't always tell. It's not so easy as that."

"I'm sure I can tell." Her face took on an expression of gravity. "I've devoted a good deal of thought to it and I've watched a great many others."

Olivia wanted to smile, but she knew she dared not if she were to keep her hold upon confidences so charming and naïve.

"And I'm sure that I'll know the man when I see him, right away, at once. It'll be like a spark, like my friendship with O'Hara, only deeper than that."

"Did you ever talk to Thérèse about love?" asked Olivia.

"No; you can't talk to her about such things. She wouldn't understand. With Thérèse everything is scientific, biological. When Thérèse marries, I think it will be some man she has picked out as the proper father, scientifically, for her children."

"That's not a bad idea."

"She might just have children by him without marrying him, the way she breeds frogs. I think that's horrible."

Again Olivia was seized with an irresistible impulse to laugh, and controlled herself heroically. She kept thinking of how silly, how ignorant, she had been at Sybil's age, silly and ignorant despite the unclean sort of sophistication she had picked up in the corridors of Continental hotels. She kept thinking how much better a chance Sybil had for happiness... Sybil, sitting there gravely, defending her warm ideas of romance against the scientific onslaughts of the swarthy, passionate Thérèse.

"It will be someone like O'Hara," continued Sybil. "Someone who is very much alive—only not middle-aged like O'Hara."

(So Sybil thought of O'Hara as middle-aged, and he was four years younger than Olivia, who felt and looked so young. The girl kept talking of O'Hara as if his life were over; but that perhaps was only because she herself was so young.)

Olivia sighed now, despite herself. "You mustn't expect too much from the world, Sybil. Nothing is perfect, not even marriage. One always has to make compromises."

"Oh, I know that; I've thought a great deal about it. All the same, I'm sure I'll know the man when I see him." She leaned forward and said earnestly, "Couldn't you tell when you were a girl?"

"Yes," said Olivia softly. "I could tell."

And then, inevitably, Sybil asked what Olivia kept praying she would not ask. She could hear the girl asking it before the words were spoken. She knew exactly what she would say.

"Didn't you know at once when you met Father?"

And in spite of every effort, the faint echo of a sigh escaped Olivia. "Yes, I knew."

She saw Sybil give her one of those quick, piercing looks of inquiry

LOUIS BROMFIELD

and then bow her head abruptly, as if pretending to study the pattern on her plate.

When she spoke again, she changed the subject abruptly, so that Olivia knew she suspected the truth, a thing which she had guarded with a fierce secrecy for so long.

"Why don't you take up riding again, Mother?" she asked "I'd love to have you go with me. We would go with O'Hara in the mornings, and then Aunt Cassie couldn't have anything to say about my getting involved with him." She looked up. "You'd like him. You couldn't help it."

She saw that Sybil was trying to help her in some way, to divert her and drive away the unhappiness.

"I like him already," said Olivia, "very much."

Then she rose, saying, "I promised Sabine to motor into Boston with her today. We're leaving in twenty minutes."

She went quickly away because she knew it was perilous to sit there any longer talking of such things while Sybil watched her, eager with the freshness of youth which has all life before it.

Out of all their talk two things remained distinct in her mind: one that Sybil thought of O'Hara as middle-aged—almost an old man, for whom there was no longer any chance of romance; the other the immense possibility for tragedy that lay before a girl who was so certain that love would be a glorious romantic affair, so certain of the ideal man whom she would find one day. What was she to do with Sybil? Where was she to find that man? And when she found him, what difficulties would she have to face with John Pentland and Anson and Aunt Cassie and the host of cousins and connections who would be marshaled to defeat her?

For she saw clearly enough that this youth for whom Sybil was waiting would never be their idea of a proper match. It would be a man with qualities which O'Hara possessed, and even Higgins, the groom. She saw perfectly why Sybil had a fondness for these two outsiders; she had come to see it more and more clearly of late. It was because they possessed a curious, indefinable solidity that the others at Pentlands all lacked, and a certain fire and vitality. Neither blood, nor circumstance, nor tradition, nor wealth, had made life for them an atrophied, empty affair, in which there was no need for effort, for struggle, for combat. They had not been lost in a haze of transcendental maunderings. O'Hara, with his career and his energy, and Higgins, with his rabbit-like love-affairs and his nearness to all that was earthy, still carried about them a sense of the great zest in life. They reached down somehow into the roots of things where there was still savor and fertility.

And as she walked along the hallway, she found herself laughing aloud over the titles of the only three books which the Pentland family had ever produced—"The Pentland Family and the Massachusetts Bay Colony" and Mr. Struthers' two books, "Cornices of Old Boston Houses" and "Walks and Talks in New England Churchyards." She thought suddenly of what Sabine had once said acidly of New England—that it was a place where thoughts were likely to grow "higher and fewer."

But she was frightened, too, because in the life of enchantment which surrounded her, the virtues of O'Hara and Higgins seemed to her the only things in the world worth possessing. She wanted desperately to be alive, as she had never been, and she knew that this, too, was what Sybil sought in all her groping, half-blind romantic youth. It was something which the girl sensed and had never clearly understood, something which she knew existed and was awaiting her.

III

SABINE, WATCHING O'HARA AS HE crossed the fields through the twilight, had penetrated in a sudden flash of intuition the depths of his character. His profound loneliness was, perhaps, the key which unlocked the whole of his soul, a key which Sabine knew well enough, for there had never been a time in all her existence, save for a sudden passionate moment or two in the course of her life with Callendar, when she was free of a painful feeling that she was alone. Even with her own daughter, the odd Thérèse, she was lonely. Watching life with the same passionate intensity with which she had watched the distant figure of O'Hara moving away against the horizon, she had come long ago to understand that loneliness was the curse of those who were free, even of all those who rose a little above the level of ordinary humanity. Looking about her she saw that old John Pentland was lonely, and Olivia, and even her own daughter Thérèse, rambling off independently across the marshes in search of bugs and queer plants. She saw that Anson Pentland was never lonely, for he had his friends who were so like him as to be very nearly indistinguishable, and he had all the traditions and fetishes which he shared with Aunt Cassie. They were part of a fabric, a small corner in the whole tapestry of life, from which they were inseparable.

Of them all, it seemed to her, as she came to see more and more of O'Hara, that he was the most lonely. He had friends, scores, even hundreds of them, in a dozen circles, ranging from the docks where he had spent his boyhood to the world about Durham where there were others who treated him less coldly than the Pentland family had done. He had friends because there was a quality about him which was irresistible. It lurked somewhere in the depths of the humorous blue eyes and at the corners of the full, rather sensual mouth—a kind of universal sympathy which made him understand the fears, the hopes, the ambitions, the weaknesses of other people. It was that quality, so invaluable in politics, which led enemies unjustly to call him all things to all people. He must have had the gift of friendship, for there were whole sections of Boston which would have followed him anywhere; and yet behind these easy, warm ties there was always a sort of veil shutting him away from them. He had a way of being at home in a barroom or at a hunt breakfast with equal ease, but there was a part of him—the part which was really O'Hara—which the world never saw at all, a strangely warm, romantic, impractical, passionate, headlong, rather unscrupulous Irishman, who lay shut away where none could penetrate. Sabine knew this O'Hara; he had been revealed to her swiftly in a sudden flash at the mention of Olivia Pentland. And afterward when she thought of it, she (Sabine Callendar), who was so hard, so bitter, so unbelieving, surrendered to him as so many had done before her.

Standing there in her sittingroom, so big and powerful and self-reliant, he had seemed suddenly like a little boy, like the little boy whom she had found once late at night long ago, sitting alone and quite still on the curb in front of her house in the Rue de Tilsitt. She had stopped for a moment and watched him, and presently she had approached and asked, "What are you doing here on the curb at this hour of the night?" And the little boy, looking up, had said gravely, "I'm playing."

It had happened years ago—the little boy must have grown into a young man by now—but she remembered him suddenly during the moment when O'Hara had turned and said to her, "It will mean a great deal to me, more than you can imagine."

O'Hara was like that, she knew—sad and a little lonely, as if in the midst of all his success, with his career and his big new house and his dogs and horses and all the other shiny accoutrements of a gentleman, he had looked up at her and said gravely, "I'm playing."

Long ago Sabine had come to understand that one got a savor out of life by casting overboard all the little rules which clutter up existence, all the ties, and beliefs and traditions in which she had been given a training so intense and severe that in the end she had turned a rebel. Behind all the indifference of countenance and the intricacy of brain, there lay a foundation of immense candor which had driven her to seek her companions, with the directness of an arrow, only among the persons whom she had come to designate as "complete." It was a label which she did not trouble to define to anyone, doubting perhaps that anyone save herself would find any interest in it; even for herself, it was a label lacking in definiteness. Vaguely she meant by "complete" the persons who stood on their own, who had an existence sufficiently strong to survive the assault or the collapse of any environment, persons who might exist independent of any concrete world, who possessed a proud sense of individuality, who might take root and work out a successful destiny wherever fate chanced to drop them. They were rare, she had come to discover, and yet they existed everywhere, such persons as John Pentland and O'Hara, Olivia and Higgins.

So she had come to seek her life among them, drawing them quietly about her wherever in the world she happened to pause for a time. She did it quietly and without loud cries of "Freedom" and "Free Love" and "The Right to Lead One's Life," for she was enough civilized to understand the absurdity of making a spectacle in the marketplace, and she was too intense an individualist ever to turn missionary. Here perhaps lay her quiet strength and the source of that vague distrust and uneasiness which her presence created in people like Anson and Aunt Cassie. It was unbearable for Aunt Cassie to suspect that Sabine really did not trouble even to scorn her, unbearable to an old woman who had spent all her life in arranging the lives of others to find that a chit of a woman like Sabine could discover in her only a subject of mingled mirth and pity. It was unbearable not to have the power of jolting Sabine out of her serene and insolent indifference, unbearable to know that she was always watching you out of those green eyes, turning you over and over as if you were a bug and finding you in the end an inferior sort of insect. Those who had shared the discovery of her secret were fond of her, and those who had not were bitter against her. And it was, after all, a very simple secret, that one has only to be simple and friendly and human and "complete." She had no patience with sentimentality, and affectation and false piety.

And so the presence of Sabine began slowly to create a vaguely defined rift in a world hitherto set and complacent and even proud of itself. Something in the sight of her cold green eyes, in the sound of her metallic voice, in the sudden shrewd, disillusioning observations which she had a way of making at disconcerting moments, filled people like Aunt Cassie with uneasiness and people like Olivia with a smoldering sense of restlessness and rebellion. Olivia herself became more and more conscious of the difference with the passing of each day into the next and there were times when she suspected that that fierce old man, her father-in-law, was aware of it. It was potent because Sabine was no outsider; the mockery of an outsider would have slipped off the back of the Durham world like arrows off the back of an armadillo. But Sabine was one of them: it was that which made the difference: she was always inside the shell.

IV

ONE HOT, BREATHLESS NIGHT IN June Sabine overcame her sense of bored indolence enough to give a dinner at Brook Cottage—a dinner well served, with delicious food, which it might have been said she flung at her guests with a superb air of indifference from the seat at the head of the table, where she sat painted, ugly and magnificently dressed, watching them all in a perverse sort of pleasure. It was a failure as an entertainment, for it had been years since Sabine had given a dinner where the guests were not clever enough to entertain themselves, and now that she was back again in a world where people were invited for every sort of reason save that you really wanted their company, she declined to make any effort. It was a failure, too, because Thérèse, for whom it was given, behaved exactly as she had behaved on the night of the ball. There was an uneasiness and a strain, a sense of awkwardness among the callow young men and a sense of weariness in Sabine and Olivia. O'Hara was there, for Sabine had kept her half-promise; but even he sat quietly, all his boldness and dash vanished before a boyish shyness. The whole affair seemed to be drowned in the lassitude, the enchantment that enveloped the old house on the other bank of the river.

Olivia had come, almost against her will, reduced to a state of exhaustion after a long call from Aunt Cassie on the subject of the rumored affair between Sybil and their Irish neighbor. And when they rose, she slipped quietly away into the garden, because she could not bear the thought of making strained and artificial conversation. She wanted, horribly, to be left in peace.

It was a superb night—hot, as a summer night should be—but clear, too, so that the whole sky was like a sapphire dome studded with diamonds. At the front of the cottage, beyond the borders of the little terraced garden, the marshes spread their dark carpet toward the distant dunes, which with the descent of darkness had turned dim and blue against the purer white of the line made by the foaming surf. The feel of the damp thick grass against the sole of her silver slippers led her to stop for a moment, breathing deeply, and filled her with a mild, half-mystical desire to blend herself into all the beauty that surrounded her, into the hot richness of the air, the scents of the opening blossoms and of pushing green stems, into the grass and the sea and the rich-smelling marshes, to slip away into a state which was nothing and yet everything, to float into eternity. She had abruptly an odd, confused sense of the timelessness of all these forces and sensations, of the sea and the marshes, the pushing green stems and the sapphire dome powdered with diamonds above her head. She saw for the first time in all her existence the power of something which went on and on, ignoring pitiful small creatures like herself and all those others in the cottage behind her, a power which ignored cities and armies and nations, which would go on and on long after the grass had blanketed the ruins of the old house at Pentland. It was sweeping past her, leaving her stranded somewhere in the dull backwaters. She wanted suddenly, fiercely, to take part in all the great spectacle of eternal fertility, a mystery which was stronger than any of them or all of them together, a force which in the end would crush all their transient little prides and beliefs and traditions.

And then she thought, as if she were conscious of it for the first time, "I am tired, tired to death, and a little mad."

Moving across the damp grass she seated herself on a stone bench which O'Hara had placed beneath one of the ancient apple-trees left standing from the orchard which had covered all the land about Brook Cottage in the days when Savina Pentland was still alive; and for a long time (she never knew how long) she remained there lost in one of those strange lapses of consciousness when one is neither awake nor asleep but in the vague borderland where there is no thought, no care, no troubles. And then slowly she became aware of someone standing there quite near her, beneath the ancient, gnarled tree. As if the presence were materialized somehow out of a dream, she noticed first the faint, insinuating masculine odor of cigar-smoke blending itself with the scent of the growing flowers in Sabine's garden, and then turning she saw a black figure which she recognized at once as that of O'Hara. There was no surprise in the sight of him; it seemed in a queer way as if she had been expecting him.

As she turned, he moved toward her and spoke. "Our garden has flourished, hasn't it?" he asked. "You'd never think it was only a year old."

"Yes," she said. "It has flourished marvelously." And then, after a little pause, "How long have you been standing there?"

"Only a moment. I saw you come out of the house." They listened for a time to the distant melancholy pounding of the surf, and presently he said softly, with a kind of awe in his voice: "It is a marvelous night. . . a night full of splendor."

She made an effort to answer him, but somehow she could think of nothing to say. The remark, uttered so quietly, astonished her, because she had never thought of O'Hara as one who would be sensitive to the beauty of a night. It was too dark to distinguish his face, but she kept seeing him as she remembered him, seeing him, too, as the others thought of him—rough and vigorous but a little common, with the scar on his temple and the intelligent blue eyes, and the springy walk, so unexpectedly easy and full of grace for a man of his size. No, one might as well have expected little Higgins the groom to say: "It is a night full of splendor." The men she knew—Anson's friends—never said such things. She doubted whether they would ever notice such a night, and if they did notice it, they would be a little ashamed of having done anything so unusual.

"The party is not a great success," he was saying.

"No."

"No one seems to be getting on with anyone else. Mrs. Callendar ought not to have asked me. I thought she was shrewder than that."

Olivia laughed softly. "She may have done it on purpose. You can never tell why she does anything."

For a time he remained silent, as if pondering the speech, and then he said, "You aren't cold out here?"

"No, not on a night like this."

There was a silence so long and so vaguely perilous that she felt the need of making some speech, politely and with banality, as if they were two strangers seated in a drawing room after dinner instead of in the garden which together they had made beneath the ancient apple-trees.

"I keep wondering," she said, "how long it will be until the bungalows of Durham creep down and cover all this land."

"They won't, not so long as I own land between Durham and the sea."

In the darkness she smiled at the thought of an Irish Roman Catholic politician as the protector of this old New England countryside, and aloud she said, "You're growing to be like all the others. You want to make the world stand still."

"Yes, I can see that it must seem funny to you." There was no bitterness in his voice, but only a sort of hurt, which again astonished her, because it was impossible to think of O'Hara as one who could be hurt.

"There will always be the Pentland house, but, of course, all of us will die some day and then what?"

"There will always be our children."

She was aware slowly of slipping back into that world of cares and troubles behind her from which she had escaped a little while before. She said, "*You* are looking a long way into the future."

"Perhaps, but I mean to have children one day. And at Pentlands there is always Sybil, who will fight for it fiercely. She'll never give it up."

"But it's Jack who will own it, and I'm not so sure about him."

Unconsciously she sighed, knowing now that she was pretending again, being dishonest. She was pretending again that Jack would live to have Pentlands for his own, that he would one day have children who would carry it on. She kept saying to herself, "It is only the truth that can save us all." And she knew that O'Hara understood her feeble game of pretending. She knew because he stood there silently, as if Jack were already dead, as if he understood the reason for the faint bitter sigh and respected it.

"You see a great deal of Sybil, don't you?" she asked.

"Yes, she is a good girl. One can depend on her."

"Perhaps if she had a little of Thérèse or Mrs. Callendar in her, she'd be safer from being hurt."

He did not answer her at once, but she knew that in the darkness he was standing there, watching her.

"But that was a silly thing to say," she murmured. "I don't suppose you know what I mean."

He answered her quickly. "I do know exactly. I know and I'm sure

Mrs. Callendar knows. We've both learned to save ourselves—not in the same school, but the same lesson, nevertheless. But as to Sybil, I think that depends upon whom she marries."

("So now," thought Olivia, "it is coming. It is Sybil whom he loves. He wants to marry her. That is why he has followed me out here.") She was back again now, solidly enmeshed in all the intricacies of living. She had a sudden, shameful, twinge of jealousy for Sybil, who was so young, who had pushed her so completely into the past along with all the others at Pentlands.

"I was wondering," she said, "whether she was not seeing too much of you, whether she might not be a bother."

"No, she'll never be that." And then in a voice which carried a faint echo of humor, he added, "I know that in a moment you are going to ask my intentions."

"No," she said, "no"; but she could think of nothing else to say. She felt suddenly shy and awkward and a little idiotic, like a young girl at her first dance.

"I shall tell you what my intentions are," he was saying, and then he broke off suddenly. "Why is it so impossible to be honest in this world, when we live such a little while? It would be such a different place if we were all honest wouldn't it?"

He hesitated, waiting for her to answer, and she said, "Yes," almost mechanically, "very different."

When he replied there was a faint note of excitement in his voice. It was pitched a little lower and he spoke more quickly. In the darkness she could not see him, and yet she was sharply conscious of the change.

"I'll tell you, then," he was saying. "I've been seeing a great deal of Sybil in the hope that I should see a little of her mother."

She did not answer him. She simply sat there, speechless, overcome by confusion, as if she had been a young girl with her first lover. She was even made a little dizzy by the sound of his voice.

"I have offended you. I'm sorry. I only spoke the truth. There is no harm in that."

With a heroic effort to speak intelligently, she succeeded in saying, "No, I am not offended." (It all seemed such a silly, helpless, pleasant feeling.) "No, I'm not offended. I don't know. . ."

Of only one thing was she certain; that this strange, dizzy, intoxicated state was like nothing she had ever experienced. It was sinister and overwhelming in a bitter-sweet fashion. She kept thinking, "I can begin to understand how a young girl can be seduced, how she cannot know what she is doing."

"I suppose," he was saying, "that you think me presumptuous."

"No, I only think everything is impossible, insane."

"You think me a kind of ruffian, a bum, an Irishman, a Roman Catholic, someone you have never heard of." He waited, and then added: "I *am* all that, from one point of view."

"No, I don't think that; I don't think that."

He sat down beside her quietly on the stone bench. "You have every right to think it," he continued softly. "Every right in the world, and still things like that make no difference, nothing makes any difference."

"My father," she said softly, "was a man very like you. His enemies sometimes used to call him 'shanty Irish.' . . ."

She knew all the while that she should have risen and sought indignant refuge in the house. She knew that perhaps she was being absurd, and yet she stayed there quietly. She was so tired and she had waited for so long (she only knew it now in a sudden flash) to have someone talk to her in just this way, as if she were a woman. She needed someone to lean upon, so desperately.

"How can you know me?" she asked out of a vague sense of helplessness. "How can you know anything about me?"

He did not touch her. He only sat there in the darkness, making her feel by a sort of power which was too strong for her, that all he said was terribly the truth.

"I know, I know, all about you, everything. I've watched you. I've understood you, even better than the others. A man whose life has been like mine sees and understands a great deal that others never notice because for him everything depends upon a kind of second sight. It's the one great weapon of the opportunist." There was a silence and he asked, "Can you understand that? It may be hard, because your life has been so different."

"Not so different, as you might think, only perhaps I've made more of a mess of it." And straightening her body, she murmured, "It is foolish of me to let you talk this way."

He interrupted her with a quick burst of almost boyish eagerness. "But you're glad, aren't you? You're glad, all the same, whether you care anything for me or not. You've deserved it for a long time."

She began to cry softly, helplessly, without a sound, the tears running down her cheeks, and she thought, "Now I'm being a supreme fool. I'm pitying myself." But she could not stop.

It appeared that even in the darkness he was aware of her tears, for he chose not to interrupt them. They sat thus for a long time in silence, Olivia conscious with a terrible aching acuteness, of the beauty of the night and finding it all strange and unreal and confused.

"I wanted you to know," he said quietly, "that there was someone near you, someone who worships you, who would give up everything for you." And after a time, "Perhaps we had better go in now. You can go in through the piazza and powder your nose. I'll go in through the door from the garden."

And as they walked across the damp, scented grass, he said, "It would be pleasant if you would join Sybil and me riding in the morning."

"But I haven't been on a horse in years," said Olivia.

THROUGHOUT THE REST OF THE evening, while she sat playing bridge with Sabine and O'Hara and the Mannering boy, her mind kept straying from the game into unaccustomed byways. It was not, she told herself, that she was even remotely in love with O'Hara; it was only that someone—a man who was no creature of ordinary attractions—had confessed his admiration for her, and so she felt young and giddy and elated. The whole affair was silly. . . and yet, yet, in a strange way, it was not silly at all. She kept thinking of Anson's remarks about his father and old Mrs. Soames, "It's a silly affair" and of Sybil saying gravely, "Only not middle-aged, like O'Hara," and it occurred to her at the same time that in all her life she felt really young for the first time. She had been young as she sat on the stone bench under the ancient apple-tree, young in spite of everything.

And aloud she would say, "Four spades," and know at once that she should have made no such bid.

She was unnerved, too, by the knowledge that there were, all the while, two pairs of eyes far more absorbed in her than in the game of bridge—the green ones of Sabine and the bright blue ones of O'Hara. She could not look up without encountering the gaze of one or the other; and to protect herself she faced them with a hard, banal little smile which she put in place in the mechanical way used by Miss Egan. It was the sort of smile which made her face feel very tired, and for the first time she had a half-comic flash of pity for Miss Egan. The face of the nurse must at times have grown horribly tired.

THE GIDDINESS STILL CLUNG TO her as she climbed into the motor beside Sybil and they drove off down the lane which led from Brook Cottage to Pentlands. The road was a part of a whole tracery of lanes, bordered by hedges and old trees, which bound together the houses of the countryside, and at night they served as a promenade and meeting-place for the servants of the same big houses. One came upon them in little groups of three or four, standing by gates or stone walls, gossiping and giggling together in the darkness, exchanging tales of the life that passed in the houses of their masters, stories of what the old man did yesterday, and how Mrs. So-and-so only took one bath a week. There was a whole world which lay beneath the solid, smooth, monotonous surface that shielded the life of the wealthy, a world which in its way was full of mockery and dark secrets and petty gossip, a world perhaps fuller of truth because it lay hidden away where none— save perhaps Aunt Cassie, who knew how many fascinating secrets servants had—ever looked, and where there was small need for the sort of pretense which Olivia found so tragic. It circulated the dark lanes at night after the dinners of the neighborhood were finished, and sometimes the noisy echoes of its irreverent mockery rose in wild Irish laughter that echoed back and forth across the mist-hung meadows.

The same lanes were frequented, too, by lovers, who went in pairs instead of groups of three or four, and at times there were echoes of a different sort of merriment—the wild, half-hysterical laughter of some kitchen-maid being wooed roughly and passionately in some dark corner by a groom or a house-servant. It was a world which blossomed forth only at nightfall. Sometimes in the darkness the masters, motoring home from a ball or a dinner, would come upon an amorous couple, bathed in the sudden brilliant glare of motor-lights, sitting with their arms about each other against a tree, or lying half-hidden among a tangle of hawthorn and elder-bushes.

Tonight, as Olivia and Sybil drove in silence along the road the hot air was filled with the thick scent of the hawthorn-blossoms and the rich, dark odor of cattle, blown toward them across the meadows by the faint salt breeze from the marshes. It was late and the lights of the motor encountered no strayed lovers until at the foot of the hill by the old bridge the glare illuminated suddenly the figures of a man and

LOUIS BROMFIELD

a woman seated together against the stone wall. At their approach the woman slipped quickly over the wall, and the man, following, leaped lightly as a goat to the top and into the field beyond. Sybil laughed and murmured, "It's Higgins again."

It *was* Higgins. There was no mistaking the stocky, agile figure clad in riding-breeches and sleeveless cotton shirt, and as he leaped the wall the sight of him aroused in Olivia a nebulous fleeting impression that was like a half-forgotten memory. A startled fawn, she thought, must have scuttled off into the bushes in the same fashion. And she had suddenly that same strange, prickly feeling of terror that had affected Sabine on the night she discovered him hidden in the lilacs watching the ball.

She shivered, and Sybil asked, "You're not cold?"

"No."

She was thinking of Higgins and hoping that this was not the beginning of some new scrape. Once before a girl had come to her in trouble—a Polish girl, whom she helped and sent away because she could not see that forcing Higgins to marry her would have brought anything but misery for both of them. It never ceased to amaze her that a man so gnarled and ugly, such a savage, hairy little man as Higgins, should have half the girls of the countryside running after him.

In her own room she listened in the darkness until she heard the sound of Jack's gentle breathing and then, after undressing, she sat for a long time at the window looking out across the meadows toward the marshes. There was a subdued excitement which seemed to run through all her body and would not let her sleep. She no longer felt the weariness of spirit which had let her slip during these last few months into a kind of lethargy. She was alive, more alive than she had ever been, even as a young girl; her cheeks were hot and flushed, so that she placed her white hands against them to feel a coolness that was missing from the night air; but they, too, were hot with life.

And as she sat there, the sounds from Sybil's room across the hall died away and at last the night grew still save for the sound of her son's slow breathing and the familiar ghostly creakings of the old house. She was alone now, the only one who was not sleeping; and sitting above the mist-hung meadows she grew more quiet. The warm rich scents of the night drifted in at the window, and again she became aware of a kind of voluptuousness which she had sensed in the air as she sat, hours earlier, on Sabine's terrace above the sea. It had assailed her again as they drove through the lane across the low, marshy pastures by the river. And then in the figure of Higgins, leaping the wall like a goat, it had come with a shock to a sudden climax of feeling, with a sudden acuteness which even terrified her. It still persisted a little, the odd feeling of some tremendous, powerful force at work all about her, moving swiftly and quietly, thrusting aside and annihilating those who opposed it.

She thought again, "I am a little mad tonight. What has come over me?" And she grew frightened, though it was a different sort of terror from that which afflicted her at the odd moments when she felt all about her the presence of the dead who lived on and on at Pentlands. What she knew now was no terror of the dead; it was rather a terror of warm, passionate life. She thought, "This is what must have happened to the others. This is how they must have felt before they died."

It was not physical death that she meant, but a death somehow of the soul, a death which left behind it such withered people as Aunt Cassie and Anson, the old woman in the north wing, and even a man so rugged and powerful as John Pentland, who had struggled so much more fiercely than the others. And she got a sudden sense of being caught between two dark struggling forces in fierce combat. It was confused and vague, yet it made her feel suddenly ill in a physical sense. The warm feeling of life and excitement flowed away leaving her chilled and relaxed, weary all at once, and filled with a soft lassitude, still looking out into the night, still smelling the thick odor of cattle and hawthorn-blossoms.

SHE NEVER KNEW WHETHER OR not she had fallen asleep in the bergère by the window, but she did know that she was roused abruptly by the sound of footsteps. Outside the door of her room, in the long hallway, there was someone walking, gently, cautiously. It was not this time merely the creaking of the old house; it was the sound of footfalls, regular, measured, inevitable, those of some person of almost no weight at all. She listened, and slowly, cautiously, almost as if the person were blind and groping his way in the darkness, the step advanced until presently it came opposite her and thin slivers of light outlined the door that led into the hall. Quietly she rose and, still lost in a vague sense of moving in a nightmare, she went over to the door and opened it. Far down the long hall, at the door which opened into the stairway leading to the attic of the house, there was a small circle of light cast by an electric torch. It threw into a black silhouette the figure of an old woman with white hair whom Olivia recognized at once. It was the old woman escaped from the north wing. While she stood watching her, the figure, fumbling at the door, opened it and disappeared quickly into the stairway.

There was no time to be lost, not time even to go in search of the starched Miss Egan. The poor creature might fling herself from the upper windows. So, without stopping even to throw a dressing-gown about her, Olivia went quickly along the dark hall and up the stairway where the fantastic creature in the flowered wrapper had vanished.

The attic was an enormous, unfinished room that covered the whole of the house, a vast cavern of a place, empty save for a few old trunks and pieces of broken furniture. The flotsam and jetsam of Pentland life had been stowed away there, lost and forgotten in the depths of the big room, for more than a century. No one entered it. Since Sybil and Jack had grown, it remained half-forgotten. They had played there on rainy days as small children, and before them Sabine and Anson had played in the same dark, mysterious corners among broken old trunks and sofas and chairs.

Olivia found the place in darkness save for the patches of blue light where the luminous night came in at the double row of dormer windows, and at the far end, by a group of old trunks, the circle of light from the torch that moved this way and that, as if old Mrs. Pentland were searching for something. In the haste of her escape and flight, her thin white hair had come undone and fell about her shoulders. A sickly smell of medicine hung about her.

Olivia touched her gently and said, "What have you lost, Mrs. Pentland? Can I help you?"

The old woman turned and, throwing the light of the torch full into Olivia's face, stared at her with the round blue eyes, murmuring, "Oh, it's you, Olivia. Then it's all right. Perhaps you can help me."

"What was it you lost? We might look for it in the morning."

"I've forgotten what it was now. You startled me, and you know my poor brain isn't very good, at best. It never has been since I married." Sharply she looked at Olivia. "It didn't affect you that way, did it? You don't ever drift away and feel yourself growing dimmer and dimmer, do you? It's odd. Perhaps it's different with your husband."

Olivia saw that the old woman was having one of those isolated moments of clarity and reason which were more horrible than her insanity because for a time she made you see that, after all, she was like yourself, human and capable of thought. To Olivia these moments were almost as if she witnessed the rising of the dead.

"No," said Olivia. "Perhaps if we went to bed now, you'd remember in the morning."

Old Mrs. Pentland shook her head violently. "No, no, I must find them now. It may be all different in the morning and I won't know anything and that Irish woman won't let me out. Say over the names of a few things like prunes, prisms, persimmons. That's what Mr. Dickens used to have his children do when he couldn't think of a word."

"Let me have the light," said Olivia; "perhaps I can find what it is you want."

With the meekness of a child, the old woman gave her the electric torch and Olivia, turning it this way and that, among the trunks and old rubbish, made a mock search among the dollhouses and the toy dishes left scattered in the corner of the attic where the children had played house for the last time.

While she searched, the old woman kept up a running comment, half to herself: "It's something I wanted to find very much. It'll make a great difference here in the lives of all of us. I thought I might find Sabine here to help me. She was here yesterday morning, playing with Anson. It rained all day and they couldn't go out. I hid it here yesterday when I came up to see them."

Olivia again attempted wheedling.

"It's late now, Mrs. Pentland. We ought both to be in bed. You try to remember what it is you want, and in the morning I'll come up and find it for you."

For a moment the old woman considered this, and at last she said, "You wouldn't give it to me if you found it. I'm sure you wouldn't. You're too afraid of them all."

"I promise you I will. You can trust me, can't you?"

"Yes, yes, you're the only one who doesn't treat me as if I wasn't quite bright. Yes, I think I can trust you." Another thought occurred to her abruptly. "But I wouldn't remember again. I might forget. Besides, I don't think Miss Egan would let me."

Olivia took one of the thin old hands in hers and said, as if she were talking to a little child, "I know what we'll do. Tomorrow you write it out on a bit of paper and then I'll find it and bring it to you."

"I'm sure little Sabine could find it," said the old woman. "She's very good at such things. She's such a clever child."

"I'll go over and fetch Sabine to have her help me."

The old woman looked at her sharply. "You'll promise that?" she asked. "You'll promise?"

"Of course, surely."

"Because all the others are always deceiving me."

And then quite gently she allowed herself to be led across the moonlit patches of the dusty floor, down the stairs and back to her room. In the hall of the north wing they came suddenly upon the starched Miss Egan, all her starch rather melted and subdued now, her red face purple with alarm.

"I've been looking for her everywhere, Mrs. Pentland," she told Olivia. "I don't know how she escaped. She was asleep when I left. I went down to the kitchen for her orange-juice, and while I was gone she disappeared."

It was the old woman who answered. Looking gravely at Olivia, she said, with an air of confidence, "You know I never speak to her at all. She's common. She's a common Irish servant. They can shut me up with her, but they can't make me speak to her." And then she began to drift back again into the hopeless state that was so much more familiar. She began to mumble over and over again a chain of words and names which had no coherence.

Olivia and Miss Egan ignored her, as if part of her—the vaguely *rational* old woman—had disappeared, leaving in her place this pitiful chattering creature who was a stranger.

Olivia explained where it was she found the old woman and why she had gone there.

"She's been talking on the subject for days," said Miss Egan. "I think it's letters that she's looking for, but it may be nothing at all. She mixes everything terribly."

Olivia was shivering now in her nightdress, more from weariness and nerves than from the chill of the night.

"I wouldn't speak of it to any of the others, Miss Egan," she said. "It will only trouble them. And we must be more careful about her in the future."

The old woman had gone past them now, back into the dark room where she spent her whole life, and the nurse had begun to recover a little of her defiant confidence. She even smiled, the hard, glittering smile which always said, "You cannot do without me, whatever happens."

Aloud she said, "I can't imagine what happened, Mrs. Pentland."

"It was an accident, never mind," said Olivia. "Goodnight. Only I think it's better not to speak of what has happened. It will only alarm the others."

But she was puzzled, Olivia, because underneath the dressing-gown Miss Egan had thrown about her shoulders she saw that the nurse was dressed neither in night-clothes nor in her uniform, but in the suit of blue serge that she wore on the rare occasions when she went into the city.

V

SHE SPOKE TO NO ONE of what had happened, either on the terrace or in the lane or in the depths of the old attic, and the days came to resume again their old monotonous round, as if the strange, hot, disturbing night had had no more existence than a dream. She did not see O'Hara, yet she heard of him, constantly, from Sybil, from Sabine, even from Jack, who seemed stronger than he had ever been and able for a time to go about the farm with his grandfather in the trap drawn by an old white horse. There were moments when it seemed to Olivia that the boy might one day be really well, and yet there was never any real joy in those moments, because always in the back of her mind stood the truth. She knew it would never be, despite all that fierce struggle which she and the old man kept up perpetually against the thing which was stronger than either of them. Indeed, she even found a new sort of sadness in the sight of the pale thin boy and the rugged old man driving along the lanes in the trap, the eyes of the grandfather bright with a look of deluding hope. It was a look which she found unbearable because it was the first time in years, almost since that first day when Jack, as a tiny baby who did not cry enough, came into the world, that the expression of the old man had changed from one of grave and uncomplaining resignation.

Sometimes when she watched them together she was filled with a fierce desire to go to John Pentland and tell him that it was not her fault that there were not more children, other heirs to take the place of Jack. She wanted to tell him that she would have had ten children if it were possible, that even now she was still young enough to have more children. She wanted to pour out to him something of that hunger of life which had swept over her on the night in Sabine's garden beneath the apple-tree, a spot abounding in fertility. But she knew, too, how impossible it was to discuss a matter which old John Pentland, in the depths of his soul believed to be "indelicate." Such things were all hidden behind a veil which shut out so much of truth from all their lives. There were times when she fancied he understood it all, those times when he took her hand and kissed her affectionately. She fancied that he understood and that the knowledge lay somehow at the root of the old man's quiet contempt for his own son.

But she saw well enough the tragedy that lay deep down at the root of the whole matter. She understood that it was not Anson who was to blame. It was that they had all been caught in the toils of something stronger than any of them, a force which with a cruel injustice compelled her to live a dry, monotonous, barren existence when she would have embraced life passionately, which compelled her to watch her own son dying slowly before her eyes.

Always she came back to the same thought, that the boy must be kept alive until his grandfather was dead; and sometimes, standing on the terrace, looking out across the fields, Olivia saw that old Mrs. Soames, dressed absurdly in pink, with a large picture-hat, was riding in the trap with the old man and his grandson, as if in reality she were the grandmother of Jack instead of the mad old woman above stairs.

The days came to resume their round of dull monotony, and yet there was a difference, odd and indefinable, as if in some way the sun were brighter than it had been, as if those days, when even in the bright sunlight the house had seemed a dull gray place, were gone now. She could no longer look across the meadows toward the bright new chimneys of O'Hara's house without a sudden quickening of breath, a warm pleasant sensation of no longer standing quite alone.

She was not even annoyed any longer by the tiresome daily visits of Aunt Cassie, nor by the old woman's passion for pitying her and making wild insinuations against Sabine and O'Hara and complaining of Sybil riding with him in the mornings over the dew-covered fields. She was able now simply to sit there politely as she had once done, listening while the old woman talked on and on; only now she did not even listen with attention. It seemed to her at times that Aunt Cassie was like some insect beating itself frantically against a pane of glass, trying over and over again with an unflagging futility to enter where it was impossible to enter.

It was Sabine who gave her a sudden glimpse of penetration into this instinct about Aunt Cassie, Sabine who spent all her time finding out about people. It happened one morning that the two clouds of dust, the one made by Aunt Cassie and the other by Sabine, met at the very foot of the long drive leading up to Pentlands, and together the two women—one dressed severely in shabby black, without so much as a fleck of powder on her nose, the other dressed expensively in what some Paris dressmaker chose to call a *costume de sport*, with her face made up like a Parisian—arrived together to sit on the piazza of Pentlands insulting each other subtly for an hour. When at last Sabine managed to outstay Aunt Cassie (it was always a contest between them, for each knew that the other would attack her as soon as she was out of hearing) she turned to Olivia and said abruptly, "I've been thinking about Aunt Cassie, and I'm sure now of one thing. Aunt Cassie is a virgin!"

There was something so cold-blooded and sudden in the statement that Olivia laughed.

"I'm sure of it," persisted Sabine with quiet seriousness. "Look at her. She's always talking about the tragedy of her being too frail ever to have had children. She never tried. That's the answer. She never tried." Sabine tossed away what remained of the cigarette she had lighted to annoy Aunt Cassie and continued. "You never knew my Uncle Ned Struthers when he was young. You only knew him as an old man with no spirit left. But he wasn't that way always. It's what she did to him. She destroyed him. He was a full-blooded kind of man who liked drinking and horses and he must have liked women, too, but she cured him of that. He would have liked children, but instead of a wife he only got a woman who couldn't bear the thought of not being married and yet couldn't bear what marriage meant. He got a creature who fainted and wept and lay on a sofa all day, who got the better of him because he was a nice, stupid, chivalrous fellow."

Sabine was launched now with all the passion which seized her when she had laid bare a little patch of life and examined it minutely.

"He didn't even dare to be unfaithful to her. If he looked at another woman she fainted and became deathly ill and made terrible scenes. I can remember some of them. I remember that once he called on Mrs. Soames when she was young and beautiful, and when he came home Aunt Cassie met him in hysterics and told him that if it ever happened again she would go out, 'frail and miserable as she was,' and commit adultery. I remember the story because I overheard my father telling it when I was a child and I was miserable until I found out what 'committing adultery' meant. In the end she destroyed him. I'm sure of it."

LOUIS BROMFIELD

Sabine sat there, with a face like stone, following with her eyes the cloud of dust that moved along the lane as Aunt Cassie progressed on her morning round of visits, a symbol in a way of all the forces that had warped her own existence.

"It's possible," murmured Olivia.

Sabine turned toward her with a quick, sudden movement. "That's why she is always so concerned with the lives of other people. She has never had any life of her own, never. She's always been afraid. It's why she loves the calamities of other people, because she's never had any of her own. Not even her husband's death was a calamity. It left her free, completely free of troubles as she had always wanted to be."

And then a strange thing happened to Olivia. It was as if a new Aunt Cassie had been born, as if the old one, so full of tears and easy sympathy who always appeared miraculously when there was a calamity in the neighborhood, the Aunt Cassie who was famous for her good works and her tears and words of religious counsel, had gone down the lane for the last time, never to return again. Tomorrow morning a new Aunt Cassie would arrive, one who outwardly would be the same; only to Olivia she would be different, a woman stripped of all those veils of pretense and emotions with which she wrapped herself, an old woman naked in her ugliness who, Olivia understood in a blinding flash of clarity, was like an insect battering itself against a pane of glass in a futile attempt to enter where it was impossible for her ever to enter. And she was no longer afraid of Aunt Cassie now. She did not even dislike her; she only pitied the old woman because she had missed so much, because she would die without ever having lived. And she must have been young and handsome once, and very amusing. There were still moments when the old lady's charm and humor and sharp tongue were completely disarming.

Sabine was talking again, in a cold, unrelenting voice. "She lay there all those years on the sofa covered with a shawl, trying to arrange the lives of everyone about her. She killed Anson's independence and ruined my happiness. She terrorized her husband until in the end he died to escape her. He was a good-natured man, horrified of scenes and scandals." Sabine lighted a cigarette and flung away the match with a sudden savage gesture. "And now she goes about like an angel of pity, a very brisk angel of pity, a harpy in angel's clothing. She has played her role well. Everyone believes in her as a frail, good, unhappy woman. Some of the saints must have been very like her. Some of them must have been trying old maids."

She rose and, winding the chiffon scarf about her throat, opened her yellow parasol, saying, "I know I'm right. She's a virgin. At least," she added, "in the technical sense, she's a virgin. I know nothing about her mind."

And then, changing abruptly, she said, "Will you go up to Boston with me tomorrow? I'm going to do something about my hair. There's gray beginning to come into it."

Olivia did not answer her at once, but when she did speak it was to say, "Yes; I'm going to take up riding again and I want to order clothes. My old ones would look ridiculous now. It's been years since I was on a horse."

Sabine looked at her sharply and, looking away again, said, "I'll stop for you about ten o'clock."

Chapter VI

Heat, damp and overwhelming, and thick with the scent of fresh-cut hay and the half-fetid odor of the salt marshes, settled over Durham, reducing all life to a state of tropical relaxation. Even in the mornings when Sybil rode with O'Hara across the meadows, there was no coolness and no dew on the grass. Only Aunt Cassie, thin and wiry, and Anson, guided perpetually by a sense of duty which took no reckoning of such things as weather, resisted the muggy warmth. Aunt Cassie, alike indifferent to heat and cold, storm or calm, continued her indefatigable rounds. Sabine, remarking that she had always known that New England was the hottest place this side of Sheol, settled into a state of complete inertia, not stirring from the house until after the sun had disappeared. Even then her only action was to come to Pentlands to sit in the writingroom playing bridge languidly with Olivia and John Pentland and old Mrs. Soames.

The old lady grew daily more dazed and forgetful and irritating as a fourth at bridge. John Pentland always insisted upon playing with her, saying that they understood each other's game; but he deceived no one, save Mrs. Soames, whose wits were at best a little dim; the others knew that it was to protect her. They saw him sit calmly and patiently while she bid suits she could not possibly make, while she trumped his tricks and excused herself on the ground of bad eyesight. She had been a great beauty once and she was still, with all her paint and powder, a vain woman. She would not wear spectacles and so played by looking through lorgnettes, which lowered the whole tempo of the game and added to the confusion. At times, in the midst of the old lady's blunders, a look of murder came into the green eyes of Sabine, but Olivia managed somehow to prevent any outburst; she even managed to force Sabine into playing on, night after night. The patience and tenderness of the old man towards Mrs. Soames moved her profoundly, and she fancied that Sabine, too,—hard, cynical, intolerant Sabine—was touched by it. There was a curious, unsuspected soft spot in Sabine, as if in some way she understood the bond between the two old people. Sabine, who allowed herself to be bored by no one, presently became willing to sit there night after night bearing this special boredom patiently.

Once when Olivia said to her, "We'll all be old someday. Perhaps we'll be worse than old Mrs. Soames," Sabine replied with a shrug of bitterness, "Old age is a bore. That's the trouble with us, Olivia. We'll never give up and become old ladies. It used to be the beauties who clung to youth, and now all of us do it. We'll probably be painted old horrors. . . like her."

"Perhaps," replied Olivia, and a kind of terror took possession of her at the thought that she would be forty on her next birthday and that nothing lay before her, even in the immediate future, save evenings like these, playing bridge with old people until presently she herself was old, always in the melancholy atmosphere of the big house at Pentlands.

"But I shan't take to drugs," said Sabine. "At least I shan't do that."

Olivia looked at her sharply. "Who takes drugs?" she asked.

"Why, she does. . . old Mrs. Soames. She's taken drugs for years. I thought everyone knew it."

"No," said Olivia sadly. "I never knew it."

Sabine laughed. "You are an innocent," she answered.

And after Sabine had gone home, the cloud of melancholy clung to her for hours. She felt suddenly that Anson and Aunt Cassie might be right, after all. There was something dangerous in a woman like Sabine, who tore aside every veil, who sacrificed everything to her passion for the truth. Somehow it riddled a world which at its best was not too cheerful.

THERE WERE EVENINGS WHEN MRS. SOAMES sent word that she was feeling too ill to play, and on those occasions John Pentland drove over to see her, and the bridge was played instead at Brook Cottage with O'Hara and a fourth recruited impersonally from the countryside. To Sabine, the choice was a matter of indifference so long as the chosen one could play well.

It happened on these occasions that O'Hara and Olivia came to play together, making a sort of team, which worked admirably. He played as she knew he would play, aggressively and brilliantly, with a fierce concentration and a determination to win. It fascinated her that a man who had spent most of his life in circles where bridge played no part, should have mastered the intricate game so completely. She fancied him taking lessons with the same passionate application which he had given to his career.

He did not speak to her again of the things he had touched upon during that first hot night on the terrace, and she was careful never to find herself alone with him. She was ashamed at the game she played—

of seeing him always with Sabine or riding with Sybil and giving him no chance to speak; it seemed to her that such behavior was cheap and dishonest. Yet she could not bring herself to refuse seeing him, partly because to refuse would have aroused the suspicions of the already interested Sabine, but more because she *wanted* to see him. She found a kind of delight in the way he looked at her, in the perfection with which they came to understand each other's game; and though he did not see her alone, he kept telling her in a hundred subtle ways that he was a man in love, who adored her.

She told herself that she was behaving like a silly schoolgirl, but she could not bring herself to give him up altogether. It seemed to her unbearable that she should lose these rare happy evenings. And she was afraid, too, that Sabine would call her a fool.

As early summer turned into July, old Mrs. Soames came less and less frequently to play bridge and there were times when Sabine, dining out or retiring early, left them without any game at all and the old familiar stillness came to settle over the drawing room at Pentlands. . . evenings when Olivia and Sybil played double patience and Anson worked at Mr. Lowell's desk over the mazes of the Pentland Family history.

On one of these evenings, when Olivia's eyes had grown weary of reading, she closed her book and, turning toward her husband, called his name. When he did not answer her at once she spoke to him again, and waited until he looked up. Then she said, "Anson, I have taken up riding again. I think it is doing me good."

But Anson, lost somewhere in the chapter about Savina Pentland and her friendship with Ingres, was not interested and made no answer.

"I go in the mornings," she repeated, "before breakfast, with Sybil."

Anson said, "Yes," again, and then, "I think it an excellent idea— your color is better," and went back to his work.

So she succeeded in telling him that it was all right about Sybil and O'Hara. She managed to tell him without actually saying it that she would go with them and prevent any entanglement. She had told him, too, without once alluding to the scene of which he was ashamed. And she knew, of course, now, that there was no danger of any entanglement, at least not one which involved Sybil.

Sitting with the book closed in her lap, she remained for a time watching the back of her husband's head—the thin gray hair, the cords that stood out weakly under the desiccated skin, the too small ears set too close against the skull; and in reality, all the while she was seeing another head set upon a full muscular neck, the skin tanned and glowing with the flush of health, the thick hair short and vigorous; and she felt an odd, inexplicable desire to weep, thinking at the same time, "I am a wicked woman. I must be really bad." For she had never known before what it was to be in love and she had lived for nearly twenty years in a family where love had occupied a poor forgotten niche.

She was sitting thus when John Pentland came in at last, looking more yellow and haggard than he had been in days. She asked him quietly, so as not to disturb Anson, whether Mrs. Soames was really ill. "No," said the old man, "I don't think so; she seems all right, a little tired, that's all. We're all growing old."

He seated himself and began to read like the others, pretending clearly an interest which he did not feel, for Olivia caught him suddenly staring before him in a line beyond the printed page. She saw that he was not reading at all, and in the back of her mind a little cluster of words kept repeating themselves—*a little tired, that's all, we're all growing old; a little tired, that's all, we're all growing old*—over and over again monotonously, as if she were hypnotizing herself. She found herself, too, staring into space in the same enchanted fashion as the old man. And then, all at once, she became aware of a figure standing in the doorway beckoning to her, and, focusing her gaze, she saw that it was Nannie, clad in a dressing-gown, her old face screwed up in an expression of anxiety. She had some reason for not disturbing the others, for she did not speak. Standing in the shadow, she beckoned; and Olivia, rising quietly, went out into the hall, closing the door behind her.

There, in the dim light, she saw that the old woman had been crying and was shaking in fright. She said, "Something had happened to Jack, something dreadful."

She had known what it was before Nannie spoke. It seemed to her that she had known all along, and now there was no sense of shock but only a hard, dead numbness of all feeling.

"Call up Doctor Jenkins," she said, with a kind of dreadful calm, and turning away she went quickly up the long stairs.

In the darkness of her own room she did not wait now to listen for the sound of breathing. It had come at last—the moment when she would enter the room and, listening for the sound, encounter only the stillness of the night. Beyond, in the room which he had occupied ever since he was a tiny baby, there was the usual dim night-light burning in the corner, and by its dull glow she was able to make out the narrow bed and his figure lying there as it had always lain, asleep. He must have been asleep, she thought, for it was impossible to have died so quietly, without moving. But she knew, of course, that he *was* dead, and she saw how near to death he had always been, how it was only a matter of slipping over, quite simply and gently.

He had escaped them at last—his grandfather and herself—in a moment when they had not been there watching; and below stairs in the drawing room John Pentland was sitting with a book in his lap by Mr. Longfellow's lamp, staring into space, still knowing nothing. And Anson's pen scratched away at the history of the Pentland Family and the Massachusetts Bay Colony, while here in the room where she stood the Pentland family had come to an end.

She did not weep. She knew that weeping would come later, after the doctor had made his silly futile call to tell her what she already knew. And now that this thing which she had fought for so long had happened, she was aware of a profound peace. It seemed to her even, that the boy, her own son, was happier now; for she had a fear, bordering upon remorse, that they had kept him alive all those years against his will. He looked quiet and still now and not at all as he had looked on those long, terrible nights when she had sat in this same chair by the same bed while, propped among pillows because he could not breathe lying down, he fought for breath and life, more to please her and his grandfather than because he wanted to live. She saw that there could be a great beauty in death. It was not as if he had died alone. He had simply gone to sleep.

She experienced, too, an odd and satisfying feeling of reality, of truth, as if in some way the air all about her had become cleared and freshened. Death was not a thing one could deny by pretense. Death was real. It marked the end of something, definitely and clearly for all time. There could be no deceptions about death.

She wished now that she had told Nannie not to speak to the others. She wanted to stay there alone in the dimly lighted room until the sky turned gray beyond the marshes.

THEY DID NOT LEAVE HER in peace with her son. There came first of all a knock which admitted old Nannie, still trembling and hysterical, followed by the starched and efficient Miss Egan, who bustled about with a hard, professional manner, and then the rattling, noisy sounds of Doctor Jenkins' Ford as he arrived from the village, and the far-off hoot of a strange motor-horn and a brilliant glare of light as a big motor rounded the corner of the lane at the foot of the drive and swept away toward Brook Cottage. The hall seemed suddenly alive with people, whispering and murmuring together, and there was a sound of hysterical sobbing from some frightened servant. Death, which ought to occur in the quiet beauty of solitude, was being robbed of all its dignity. They would behave like this for days. She knew that it was only now, in the midst of all that pitiful hubbub, that she had lost her son. He had been hers still, after a fashion, while she was alone there in the room.

Abruptly, in the midst of the flurry, she remembered that there were others besides herself. There was Sybil, who had come in and stood beside her, grave and sympathetic, pressing her mother's hand in silence; and Anson, who stood helplessly in the corner, more awkward and useless and timid than ever in the face of death. But most of all, there was John Pentland. He was not in the room. He was nowhere to be seen.

She went to search for him, because she knew that he would never come there to face all the others; instead, he would hide himself away like a wounded animal. She knew that there was only one person whom he could bear to see. Together they had fought for the life of the boy and together they must face the cold, hard fact of his death.

She found him standing on the terrace, outside the tall windows that opened into the drawing room, and as she approached, she saw that he was so lost in his sorrow that he did not even notice her. He was like a man in a state of enchantment. He simply stood there, tall and stiff and austere, staring across the marshes in the direction of the sea, alone as he had always been, surrounded by the tragic armor of loneliness that none of them, not even herself, had ever succeeded in piercing. She saw then that there was a grief more terrible than her own. She had lost her son but for John Pentland it was the end of everything. She saw that the whole world had collapsed about him. It was as if he, too, had died.

She did not speak to him at first, but simply stood beside him, taking his huge, bony hand in hers, aware that he did not look at her, but kept staring on and on across the marshes in the direction of the sea. And at last she said softly, "It has happened, at last."

Still he did not look at her, but he did answer, saying, "I knew," in a whisper that was barely audible. There were tears on his leathery old cheeks. He had come out into the darkness of the scented garden to weep. It was the only time that she had ever seen tears in the burning black eyes.

NOT UNTIL LONG AFTER MIDNIGHT did all the subdued and vulgar hubbub that surrounds death fade away once more into silence, leaving Olivia alone in the room with Sybil. They did not speak to each other, for they knew well enough the poverty of words, and there was between them no need for speech.

At last Olivia said, "You had best get some sleep, darling; tomorrow will be a troublesome day."

And then, like a little girl, Sybil came over and seating herself on her mother's lap put her arms about her neck and kissed her.

The girl said softly, "You are wonderful, Mother. I know that I'll never be so wonderful a woman. We should have spared you tonight, all of us, and instead of that, it was you who managed everything." Olivia only kissed her and even smiled a little at Sybil. "I think he's happier. He'll never be tired again as he used to be."

She had risen to leave when both of them heard, far away, somewhere in the distance, the sound of music. It came to them vaguely and in snatches borne in by the breeze from the sea, music that was filled with a wild, barbaric beat, that rose and fell with a passionate sense of life. It seemed to Olivia that there was in the sound of it some dark power which, penetrating the stillness of the old house, shattered the awesome silence that had settled down at last with the approach of death. It was as if life were celebrating its victory over death, in a savage, wild, exultant triumph.

It was music, too, that sounded strange and passionate in the thin, clear air of the New England night, such music as none of them had ever heard there before; and slowly, as it rose to a wild crescendo of sound, Olivia recognized it—the glowing barbaric music of the tribal dances in *Prince Igor*, being played brilliantly with a sense of abandoned joy.

At the same moment Sybil looked at her mother and said, "It's Jean de Cyon. . . I'd forgotten that he was arriving tonight." And then sadly, "Of course he doesn't know."

There was a sudden light in the girl's eye, the merest flicker, dying out again quickly, which had a strange, intimate relation to the passionate music. Again it was life triumphing in death. Long afterward Olivia remembered it well. . . the light of something which went on and on.

Chapter VII

I

THE NEWS REACHED AUNT CASSIE only the next morning at ten and it brought her, full of reproaches and tears, over the dusty lanes to Pentlands. She was hurt, she said, because they had not let her know at once. "I should have risen from my bed and come over immediately," she repeated. "I was sleeping very badly, in any case. I could have managed everything. You should have sent for Aunt Cassie at once."

And Olivia could not tell her that they had kept her in ignorance for that very reason—because they knew she *would* rise from her bed and come over at once.

Aunt Cassie it was who took the burden of the grief upon her narrow shoulders. She wept in the manner of a professional mourner. She drew the shades in the drawing room, because in her mind death was not respectable unless the rooms were darkened, and sat there in a corner receiving callers, as if she were the one most bereft, as if indeed she were the only one who suffered at all. She returned to her own cupolaed dwelling only late at night and took all her meals at Pentlands, to the annoyance of her brother, who on the second day in the midst of lunch turned to her abruptly and said: "Cassie, if you can't stop this eternal blubbering, I wish you'd eat at home. It doesn't help anything."

At which she had risen from the table, in a sudden climax of grief and persecution, to flee, sobbing and hurt, from the room. But she was not insulted sufficiently to take her meals at home. She stayed on at Pentlands because, she said, "They needed someone like me to help out. . ." And to the trembling, inefficient Miss Peavey, who came and went like a frightened rabbit on errands for her, she confided her astonishment that her brother and Olivia should treat death with such indifference. They did not weep; they showed no signs of grief. She was certain that they lacked sensibility. They did not feel the tragedy. And, weeping again, she would launch into memories of the days when the boy had come as a little fellow to sit, pale and listless, on the floor of her big, empty drawing room, turning the pages of the Doré Bible.

And to Miss Peavey she also said, "It's at times like this that one's breeding comes out. Olivia has failed for the first time. She doesn't understand the things one must do at a time like this. If she had been brought up properly, here among us. . ."

For with Aunt Cassie death was a mechanical, formalized affair which one observed by a series of traditional gestures.

It was a remarkable bit of luck, she said, that Bishop Smallwood (Sabine's Apostle to the Genteel) was still in the neighborhood and could conduct the funeral services. It was proper that one of Pentland blood should bury a Pentland (as if no one else were quite worthy of such an honor). And she went to see the Bishop to discuss the matter of the services. She planned that immensely intricate affair, the seating of relations and connections—all the Canes and Struthers and Mannerings and Sutherlands and Pentlands—at the church. She called on Sabine to tell her that whatever her feelings about funerals might be, it was her duty to attend this one. Sabine must remember that she was back again in a world of civilized people who behaved as ladies and gentlemen. And to each caller whom she received in the darkened drawing room, she confided the fact that Sabine must be an unfeeling, inhuman creature, because she had not even paid a visit to Pentlands.

But she did not know what Olivia and John Pentland knew—that Sabine had written a short, abrupt, almost incoherent note, with all the worn, tattered, pious old phrases missing, which had meant more to them than any of the cries and whispering and confusion that went on below stairs, where the whole countryside passed in and out in an endless procession.

When Miss Peavey was not at hand to run errands for her, she made Anson her messenger. . . Anson, who wandered about helpless and lost and troubled because death had interrupted the easy, eventless flow of a life in which usually all moved according to a set plan. Death had upset the whole household. It was impossible to know how Anson Pentland felt over the death of his son. He did not speak at all, and now that "The Pentland Family and the Massachusetts Bay Colony" had been laid aside in the midst of the confusion and Mr. Lowell's desk stood buried beneath floral offerings, there was nothing to do but wander about getting in the way of everyone and drawing upon his head the sharp reproofs of Aunt Cassie.

It was Aunt Cassie and Anson who opened the great box of roses that came from O'Hara. It was Aunt Cassie's thin, blue-veined hand that tore open the envelope addressed plainly to "Mrs. Anson Pentland." It was Aunt Cassie who forced Anson to read what was written inside:

> *Dear Mrs. Pentland,*
> *You know what I feel. There is no need to say anything more.*
> *Michael O'Hara.*

And it was Aunt Cassie who said, "Impertinent! Why should he send flowers at all?" And Aunt Cassie who read the note again and again, as if she might find in some way a veiled meaning behind the two cryptic sentences. It was Aunt Cassie who carried the note to Olivia and watched her while she read it and laid it quietly aside on her dressing-table. And when she had discovered nothing she said to Olivia, "It seems to me impertinent of him to send flowers and write such a note. What is he to us here at Pentlands?"

Olivia looked at her a little wearily and said, "What does it matter whether he is impertinent or not? Besides, he was a great friend of Jack's." And then, straightening her tired body, she looked at Aunt Cassie and said slowly, "He is also a friend of mine."

It was the first time that the division of forces had stood revealed, even for a second, the first time that Olivia had shown any feeling for O'Hara, and there was something ominous in the quietness of a speech made so casually. She ended any possible discussion by leaving the room in search of Anson, leaving Aunt Cassie disturbed by the sensation of alarm which attacked her when she found herself suddenly face to face with the mysterious and perilous calm that sometimes took possession of Olivia. Left alone in the room, she took up the note again from the dressing-table and read it through for the twentieth time. There was nothing in it. . . nothing on which one could properly even pin a suspicion.

So, in the midst of death, enveloped by the odor of tuberoses, the old lady rose triumphant, a phoenix from ashes. In some way she found in tragedy her proper role and she managed to draw most of the light from the other actors to herself. She must have known that people went away from the house saying, "Cassie rises to such occasions beautifully. She has taken everything on her own shoulders." She succeeded in conveying the double impression that she suffered far more than any of the others and that none of the others could possibly have done without her.

LOUIS BROMFIELD

And then into the midst of her triumph came the worst that could have happened. Olivia was the first to learn of the calamity as she always came to know before any of the others knowledge which old John Pentland possessed; and the others would never have known until the sad business of the funeral was over save for Aunt Cassie's implacable curiosity.

On the second day, Olivia, summoned by her father-in-law to come to the library, found him there as she had found him so many times before, grim and silent and repressed, only this time there was something inexpressibly tragic and broken in his manner.

She did not speak to him; she simply waited until, looking up at last, he said almost in a whisper, "Horace Pentland's body is at the Durham station."

And he looked at her with the quick, pitiful helplessness of a strong man who has suddenly grown weak and old, as if at last he had come to the end of his strength and was turning now to her. It was then for the first rime that she began to see how she was in a way a prisoner, that from now on, as one day passed into another, the whole life at Pentlands would come to be more and more her affair. There was no one to take the place of the old man. . . no one, save herself.

"What shall we do?" he asked in the same low voice. "I don't know. I am nearly at the end of things."

"We could bury them together," said Olivia softly. "We could have a double funeral."

He looked at her in astonishment. "You wouldn't mind that?" and when she shook her head in answer, he replied: "But we can't do it. There seems to me something wrong in such an idea. . . I can't explain what I mean. . . It oughtn't to be done. . . A boy like Jack and an old reprobate like Horace."

They would have settled it quietly between them as they had settled so many troubles in the last years when John Pentland had come to her for strength, but at that moment the door opened suddenly and, without knocking, Aunt Cassie appeared, her eyes really blazing with an angry, hysterical light, her hair all hanging in little iron-gray wisps about her narrow face.

"What is it?" she asked. "What has gone wrong? I know there's something, and you've no right to keep it from me." She was shrill and brittle, as if in those two days all the pleasure and activity surrounding death had driven her into an orgy of excitement. At the sound of her voice, both Olivia and John Pentland started abruptly. She had touched them on nerves raw and worn.

The thin, high-pitched voice went on. "I've given up all my time to arranging things. I've barely slept. I sacrifice myself to you all day and night and I've a right to know." It was as if she had sensed the slow breaking up of the old man and sought now to hurl him aside, to depose him as head of the family, in one great *coup d'état*, setting herself up there in his place, a thin, fiercely intolerant tyrant; as if at last she had given up her old subtle way of trying to gain her ends by intrigue through the men of the family. She stood ready now to set up a matriarchy, the last refuge of a family whose strength was gone. She had risen thus in the same way once before within the memory of Olivia, in those long months when Mr. Struthers, fading slowly into death, yielded her the victory.

John Pentland sighed, profoundly, wearily, and murmured, "It's nothing, Cassie. It would only trouble you. Olivia and I are settling it."

But she did not retreat. Standing there, she held her ground and continued the tirade, working herself up to a pitch of hysteria. "I won't be put aside. No one ever tells me anything. For years now I've been shut out as if I were half-witted. Frail as I am, I work myself to the bone for the family and don't even get a word of thanks. . . Why is Olivia always preferred to your own sister?" And tears of luxurious, sensual, self-pity began to stream down her withered face. She began even to mumble and mix her words, and she abandoned herself completely to the fleshly pleasure of hysterics.

Olivia, watching her quietly, saw that this was no usual occasion. This was, in truth, the new Aunt Cassie whom Sabine had revealed to her a few days before. . . the aggressively virginal Aunt Cassie who had been born in that moment on the terrace to take the place of the old Aunt Cassie who had existed always in an aura of tears and good works and sympathy. She understood now what she had never understood before—that Aunt Cassie was not merely an irrational hypochondriac, a harmless, pitiful creature, but a ruthless and unscrupulous force. She knew that behind this emotional debauch there lay some deeply conceived plan. Vaguely she suspected that the plan was aimed at subduing herself, or bringing her (Olivia) completely under the will of the old woman. It was the insect again beating its wings frantically against the windows of a world which she could never enter. . .

And softly Olivia said, "Surely, Aunt Cassie, there is no need to make a scene. . . there's no need to be vulgar. . . at a time like this."

The old woman, suddenly speechless, looked at her brother, but from him there came no sign of aid or succor; she must have seen, plainly, that he had placed himself on the side of Olivia. . . the outsider, who had dared to accuse a Pentland of being vulgar.

"You heard what she said, John. . . You heard what she said! She called your sister vulgar!" But her hysterical mood began to abate suddenly, as if she saw that she had chosen, after all, the wrong plan of attack. Olivia did not answer her. She only sat there, looking pale and patient and beautiful in her black clothes, waiting. It was a moment unfair to Aunt Cassie. No man, even Anson, would have placed himself against Olivia just then.

"If you must know, Cassie. . ." the old man said slowly. "It's a thing you won't want to hear. But if you must know, it is simply that Horace Pentland's body is at the station in Durham."

Olivia had a quick sense of the whited sepulcher beginning to crack, to fall slowly into bits.

At first Aunt Cassie only stared at them, snuffling and wiping her red eyes, and then she said, in an amazingly calm voice, "You see. . . You never tell me anything. I never knew he was dead." There was a touch of triumph and vindication in her manner.

"There was no need of telling you, Cassie," said the old man. "You wouldn't let his name be spoken in the family for years. It was you— you and Anson—who made me threaten him into living abroad. Why should you care when he died?"

Aunt Cassie showed signs of breaking down once more. "You see, I'm always blamed for everything. I was thinking of the family all these years. We couldn't have Horace running around loose in Boston." She broke off with a sudden, fastidious gesture of disgust, as if she were washing her hands of the whole affair. "I could have managed it better myself. He ought never to have been brought home. . . to stir it all up again."

Still Olivia kept silent and it was the old man who answered Aunt Cassie. "He wanted to be buried here. . . He wrote to ask me, when he was dying."

"He had no right to make such a request. He forfeited all rights by his behavior. I say it again and I'll keep on saying it. He ought never to have been brought back here. . . after people even forgot whether he was alive or dead."

The perilous calm had settled over Olivia. . . She had been looking out of the window across the marshes into the distance, and when she turned she spoke with a terrible quietness. She said: "You may do with Horace Pentland's body what you like. It is more your affair than mine, for I never saw him in my life. But it is *my* son who is dead. . . *my* son, who belongs to *me* more than to any of you. You may bury Horace Pentland on the same day. . . at the same service, even in the same grave. Things like that can't matter very much after death. You can't go on pretending forever. . . Death is too strong for that. It's stronger than any of us puny creatures because it's the one truth we can't avoid. It's got nothing to do with prejudices and pride and respectability. In a hundred years—even in a year, in a month, what will it matter what we've done with Horace Pentland's body?"

She rose, still enveloped in the perilous calm, and said: "I'll leave Horace Pentland to you two. There is none of his blood in my veins. Whatever you do, I shall not object. . . only I wouldn't be too shabby in dealing with death."

She went out, leaving Aunt Cassie exhausted and breathless and confused. The old woman had won her battle about the burial of Horace Pentland, yet she had suffered a great defeat. She must have seen that she had really lost everything, for Olivia somehow had gone to the root of things, in the presence of John Pentland, who was himself so near to death. (Olivia daring to say proudly, as if she actually scorned the Pentland name, "There is none of his blood in my veins.")

But it was a defeat which Olivia knew she would never admit: that was one of the qualities which made it impossible to deal with Aunt Cassie. Perhaps, even as she sat there dabbing at her eyes, she was choosing new weapons for a struggle which had come at last into the open because it was impossible any longer to do battle through so weak and shifting an ally as Anson.

She was a natural martyr, Aunt Cassie. Martyrdom was the great feminine weapon of her Victorian day and she was practised in it; she had learned all its subtleties in the years she had lain wrapped in a shawl on a sofa subduing the full-blooded Mr. Struthers.

And Olivia knew as she left the room that in the future she would have to deal with a poor, abused, invalid aunt who gave all her strength in doing good works and received in return only cruelty and heartlessness from an outsider, from an intruder, a kind of adventuress who had wormed her way into the heart of the Pentland family. Aunt Cassie, by a kind of art of which she possessed the secret, would somehow make it all seem so.

　　　　　　　　　　　　　　　　　　　　　　　LOUIS BROMFIELD

THE HEAT DID NOT GO away. It hung in a quivering cloud over the whole countryside, enveloping the black procession which moved through the lanes into the highroad and thence through the clusters of ugly stucco bungalows inhabited by the millworkers, on its way past the deserted meeting house where Preserved Pentland had once harangued a tough and sturdy congregation and the Rev. Josiah Milford had set out with his flock for the Western Reserve. . . . It enveloped the black slow-moving procession to the very doors of the cool, ivy-covered stone church (built like a stage piece to imitate some English county church) where the Pentlands worshiped the more polite, compromising gods scorned and berated by the witch-burner. On the way, beneath the elms of High Street, Polish women and children stopped to stare and cross themselves at the sight of the grand procession.

The little church seemed peaceful after the heat and the stir of the Durham street, peaceful and hushed and crowded to the doors by the relatives and connections of the family. Even the back pews were filled by the poor half-forgotten remnants of the family who had no wealth to carry them smoothly along the stream of life. Old Mrs. Featherstone (who did washing) was there sobbing because she sobbed at all funerals, and old Miss Haddon, the genteel Pentland cousin, dressed even in the midst of summer in her inevitable cape of thick black broadcloth, and Mrs. Malson, shabby-genteel in her foulards and high-pitched bonnet, and Miss Murgatroyd whose bullfinch house was now "Ye Witch's Broome" where one got bad tea and melancholy sandwiches. . .

Together Bishop Smallwood and Aunt Cassie had planned a service calculated skilfully to harrow the feelings and give full scope to the vast emotional capacities of their generation and background.

They chose the most emotional of hymns, and Bishop Smallwood, renowned for his effect upon pious and sentimental old ladies, said a few insincere and pompous words which threw Aunt Cassie and poor old Mrs. Featherstone into fresh excesses of grief. The services for the boy became a barbaric rite dedicated not to his brief and pathetic existence but to a glorification of the name he bore and of all those traits—the narrowness, the snobbery, the lower middle-class respect for property—which had culminated in the lingering tragedy of his sickly life. In their respective pews Anson and Aunt Cassie swelled with pride at the mention of the Pentland ancestry. Even the sight of the vigorous, practical, stocky Polish women staring round-eyed at the funeral procession a little before, returned to them now in a wave of pride and secret elation. The same emotion in some way filtered back through the little church from the pulpit where Bishop Smallwood (with the sob in his voice which had won him prizes at the seminary) stood surrounded by midsummer flowers, through all the relatives and connections, until far in the back among the more obscure and remote ones it became simply a pride in their relation to New England and the ancient dying village that was fast disappearing beneath the inroads of a more vigorous world. Something of the Pentland enchantment engulfed them all, even old Mrs. Featherstone, with her poor back bent from washing to support the four defective grandchildren who ought never to have been born. Through her facile tears (she wept because it was the only pleasure left her) there shone the light of a pride in belonging to these people who had persecuted witches and evolved transcendentalism and Mr. Lowell and Doctor Holmes and the good, kind Mr. Longfellow. It raised her somehow above the level of those hardy foreigners who worshiped the Scarlet Woman of Rome and jostled her on the sidewalks of High Street.

In all the little church there were only two or three, perhaps, who escaped that sudden mystical surge of self-satisfaction. . . O'Hara, who was forever outside the caste, and Olivia and old John Pentland, sitting there side by side so filled with sorrow that they did not even resent the antics of Bishop Smallwood. Sabine (who had come, after all, to the services) sensed the intensity of the engulfing emotion. It filled her with a sense of slow, cold, impotent rage.

As the little procession left the church, wiping its eyes and murmuring in lugubrious tones, the clouds which a little earlier had sprung up against the distant horizon began to darken the whole sky. The air became so still that the leaves on the tall, drooping elms hung as motionless as leaves in a painted picture, and far away, gently at first, and then with a slow, increasing menace, rose the sound of distant echoing thunder. Ill at ease, the mourners gathered in little groups about the steps, regarding alternately the threatening sky and the waiting hearse, and presently, one by one, the more timorous ones began to drift sheepishly away. Others followed them slowly until by the time the coffin was borne out, they had all melted away save for the members of the "immediate family" and one or two others. Sabine remained, and O'Hara and old Mrs. Soames (leaning on John Pentland's arm as if it were her grandson who was dead), and old Miss Haddon in her black cape, and the pall-bearers, and of course Bishop Smallwood and the country rector who, in the presence of this august and saintly pillar of the church, had faded to insignificance. Besides these there were one or two other relatives, like Struthers Pentland, a fussy little bald man (cousin of John Pentland and of the disgraceful Horace), who had never married but devoted himself instead to fathering the boys of his classes at Harvard.

It was this little group which entered the motors and hurried off after the hearse in its shameless race with the oncoming storm.

THE TOWN BURIAL-GROUND LAY AT the top of a high, bald hill where the first settlers of Durham had chosen to dispose of their dead, and the ancient roadway that led up to it was far too steep and stony to permit the passing of motors, so that part way up the hill the party was forced to descend and make the remainder of the journey on foot. As they assembled, silently but in haste, about the open, waiting grave, the sound of the thunder accompanied now by wild flashes of lightning, drew nearer and nearer, and the leaves of the stunted trees and shrubs which a moment before had been so still, began to dance and shake madly in the green light that preceded the storm.

Bishop Smallwood, by nature a timorous man, stood beside the grave opening his jewel-encrusted Prayer Book (he was very High Church and fond of incense and precious stones) and fingering the pages nervously, now looking down at them, now regarding the stolid Polish gravediggers who stood about waiting to bury the last of the Pentlands. There were irritating small delays, but at last everything was ready and the Bishop, reading as hastily as he dared, began the service in a voice less rich and theatrical than usual.

"I am the Resurrection and the Life, saith the Lord . . ."

And what followed was lost in a violent crash of thunder so that the Bishop was able to omit a line or two without being discovered. The few trees on the bald hill began to sway and rock, bending low toward the earth, and the crape veils of the women performed wild black writhings. In the uproar of wind and thunder only a sentence or two of the service became audible. . .

"For a thousand years in Thy sight are but as yesterday, seeing that the past is as a watch in the night . . ."

And then again a wild, angry Nature took possession of the services, drowning out the anxious voice of the Bishop and the loud theatrical sobs of Aunt Cassie, and again there was a sudden breathless hush and the sound of the Bishop's voice, so pitiful and insignificant in the midst of the storm, reading. . .

"O teach us to number our days that we may apply our hearts unto wisdom."
And again:
"For as much as it hath pleased Almighty God in His Providence to take out of the world, the soul of our deceased brother."

And at last, with relief, the feeble, reed-like voice, repeating with less monotony than usual: *"The Grace of our Lord Jesus Christ and the Love of God and the Fellowship of the Holy Ghost be with us all evermore. Amen."*

Sabine, in whose hard nature there lay some hidden thing which exulted in storms, barely heard the service. She stood there watching the wild beauty of the sky and the distant sea and the marshes and thinking how different a thing the burial of the first Pentland must have been from the timorous, hurried rite that marked the passing of the last. She kept seeing those first fanatical, hard-faced, rugged Puritans standing above their tombs like ghosts watching ironically the genteel figure of the Apostle to the Genteel and his jeweled Prayer Book. . .

THE POLISH GRAVEDIGGERS SET ABOUT their work stolidly indifferent to the storm, and before the first motor had started down the steep and stony path, the rain came with a wild, insane violence, sweeping inward in a wall across the sea and the black marshes. Sabine, at the door of her motor, raised her head and breathed deeply, as if the savage, destructive force of the storm filled her with a kind of ecstasy.

ON THE FOLLOWING DAY, COOL after the storm and bright and clear, a second procession made its way up the stony path to the top of the bald hill, only this time Bishop Smallwood was not there, nor Cousin Struthers Pentland, for they had both been called away suddenly and mysteriously. And Anson Pentland was not there because he would have nothing to do with a blackguard like Horace Pentland, even in death. In the little group about the open grave stood Olivia and John Pentland and Aunt Cassie, who had come because, after all, the dead man's name was Pentland, and Miss Haddon (in her heavy broadcloth cape), who never missed any funeral and had learned about this one from her friend, the undertaker, who kept her perpetually *au courant*. There were not even any friends to carry the coffin to the grave, and so this labor was divided between the undertaker's men and the gravediggers. . .

LOUIS BROMFIELD

And the service began again, read this time by the rector, who since the departure of the Bishop seemed to have grown a foot in stature. . .

"I am the Resurrection and the Life, saith the Lord . . .

"For a thousand years in Thy sight are but as yesterday, seeing that is past as a watch in the night . . .

"O teach us to number our days that we may apply our hearts unto wisdom."

Aunt Cassie wept again, though the performance was less good than on the day before, but Olivia and John Pentland stood in silence while Horace Pentland was buried at last in the midst of that little colony of grim and respectable dead.

Sabine was there, too, standing at a little distance, as if she had a contempt for all funerals. She had known Horace Pentland in life and she had gone to see him in his long exile whenever her wanderings led her to the south of France, less from affection than because it irritated the others in the family. (He must have been happier in that warm, rich country than he could ever have been in this cold, stony land.) But she had come today less for sentimental reasons than because it gave her the opportunity of a triumph over Aunt Cassie. She could watch Aunt Cassie out of her cold green eyes while they all stood about to bury the family skeleton. Sabine, who had not been to a funeral in the twenty-five years since her father's death, had climbed the stony hill to the Durham town burial-ground twice in as many days. . .

The rector was speaking again. . .

"The Grace of our Lord Jesus Christ and the Love of God and the Fellowship of the Holy Ghost be with us all evermore. Amen."

The little group turned away in silence, and in silence disappeared over the rim of the hill down the steep path. The secret burial was finished and Horace Pentland was left alone with the Polish gravediggers, come home at last.

III

THE PEACE WHICH HAD TAKEN possession of Olivia as she sat alone by the side of her dead son, returned to her slowly with the passing of the excitement over the funeral. Indeed, she was for once thankful for the listless, futile enchantment which invested the quiet old world. It soothed her at a moment when, all interest having departed from life, she wanted merely to be left in peace. She came to see for a certainty that there was no tragedy in her son's death; the only tragedy had been that he had ever lived at all such a baffled, painful, hopeless existence. And now, after so many years of anxiety, there was peace and a relaxation that seemed strange and in a way delicious. . . moments when, lying in the chaise longue by the window overlooking the marshes, she was enveloped by deep and healing solitude. Even the visits of Aunt Cassie, who would have forced her way into Olivia's room in the interests of "duty," made only a vague, dreamlike impression. The old lady became more and more a droning, busy insect, the sound of whose buzzing grew daily more distant and vague, like the sound of a fly against a windowpane heard through veils of sleep.

From her window she sometimes had a distant view of the old man, riding alone now, in the trap across the fields behind the old white horse, and sometimes she caught a glimpse of his lean figure riding the savage red mare along the lanes. He no longer went alone with the mare; he had yielded to Higgins' insistent warnings of her bad temper and permitted the groom to go with him, always at his side or a little behind to guard him, riding a polo pony with an ease and grace which made horse and man seem a single creature. . . a kind of centaur. On a horse the ugliness of the robust, animal little man seemed to flow away. It was as if he had been born thus, on a horse, and was awkward and ill at ease with his feet on the earth.

And Olivia knew the thought that was always in the mind of her father-in-law as he rode across the stony, barren fields. He was thinking all the while that all this land, all this fortune, even Aunt Cassie's carefully tended pile, would one day belong to a family of someother name, perhaps a name which he had never even heard.

There were no more Pentlands. Sybil and her husband would be rich, enormously so, with the Pentland money and Olivia's money. . . but there would never be anymore Pentlands. It had all come to an end in this. . . futility and oblivion. In another hundred years the name would exist, if it existed at all, only as a memory, embalmed within the pages of Anson's book.

The new melancholy which settled over the house came in the end even to touch the spirit of Sybil, so young and so eager for experience, like a noxious mildew. Olivia noticed it first in a certain shadowy listlessness that seemed to touch every action of the girl, and then in an occasional faint sigh of weariness, and in the visits the girl paid her in her room, and in the way she gave up willingly evenings at Brook Cottage to stay at home with her mother. She saw that Sybil, who had

LOUIS BROMFIELD

always been so eager, was touched by the sense of futility which she (Olivia) had battled for so long. And Sybil, Sybil of them all, alone possessed the chance of being saved.

She thought, "I must not come to lean on her. I must not be the sort of mother who spoils the life of her child."

And when John Pentland came to sit listlessly by her side, sometimes in silence, sometimes making empty speeches that meant nothing in an effort to cover his despair, she saw that he, too, had come to her for the strength which she alone could give him. Even old Mrs. Soames had failed him, for she lay ill again and able to see him only for a few minutes each day. (It was Sabine's opinion, uttered during one of her morning visits, that these strange sudden illnesses came from overdoses of drugs.)

So she came to see that she was being a coward to abandon the struggle now, and she rose one morning almost at dawn to put on her riding-clothes and set out with Sybil across the wet meadows to meet O'Hara. She returned with something of her pallor gone and a manner almost of gaiety, her spirit heightened by the air, the contact with O'Hara and the sense of having taken up the struggle once more.

Sabine, always watchful, noticed the difference and put it down to the presence of O'Hara alone, and in this she was not far wrong, for set down there in Durham, he affected Olivia powerfully as one who had no past but only a future. With him she could talk of things which lay ahead—of his plans for the farm he had bought, of Sybil's future, of his own reckless, irresistible career.

O'HARA HIMSELF HAD COME TO a dangerous state of mind. He was one of those men who seek fame and success less for the actual rewards than for the satisfaction of the struggle, the fierce pleasure of winning with all the chances against one. He had won successes already. He had his house, his horses, his motor, his well-tailored clothes, and he knew the value of these things, not only in the world of Durham, but in the slums and along the wharves of Boston. He had no illusions about the imperfect workings of democracy. He knew (perhaps because, having begun at the very bottom, he had fought his way very near to the top) that the poor man expects a politician to be something of a splendorous affair, especially when he has begun his career as a very common and ordinary sort of poor man. O'Hara was not playing his game foolishly or recklessly. When he visited the slums or sat in at political meetings, he was a sort of universal common man, a brother to all. When he addressed a large meeting or presided at an assembly, he arrived in a glittering motor and appeared in the elegant clothes suitable to a representative of the government, of power; and so he reflected credit on those men who had played with him as boys along India Wharf and satisfied the universal hunger in man for something more splendorous than the machinery of a perfect democracy.

He understood the game perfectly and made no mistakes, for he had had the best of all training—that of knowing all sorts of people in all sorts of conditions. In himself, he embodied them all, if the simple and wholly kindly and honest were omitted; for he was really not a simple man nor a wholly honest one and he was too ruthless to be kindly. He understood people (as Sabine had guessed), with their little prides and vanities and failings and ambitions.

Aunt Cassie and Anson in the rigidity of their minds had been unjust in thinking that their world was the goal of his ambitions. They had, in the way of those who depend on their environment as a justification for their own existence, placed upon it a value out of all proportion in the case of a man like O'Hara. To them it was everything, the ultimate to be sought on this earth, and so they supposed it must seem to O'Hara. It would have been impossible for them to believe that he considered it only as a small part of his large scheme of life and laid siege to it principally for the pleasure that he found in the battle; for it was true that O'Hara, once he had won, would not know what to do with the fruits of his victory.

Already he himself had begun to see this. He had begun to understand that the victory was so easy that the battle held little savor for him. Moments of satisfaction such as that which had overtaken him as he sat talking to Sabine were growing more and more rare. . . moments when he would stop and think, "Here am I, Michael O'Hara, a nobody. . . son of a laborer and a housemaid, settled in the midst of such a world as Durham, talking to such a woman as Mrs. Cane Callendar."

No, the savor was beginning to fail, to go out of the struggle. He was beginning to be bored, and as he grew bored he grew also restless and unhappy.

Born in the Roman Catholic church, he was really neither a very religious nor a very superstitious man. He was skeptic enough not to believe all the faiths the church sought to impose upon him, yet he was not skeptic enough to find peace of mind in an artificial will to believe.

For so long a time he had relied wholly upon himself that the idea of leaning for support, even in lonely, restless moments, upon a God or a church, never even occurred to him. He remained outwardly a Roman Catholic because by denying the faith he would have incurred the enmity of the church and many thousands of devout Irish and Italians. The problem simply did not concern him deeply one way or the other.

And so he had come, guided for the moment by no very strong passion, into the doldrums of confusion and boredom. Even his fellow-politicians in Boston saw the change in him and complained that he displayed no very great interest in the campaign to send him to Congress. He behaved at times as if it made not the slightest difference to him whether he was elected to Congress or not. . . he, this Michael O'Hara who was so valuable to his party, so engaging and shrewd, who could win for it almost anything he chose.

And though he took care that no one should divine it, this strange state of mind troubled him more deeply than any of his friends. He was assailed by the certainty that there was something lacking from his life, something very close to the foundations. Now that he was inactive and bored, he had begun to think of himself for the first time. The fine, glorious burst of first youth, when everything seemed part of a splendid game, was over and done now, and he felt himself slipping away toward the borderland of middle-age. Because he was a man of energy and passion, who loved life, he felt the change with a keen sense of sadness. There was a kind of horror for him in the idea of a lowered tempo of life—a fear that filled him at times with a passionately satisfactory sort of Gaelic melancholy.

In such moments, he had quite honestly taken stock of all he possessed, and found the amassed result bitterly unsatisfactory. He had a good enough record. He was decidedly more honorable than most men in such a dirty business as politics—indeed, far more honorable and freer from spites and nastinesses than many of those who had come out of this very sacred Durham world. He had made enough money in the course of his career, and he was winning his battle in Durham. Yet at thirty-five life had begun to slacken, to lose some of that zest which once had led him to rise every morning bursting with animal spirits, his brain all a-glitter with fascinating schemes.

And then, in the very midst of this perilous state of mind, he discovered one morning that the old sensation of delight at rising had returned to him, only it was not because his brain was filled with fascinating schemes. He arose with an interest in life because he knew that in a little while he would see Olivia Pentland. He arose, eager to fling himself on his horse and, riding across the meadows, to wait by the abandoned gravel-pit until he saw her coming over the dew-covered fields, radiant, it seemed to him, as the morning itself. On the days when she did not come it was as if the bottom had dropped out of his whole existence.

It was not that he was a man encountering the idea of woman for the first time. There had been women in his life always, since the very first bedraggled Italian girl he had met as a boy among the piles of lumber along the wharves. There had been women always because it was impossible for a man so vigorous and full of zest, so ruthless and so scornful, to have lived thirty-five years without them, and because he was an attractive man, filled when he chose to be, with guile and charm, whom women found it difficult to resist. There had been plenty of women, kept always in the background, treated as a necessity and prevented skilfully from interfering with the more important business of making a career.

But with Olivia Pentland, something new and disturbing had happened to him. . . something which, in his eagerness to encompass all life and experience, possessed an overwhelming sensuous fascination. She was not simply another woman in a procession of considerable length. Olivia Pentland, he found, was different from any of the others. . . a woman of maturity, poised, beautiful, charming and intelligent, and besides all these things she possessed for him a kind of fresh and iridescent bloom, the same freshness, only a little saddened, that touched her young daughter.

In the beginning, when they had talked together while she planned the garden at Brook Cottage, he had found himself watching her, lost in a kind of wonder, so that he scarcely understood what she was saying. And all the while he kept thinking, "Here is a wonderful woman. . . the most wonderful I've ever seen or will ever see again. . . a woman who could make life a different affair for me, who would make of love something which people say it is."

She had affected him thus in a way that swept aside all the vulgar and cynical coarseness with which a man of such experience is likely to invest the whole idea of woman. Until now women had seemed to him made to entertain men or to provide children for them, and now he saw that there was, after all, something in this sentiment with which

LOUIS BROMFIELD

people surrounded a love affair. For a long time he searched for a word to describe Olivia and in the end he fell back upon the old well-worn one which she always brought to mind. She was a "lady"—and as such she had an overwhelming effect upon his imagination.

He had said to himself that here was a woman who could understand him, not in the aloof, analytical fashion of a clever woman like Sabine Callendar, but in quite another way. She was a woman to whom he could say, "I am thus and so. My life has been of this kind. My motives are of this sort," and she would understand, the bad with the good. She would be the one person in the world to whom he could pour out the whole burden of secrets, the one woman who could ever destroy the weary sense of loneliness which sometimes afflicted him. She made him feel that, for all his shrewdness and hard-headed scheming, she was far wiser than he would ever be, that in a way he was a small boy who might come to her and, burying his head in her lap, have her stroke his thick black hair. She would understand that there were times when a man wanted to be treated thus. In her quiet way she was a strong woman, unselfish, too, who did not feed upon flattery and perpetual attention, the sort of woman who is precious to a man bent upon a career. The thought of her filled him with a poignant feeling of sadness, but in his less romantic moments he saw, too, that she held the power of catching him up out of his growing boredom. She would be of great value to him.

And so Sabine had not been far wrong when she thought of him as the small boy sitting on the curbstone who had looked up at her gravely and said, "I'm playing." He was at times very like such an image.

But in the end he was always brought up abruptly against the hard reality of the fact that she was already married to a man who did not want her himself but who would never set her free, a man who perhaps would have sacrificed everything in the world to save a scandal in his family. And beyond these hard, tangible difficulties he discerned, too, the whole dark decaying web, less obvious but none the less potent, in which she had become enmeshed.

Yet these obstacles only created a fascination to a mind so complex, so perverse, for in the solitude of his mind and in the bitterness of the long struggle he had known, he came to hold the whole world in contempt and saw no reason why he should not take what he wanted from this Durham world. Obstacles such as these provided the material for a new battle, a new source of interest in the turbulent stream of his existence; only this time there was a difference. . . that he coveted the prize itself more than the struggle. He wanted Olivia Pentland, strangely enough, not for a moment or even for a month or a year, but for always.

He waited because he understood, in the shrewdness of his long experience, that to be insistent would only startle such a woman and cause him to lose her entirely, and because he knew of no plan of action which could overcome the obstacles which kept them apart. He waited, as he had done many times in his career, for circumstances to solve themselves. And while he waited, with each time that he saw her she grew more and more desirable, and his own invincible sense of caution became weaker and weaker.

IV

IN THOSE LONG DAYS SPENT in her room, Olivia had come slowly to be aware of the presence of the newcomer at Brook Cottage. It had begun on the night of Jack's death with the sound of his music drifting across the marshes, and after the funeral Sabine had talked of him to Olivia with an enthusiasm curiously foreign to her. Once or twice she had caught a glimpse of him crossing the meadows toward O'Hara's shining chimneys or going down the road that led through the marshes to the sea—a tall, red-haired young man who walked with a slight limp. Sybil, she found, was strangely silent about him, but when she questioned the girl about her plans for the day she found, more often than not, that they had to do with him. When she spoke of him, Sybil had a way of blushing and saying, "He's very nice, Mother. I'll bring him over when you want to see people. . . I used to know him in Paris."

And Olivia, wisely, did not press her questions. Besides, Sabine had told her almost all there was to know. . . perhaps more than Sybil herself knew.

Sabine said, "He belongs to a rather remarkable family. . . wilful, reckless and full of spirit. His mother is probably the most remarkable of them all. She's a charming woman who has lived luxuriously in Paris most of her life. . . not one of the American colony. She doesn't ape anyone and she's incapable of pretense of any sort. She's lived, rather alone, over there on money. . . quite a lot of money. . . which seems to come out of steel-mills in some dirty town of the Middle West. She's one of my great friends. . . a woman of no intellect, but very beautiful and blessed with a devastating charm. She is one of the women who was born for men. . . She's irresistible to them, and I imagine there have been men in her life always. She was made for men, but her taste is perfect, so her morals don't matter."

The woman. . . indeed all Jean de Cyon's family. . . seemed to fascinate Sabine as she sat having tea with Olivia, for she went on and on, talking far more than usual, describing the house of Jean's mother, her friends, the people whom one met at her dinners, all there was to tell about her.

"She's the sort of woman who has existed since the beginning of time. There's some mystery about her early life. It has something to do with Jean's father. I don't think she was happy with him. He's never mentioned. Of course, she's married again now to a Frenchman. . . much older than herself. . . a man, very distinguished, who has been in three cabinets. That's where the boy gets his French name. The old man has adopted him and treats him like his own son. De Cyon is a good name in France, one of the best; but of course Jean hasn't any French blood. He's pure American, but he's never seen his own country until now."

Sabine finished her tea and putting her cup back on the Regence table (which had come from Olivia's mother and so found its graceful way into a house filled with stiff early American things), she added, "It's a remarkable family. . . wild and restless. Jean had an aunt who died in the Carmelite convent at Lisieux, and his cousin is Lilli Barr. . . a really great musician." She looked out of the window and after a moment said in a low voice, "Lilli Barr is the woman whom my husband married. . . but she divorced him, too, and now we are friends. . . she and I." The familiar hard, metallic laugh returned and she added, "I imagine our experience with him made us sympathetic. . . You see, I know the family very well. It's the sort of blood which produces people with a genius for life. . . for living in the moment."

She did not say that Jean and his mother and the ruthless cousin Lilli Barr fascinated her because they stood in a way for the freedom toward which she had been struggling through all the years since she escaped from Durham. They were free in a way from countries, from towns, from laws, from prejudices, even in a way from nationality. She had hoped once that Jean might interest himself in her own sullen, independent, clever Thérèse, but in her knowledge of the world she had long ago abandoned that hope, knowing that a boy so violent and romantic, so influenced by an upbringing among Frenchmen, a youth so completely masculine, was certain to seek a girl more soft and gentle and feminine than Thérèse. She knew it was inevitable that he should fall in love with a girl like Sybil, and in a way she was content because it fell in admirably with her own indolent plans. The Pentlands were certain to look upon Jean de Cyon as a sort of gipsy, and when they knew the whole truth. . .

The speculation fascinated her. The summer in Durham, even with the shadow of Jack's death flung across it, was not proving as dreadful as she had feared; and this new development interested her as something she had never before observed. . . an idyllic love affair between two young people who each seemed to her a perfect, charming creature.

V

IT HAD ALL BEGUN ON the day nearly a year earlier when all Paris was celebrating the anniversary of the Armistice, and in the morning Sybil had gone with Thérèse and Sabine to lay a wreath beside the flame at the Arc de Triomphe (for the war was one of the unaccountable things about which Sabine chose to make a display of sentiment). And afterward she played in the garden with the dogs which they would not let her keep at the school in Saint-Cloud, and then she had gone into the house to find there a fascinating and beautiful woman of perhaps fifty—a Madame de Cyon, who had come to lunch, with her son, a young man of twenty-four, tall, straight and slender, with red hair and dark blue eyes and a deep, pleasant voice. On account of the day he was dressed in his cuirassier's uniform of black and silver, and because of an old wound he walked with a slight limp. Almost at once (she remembered this when she thought of him) he had looked at her in a frank, admiring way which gave her a sense of pleasurable excitement wholly new in her experience.

Something in the sight of the uniform, or perhaps in the feel of the air, the sound of the military music, the echoes of the *Marseillaise* and the *Sambre et Meuse*, the sight of the soldiers in the street and the great Arc with the flame burning there. . . something in the feel of Paris, something which she loved passionately, had taken possession of her. It was something which, gathering in that moment, had settled upon the strange young man who regarded her with such admiring eyes.

She knew vaguely that she must have fallen in love in the moment she stood there in Sabine Callendar's salon bowing to Lily de Cyon. The experience had grown in intensity when, after lunch, she took him into the garden to show him her dogs and watched him rubbing the ears of the Doberman "Imp" and talking to the dog softly in a way which made her know that he felt about animals as she did. He had been so pleasant in his manner, so gentle in his bigness, so easy to talk to, as if they had always been friends.

And then almost at once he had gone away to the Argentine, without even seeing her again, on a trip to learn the business of cattle-raising because he had the idea that one day he might settle himself as a rancher. But he left behind him a vivid image which with the passing of time grew more and more intense in the depths of a romantic nature which revolted at the idea of Thérèse choosing a father scientifically for her child. It was an image by which she had come, almost unconsciously, to measure other men, even to such small details as the set of their shoulders and the way they used their hands and the timbre of their voices. It was this she had really meant when she said to her mother, "I know what sort of man I want to marry. I know exactly." She had meant, quite without knowing it, that it must be a man like Jean de Cyon. . . charming, romantic and a little wild.

She had not forgotten him, though there were moments at the school in Saint-Cloud when she had believed she would never see him again—moments when she was swept by a delicious sense of hopeless melancholy in which she believed that her whole life had been blighted, and which led her to make long and romantic entries in the diary that was kept hidden beneath her mattress. And so as she grew more hopeless, the aura of romance surrounding him took on colors deeper and more varied and intense. She had grown so pale that Mademoiselle Vernueil took to dosing her, and Thérèse accused her abruptly of having fallen in love, a thing she denied vaguely and with overtones of romantic mystery.

And then with the return to Pentlands (a return advised by her mother on account of Jack's health) the image dimmed a little in the belief that even by the wildest flights of imagination there was no chance of her seeing him again. It became a hopeless passion; she prepared herself to forget him and, in the wisdom of her young mind, grow accustomed to the idea of marrying one of the tame young men who were so much more suitable and whom her family had always known. She had watched her admirers carefully, weighing them always against the image of the young man with red hair, dressed in the black and silver of the cuirassiers, and beside that image they had seemed to her—even the blond, good-looking Mannering boy—like little boys, rather naughty and not half so old and wise as herself. She had reconciled herself secretly and with gravity to the idea of making one of the matches common in her world—a marriage determined by property and the fact that her fiancé would be "the right sort of person."

And so the whole affair had come to take on the color of a tragic romance, to be guarded secretly. Perhaps when she was an old woman she would tell the story to her grandchildren. She believed that whomever she married, she would be thinking always of Jean de Cyon. It was one of those half-comic illusions of youth in which there is more than a grain of melancholy truth.

And then abruptly had come the news of his visit to Brook Cottage. She still kept her secret, but not well enough to prevent her mother and Sabine from suspecting it. She had betrayed herself first on the very night of Jack's death when she had said, with a sudden light in her eye, "It's Jean de Cyon. . . I'd forgotten he was arriving tonight." Olivia had noticed the light because it was something which went on and on.

AND AT BROOK COTTAGE YOUNG de Cyon, upset by the delay caused by the funeral and the necessity of respecting the mourning at Pentlands, had sulked and behaved in such a way that he would have been a nuisance to anyone save Sabine, who found amusement in the spectacle. Used to rushing headlong toward anything he desired (as he had rushed into the French army at seventeen and off to the Argentine nine months ago), he turned ill-tempered and spent his days out of doors, rowing on the river and bathing in the solitude of the great white beach. He quarreled with Thérèse, whom he had known since she was a little girl, and tried to be as civil as possible toward the amused Sabine.

She knew by now that he had not come to Durham through any great interest in herself or Thérèse. She knew now how wise she had been (for the purposes of her plan) to have included in her invitation to him the line. . . "Sybil Pentland lives on the next farm to us. You may remember her. She lunched with us last Armistice Day."

She saw that he rather fancied himself as a man of the world who was being very clever in keeping his secret. He asked her about Sybil Pentland in a casual way that was transparently artificial, and consulted her on the lapse of time decently necessary before he broke in upon the mourning at Pentlands, and had Miss Pentland shown any admiration for the young men about Durham? If he had not been so charming and impatient he would have bored Sabine to death.

LOUIS BROMFIELD

The young man was afraid of only one thing. . . that perhaps she had changed in some way, that perhaps she was not in the reality as charming as she had seemed to him in the long months of his absence. He was not without experience (indeed, Sabine believed that he had gone to the Argentine to escape from some Parisian complication) and he knew that such calamitous disappointments *could* happen. Perhaps when he came to know her better the glamour would fade. Perhaps she did not remember him at all. But she seemed to him, after months of romantic brooding, the most desirable woman he had ever seen.

It was a new world in which he discovered himself, in some way a newer and more different world than the vast grass-covered plains from which he had just come. People about Durham, he learned, had a way of saying that Boston and Durham were like England, but this he put down quietly as a kind of snobbery, because Boston and Durham weren't like England at all, so far as he could see; in spots Boston and Durham seemed old, but there wasn't the same richness, the same glamour about them. They should have been romantic and yet they were not; they were more, it seemed to him, like the illustrations in a school history. They were dry. . . *sec*, he thought, considering the French word better in this case on account of its sound.

And it wasn't the likeness to England that he found interesting, but rather the difference. . . the bleak rawness of the countryside and the sight of whole colonies of peoples as strange and foreign as the Czechs and Poles providing a sort of alien background to the whole picture.

He had gone about the business of becoming acquainted with his own country in a thorough, energetic fashion, and being a sensuous youth, filled with a taste for colors and sounds and all the emanations of the spectacle of life, he was acutely conscious of it.

To Sabine, he said, "You know the funny thing is that it seems to me like coming home. It makes me feel that I belong in America. . . not in Durham, but in New York or some of those big roaring towns I've passed through."

He spoke, naturally enough, not at all like an American but in the clipped English fashion, rather swallowing his words, and now and then with a faint trace of French intonation. His voice was deeper and richer than the New England voices, with their way of calling Charles Street "Challs Street" and sacred Harvard. . . "Havaad."

It was the spectacle of New York which had fascinated him more than any other because it surpassed all his dreams of it and all the descriptions people had given him of its immense force and barbaric splendor and the incredible variety of tongues and people. New York, Sabine told him with a consciousness of uttering treason, *was* America, far more than the sort of life he would encounter in Durham.

As he talked to Sabine of New York, he would rise to that pitch of excitement and enthusiasm which comes to people keenly alive. He even confided in her that he had left Europe never to return there to live.

"It's old country," he said, "and if one has been brought up there, as I've been, there's no reason for going back there to live. In a way it's a dead world. . . dead surely in comparison to the Americas. And it's the future that interests me. . . not the past. I want to be where the most is going on. . . in the center of things."

When he was not playing the piano wildly, or talking to Sabine, or fussing about with Thérèse among the frogs and insects of the laboratory she had rigged up on the glass-enclosed piazza, he was walking about the garden in a state of suppressed excitement, turning over and over in his young mind his own problem and the plans he had for adjusting himself in this vigorous country. To discover it now, at the age of twenty-five, was an exciting experience. He was beginning to understand those young Americans he had encountered occasionally in Europe (like his cousin Fergus Tolliver, who died in the war), who seemed so alive, so filled with a reckless sense of adventure. . . young men irresistible in such an old, tired world, because Nature itself was on their side.

To ease his impatience he sought refuge in a furious physical activity, rowing, swimming and driving with Sabine about the Durham countryside. He could not walk far, on account of the trouble caused by his old wound, but he got as far as O'Hara's house, where he met the Irishman and they became friends. O'Hara turned over to him a canoe and a rowing-scull and told him that whenever his leg was better he might have a horse from his stables.

One morning as he pulled his canoe up the muddy bank of the river after his early exercise, he heard the sound of hoofs in the thick mud near at hand and, turning, he saw Sybil Pentland on her mare Andromache coming out of the thicket almost at his side.

It was a superb morning—cool for Durham in mid-August—and on the lazy river the nympheas spread their waxy white blossoms in starlike clusters against a carpet of green pads. It was a morning made for delights, with the long rays of the rising sun striking to silver the dew-hung spider-webs that bound together the tangled masses of wild-grape vines; and young de Cyon, standing on the edge of the path, flushed with health and the early morning exercise, his thick red hair all rumpled, was overcome swiftly by a sense of tremendous physical well-being and strength. A whole world lay before him waiting to be conquered; and into it, out of the tangled thicket, had come Sybil Pentland, more charming in the flesh than she had seemed to him even on the long starlit nights when he lay awake on the pampas thinking of her.

For a second neither of them said anything. The girl, startled and blushing a little, but touched, too, by a quiet sense of dignity, drew in her mare; and Jean, looking up at her, said in a falsely casual way (for his veins were throbbing with excitement), "Oh! Hello! You're Miss Pentland."

"Yes." But she looked suddenly disappointed, as if she *really* believed that he had almost forgotten her.

Standing clad only in trousers and a rowing-shirt, he looked down at his costume and said, grinning, "I'm not dressed to receive visitors."

Somehow this served to break the sense of restraint, and they fell into conversation, exchanging a few banal remarks on the beauty of the morning, and Jean, standing by Andromache, rubbing her nose with the same tenderness he had shown toward Sybil's dogs, looked at her out of the candid blue eyes and said, "I should have come to see you sooner, only I thought you mightn't want to see me."

A quivering note of warmth colored his voice.

"It would have made no difference," she said. "And now you must come often. . . as often as you like. How long are you staying at Brook Cottage?"

For a second he hesitated. "A fortnight. . . perhaps. Perhaps. . . longer."

And looking down at him, she thought, "I must make him stay. If I lose him again now. . . I must make him stay. I like him more than anyone in the world. I can't lose him now."

And she began to reason with herself that Fate was on her side, that destiny had delivered him again into her hands. It was like a thing ordained, and life with him would be exciting, a thrilling affair. The quiet stubbornness, come down to her from Olivia, began to rise and take possession of her. She was determined not to lose him.

They moved away up the river, still talking in a rather stiff fashion, while Jean walked beside Andromache, limping a little. One banality followed another as they groped toward each other, each proud and fearful of showing his feelings, each timid and yet eager and impatient. It was the excitement of being near to each other that made the conversation itself take on a sense of importance. Neither of them really knew what they were saying. In one sense they seemed strange and exciting to each other, but in another they were not strange at all because there lay between them that old feeling, which Sybil had recognized in the garden of the Rue de Tilsitt, that they had known each other always. There were no hesitations or doubts or suspicions.

The sky was brilliant; the scent of the mucky river and growing weeds was overwhelming. There came to both of them a quickening of the senses, a sort of heightened ecstasy, which shut out all the world. It was a kind of enchantment, but different from the enchantment which enveloped the dead house at Pentlands.

VI

EACH TIME THAT OLIVIA ROSE at dawn to ride out with Sybil and meet O'Hara at the old gravel-pit, the simple excursion became more glamorous to her. There was a youth in the contact with Sybil and the Irishman which she had almost forgotten, a feeling of strength for which she had long been hungering. It was, she found, a splendid way to begin the day—in the cool of the morning, riding away over the drenched grass; it made a freshening contrast to the rest of a day occupied largely by such old people as her father-in-law and Anson (who was really an old man) and the old woman in the north wing and by the persistent fluttering attacks of Aunt Cassie. And Olivia, who was not without a secret vanity, began to notice herself in the mirror. . . that her eyes were brighter and her skin was more clear. She saw that she was even perhaps beautiful, and that the riding-habit became her in a romantic fashion.

She knew, too, riding across the fields between Sybil and O'Hara, that he sometimes watched her with a curious bright light in his blue eyes. He said nothing; he betrayed in no way the feeling behind all that sudden, quiet declaration on the terrace of Brook Cottage. She began to see that he was (as Sabine had discovered almost at once) a very clever and dangerous man. It was not alone because of the strange, almost physical, effect he had upon people—an effect which was almost as if his presence took possession of you completely—but because he had patience and knew how to be silent. If he had rushed in, recklessly and clumsily, everything would have been precipitated and ruined at once. There would have been a scene ending with his dismissal and Olivia, perhaps, would have been free; but he had never touched her. It was simply that he was always there, assuring her in some mysterious way that his emotions had not changed, that he still wanted her more than anything in all the world. And to a woman who was romantic by nature and had never known any romance, it was a dangerous method.

There came a morning when, waiting by the gravel-pit, O'Hara saw that there was only one rider coming toward him across the fields from Pentlands. At first it occurred to him that it must be Sybil coming alone, without her mother, and the old boredom and despair engulfed him swiftly. It was only when the rider came nearer and he saw the white star in the forehead of her horse that he knew it was Olivia herself. That she came alone, knowing what he had already told her, he took as a sign of immense importance.

This time he did not wait or ride slowly toward her. He galloped impatiently as a boy across the wet fields to meet her.

She had the old look of radiance about her and a shyness, too, that made her seem at first a trifle cool and withdrawn. She told him quietly, "Sybil didn't come this morning. She went out very early to fish with Jean de Cyon. The mackerel are beginning to run in the open water off the marshes."

There was an odd, strained silence and O'Hara said, "He's a nice boy. . . de Cyon." And then, with a heroic effort to overcome the shyness which she always managed to impose upon him, he said in a low voice, "But I'm glad she didn't come. I've wanted it to be like this all along."

She did not say archly that he must not talk in this vein. It was a part of her fascination that she was too honest and intelligent not to dispense with such coquetry. He had had enough of coquetry from cheap women and had wearied of it long ago. Besides, she had wanted it "like this" herself and she knew that with O'Hara it was silly to pretend, because sooner or later he always found her out. They were not children, either of them. They both knew what they were doing, that it was a dangerous, even a reckless thing; and yet the very sense of excitement made the adventure as irresistible to the one as to the other.

For a little time they rode in silence, watching the dark hoofs of the horses as they sent up little showers of glittering dew from the knee-deep grass and clover, and presently as they turned out of the fields into the path that led into the birch woods, he laughed and said, "A penny for your thoughts."

Smiling, she replied, "I wouldn't sell them for millions."

"They must be very precious."

"Perhaps. . . precious to me, and to no one else."

"Not to anyone at all. . ."

"No. . . I don't think they'd interest anyone. They're not too cheerful."

At this he fell silent again, with an air of brooding and disappointment. For a time she watched him, and presently she said, "You mustn't sulk on a morning like this."

"I'm not sulking. . . I was only. . . thinking."

She laughed. "A penny for your thoughts."

He did not laugh. He spoke with a sudden intensity. "They, too, are worth a million. . . more than that. . . only I'll share them with you. I wouldn't share them with anyone else."

At the sound of his voice, a silly wave of happiness swept through Olivia. She thought, "I'm being young and ridiculous and enjoying myself."

Aloud she said, "I haven't a penny, but if you'll trust me until tomorrow?"

And then he turned to her abruptly, the shyness gone and in its place an emotion close to irritation and anger. "Why buy them?" he asked. "You know well enough what they are. You haven't forgotten what I told you on the terrace at Brook Cottage. . . It's grown more true everyday. . . all of it." When he saw that she had become suddenly grave, he said, "And what about you?"

"You know how impossible it is."

"Nothing is impossible. . . nothing. Besides, I don't mean the difficulties. Those will come later. . . I only mean your own feelings."

"Can't you see that I like you? . . . I must like you else I wouldn't have come alone this morning."

"Like me," he echoed with bitterness. "I'm not interested in having you like me!" And when she made no reply, he added, almost savagely,

"Why do you keep me away from you? Why do you always put a little wall about yourself?"

"Do I?" she asked, stupidly, and with a sense of pain.

"You are cool and remote even when you laugh."

"I don't want to be—I hate cold people."

For a moment she caught a quick flash of the sudden bad temper which sometimes betrayed him. "It's because you're so damned ladylike. Sometimes I wish you were a servant or a scrubwoman."

"And then I wouldn't be the same—would I?"

He looked up quickly, as if to make a sudden retort, and then, checking himself, rode on in silence. Stealing a glance at him, Olivia caught against the wall of green a swift image of the dark, stubborn tanned head—almost, she thought, like the head of a handsome bull—bent a little, thoughtfully, almost sadly; and again a faint, weak feeling attacked her—the same sensation that had overcome her on the night of her son's death when she sat regarding the back of Anson's head and not seeing it at all. She thought, "Why is it that this man—a stranger—seems nearer to me than Anson has ever been? Why is it that I talk to him in a way I never talked to Anson?" And a curious feeling of pity seized her at the sight of the dark head. In a quick flash of understanding she saw him as a little boy searching awkwardly for something which he did not understand; she wanted to stroke the thick, dark hair in a comforting fashion.

He was talking again. "You know nothing about me," he was saying. "And sometimes I think you ought to know it all." Looking at her quickly he asked, "Could you bear to hear it. . . a little of it?"

She smiled at him, certain that in some mysterious, clairvoyant fashion she had penetrated the very heart of his mood, and she thought, "How sentimental I'm being. . . how sickeningly sentimental!" Yet it was a rich, luxuriant mood in which her whole being relaxed and bathed itself. She thought again, "Why should I not enjoy this? I've been cautious all my life."

And seeing her smile, he began to talk, telling her, as they rode toward the rising sun, the story of his humble origin and of those early bitter days along India Wharf, and from time to time she said, "I understand. My own childhood wasn't happy," or, "Go on, please. It fascinates me. . . more than you can imagine."

So he went on, telling her the story of the long scar on his temple, telling her as he had known he would, of his climb to success, confessing everything, even the things of which he had come to be a little ashamed, and betraying from time to time the bitterness which afflicts those who have made their own way against great odds. The shrewd, complex man became as naïve as a little boy; and she understood, as he had known she would. It was miraculous how right he had been about her.

Lost in this mood, they rode on and on as the day rose and grew warm, enveloped all the while in the odor of the dark, rich, growing thicket and the acrid smell of the tall marsh ferns, until Olivia, glancing at her watch, said, "It is very late. I shall have missed the family breakfast." She meant really that Anson would have gone up to Boston by now and that she was glad—only it was impossible to say a thing like that.

AT THE GRAVEL-PIT, SHE BADE him goodbye, and turning her mare toward Pentlands she felt the curious effect of his nearness slipping away from her with each new step; it was as if the hot August morning were turning cold. And when she came in sight of the big red brick house sitting so solidly among the ancient elms, she thought, "I must never do this again. I have been foolish." And again, "Why should I not do it? Why should I not be happy? They have no right to any claim upon me."

But there was one claim, she knew; there was Sybil. She must not make a fool of herself for the sake of Sybil. She must do nothing to interfere with what had been taking place this very morning in the small fishing-boat far out beyond the marshes somewhere near the spot where Savina Pentland had been drowned. She knew well enough why Sybil had chosen to go fishing instead of riding; it was so easy to look at the girl and at young de Cyon and know what was happening there. She herself had no right to stand in the way of this other thing which was so much younger and fresher, so much more nearly perfect.

As she put her mare over the low wall by the stables she looked up and chanced to see a familiar figure in rusty black standing in the garden, as if she had been there all the while looking out over the meadows, watching them. As she drew near, Aunt Cassie came forward with an expression of anxiety on her face, saying in a thin, hushed voice, as if she might be overheard, "I thought you'd never come back, Olivia dear. I've been looking everywhere for you."

Aware from the intense air of mystery that some new calamity had occurred, Olivia replied, "I was riding with O'Hara. We went too far and it was too hot to hurry the horses."

"I know," said Aunt Cassie. "I saw you." ("Of course she would," thought Olivia. "Does anything ever escape her?") "It's about *her*. She's been violent again this morning and Miss Egan says you may be able to do something. She keeps raving about something to do with the attic and Sabine."

"Yes, I know what it is. I'll go right up."

Higgins appeared, grinning and with a bright birdlike look in his sharp eyes, as if he knew all that had been happening and wanted to say, "Ah, you were out with O'Hara this morning. . . alone. . . Well, you can't do better, Ma'am. I hope it brings you happiness. You ought to have a man like that."

As he took the bridle, he said, "That's a fine animal Mr. O'Hara rides, Ma'am. I wish we had him in our stables. . ."

She murmured something in reply and without even waiting for coffee hastened up the dark stairs to the north wing. On the way past the row of tall deep-set windows she caught a swift glimpse of Sabine, superbly dressed and holding a bright yellow parasol over her head, moving indolently up the long drive toward the house, and again she had a sudden unaccountable sense of something melancholy, perhaps even tragic, a little way off. It was one of those quick, inexplicable waves of depression that sweeps over one like a shadow. She said to herself, "I'm depressed now because an hour ago I was too happy."

And immediately she thought, "But it was like Aunt Cassie to have such a thought as that. I must take care or I'll be getting to be a true Pentland. . . believing that if I'm happy a calamity is soon to follow."

She had moments of late when it seemed to her that something in the air, some power hidden in the old house itself, was changing her slowly, imperceptibly, in spite of herself.

MISS EGAN MET HER OUTSIDE the door, with the fixed eternal smile which today seemed to Olivia the sort of smile that the countenance of Fate itself might wear.

"The old lady is more quiet," she said. "Higgins helped me and we managed to bind her in the bed so that she couldn't harm herself. It's surprising how much strength she has in her poor thin body." She explained that old Mrs. Pentland kept screaming, "Sabine! Sabine!" for

Mrs. Callendar and that she kept insisting on being allowed to go into the attic.

"It's the old idea that she's lost something up there," said Miss Egan. "But it's probably only something she's imagined." Olivia was silent for a moment. "I'll go and search," she said. "It might be there is something and if I could find it, it would put an end to these spells."

SHE FOUND THEM EASILY, ALMOST at once, now that there was daylight streaming in at the windows of the cavernous attic. They lay stuffed away beneath one of the great beams. . . a small bundle of ancient yellowed letters which had been once tied together with a bit of mauve ribbon since torn in haste by someone who thrust them in this place of concealment. They had been opened carelessly and in haste, for the moldering paper was all cracked and torn along the edges. The ink, violet once, had turned to a dirty shade of brown.

Standing among the scattered toys left by Jack and Sybil the last time they had played house, Olivia held the letters one by one up to the light. There were eleven in all and each one was addressed to Mrs. J. Pentland, at Pentlands. Eight of them had been sent through the Boston post-office and the other three bore no stamps of any kind, as if they had been sent by messengers or in a bouquet or between the leaves of a book. The handwriting was that of a man, large, impetuous, sprawling, which showed a tendency to blur the letters together in a headlong, impatient way.

She thought at once, "They are addressed to Mrs. J. Pentland, which means Mrs. Jared Pentland. Anson will be delighted, for these must be the letters which passed between Savina Pentland and her cousin, Toby Cane. Anson needed them to complete the book."

And then it occurred to her that there was something strange about the letters—in their having been hidden and perhaps found by the old lady below stairs and then hidden away a second time. Old Mrs. Pentland must have found them there nearly forty years ago, when they still allowed her to wander about the house. Perhaps it had been on one of those rainy days when Anson and Sabine had come into the attic to play in this very corner with these same old toys—the days when Sabine refused to pretend that muddy water was claret. And now the old lady was remembering the discovery after all these years because the return of Sabine and the sound of her name had lighted some train of long-forgotten memories.

　　　　　　　　　　　　　　　　　　　LOUIS BROMFIELD

Seating herself on a broken, battered old trunk, she opened the first of the letters reverently so as not to dislodge the bits of violet sealing-wax that still clung to the edges, and almost at once she read with a swift sense of shock:

Carissima,
I waited last night in the cottage until eleven and when you didn't
come I knew he had not gone to Salem, after all, and was still
there at Pentlands with you . . .

She stopped reading. She understood it now. . . The scamp Toby Cane had been more than merely a cousin to Savina Pentland; he had been her lover and that was why she had hidden the letters away beneath the beams of the vast unfinished attic, intending perhaps to destroy them one day. And then she had been drowned before there was time and the letters lay in their hiding-place until John Pentland's wife had discovered them one day by chance, only to hide them again, forgetting in the poor shocked mazes of her mind what they were or where they were hidden. They were the letters which Anson had been searching for.

But she saw at once that Anson would never use the letters in his book, for he would never bring into the open a scandal in the Pentland family, even though it was a scandal which had come to an end, tragically, nearly a century earlier and was now almost pure romance. She saw, of course, that a love affair between so radiant a creature as Savina Pentland and a scamp like Toby Cane would seem rather odd in a book called "The Pentland Family and the Massachusetts Bay Colony." Perhaps it was better not to speak of the letters at all. Anson would manage somehow to destroy all the value there was in them; he would sacrifice truth to the gods of Respectability and Pretense.

Thrusting the letters into her pocket, she descended the dark stairway, and in the north wing Miss Egan met her to ask, almost with an air of impatience, "I suppose you didn't find anything?"

"No," said Olivia quickly, "nothing which could possibly have interested her."

"It's some queer idea she's hatched up," replied Miss Egan, and looked at Olivia as if she doubted the truth of what she had said.

SHE DID NOT GO DOWNSTAIRS at once. Instead, she went to her own room and after bathing, seated herself in the chaise longue by the open window above the terrace, prepared to read the letters one by one. From below there arose a murmur of voices, one metallic and hard, the other nervous, thin, and high-pitched—Sabine's and Aunt Cassie's—as they sat on the terrace in acid conversation, each trying to outstay the other. Listening, Olivia decided that she was a little weary of them both this morning; it was the first time it had ever occurred to her that in a strange way there was a likeness between two women who seemed so different. That curious pair, who hated each other so heartily, had the same way of trying to pry into her life.

None of the letters bore any dates, so she fell to reading them in the order in which they had been found, beginning with the one which read:

> *Carissima,*
> *I waited last night in the cottage until eleven and when you didn't come I knew he had not gone to Salem, after all, and, was still there at Pentlands with you . . .*

She read on:

> *It's the thought of his being there beside you, even taking possession of you sometimes, that I can't bear. I see him sitting there in the drawing room, looking at you—eating you with his eyes and pretending all the while that he is above the lusts of the flesh. The flesh! The flesh! You and I, dearest, know the glories of the flesh. Sometimes I think I'm a coward not to kill him at once.*
>
> *For God's sake, get rid of him somehow tonight. I can't pass another evening alone in the dark gloomy cottage waiting in vain. It is more than I can bear to sit there knowing that every minute, every second, may bring the sound of your step. Be merciful to me. Get rid of him somehow.*
>
> *I have not touched a drop of anything since I last saw you. Are you satisfied with that?*
>
> *I am sending this in a book by black Hannah. She will wait for an answer.*

Slowly, as she read on and on through the mazes of the impetuous, passionate writing, the voices from the terrace below, the one raised now and a little angry, the other still metallic, hard and indifferent, grew more and more distant until presently she did not hear them at all and in the place of the sound her senses received another impression—that of a curious physical glow, stealing slowly through her whole body. It was as if there lay in that faded brown writing a smoldering fire that had never wholly died out and would never be extinguished until the letters themselves had been burned into ashes.

Word by word, line by line, page by page, the whole tragic, passionate legend came to recreate itself, until near the end she was able to see the three principal actors in it with the reality of life, as if they had never died at all but had gone on living in this old house, perhaps in this very room where she sat. . . the very room which once must have belonged to Savina Pentland.

She saw the husband, that Jared Pentland of whom no portrait existed because he would never spend money on such a luxury, as he must have been in life—a sly man, shrewd and pious and avaricious save when the strange dark passion for his wife made of him an unbalanced creature. And Savina Pentland herself was there, as she looked out of the Ingres portrait—dark, voluptuous, reckless, with her bad enticing eyes—a woman who might easily be the ruin of a man like Jared Pentland. And somehow she was able to get a clear and vivid picture of the writer of those smoldering letters—a handsome scamp of a lover, dark like his cousin Savina, and given to drinking and gambling. But most of all she was aware of that direct, unashamed and burning passion that never had its roots in this stony New England soil beyond the windows of Pentlands. A man who frankly glorified the flesh! A waster! A seducer! And yet a man capable of this magnificent fire which leaped up from the yellow pages and warmed her through and through. It occurred to her then for the first time that there was something heroic and noble and beautiful in a passion so intense. For a moment she was even seized by the feeling that reading these letters was a kind of desecration.

They revealed, too, how Jared Pentland had looked upon his beautiful wife as a fine piece of property, an investment which gave him a sensual satisfaction and also glorified his house and dinnertable. (What Sabine called the "lower middle-class sense of property.") He must have loved her and hated her at once, in the way Higgins loved and hated the handsome red mare. He must have been proud of her and yet hated her because she possessed so completely the power of making a fool of him.

The whole story moved against a background of family. . . the Pentland family. There were constant references to cousins and uncles and aunts and their suspicions and interference.

"It must have begun," thought Olivia, "even in those days."

Out of the letters she learned that the passion had begun in Rome when Savina Pentland was sitting for her portrait by Ingres. Toby Cane had been there with her and afterwards she had gone with him to his lodgings; and when they had returned to the house at Durham (almost new then and the biggest country seat in all New England) they had met in the cottage—Brook Cottage, which still stood there within sight of Olivia's window—Brook Cottage, which after the drowning had been bought by Sabine's grandfather and then fallen into ruins and been restored again by the too-bright, vulgar, resplendent touch of O'Hara. It was an immensely complicated and intricate story which went back, back into the past and seemed to touch them all here in Durham.

"The roots of life at Pentlands," thought Olivia, "go down, down into the past. There are no new branches, no young, vigorous shoots."

She came at length to the last of the letters, which had buried in its midst the terrible revealing lines—

If you knew what delight it gives me to have you write that the child is ours beyond any doubt, that there cannot be the slightest doubt of it! The baby belongs to us. . . to us alone! It has nothing to do with him. I could not bear the idea of his thinking that the child is his if it was not that it makes your position secure. The thought tortures me but I am able to bear it because it leaves you safe and above suspicion.

Slowly, thoughtfully, as if unable to believe her eyes, she reread the lines through again, and then placed her hands against her head with a gesture of feeling suddenly weak and out of her mind.

She tried to think clearly. "Savina Pentland never had but one child, so far as I know. . . never but one. And that must have been Toby Cane's child."

There could be no doubt. It was all there, in writing. The child was the child of Toby Cane and a woman who was born Savina Dalgedo. He was not a Pentland and none of his descendants had been Pentlands. . . not one.

They were not Pentlands at all save as the descendants of Savina and her lover had married among the Brahmins where Pentland blood was in every family. They were not Pentlands by blood and yet they were Pentlands beyond any question, in conduct, in point of view, in tradition. It occurred to Olivia for the first time how immense and terrible a thing was that environment, that air which held them all enchanted. . . all the cloud of prejudices and traditions and prides and small anxieties. It was a world so set, so powerful, so iron-bound that it had made Pentlands of people like Anson and Aunt Cassie, even like her father-in-law. It made Pentlands of people who were not Pentlands at all. She saw it now as an overwhelming, terrifying power that was a part of the old house. It stood rooted in the very soil of all the landscape that spread itself beyond her windows.

And in the midst of this realization she had a swift impulse to laugh, hysterically, for the picture of Anson had come to her suddenly. . . Anson pouring his whole soul into that immense glorification to be known as "The Pentland Family and the Massachusetts Bay Colony."

Slowly, as the first shock melted away a little, she began to believe that the yellowed bits of paper were a sort of infernal machine, an instrument with the power of shattering a whole world. What was she to do with this thing—this curious symbol of a power that always won every struggle in one way or another, directly as in the case of Savina and her lover, or by taking its vengeance upon body or soul as it had done in the case of Aunt Cassie's poor, prying, scheming mind? And there was, too, the dark story of Horace Pentland, and the madness of the old woman in the north wing, and even those sudden terrible bouts of drinking which made so fine a man as John Pentland into something very near to a beast.

It was as if a light of blinding clarity had been turned upon all the long procession of ancestors. She saw now that if "The Pentland Family and the Massachusetts Bay Colony" was to have any value at all as truth it must be rewritten in the light of the struggle between the forces glorified by that drunken scamp Toby Cane and this other terrible force which seemed to be all about her everywhere, pressing even herself slowly into its own mold. It was an old struggle between those who chose to find their pleasure in this world and those who looked for the vague promise of a glorified future existence.

She could see Anson writing in his book, "In the present generation (192-) there exists Cassandra Pentland Struthers (Mrs. Edward Cane

Struthers), a widow who has distinguished herself by her devotion to the Episcopal Church and to charity and good works. She resides in winter in Boston and in summer at her country house near Durham on the land claimed from the wilderness by the first Pentland, distinguished founder of the American family."

Yes, Anson would write just those words in his book. He would describe thus the old woman who sat below stairs hoping all the while that Olivia would descend bearing the news of some new tragedy. . . that virginal old woman who had ruined the whole life of her husband and kept poor half-witted Miss Peavey a prisoner for nearly thirty years.

THE MURMUR OF VOICES DIED away presently and Olivia, looking out of the window, saw that it was Aunt Cassie who had won this time. She was standing in the garden looking down the drive with that malignant expression which sometimes appeared on her face in moments when she thought herself alone. Far down the shadow-speckled drive, the figure of Sabine moved indolently away in the direction of Brook Cottage. Sabine, too, belonged in a way to the family; she had grown up enveloped in the powerful tradition which made Pentlands of people who were not Pentlands at all. Perhaps (thought Olivia) the key to Sabine's restless, unhappy existence also lay in the same dark struggle. Perhaps if one could penetrate deeply enough in the long family history one would find there the reasons for Sabine's hatred of this Durham world and the reasons why she had returned to a people she disliked with all the bitter, almost fanatic passion of her nature. There was in Sabine an element of cold cruelty.

At the sight of Olivia coming down the steps into the garden, Aunt Cassie turned and moved forward quickly with a look of expectancy, asking, "And how is the poor thing?"

And at Olivia's answer, "She's quiet now. . . sleeping. It's all passed," the looked changed to one of disappointment.

She said, with an abysmal sigh, "Ah, she will go on forever. She'll be alive long after I've gone to join dear Mr. Struthers."

"Invalids are like that," replied Olivia, by way of saying something. "They take such care of themselves." And almost at once, she thought, "Here I am playing the family game, pretending that she's not mad but only an invalid."

She had no feeling of resentment against the busy old woman; indeed it seemed to her at times that she had almost an affection for

Aunt Cassie—the sort of affection one has for an animal or a bit of furniture which has been about almost as long as one can remember. And at the moment the figure of Aunt Cassie, the distant sight of Sabine, the bright garden full of flowers. . . all these things seemed to her melodramatic and unreal, for she was still living in the Pentlands of Savina and Toby Cane. It was impossible to fix her attention on Aunt Cassie and her flutterings.

The old lady was saying, "You all seem to have grown very fond of this man O'Hara."

(What was she driving at now?) Aloud, Olivia said, "Why not? He's agreeable, intelligent. . . even distinguished in his way."

"Yes," said Aunt Cassie. "I've been discussing him with Sabine, and I've come to the conclusion that I may have been wrong about him. She thinks him a clever man with a great future." There was a pause and she added with an air of making a casual observation, "But what about his past? I mean where does he come from."

"I know all about it. He's been telling me. That's why I was late this morning."

For a time Aunt Cassie was silent, as if weighing some deep problem. At last she said, "I was wondering about seeing too much of him. He has a bad reputation with women. . . At least, so I'm told."

Olivia laughed. "After all, Aunt Cassie, I'm a grown woman. I can look out for myself."

"Yes. . . I know." She turned with a disarming smile of Christian sweetness. "I don't want you to think that I'm interfering, Olivia. It's the last thing I'd think of doing. But I was considering your own good. It's harmless enough, I'm sure. No one would ever think otherwise, knowing you, my dear. But it's what people will say. There was a scandal I believe about eight years ago. . . a road-house scandal!" She said this with an air of great suffering, as if the words "road-house scandal" seared her lips.

"I suppose so. Most men. . . politicians, I mean. . . have scandals connected with their names. It's part of the business, Aunt Cassie."

And she kept thinking with amazement of the industry of the old lady—that she should have taken the trouble of going far back into O'Hara's past to find some definite thing against him. She did not doubt the ultimate truth of Aunt Cassie's insinuation. Aunt Cassie did not lie deliberately; there was always a grain of truth in her implications, though sometimes the poor grain lay buried so deeply beneath exaggerations that it was almost impossible to discover it. And a thing like that might easily be true about O'Hara. With a man like him you couldn't expect women to play the role they played with a man like Anson.

"It's only on account of what people will say," repeated Aunt Cassie.

"I've almost come to the conclusion that what people say doesn't really matter any longer. . ."

Aunt Cassie began suddenly to pick a bouquet from the border beside her. "Oh, it's not you I'm worrying about, Olivia dear. But we have to consider others sometimes. . . There's Sybil and Anson, and even the very name of Pentland. There's never been any such suspicion attached to it. . . ever."

It was incredible (thought Olivia) that anyone would make such a statement, incredible anywhere else in the world. She wanted to ask, "What about your brother and old Mrs. Soames?" And in view of those letters that lay locked in her dressing-table. . .

At that moment lunch was announced by Peters' appearance in the doorway. Olivia turned to Aunt Cassie, "You're staying, of course."

"No, I must go. You weren't expecting me."

So Olivia began the ancient game, played for so many years, of pressing Aunt Cassie to stay to lunch.

"It makes no difference," she said, "only another plate." And so on through a whole list of arguments that she had memorized long ago. And at last Aunt Cassie, with the air of having been pressed beyond her endurance, yielded, and to Peters, who had also played the game for years, Olivia said, "Lay another place for Mrs. Struthers."

She had meant to stay all along. Lunching out saved both money and trouble, for Miss Peavey ate no more than a bird, at least not openly; and, besides, there were things she must find out at Pentlands, and other things which she must plan. In truth, wild horses could not have dragged her away.

As they entered the house, Aunt Cassie, carrying the bouquet she had plucked, said casually, "I met the Mannering boy on the road this morning and told him to come in tonight. I thought you wouldn't mind. He's very fond of Sybil, you know."

"No, of course not," replied Olivia. "I don't mind. But I'm afraid Sybil isn't very interested in him."

Chapter VIII

I

THE DEATH OF HORACE PENTLAND was not an event to be kept quiet by so simple a means as a funeral that was almost secret; news of it leaked out and was carried here and there by ladies eager to rake up an old Pentland scandal in vengeance upon Aunt Cassie, the community's principal disseminator of calamities. It even penetrated at last the offices of the *Transcript*, which sent a request for an obituary of the dead man, for he was, after all, a member of one of Boston's proudest families. And then, without warning, the ghost of Horace Pentland reappeared suddenly in the most disconcerting of all quarters—Brook Cottage.

The ghost accompanied Sabine up the long drive one hot morning while Olivia sat listening to Aunt Cassie. Olivia noticed that Sabine approached them with an unaccustomed briskness, that all trace of the familiar indolence had vanished. As she reached the edge of the terrace, she called out with a bright look in her eyes, "I have news. . . of Cousin Horace."

She was enjoying the moment keenly, and the sight of her enjoyment must have filled Aunt Cassie, who knew her so well, with uneasiness. She took her own time about revealing the news, inquiring first after Aunt Cassie's health, and settling herself comfortably in one of the wicker chairs. She was an artist in the business of tormenting the old lady and she waited now to squeeze every drop of effect out of her announcement. She was not to be hurried even by the expression which Aunt Cassie's face inevitably assumed at the mention of Horace Pentland—the expression of one who finds himself in the vicinity of a bad smell and is unable to escape.

At last, after lighting a cigarette and moving her chair out of the sun, Sabine announced in a flat voice, "Cousin Horace has left everything he possesses to me."

A look of passionate relief swept Aunt Cassie's face, a look which said, "Pooh! Pooh! Is that all?" She laughed—it was almost a titter, colored by mockery—and said, "Is that all? I imagine it doesn't make you a great heiress."

("Aunt Cassie," thought Olivia, "ought not to have given Sabine such an opportunity; she has said just what Sabine wanted her to say.")

Sabine answered her: "But you're wrong there, Aunt Cassie. It's not money that he's left, but furniture. . . furniture and bibelots. . . and it's a wonderful collection. I've seen it myself when I visited him at Mentone."

"You ought never to have gone. . . You certainly have lost all moral sense, Sabine. You've forgotten all that I taught you as a little girl."

Sabine ignored her. "You see, he worshiped such things, and he spent twenty years of his life collecting them."

"It seems improbable that they could be worth much. . . with as little money as Horace Pentland had. . . only what we let him have to live on."

Sabine smiled again, sardonically, perhaps because the tilt with Aunt Cassie proved so successful. "You're wrong again, Aunt Cassie. . . They're worth a great deal. . . far more than he paid for them, because there are things in his collection which you couldn't buy elsewhere for any amount of money. He took to trading pieces off until his collection became nearly perfect." She paused for a moment, allowing the knife to rest in the wound. "It's an immensely valuable collection. You see, I know about it because I used to see Cousin Horace every winter when I went to Rome. I knew more about him than any of you. He was a man of perfect taste in such things. He really knew."

Olivia sat all the while watching the scene with a quiet amusement. The triumph on this occasion was clearly Sabine's, and Sabine knew it. She sat there enjoying every moment of it, watching Aunt Cassie writhe at the thought of so valuable a heritage going out of the direct family, to so remote and hostile a connection. It was clearly a disaster ranking in importance with the historic loss of Savina Pentland's parure of pearls and emeralds at the bottom of the Atlantic Ocean. It was property lost forever that should have gone into the family fortune.

Sabine was opening the letter slowly, allowing the paper to crackle ominously, as if she knew that every crackle ran painfully up and down the spine of the old lady.

"It's the invoice from the Custom House," she said, lifting each of the five long sheets separately. "Five pages long. . . total value perhaps as much as seventy-five thousand dollars. . . Of course there's not even any duty to pay, as they're all old things."

Aunt Cassie started, as if seized by a sudden pain, and Sabine continued, "He even left provision for shipping it. . . all save four or five big pieces which are being held at Mentone. There are eighteen cases in all."

She began to read the items one by one. . . cabinets, commodes, chairs, lusters, tables, pictures, bits of bronze, crystal and jade. . . all the long list of things which Horace Pentland had gathered with the loving care of a connoisseur during the long years of his exile; and in the midst of the reading, Aunt Cassie, unable any longer to control herself, interrupted, saying, "It seems to me he was an ungrateful, disgusting man. It ought to have gone to my dear brother, who supported him all these years. I don't see why he left it all to a remote cousin like you."

Sabine delved again into the envelope. "Wait," she said. "He explains that point himself. . . in his own will." She opened a copy of this document and, searching for a moment, read, "To my cousin, Sabine Callendar (Mrs. Cane Callendar), of—Rue de Tilsitt, Paris, France, and Newport, Rhode Island, I leave all my collections of furniture, tapestries, bibelots, etc., in gratitude for her kindness to me over a period of many years and in return for her faith and understanding at a time when the rest of my family treated me as an outcast."

Aunt Cassie was beside herself. "And how should he have been treated if not as an outcast? He was an ungrateful, horrible wretch! It was Pentland money which supported him all his miserable life." She paused a moment for breath. "I always told my dear brother that twenty-five hundred a year was far more than Horace Pentland needed. And that is how he has spent it, to insult the very people who were kind to him."

Sabine put the papers back in the envelope and, looking up, said in her hard, metallic voice: "Money's not everything, as I told you once before, Aunt Cassie. I've always said that the trouble with the Pentlands. . . with most of Boston, for that matter. . . lies in the fact that they were lower middle-class shopkeepers to begin with and they've never lost any of the lower middle-class virtues. . . especially about money. They've been proud of living off the income of their incomes. . . No, it wasn't money that Horace Pentland wanted. It was a little decency and kindness and intelligence. I fancy you got your money's worth out of the poor twenty-five hundred dollars you sent him every year. It was worth a great deal more than that to keep the truth under a bushel."

A long and painful silence followed this speech and Olivia, turning toward Sabine, tried to reproach her with a glance for speaking thus to the old lady. Aunt Cassie was being put to rout so pitifully, not only by Sabine, but by Horace Pentland, who had taken his vengeance shrewdly, long after he was dead, by striking at the Pentland sense of possessions, of property.

The light of triumph glittered in the green eyes of Sabine. She was paying back, bit by bit, the long account of her unhappy childhood; and she had not yet finished.

Olivia, watching the conflict with disinterest, was swept suddenly by a feeling of pity for the old lady. She broke the painful silence by asking them both to stay for lunch, but this time Aunt Cassie refused, in all sincerity, and Olivia did not press her, knowing that she could not bear to face the ironic grin of Sabine until she had rested and composed her face. Aunt Cassie seemed suddenly tired and old this morning. The indefatigable, meddling spirit seemed to droop, no longer flying proudly in the wind.

The queer, stuffy motor appeared suddenly on the drive, the back seat filled by the rotund form of Miss Peavey surrounded by four yapping Pekinese. The intricate veils which she wore on entering a motor streamed behind her. Aunt Cassie rose and, kissing Olivia with ostentation, turned to Sabine and went back again to the root of the matter. "I always told my dear brother," she repeated, "that twenty-five hundred a year was far too much for Horace Pentland."

The motor rattled off, and Sabine, laying the letter on the table beside her, said, "Of course, I don't want all this stuff of Cousin Horace's, but I'm determined it shan't go to her. If she had it the poor old man wouldn't rest in his grave. Besides, she wouldn't know what to do with it in a house filled with tassels and antimacassars and souvenirs of Uncle Ned. She'd only sell it and invest the money in invincible securities."

"She's not well. . . the poor old thing," said Olivia. "She wouldn't have had the motor come for her if she'd been well. She's pretended all her life, and now she's really ill—she's terrified at the idea of death. She can't bear it."

The old relentless, cruel smile lighted Sabine's face. "No, now that the time has come she hasn't much faith in the Heaven she's preached all her life." There was a brief silence and Sabine added grimly, "She will certainly be a nuisance to Saint Peter."

But there was only sadness in Olivia's dark eyes, because she kept thinking what a shallow, futile life Aunt Cassie's had been. She had turned her back upon life from the beginning, even with the husband whom she married as a convenience. She kept thinking what a poor barren thing that life had been; how little of richness, of memories, it held, now that it was coming to an end.

Sabine was speaking again. "I know you're thinking that I'm heartless, but you don't know how cruel she was to me. . . what things she did to me as a child." Her voice softened a little, but in pity for herself and not for Aunt Cassie. It was as if the ghost of the queer, unhappy, red-haired little girl of her childhood had come suddenly to stand there beside them where the ghost of Horace Pentland had stood a little while before. The old ghosts were crowding about once more, even there on the terrace in the hot August sunlight in the beauty of Olivia's flowery garden.

"She sent me into the world," continued Sabine's hard voice, "knowing nothing but what was false, believing—the little I believed in anything—in false gods, thinking that marriage was no more than a business contract between two young people with fortunes. She called ignorance by the name of innocence and quoted the Bible and that milk-and-water philosopher Emerson. . . 'dear Mr. Emerson' . . . whenever I asked her a direct, sensible question. . . And all she accomplished was to give me a hunger for facts—hard, unvarnished facts—pleasant or unpleasant."

A kind of hot passion entered the metallic voice, so that it took on an unaccustomed warmth and beauty. "You don't know how much she is responsible for in my life. She. . . and all the others like her. . . killed my chance of happiness, of satisfaction. She cost me my husband. . . What chance had I with a man who came from an older, wiser world. . . a world in which things were looked at squarely, and honestly as truth. . . a man who expected women to be women and not timid icebergs? No, I don't think I shall ever forgive her." She paused for a moment, thoughtfully, and then added, "And whatever she did, whatever cruelties she practised, whatever nonsense she preached, was always done in the name of duty and always 'for your own good, my dear.'"

Then abruptly, with a bitter smile, her whole manner changed and took on once more the old air of indolent, almost despairing, boredom. "I couldn't begin to tell you all, my dear. . . It goes back too far. We're all rotten here. . . not so much rotten as desiccated, for there was never much blood in us to rot. . . The roots go deep. . . But I shan't bore you again with all this, I promise."

Olivia, listening, wanted to say, "You don't know how much blood there is in the Pentlands. . . You don't know that they aren't Pentlands at all, but the children of Savina Dalgedo and Toby Cane. . . But even that hasn't mattered. . . The very air, the very earth of New England, has changed them, dried them up."

But she could not say it, for she knew that the story of those letters must never fall into the hands of the unscrupulous Sabine.

"It doesn't bore me," said Olivia quietly. "It doesn't bore me. I understand it much too well."

"In any case, we've spoiled enough of one fine day with it." Sabine lighted another cigarette and said with an abrupt change of tone, "About this furniture, Olivia. . . I don't want it. I've a house full of such things in Paris. I shouldn't know what to do with it and I don't think I have the right to break it up and sell it. I want you to have it here at Pentlands. . . Horace Pentland would be satisfied if it went to you and Cousin John. And it'll be an excuse to clear out some of the Victorian junk and some of the terrible early American stuff. Plenty of people will buy the early American things. The best of them are only bad imitations of the real things Horace Pentland collected, and you might as well have the real ones."

Olivia protested, but Sabine pushed the point, scarcely giving her time to speak. "I want you to do it. It will be a kindness to me. . . and after all, Horace Pentland's furniture ought to be here. . . in Pentlands. I'll take one or two things for Thérèse, and the rest you must keep, only nothing. . . not so much as a medallion or a snuff-box. . . is to go to Aunt Cassie. She hated him while he was alive. It would be wrong for her to possess anything belonging to him after he is dead. Besides," she added, "a little new furniture would do a great deal toward cheering up the house. It's always been rather spare and cold. It needs a little elegance and sense of luxury. There has never been any splendor in the Pentland family—or in all New England, for that matter."

II

AT ALMOST THE SAME MOMENT that Olivia and Sabine entered the old house to lunch, the figures of Sybil and Jean appeared against the horizon on the rim of the great, bald hill crowned by the town burial-ground. Escaped at length from the eye of the curious, persistent Thérèse, they had come to the hill to eat their lunch in the open air. It was a brilliantly clear day and the famous view lay spread out beneath them like some vast map stretching away for a distance of nearly thirty miles. The marshes appeared green and dark, crossed and recrossed by a reticulation of tidal inlets frequented at nightfall by small boats which brought in whisky and rum from the open sea. There were, distantly visible, great piles of reddish rock rising from the endless white ribbon of beach, and far out on the amethyst sea a pair of white-sailed fishing-boats moved away in the direction of Gloucester. The white sails, so near to each other, carried a warm friendliness in a universe magnificent but also bleak and a little barren.

Coming over the rim of the hill the sudden revelation of the view halted them for a moment. The day was hot, but here on the great hill, remote from the damp, low-lying meadows, there was a fresh cool wind, almost a gale, blowing in from the open sea. Sybil, taking off her hat, tossed it to the ground and allowed the wind to blow her hair in a dark, tangled mass about the serious young face; and at the same moment Jean, seized by a sudden quick impulse, took her hand quietly in his. She did not attempt to draw it away; she simply stood there quietly, as if conscious only of the wild beauty of the landscape spread out below them and the sense of the boy's nearness to her. The old fear of depression and loneliness seemed to have melted away from her; here on this high brown hill, with all the world spread out beneath, it seemed to her that they were completely alone. . . the first and the last two people in all the world. She was aware that a perfect thing had happened to her, so perfect and so far beyond the realm of her most romantic imaginings that it seemed scarcely real.

A flock of glistening white gulls, sweeping in from the sea, soared toward them screaming wildly, and she said, "We'd better find a place to eat."

She had taken from the hands of Sabine the task of showing Jean this little corner of his own country, and today they had come to see the view from the burial-ground and read the moldering queer old inscriptions on the tombstones. On entering the graveyard they came almost at once to the little corner allotted long ago to immigrants with the name of Pentland—a corner nearly filled now with neat rows of graves. By the side of the latest two, still new and covered with fresh sod, they halted, and she began in silence to separate the flowers she had brought from her mother's garden into two great bunches.

"This," she said, pointing to the grave at her feet, "is his. The other grave is Cousin Horace Pentland's, whom I never saw. He died in Mentone. . . He was a first cousin of my grandfather."

Jean helped her to fill the two vases with water and place the flowers in them. When she had finished she stood up, with a sigh, very straight and slender, saying, "I wish you had known him, Jean. You would have liked him. He was always good-humored and he liked everything in the world. . . only he was never strong enough to do much but lie in bed or sit on the terrace in the sun."

The tears came quietly into her eyes, not at sorrow over the death of her brother, but at the pathos of his poor, weak existence; and Jean, moved by a quick sense of pity, took her hand again and this time kissed it, in the quaint, dignified foreign way he had of doing such things.

They knew each other better now, far better than on the enchanted morning by the edge of the river; and there were times, like this, when to have spoken would have shattered the whole precious spell. There was less of shyness between them than of awe at the thing which had happened to them. At that moment he wanted to keep her forever thus, alone with him, on this high barren hill, to protect her and feel her always there at his side touching his arm gently. Here, in such a place, they would be safe from all the unhappiness and the trouble which in a vague way he knew was inevitably a part of living.

As they walked along the narrow path between the rows of chipped, worn old stones they halted now and then to read some half-faded, crumbling epitaph set forth in the vigorous, Biblical language of the first hardy settlers—sometimes amused, sometimes saddened, by the quaint sentiments. They passed rows of Sutherlands and Featherstones and Canes and Mannerings, all turned to dust long ago, the good New England names of that little corner of the world; and at length they came to a little colony of graves with the name Milford cut into each stone. Here there were no new monuments, for the family had disappeared long ago from the Durham world.

In the midst of these Jean halted suddenly and, bending over one of the stones, said, "Milford. . . Milford. . . That's odd. I had a great-grandfather named Milford who came from this part of the country."

"There used to be a great many Milfords here, but there haven't been any since I can remember."

"My great-grandfather was a preacher," said Jean. "A Congregationalist. He led all his congregation into the Middle West. They founded the town my mother came from."

For a moment Sybil was silent. "Was his name Josiah Milford?" she asked.

"Yes. . . That was his name."

"He came from Durham. And after he left, the church died slowly. It's still standing. . . the big white church with the spire, on High Street. It's only a museum now."

Jean laughed. "Then we're not so far apart, after all. It's almost as if we were related."

"Yes, because a Pentland did marry a Milford once, a long time ago. . . more than a hundred years, I suppose."

The discovery made her happy in a vague way, perhaps because she knew it made him seem less what they called an "outsider" at Pentlands. It wouldn't be so hard to say to her father, "I want to marry Jean de Cyon. You know his ancestors came from Durham." The name of Milford would make an impression upon a man like her father, who made a religion of names; but, then, Jean had not even asked her to marry him yet. For some reason he had kept silent, saying nothing of marriage, and the silence clouded her happiness at being near him.

"It's odd," said Jean, suddenly absorbed, in the way of men, over this concrete business of ancestry. "Some of these Milfords must be direct ancestors of mine and I've no idea which ones they are."

"When we go down the hill," she said, "I'll take you to the meeting house and show you the tablet that records the departure of the Reverend Josiah Milford and his congregation."

She answered him almost without thinking what she was saying, disappointed suddenly that the discovery should have broken in upon the perfection of the mood that united them a little while before.

THEY FOUND A GRASSY SPOT sheltered from the August sun by the leaves of a stunted wild-cherry tree, all twisted by the sea winds, and there Sybil seated herself to open their basket and spread the lunch—the chicken, the crisp sandwiches, the fruit. The whole thing seemed an adventure, as if they were alone on a desert island, and the small act gave her a new kind of pleasure, a sort of primitive delight in serving him while he stood looking down at her with a frank grin of admiration.

When she had finished he flung himself down at full length on the grass beside her, to eat with the appetite of a great, healthy man given to violent physical exercise. They ate almost in silence, saying very little, looking out over the marshes and the sea. From time to time she grew aware that he was watching her with a curious light in his blue eyes, and when they had finished, he sat up cross-legged like a tailor, to smoke; and presently, without looking at her he said, "A little while ago, when we first came up the hill, you let me take your hand, and you didn't mind."

"No," said Sybil swiftly. She had begun to tremble a little, frightened but wildly happy.

"Was it because. . . because. . ." He groped for a moment for words and, finding them, went quickly on, "because you feel as I do?"

She answered him in a whisper. "I don't know," she said, and suddenly she felt an overwhelming desire to weep.

"I mean," he said quietly, "that I feel we were made for each other. . . perfectly."

"Yes. . . Jean."

He did not wait for her to finish. He rushed on, overwhelming her in a quick burst of boyish passion. "I wish it wasn't necessary to talk. Words spoil everything. . . They aren't good enough. . . No, you must take me, Sybil. Sometimes I'm disagreeable and impatient and selfish. . . but you must take me. I'll do my best to reform. I'll make you happy. . . I'll do anything for you. And we can go away together anywhere in the world. . . always together, never alone. . . just as we are here, on the top of this hill."

Without waiting for her to answer, he kissed her quickly, with a warm tenderness that made her weep once more. She said over and over again, "I'm so happy, Jean. . . so happy." And then, shamefacedly, "I must confess something. . . I was afraid you'd never come back, and I wanted you always. . . from the very beginning. I meant to have you from the beginning. . . from that first day in Paris."

He lay with his head in her lap while she stroked the thick, red hair, in silence. There in the graveyard, high above the sea, they lost themselves in the illusion which overtakes such young lovers. . . that they had come already to the end of life. . . that, instead of beginning, it was already complete and perfect.

"I meant to have you always. . . Jean. And after you came here and didn't come over to see me. . . I decided to go after you. . . for fear that you'd escape again. I was shameless. . . and a fraud, too. . . That morning by the river. . . I didn't come on you by accident. I knew you were there all the while. I hid in the thicket and waited for you."

"It wouldn't have made the least difference. I meant to have you, too." A sudden impatient frown shadowed the young face. "You won't let anything change you, will you? Nothing that anyone might say. . . nothing that might happen. . . not anything?"

"Not anything," she repeated. "Not anything in the world. Nothing could change me."

"And you wouldn't mind going away from here with me?"

"No. . . I'd like that. It's what I have always wanted. I'd be glad to go away."

LOUIS BROMFIELD

"Even to the Argentine?"

"Anywhere. . . anywhere at all."

"We can be married very soon. . . before I leave. . . and then we can go to Paris to see my mother." He sat up abruptly with an odd, troubled look on his face. "She's a wonderful woman, darling. . . beautiful and kind and charming."

"I thought she was lovely. . . that day in Paris. . . the most fascinating woman I'd ever seen, Jean dear."

He seemed not to be listening to her. The wind was beginning to die away with the heat of the afternoon, and far out on the amethyst sea the two sailing ships lay becalmed and motionless. Even the leaves of the twisted wild-cherry tree hung listlessly in the hot air. All the world about them had turned still and breathless.

Turning, he took both her hands and looked at her. "There's something I must tell you. . . Sybil. . . something you may not like. But you mustn't let it make any difference. . . In the end things like that don't matter."

She interrupted him. "If it's about women. . . I don't care. I know what you are, Jean. . . I'll never know any better than I know now. . . I don't care."

"No. . . what I want to tell you isn't about women. It's about my mother." He looked at her directly, piercingly. "You see. . . my mother and my father were never married. Good old Monsieur de Cyon only adopted me. . . I've no right to the name. . . really. My name is really John Shane. . . They were never married, only it's not the way it sounds. She's a great lady, my mother, and she refused to marry my father because. . . she says. . . she says she found out that he wasn't what she thought him. He begged her to. He said it ruined his whole life. . . but she wouldn't marry him. . . not because she was weak, but because she was strong. You'll understand that when you come to know her."

What he said would have shocked her more deeply if she had not been caught in the swift passion of a rebellion against all the world about her, all the prejudices and the misunderstandings that in her young wisdom she knew would be ranged against herself and Jean. In this mood, the mother of Jean became to her a sort of heroic symbol, a woman to be admired.

She leaned toward him. "It doesn't matter. . . not at all, Jean. . . things like that don't matter in the end. . . All that matters is the future. . ." She looked away from him and added in a low voice, "Besides, what I have to tell you is much worse." She pressed his hand savagely. "You won't let it change you? You'll not give me up? Maybe you know it already. . . that I have a grandmother who is mad. . . She's been mad for years. . . almost all her life."

He kissed her quickly. "No, it won't matter. . . Nothing could make me think of giving you up. . . nothing in the world."

"I'm so happy, Jean. . . and so peaceful. . . as if you had saved me. . . as if you'd changed all my life. I've been frightened sometimes. . ."

But a sudden cloud had darkened the happiness. . . the cloud that was never absent from the house at Pentlands.

"You won't let your father keep us apart, Sybil. . . He doesn't like me. . . It's easy to see that."

"No, I shan't let him." She halted abruptly. "What I am going to say may sound dreadful. . . I shouldn't take my father's word about anything. I wouldn't let him influence me. He's spoiled his own life and my mother's too. . . I feel sorry for my father. . . He's so blind. . . and he fusses so. . . always about things which don't matter."

For a long time they sat in silence, Sybil with her eyes closed leaning against him, when suddenly she heard him saying in a fierce whisper, "That damned Thérèse!" and looking up she saw at the rim of the hill beyond the decaying tombstones, the stocky figure of Thérèse, armed with an insect-net and a knapsack full of lunch. She was standing with her legs rather well apart, staring at them out of her queer gray eyes with a mischievous, humorous expression. Behind her in a semicircle stood a little army of dirty Polish children she had recruited to help her collect bugs. They knew that she had followed them deliberately to spy on them, and they knew that she would pretend blandly that she had come upon them quite by accident.

"Shall we tell her?" asked Jean in a furious whisper.

"No. . . never tell anything in Durham."

The spell was broken now and Jean was angry. Rising, he shouted at Thérèse, "Go and chase your old bugs and leave us in peace!" He knew that, like her mother, Thérèse was watching them scientifically, as if they were a pair of insects.

III

ANSON PENTLAND WAS NOT BY nature a malicious man or even a very disagreeable one; his fussy activities on behalf of Morality arose from no suppressed, twisted impulse of his own toward vice. Indeed, he was a man of very few impulses—a rather stale, flat man who espoused the cause of Morality because it belonged to his tradition and therefore should be encouraged. He was, according to Sabine, something far worse than an abandoned lecher; he was a bore, and a not very intelligent one, who only saw straight along his own thin nose the tiny sector of the universe in which circumstance had placed him. After forty-nine years of staring, his gaze had turned myopic, and the very physical objects which surrounded him—his house, his office, his table, his desk, his pen—had come to be objects unique and glorified by their very presence as utensils of a society the most elevated and perfect in existence. Possessed of an immense and intricate *savoir-faire* he lacked even a suspicion of *savoir-vivre*, and so tradition, custom, convention, had made of his life a shriveled affair, without initiative or individuality, slipping along the narrow groove of ways set and uninteresting. It was this, perhaps, which lay at the root of Sybil's pity for him.

Worshiping the habit of his stale world, he remained content and even amiable so long as no attack was made upon his dignity—a sacred and complicated affair which embraced his house, his friends, his clubs, his ancestors, even to the small possessions allowed him by his father. Yet this dignity was also a frail affair, easily subject to collapse. . . a sort of thin shell enclosing and protecting him. He guarded it with a maidenly and implacable zeal. When all the threats and pleadings of Aunt Cassie moved him to nothing more definite than an uneasy sort of evasion, a threat at any of the things which came within the realm of his dignity set loose an unsuspected, spiteful hatred.

He resented O'Hara because he knew perhaps that the Irishman regarded him and his world with cynicism; and it was O'Hara and Irishmen like him—Democrats (thought Anson) and therefore the scum of the earth—who had broken down the perfect, chilled, set model of Boston life. Sabine he hated for the same reasons; and from the very beginning he had taken a dislike to "that young de Cyon" because the young man seemed to stand entirely alone, independent of such dignities, without sign even of respect for them. And he was, too, inextricably allied with O'Hara and Sabine and the "outlandish Thérèse."

Olivia suspected that he grew shrill and hysterical only at times when he was tormented by a suspicion of their mockery. It was then that he became unaccountable for what he said and did. . . unaccountable as he had been on that night after the ball. She understood that each day made him more acutely sensitive of his dignity, for he was beginning to interpret the smallest hint as an attack upon it.

Knowing these things, she had come to treat him always as a child, humoring and wheedling him until in the end she achieved what she desired, painlessly and surely. She treated him thus in the matter of refurnishing the house. Knowing that he was absorbed in finishing the final chapters of "The Pentland Family and the Massachusetts Bay Colony," she suggested that he move his table into the distant "writingroom" where he would be less disturbed by family activities; and Anson, believing that at last his wife was impressed by the importance and dignity of his work, considered the suggestion an excellent one. He even smiled and thanked her.

Then, after having consulted old John Pentland and finding that he approved the plan, she began bit by bit to insinuate the furniture of Horace Pentland into the house. Sabine came daily to watch the progress of the change, to comment and admire and suggest changes. They found an odd excitement in the emergence of one beautiful object after another from its chrysalis of *emballage*; out of old rags and shavings there appeared the most exquisite of tables and cabinets, bits of chinoiserie, old books and engravings. One by one the ugly desk used by Mr. Lowell, the monstrous lamp presented by Mr. Longfellow, the anemic watercolors of Miss Maria Pentland. . . all the furnishings of the museum were moved into the vast old attic; until at length a new drawing room emerged, resplendent and beautiful, civilized and warm and even a little exotic, dressed in all the treasures which Horace Pentland had spent his life in gathering with passionate care. Quietly and almost without its being noticed, the family skeleton took possession of the house, transforming its whole character.

The change produced in Aunt Cassie a variety of confused and conflicting emotions. It seemed sacrilege to her that the worn, familiar, homely souvenirs of her father's "dear friends" should be relegated into the background, especially by the hand of Horace Pentland; yet it was impossible for her to overlook the actual value of the collection. She saw the objects less as things of rare beauty than in terms of dollars and cents. And, as she had said, "Pentland things ought to find a place in a Pentland house." She suspected Sabine of Machiavellian tactics and could not make up her mind whether Sabine and Horace Pentland had not triumphed in the end over herself and "dear Mr. Lowell" and "good, kind Mr. Longfellow."

Anson, strangely enough, liked the change, with reservations. For a long time he had been conscious of the fact that the drawing room and much of the rest of the house seemed shabby and worn, and so, unworthy of such dignity as attached to the Pentland name.

He stood in the doorway of the drawing room, surveying the transformation, and remarked, "The effect seems good. . . a little flamboyant, perhaps, and undignified for such a house, but on the whole. . . good. . . quite good. I myself rather prefer the plain early American furniture. . ."

To which Sabine replied abruptly, "But it makes hard sitting."

Until now there had never been any music at Pentlands, for music was regarded in the family as something you listened to in concert-halls, dressed in your best clothes. Aunt Cassie, with Miss Peavey, had gone regularly for years each Friday afternoon, to sit hatless with a scarf over her head in Symphony Hall listening to "dear Colonel Higginson's orchestra" (which had fallen off so sadly since his death), but she had never learned to distinguish one melody from another. . . Music at Pentlands had always been a cultural duty, an exercise something akin to attending church. It made no more impression on Aunt Cassie than those occasional trips to Europe when, taking her own world with her, she stayed always at hotels where she would encounter friends from Boston and never be subjected to the strain of barbaric, unsympathetic faces and conversations.

And now, quite suddenly, music at Pentlands became something alive and colorful and human. The tinny old square piano disappeared and in its place there was a great new one bought by Olivia out of her own money. In the evenings the house echoed to the sound of Chopin and Brahms, Beethoven and Bach, and even such barbaric newcomers as Stravinsky and Ravel. Old Mrs. Soames came, when she was well enough, to sit in the most comfortable of the Regence chairs with old John Pentland at her side, listening while the shadow of youth returned to her half-blind old eyes. The sound of Jean's music penetrated sometimes as far as the room of the mad old woman in the north wing and into the writingroom, where it disturbed Anson working on "The Pentland Family and the Massachusetts Bay Colony."

And then one night, O'Hara came in after dinner, dressed in clothes cut rather too obviously along radically fashionable lines. It was the first time he had ever set foot on Pentland soil.

THERE WERE TIMES NOW WHEN Aunt Cassie told herself that Olivia's strange moods had vanished at last, leaving in their place the old docile, pleasant Olivia who had always had a way of smoothing out the troubles at Pentlands. The sudden perilous calm no longer settled over their conversations; Aunt Cassie was no longer fearful of "speaking her mind, frankly, for the good of all of them." Olivia listened to her quietly, and it is true that she was happier in one sense because life at Pentlands seemed to be working itself out; but inwardly, she went her own silent way, grieving in solitude because she dared not add the burden of her grief to that of old John Pentland. Even Sabine, more subtle in such things than Aunt Cassie, came to feel herself quietly shut out from Olivia's confidence.

Sybil, slipping from childhood into womanhood, no longer depended upon her; she even grew withdrawn and secret about Jean, putting her mother off with empty phrases where once she had confided everything. Behind the pleasant, quiet exterior, it seemed to Olivia at times that she had never been so completely, so superbly, alone. She began to see that at Pentlands life came to arrange itself into a series of cubicles, each occupied by a soul shut in from all the others. And she came, for the first time in her life, to spend much time thinking of herself.

With the beginning of autumn she would be forty years old. . . on the verge of middle-age, a woman perhaps with a married daughter. Perhaps at forty-two she would be a grandmother (it seemed likely with such a pair as Sybil and young de Cyon) . . . a grandmother at forty-two with her hair still thick and black, her eyes bright, her face unwrinkled. . . a woman who at forty-two might pass for a woman ten years younger. A grandmother was a grandmother, no matter how youthful she appeared. As a grandmother she could not afford to make herself ridiculous.

She could perhaps persuade Sybil to wait a year or two and so put off the evil day, yet such an idea was even more abhorrent to her. The very panic which sometimes seized her at the thought of turning slowly into an old woman lay also at the root of her refusal to delay Sybil's marriage. What was happening to Sybil had never happened to herself and never could happen now; she was too old, too hard, even too cynical. When one was young like Jean and Sybil, one had an endless store of faith and hope. There was still a glow over all life, and one ought to begin that way. Those first years—no matter what came afterward—would be the most precious in all their existence; and looking about her, she thought, "There are so few who ever have that chance, so few who can build upon a foundation so solid."

Sometimes there returned to her a sudden twinge of the ancient, shameful jealousy which she had felt for Sybil's youth that suffocating night on the terrace overlooking the sea. (In an odd way, all the summer unfolding itself slowly seemed to have grown out of that night.)

No, in the end she returned always to the same thought. . . that she would sacrifice everything to the perfection of this thing which existed between Sybil and the impatient, red-haired young man.

When she was honest with herself, she knew that she would have had no panic, no terror, save for O'Hara. Save for him she would have had no fear of growing old, of seeing Sybil married and finding herself a grandmother. She had prayed for all these things, even that Fate should send Sybil just such a lover; and now that her prayer was answered there were times when she wished wickedly that he had not come, or at least not so promptly. When she was honest, the answer was always the same. . . that O'Hara had come to occupy the larger part of her interest in existence.

In the most secret part of her soul, she no longer pretended that her feeling for him was only one of friendship. She was in love with him. She rose each morning joyfully to ride with him across the meadows, pleased that Sybil came with them less and less frequently; and on the days when he was kept in Boston a cloud seemed to darken all her thoughts and actions. She talked to him of his future, his plans, the progress of his campaign, as if already she were his wife or his mistress. She played traitor to all her world whose fortunes rested on the success and power of his political enemies. She came to depend upon his quick sympathy. He had a Gaelic way of understanding her moods, her sudden melancholy, that had never existed in the phlegmatic, insensitive world of Pentlands.

She was honest with herself after the morning when, riding along the damp, secret paths of the birch thicket, he halted his horse abruptly and with a kind of anguish told her that he could no longer go on in the way they were going.

He said, "What do you want me to do? I am good for nothing. I can think of nothing but you. . . all day and all night. I go to Boston and try to work and all the while I'm thinking of you. . . thinking what is to be done. You must see what hell it is for me. . . to be near you like this and yet to be treated only as a friend."

Abruptly, when she turned and saw the suffering in his eyes, she knew there was no longer any doubt. She asked sadly. "What do you want me to do? What can I do? You make me feel that I am being the cheapest, silliest sort of woman." And in a low voice she added, "I don't mean to be, Michael. . . I love you, Michael. . . Now I've told you. You are the only man I've ever loved. . . even the smallest bit."

A kind of ecstatic joy took possession of him. He leaned over and kissed her, his own tanned face dampened by her tears.

"I'm so happy," she said, "and yet so sad. . ."

"If you love me. . . then we can go our way. . . we need not think of any of the others."

"Oh, it's not so easy as that, my dear." She had never before been so conscious of his presence, of that strange sense of warmth and charm which he seemed to impose on everything about him.

"I do have to think of the others," she said. "Not my husband. . . I don't think he even cares so long as the world knows nothing. But there's Sybil. . . I can't make a fool of myself on account of Sybil."

She saw quickly that she had used the wrong phrase, that she had hurt him; striking without intention at the fear which he sometimes had that she thought him a common, vulgar Irish politician.

"Do you think that this thing between us. . . might be called 'making a fool of yourself'?" he asked with a faint shade of bitterness.

"No. . . you know me better than that. . . You know I was thinking only of myself. . . as a middle-aged woman with a daughter ready to be married."

"But she *will* be married. . . soon. . . surely. Young de Cyon isn't the sort who waits."

"Yes. . . that's true. . . but even then." She turned quickly. "What do you want me to do? . . . Do you want me to be your mistress?"

"I want you for my own. . . I want you to marry me."

"Do you want me as much as that?"

"I want you as much as that. . . I can't bear the thought of sharing you. . . of having you belong to anyone else."

"Oh. . . I've belonged to no one for a great many years now. . . not since Jack was born."

He went on, hurriedly, ardently. "It would change all my life. It would give me some reason to go on. . . Save for you. . . I'd chuck everything and go away. . . I'm sick of it."

"And you want me for my own sake. . . not just because I'll help your career and give you an interest in life."

"For your own sake. . . nothing else, Olivia."

"You see, I ask because I've thought a great deal about it. I'm older than you, Michael. I seem young now. . . But at forty. . . I'll be forty in the autumn. . . at forty being older makes a difference. It cuts short our time. . . It's not as if we were in our twenties. . . I ask you, too, because you are a clever man and must see these things, too."

"None of it makes any difference." He looked so tragically in earnest, there was such a light in his blue eyes, that her suspicions died. She believed him.

"But we can't marry. . . ever," she said, "so long as my husband is alive. He'll never divorce me nor let me divorce him. It's one of his passionate beliefs. . . that divorce is a wicked thing. Besides, there has never been a divorce in the Pentland family. There have been worse things," she said bitterly, "but never a divorce and Anson won't be the first to break any tradition."

"Will you talk to him?"

"Just now, Michael, I think I'd do anything. . . even that. But it will do no good." For a time they were both silent, caught in a profound feeling of hopelessness, and presently she said, "Can you go on like this for a little time. . . until Sybil is gone?"

"We're not twenty. . . either of us. We can't wait too long."

"I can't desert her yet. You don't know how it is at Pentlands. I've got to save her, even if I lose myself. I fancy they'll be married before winter. . . even before autumn. . . before he leaves. And then I shall be free. I couldn't. . . I couldn't be your mistress now, Michael. . . with Sybil still in there at Pentlands with me. . . I may be quibbling. . . I may sound silly, but it does make a difference. . . because perhaps I've lived among them for too long."

"You promise me that when she's gone you'll be free?"

"I promise you, Michael. . . I've told you that I love you. . . that you're the only man I've ever loved. . . even the smallest bit."

"Mrs. Callendar will help us. . . She wants it."

"Oh, Sabine. . ." She was startled. "You haven't spoken to her? You haven't told her anything?"

"No. . . But you don't need to tell her such things. She has a way of knowing." After a moment he said, "Why, even Higgins wants it. He keeps saying to me, in an offhand sort of way, as if what he said meant nothing at all, 'Mrs. Pentland is a fine woman, sir. I've known her for years. Why, she's even helped me out of scrapes. But it's a pity she's shut up in that mausoleum with all those dead ones. She ought to have a husband who's a man. She's married to a living corpse.'"

Olivia flushed. "He has no right to talk that way. . ."

"If you could hear him speak, you'd know that it's not disrespect, but because he worships you. He'd kiss the ground you walk over." And looking down, he added, "He says it's a pity that a thoroughbred like you is shut up at Pentlands. You mustn't mind his way of saying it. He's something of a horse-breeder and so he sees such things in the light of truth."

She knew, then, what O'Hara perhaps had failed to understand— that Higgins was touching the tragedy of her son, a son who should have been strong and full of life, like Jean. And a wild idea occurred to her—that she might still have a strong son, with O'Hara as the father, a son who would be a Pentland heir but without the Pentland taint. She might do what Savina Pentland had done. But she saw at once how absurd such an idea was; Anson would know well enough that it was not *his* son.

They rode on slowly and in silence while Olivia thought wearily round and round the dark, tangled maze in which she found herself. There seemed no way out of it. She was caught, shut in a prison, at the very moment when her chance of happiness had come.

They came suddenly out of the thicket into the lane that led from Aunt Cassie's gazeboed house to Pentlands, and as they passed through the gate they saw Aunt Cassie's antiquated motor drawn up at the side of the road. The old lady was nowhere to be seen, but at the sound of hoofs the rotund form and silly face of Miss Peavey emerged from the bushes at one side, her bulging arms filled with great bunches of some weed.

She greeted Olivia and nodded to O'Hara. "I've been gathering catnip for my cats," she called out. "It grows fine and thick there in the damp ground by the spring."

Olivia smiled. . . a smile that gave her a kind of physical pain. . . and they rode on, conscious all the while that Miss Peavey's china-blue eyes were following them. She knew that Miss Peavey was too silly

LOUIS BROMFIELD

and innocent to suspect anything, but she would, beyond all doubt, go directly to Aunt Cassie with a detailed description of the encounter. Very little happened in Miss Peavey's life and such an encounter loomed large. Aunt Cassie would draw from her all the tiny details, such as the fact that Olivia looked as if she had been weeping.

Olivia turned to O'Hara. "There's nothing malicious about poor Miss Peavey," she said, "but she's a fool, which is far more dangerous."

Chapter IX

I

As the month of August moved toward an end there was no longer any doubt as to the "failing" of Aunt Cassie; it was confirmed by the very silence with which she surrounded the state of her health. For forty years one had discussed Aunt Cassie's health as one discussed the weather—a thing ever present in the consciousness of man about which one could do nothing, and now Aunt Cassie ceased suddenly to speak of her health at all. She even abandoned her habit of going about on foot and took to making her round of calls in the rattling motor which she protested to fear and loathe, and she came to lean more and more heavily upon the robust Miss Peavey for companionship and support. Claiming a fear of burglars, she had Miss Peavey's bed moved into the room next to hers and kept the door open between. She developed, Olivia discovered, an almost morbid terror of being left alone.

And so the depression of another illness came to add its weight to the burden of Jack's death and the grief of John Pentland. The task of battling the cloud of melancholy which hung over the old house grew more and more heavy upon Olivia's shoulders. Anson remained as usual indifferent to any changes in the life about him, living really in the past among all the sheaves of musty papers, a man not so much cold-blooded as bloodless, for there was nothing active nor calculating in his nature, but only a great inertia, a lack of all fire. And it was impossible to turn to Sabine, who in an odd way seemed as cold and detached as Anson; she appeared to stand at a little distance, waiting, watching them all, even Olivia herself. And it was of course unthinkable to cloud the happiness of Sybil by going to her for support.

There was at least O'Hara, who came more and more frequently to Pentlands, now that the first visit had been made and the ice was broken. Anson encountered him once in the hallway, coldly; and he had become very friendly with old John Pentland. The two had a common interest in horses and dogs and cattle, and O'Hara, born in the Boston slums and knowing very little on any of these subjects, perhaps found the old gentleman a valuable source of information. He told Olivia, "I wouldn't come to the house except for you. I can't bear to think of you there. . . always alone. . . always troubled."

LOUIS BROMFIELD

And in the evenings, while they played bridge or listened to Jean's music, she sometimes caught his eye, watching her with the old admiration, telling her that he was ready to support her no matter what happened.

A week after the encounter with Miss Peavey at the catnip-bed, Peters came to Olivia's room late in the afternoon to say, with a curious blend of respect and confidence, "He's ill again, Mrs. Pentland."

She knew what Peters meant; it was a kind of code between them. . . The same words used so many times before.

She went quickly to the tall narrow library that smelled of dogs and apples and woodsmoke, knowing well enough what she would find there; and on opening the door she saw him at once, lying asleep in the big leather chair. The faint odor of whisky—a smell which had come long since to fill her always with a kind of horror—hung in the air, and on the mahogany desk stood three bottles, each nearly emptied. He slept quietly, one arm flung across his chest, the other hanging to the floor, where the bony fingers rested limply against the Turkey-red carpet. There was something childlike in the peace which enveloped him. It seemed to Olivia that he was even free now of the troubles which long ago had left their mark in the harsh, bitter lines of the old face. The lines were gone, melted away somehow, drowned in the immense quiet of this artificial death. It was only thus, perhaps, that he slept quietly, untroubled by dreams. It was only thus that he ever escaped.

Standing in the doorway she watched him for a time, quietly, and then, turning, she said to Peters, "Will you tell Higgins?" and entering the door she closed the red-plush curtains, shutting out the late afternoon sunlight.

Higgins came, as he had done so many times before, to lock the door and sit there in the room, even sleeping on the worn leather divan, until John Pentland, wakening slowly and looking about in a dazed way, discovered his groom sitting in the same room, polishing a bridle or a pair of riding-boots. The little man was never idle. Something deep inside him demanded action: he must always be doing something. And so, after these melancholy occasions, a new odor clung to the library for days. . . the fresh, clean, healthy odor of leather and harness-soap.

FOR TWO DAYS HIGGINS STAYED in the library, leaving it only for meals, and for two days the old lady in the north wing went unvisited. Save for this single room, there was no evidence of any change in the order of life at Pentlands. Jean, in ignorance of what had happened, came in the evenings to play. But Sabine knew; and Aunt Cassie, who never asked questions concerning the mysterious absence of her brother lest she be told the truth. Anson, as usual, noticed nothing. The only real change lay in a sudden display of sulking and ill-temper on the part of Miss Egan. The invincible nurse even quarreled with the cook, and was uncivil to Olivia, who thought, "What next is to happen? I shall be forced to look for a new nurse."

On the evening of the third day, just after dinner, Higgins opened the door and went in search of Olivia.

"The old gentleman is all right again," he said. "He's gone to bathe and he'd like to see you in the library in half an hour."

She found him there, seated by the big mahogany desk, bathed and spotlessly neat in clean linen; but he looked very old and weary, and beneath the tan of the leathery face there was a pallor which gave him a yellowish look. It was his habit never to refer in anyway to these sad occasions, to behave always as if he had only been away for a day or two and wanted to hear what had happened during his absence.

Looking up at her, he said gravely, "I wanted to speak to you, Olivia. You weren't busy, were you? I didn't disturb you?"

"No," she said. "There's nothing. . . Jean and Thérèse are here with Sybil. . . That's all."

"Sybil," he repeated. "Sybil. . . She's very happy these days, isn't she?" Olivia nodded and even smiled a little, in a warm, understanding way, so that he added, "Well, we mustn't spoil her happiness. We mustn't allow anything to happen to it."

A light came into the eyes of Olivia. "No; we mustn't," she repeated, and then, "She's a clever girl. . . She knows what she wants from life, and that's the whole secret. Most people never know until it's too late."

A silence followed this speech, so eloquent, so full of unsaid things, that Olivia grew uneasy.

"I wanted to talk to you about. . ." he hesitated for a moment, and she saw that beneath the edge of the table his hands were clenched so violently that the bony knuckles showed through the brown skin. "I wanted to talk to you about a great many things." He stirred and added abruptly, "First of all, there's my will."

He opened the desk and took out a packet of papers, separating them carefully into little piles before he spoke again. There was a weariness in all his movements. "I've made some changes," he said, "changes that

you ought to know about. . . and there are one or two other things."
He looked at her from under the fierce, shaggy eyebrows. "You see, I
haven't long to live. I've no reason to expect to live forever and I want to
leave things in perfect order, as they have always been."

To Olivia, sitting in silence, the conversation became suddenly
painful. With each word she felt a wall rising about her, shutting her
in, while the old man went on and on with an agonizing calmness, with
an air of being certain that his will would be obeyed in death as it had
always been in life.

"To begin with, you will all be left very rich. . . very rich. . . something
over six million dollars. And it's solid money, Olivia. . . money not
made by gambling, but money that's been saved and multiplied by
careful living. For seventy-five years it's been the tradition of the family
to live on the income of its income. We've managed to do it somehow,
and in the end we're rich. . . very rich."

As he talked he kept fingering the papers nervously, placing them in
neat little piles, arranging and rearranging them.

"And, as you know, Olivia, the money has been kept in a way so
that the principal could never be spent. Sybil's grandchildren will be
able to touch some of it. . . that is, if you are unwise enough to leave
it to them that way."

Olivia looked up suddenly. "But why me? What have I to do with it?"

"That's what I'm coming to, Olivia dear. . . It's because I'm leaving
control of the whole fortune to you."

Suddenly, fiercely, she wanted none of it. She had a quick, passionate
desire to seize all the neatly piled papers and burn them, to tear them
into small bits and fling them out of the window.

"I don't want it!" she said. "Why should you leave it to me? I'm rich
myself. I don't want it! I'm not a Pentland. . . It's not my money. I've
nothing to do with it." In spite of herself, there was a note of passionate
resentment in her voice.

The shaggy brows raised faintly in a look of surprise.

"To whom, if not to you?" he asked.

After a moment, she said, "Why, Anson. . . to Anson, I suppose."

"You don't really think that?"

"It's his money. . . Pentland money. . . not mine. I've all the money I
need and more."

"It's yours, Olivia. . ." He looked at her sharply. "You're more a
Pentland than Anson, in spite of blood. . . in spite of name. You're more

a Pentland than any of them. It's your money by every right in spite of anything you can do."

("But Anson isn't a Pentland, nor you either," thought Olivia.)

"It's you who are dependable, who are careful, who are honorable, Olivia. You're the strong one. When I die, you'll be the head of the family. . . Surely, you know that. . . already."

("I," thought Olivia, "I who have been so giddy, who am planning to betray you all. . . I am all this!")

"If I left it to Anson, it would be wasted, lost on foolish ideas. He's no idea of business. . . There's a screw loose in Anson. . . He's a crank. He'd be giving away this good money to missionaries and queer committees. . . societies for meddling in the affairs of people. That wasn't what this fortune was made for. No, I won't have Pentland money squandered like that. . ."

"And I," asked Olivia. "How do you know what I will do with it?"

He smiled softly, affectionately. "I know what you'll do with it, because I know you, Olivia, my dear. . . You'll keep it safe and intact. . . You're the Pentland of the family. You weren't when you came here, but you are now. I mean that you belong to the grand tradition of Pentlands. . . the old ones who hang out there in the hall. You're the only one left. . . for Sybil is too young. She's only a child. . . yet."

Olivia was silent, but beneath the silence there ran a torrent of cold, rebellious thoughts. Being a Pentland, then, was not a matter of blood: it was an idea, even an ideal. She thought fiercely, "I'm not a Pentland. I'm alive. I am myself. I've not been absorbed into nothing. All these years haven't changed me so much. They haven't made me into a Pentland." But for the sake of her affection, she could say none of these things. She only said, "How do you know what I'll do with it? How do you know that I mightn't squander it extravagantly—or—or even run away, taking all that was free with me. No one could stop me—no one."

He only repeated what he had said before, saying it more slowly this time, as if to impress her. "I know what you'll do with it, Olivia, because I know you, Olivia dear—you'd never do anything foolish or shameful—I know that—that's why I trust you."

And when she did not answer him, he asked, "You will accept it, won't you, Olivia? You'll have the help of a good lawyer. . . one of the best. . . John Mannering. It will please me, Olivia, and it will let the world know what I think of you, what you have been to me all these years. . . all that Anson has never been. . . nor my own sister,

LOUIS BROMFIELD

Cassie." He leaned across the table, touching her white hand gently. "You will, Olivia?"

It was impossible to refuse, impossible even to protest any further, impossible to say that in this very moment she wanted only to run away, to escape, to leave them all forever, now that Sybil was safe. Looking away, she said in a low voice, "Yes."

It was impossible to desert him now. . . an old, tired man. The bond between them was too strong; it had existed for too long, since that first day she had come to Pentlands as Anson's bride and known that it was the father and not the son whom she respected. In a way, he had imposed upon her something of his own rugged, patriarchal strength. It seemed to her that she had been caught when she meant most to escape; and she was frightened, too, by the echoing thought that perhaps she had become, after all, a Pentland. . . hard, cautious, unadventurous and a little bitter, one for whom there was no fire or glamour in life, one who worshiped a harsh, changeable, invisible goddess called Duty. She kept thinking of Sabine's bitter remark about "the lower middle-class virtues of the Pentlands" . . . the lack of fire, the lack of splendor, of gallantry. And yet this fierce old man *was* gallant, in an odd fashion. . . Even Sabine knew that.

He was talking again. "It's not only money that's been left to you. . . There's Sybil, who's still too young to be let free. . ."

"No," said Olivia with a quiet stubbornness, "she's not too young. She's to do as she pleases. I've tried to make her wiser than I was at her age. . . perhaps wiser than I've ever been. . . even now."

"Perhaps you're right, my dear. You have been so many times. . . and things aren't the same as they were in my day. . . certainly not with young girls."

He took up the papers again, fussing over them in a curious, nervous way, very unlike his usual firm, unrelenting manner. She had a flash of insight which told her that he was behaving thus because he wanted to avoid looking at her. She hated confidences and she was afraid now that he was about to tell her things she preferred never to hear. She hated confidences and yet she seemed to be a person who attracted them always.

"And leaving Sybil out of it," he continued, "there's queer old Miss Haddon in Durham whom, as you know, we've taken care of for years; and there's Cassie, who's growing old and ill, I think. We can't leave her to half-witted Miss Peavey. I know my sister Cassie has been a burden to you. . . She's been a burden to me, all my life. . ." He smiled grimly. "I suppose you know that. . ." Then, after a pause, he said, "But most of all, there's my wife."

His voice assumed a queer, unnatural quality, from which all feeling had been removed. It became like the voices of deaf persons who never hear the sounds they make.

"I can't leave her alone," he said. "Alone. . . with no one to care for her save a paid nurse. I couldn't die and know that there's no one to think of her. . . save that wretched, efficient Miss Egan. . . a stranger. No, Olivia. . . there's no one but you. . . No one I can trust." He looked at her sharply. "You'll promise me to keep her here always. . . never to let them send her away? You'll promise?"

Again she was caught. "Of course," she said. "Of course I'll promise you that." What else was she to say?

"Because," he added, looking away from her once more, "because I owe her that. . . even after I'm dead. I couldn't rest if she were shut up somewhere. . . among strangers. You see. . . once. . . once. . ." He broke off sharply, as if what he had been about to say was unbearable.

With Olivia the sense of uneasiness changed into actual terror. She wanted to cry out, "Stop! . . . Don't go on!" But some instinct told her that he meant to go on and on to the very end, painfully, despite anything she could do.

"It's odd," he was saying quite calmly, "but there seem to be only women left. . . no men. . . for Anson is really an old woman."

Quietly, firmly, with the air of a man before a confessor, speaking almost as if she were invisible, impersonal, a creature who was a kind of machine, he went on, "And of course, Horace Pentland is dead, so we needn't think of him any longer. . . But there's Mrs. Soames. . ." He coughed and began again to weave the gaunt bony fingers in and out, as if what he had to say were drawn from the depth of his soul with a great agony. "There's Mrs. Soames," he repeated. "I know that you understand about her, Olivia. . . and I'm grateful to you for having been kind and human where none of the others would have been. I fancy we've given Beacon Hill and Commonwealth Avenue subject for conversation for thirty years. . . but I don't care about that. They've watched us. . . they've known everytime I went up the steps of her brownstone house. . . the very hour I arrived and the hour I left. They have eyes, in our world, Olivia, even in the backs of their heads. You must remember that, my dear. They watch you. . . they see everything you do. They almost know

　　　　　　　　　　　　　　　LOUIS BROMFIELD

what you think. . . and when they don't know, they make it up. That's one of the signs of a sick, decaying world. . . that they get their living vicariously. . . by watching someone else live. . . that they live always in the past. That's the only reason I ever felt sorry for Horace Pentland. . . the only reason that I had sympathy for him. It was cruel that he should have been born in such a place."

The bitterness ran like acid through all the speech, through the very timbre of his voice. It burned in the fierce black eyes where the fire was not yet dead. Olivia believed that she was seeing him now for the first time, in his fulness, with nothing concealed. And as she listened, the old cloud of mystery that had always hidden him from her began to clear away like the fog lifting from the marshes in the early morning. She saw him now as he really was. . . a man fiercely masculine, bitter, clear-headed, and more human than the rest of them, who had never before betrayed himself even for an instant.

"But about Mrs. Soames. . . If anything should happen to me, Olivia. . . if I should die first, I want you to be kind to her. . . for my sake and for hers. She's been patient and good to me for so long." The bitterness seemed to flow away a little now, leaving only a kindling warmth in its place. "She's been good to me. . . She's always understood, Olivia, even before you came here to help me. You and she, Olivia, have made life worth living for me. She's been patient. . . more patient than you know. Sometimes I must have made life for her a hell on earth. . . but she's always been there, waiting, full of gentleness and sympathy. She's been ill most of the time you've known her. . . old and ill. You can't imagine how beautiful she once was."

"I know," said Olivia softly. "I remember seeing her when I first came to Pentlands. . . and Sabine has told me."

The name of Sabine appeared to rouse him suddenly. He sat up very straight and said, "Don't trust Sabine too far, Olivia. She belongs to us, after all. She's very like my sister Cassie. . . more like her than you can imagine. It's why they hate each other so. She's Cassie turned inside out, as you might say. They'd both sacrifice everything for the sake of stirring up some trouble or calamity that would interest them. They live. . . vicariously."

Olivia would have interrupted him, defending Sabine and telling of the one real thing that had happened to her. . . the tragic love for her husband; she would have told him of all the abrupt, incoherent confidences Sabine had made her; but the old man gave her no chance.

It seemed suddenly that he had become possessed, fiercely intent upon pouring out to her all the dark things he had kept hidden for so long.

(She kept thinking, "Why must I know all these things? Why must I take up the burden? Why was it that *I* should find those letters which had lain safe and hidden for so long?")

He was talking again quietly, the bony fingers weaving in and out their nervous futile pattern. "You see, Olivia. . . You see, she takes drugs now. . . and there's no use in trying to cure her. She's old now, and it doesn't really matter. It's not as if she were young with all her life before her."

Almost without thinking, Olivia answered, "I know that."

He looked up quickly. "Know it?" he asked sharply. "How could you know it?"

"Sabine told me."

The head bowed again. "Oh, Sabine! Of course! She's dangerous. She knows far too much of the world. She's known too many strange people." And then he repeated again what he had said months ago after the ball. "She ought never to have come back here."

Into the midst of the strange, disjointed conversation there came presently the sound of music drifting toward them from the distant drawing room. John Pentland, who was a little deaf, did not hear it at first, but after a little time he sat up, listening, and turning toward her, asked, "Is that Sybil's young man?"

"Yes."

"He's a nice boy, isn't he?"

"A very nice boy."

After a silence he asked, "What's the name of the thing he's playing?"

Olivia could not help smiling. "It's called *I'm in love again and the spring is a-comin'*. Jean brought it back from Paris. A friend of his wrote it. . . but names don't mean anything in music anymore. No one listens to the words."

A shadow of amusement crossed his face. "Songs have queer names nowadays."

She would have escaped, then, going quietly away. She stirred and even made a gesture toward leaving, but he raised his hand in the way he had, making her feel that she must obey him as if she were a child.

"There are one or two more things you ought to know, Olivia. . . things that will help you to understand. Someone has to know them. Someone. . ." He halted abruptly and again made a great effort to go on. The veins stood out sharply on the bony head.

LOUIS BROMFIELD

"It's about *her* chiefly," he said, with the inevitable gesture toward the north wing. "She wasn't always that way. That's what I want to explain. You see. . . we were married when we were both very young. It was my father who wanted it. I was twenty and she was eighteen. My father had known her family always. They were cousins of ours, in a way, just as they were cousins of Sabine's. He had gone to school with her father and they belonged to the same club and she was an only child with a prospect of coming into a great fortune. It's an old story, you see, but a rather common one in our world. . . All these things counted, and as for myself, I'd never had anything to do with women and I'd never been in love with anyone. I was very young. I think they saw it as a perfect match. . . made in the hard, prosperous Heaven of their dreams. She was very pretty. . . you can see even now that she must have been very pretty. . . She was sweet, too, and innocent." He coughed, and continued with a great effort. "She had. . . she had a mind like a little child's. She knew nothing. . . a flower of innocence," he added with a strange savagery.

And then, as if the effort were too much for him, he paused and sat staring out of the window toward the sea. To Olivia it seemed that he had slipped back across the years to the time when the poor old lady had been young and perhaps curiously shy of his ardent wooing. A silence settled again over the room, so profound that this time the faint, distant roaring of the surf on the rocks became audible, and then again the sound of Jean's music breaking in upon them. He was playing another tune. . . not *I'm in love again*, but one called *Ukulele Lady*.

"I wish they'd stop that damned music!" said John Pentland.

"I'll go," began Olivia, rising.

"No. . . don't go. You mustn't go. . . not now." He seemed anxious, almost terrified, perhaps by the fear that if he did not tell now he would never tell her the long story that he must tell to someone. "No, don't go. . . not until I've finished, Olivia. I must finish. . . I want you to know why such things happened as happened here yesterday and the day before in this room. . . There's no excuse, but what I have to tell you may explain it. . . a little."

He rose and opening one of the bookcases, took out a bottle of whisky. Looking at her, he said, "Don't worry, Olivia, I shan't repeat it. It's only that I'm feeling weak. It will never happen again. . . what happened yesterday. . . never. I give you my word."

He poured out a full glass and seated himself once more, drinking the stuff slowly while he talked.

"So we were married, I thinking that I was in love with her, because I knew nothing of such things. . . nothing. It wasn't really love, you see. . . Olivia, I'm going to tell you the truth. . . everything. . . all of the truth. It wasn't really love, you see. It was only that she was the only woman I had ever approached in that way. . . and I was a strong, healthy young man."

He began to speak more and more slowly, as if each word were thrust out by an immense effort of will. "And she knew nothing. . . nothing at all. She was," he said bitterly, "all that a young woman was supposed to be. After the first night of the honeymoon, she was never quite the same again. . . never quite the same, Olivia. Do you know what that means? The honeymoon ended in a kind of madness, a fixed obsession. She'd been brought up to think of such things with a sacred horror and there was a touch of madness in her family. She was never the same again," he repeated in a melancholy voice, "and when Anson was born she went quite out of her head. She would not see me or speak to me. She fancied that I had disgraced her forever. . . and after that she could never be left alone without someone to watch her. She never went out again in the world. . ."

The voice died away into a hoarse whisper. The glass of whisky had been emptied in a supreme effort to break through the shell which had closed him in from all the world, from Olivia, whom he cherished, perhaps even from Mrs. Soames, whom he had loved. In the distance the music still continued, this time as an accompaniment to the hard, loud voice of Thérèse singing, *I'm in love again and the spring is a-comin'* . . . Thérèse, the dark, cynical, invincible Thérèse for whom life, from frogs to men, held very few secrets.

"But the story doesn't end there," continued John Pentland weakly. "It goes on. . . because I came to know what being in love might be when I met Mrs. Soames. . . Only then," he said sadly, as if he saw the tragedy from far off as a thing which had little to do with him. "Only then," he repeated, "it was too late. After what I had done to *her*, it was too late to fall in love. I couldn't abandon her. It was impossible. It ought never to have happened." He straightened his tough old body and added, "I've told you all this, Olivia, because I wanted you to understand why sometimes I am. . ." He paused for a moment and then plunged ahead, "why I am a beast as I was yesterday. There have been times when it was the only way I could go on living. . . And it harmed no one. There aren't many who ever knew about it. . . I always hid myself. There was never any spectacle."

Slowly Olivia's white hand stole across the polished surface of the desk and touched the brown, bony one that lay there now, quietly, like a hawk come to rest. She said nothing and yet the simple gesture carried an eloquence of which no words were capable. It brought tears into the burning eyes for the second time in the life of John Pentland. He had wept only once before. . . on the night of his grandson's death. And they were not, Olivia knew, tears of self-pity, for there was no self-pity in the tough, rugged old body; they were tears at the spectacle of a tragedy in which he happened by accident to be concerned.

"I wanted you to know, my dear Olivia. . . that I have never been unfaithful to *her*, not once in all the years since our wedding-night. . . I know the world will never believe it, but I wanted you to know because, you see, you and Mrs. Soames are the only ones who matter to me. . . and she *knows* that it is true."

And now that she knew the story was finished, she did not go away, because she knew that he wanted her to stay, sitting there beside him in silence, touching his hand. He was the sort of man—a man, she thought, like Michael—who needed women about him.

After a long time, he turned suddenly and asked, "This boy of Sybil's—who is he? What is he like?"

"Sabine knows about him."

"It's that which makes me afraid. . . He's out of her world and I'm not so sure that I like it. In Sabine's world it doesn't matter who a person is or where he comes from as long as he's clever and amusing."

"I've watched him. . . I've talked with him. I think him all that a girl could ask. . . a girl like Sybil, I mean. . . I shouldn't recommend him to a silly girl. . . he'd give such a wife a very bad time. Besides, I don't think we can do much about it. Sybil, I think, has decided."

"Has he asked her to marry him? Has he spoken to you?"

"I don't know whether he's asked her. He hasn't spoken to me. Young men don't bother about such things nowadays."

"But Anson won't like it. There'll be trouble. . . and Cassie, too."

"Yes. . . and still, if Sybil wants him, she'll have him. I've tried to teach her that in a case like this. . . well," she made a little gesture with her white hand, "that she should let nothing make any difference."

He sat thoughtfully for a long time, and at last, without looking up and almost as if speaking to himself, he said, "There was once an elopement in the family. . . Jared and Savina Pentland were married that way."

"But that wasn't a happy match. . . not too happy," said Olivia; and immediately she knew that she had come near to betraying herself. A word or two more and he might have trapped her. She saw that it was impossible to add the burden of the letters to these other secrets.

As it was, he looked at her sharply, saying, "No one knows that. . . One only knows that she was drowned."

She saw well enough what he meant to tell her, by that vague hint regarding Savina's elopement; only now he was back once more in the terrible shell; he was the mysterious, the false, John Pentland who could only hint but never speak directly.

The music ceased altogether in the drawing room, leaving only the vague, distant, eternal pounding of the surf on the red rocks, and once the distant echo of a footstep coming from the north wing. The old man said presently, "So she wasn't falling in love with this man O'Hara, after all? There wasn't any need for worry?"

"No, she never thought of him in that way, even for a moment. . . To her he seems an old man. . . We mustn't forget how young she is."

"He's not a bad sort," replied the old man. "I've grown fond of him, and Higgins thinks he's a fine fellow. I'm inclined to trust Higgins. He has an instinct about people. . . the same as he has about the weather." He paused for a moment, and then continued, "Still, I think we'd best be careful about him. He's a clever Irishman on the make. . . and such gentlemen need watching. They're usually thinking only of themselves."

"Perhaps," said Olivia, in a whisper. "Perhaps. . ."

The silence was broken by the whirring and banging of the clock in the hall making ready to strike eleven. The evening had slipped away quickly, veiled in a mist of unreality. At last the truth had been spoken at Pentlands—the grim, unadorned, terrible truth; and Olivia, who had hungered for it for so long, found herself shaken.

John Pentland rose slowly, painfully, for he had grown stiff and brittle with the passing of the summer. "It's eleven, Olivia. You'd better go to bed and get some rest."

II

SHE DID NOT GO TO her own room, because it would have been impossible to sleep, and she could not go to the drawing room to face, in the mood which held her captive, such young faces as those of Jean and Thérèse and Sybil. At the moment she could not bear the thought of any enclosed place, of a room or even a place covered by a roof which shut out the open sky. She had need of the air and that healing sense of freedom and oblivion which the sight of the marshes and the sea sometimes brought to her. She wanted to breathe deeply the fresh salty atmosphere, to run, to escape somewhere. Indeed, for a moment she succumbed to a sense of panic, as she had done on the other hot night when O'Hara followed her into the garden.

She went out across the terrace and, wandering aimlessly, found herself presently moving beneath the trees in the direction of the marshes and the sea. This last night of August was hot and clear save for the faint, blue-white mist that always hung above the lower meadows. There had been times in the past when the thought of crossing the lonely meadows, of wandering the shadowed lanes in the darkness, had frightened her, but tonight such an adventure seemed only restful and quiet, perhaps because she believed that she could encounter there nothing more terrible than the confidences of John Pentland. She was acutely aware, as she had been on that other evening, of the breathless beauty of the night, of the velvety shadows along the hedges and ditches, of the brilliance of the stars, of the distant foaming white line of the sea and the rich, fertile odor of the pastures and marshes.

And presently, when she had grown a little more calm, she tried to bring some order out of the chaos that filled her body and spirit. It seemed to her that all life had become hopelessly muddled and confused. She was aware in some way, almost without knowing why, that the old man had tricked her, turning her will easily to his own desires, changing all the prospect of the future. She had known always that he was strong and in his way invincible, but until tonight she had never known the full greatness of his strength. . . how relentless, even how unscrupulous he could be; for he had been unscrupulous, unfair, in the way he had used every weapon at hand. . . every sentiment, every memory. . . to achieve his will. There had been no fierce struggle in the open; it was far more subtle than that. He had subdued her without her knowing it, aided perhaps by all that dark force which had the power of changing them all. . . even the children of Savina Dalgedo and Toby Cane into "Pentlands."

Thinking bitterly of what had passed, she came to see that his strength rested upon the foundation of his virtue, his *rightness*. One could say—indeed, one could believe it as one believed that the sun had risen yesterday—that all his life had been tragically foolish and quixotic, fantastically devoted to the hard, uncompromising ideal of what a Pentland ought to be; and yet. . . yet one knew that he had been right, even perhaps heroic; one respected his uncompromising strength. He had made a wreck of his own happiness and driven poor old Mrs. Soames to seek peace in the Nirvana of drugs; and yet for her, he was the whole of life: she lived only for him. This code of his was hard, cruel, inhuman, sacrificing everything to its observance. . . "Even," thought Olivia, "to sacrificing me along with himself. But I will not be sacrificed. I will escape!"

And after a long time she began to see slowly what it was that lay at the bottom of the iron power he had over people, the strength which none of them had been able to resist. It was a simple thing. . . simply that he *believed*, passionately, relentlessly, as those first Puritans had done.

The others all about her did not matter. Not one of them had any power over her. . . not Anson, nor Aunt Cassie, nor Sabine, nor Bishop Smallwood. None of them played any part in the course of her life. They did not matter. She had no fear of them; rather they seemed to her now fussy and pitiful.

But John Pentland *believed*. It was that which made the difference.

STUMBLING ALONG HALF-BLINDLY, SHE FOUND herself presently at the bridge where the lane from Pentlands crossed the river on its way to Brook Cottage. Since she had been a little girl the sight of water had exerted a strange spell upon her. . . the sight of a river, a lake, but most of all the open sea; she had always been drawn toward these things like a bit of iron toward a magnet; and now, finding herself at the bridge, she halted, and stood looking over the stone parapet in the shadow of the hawthorn-bushes that grew close to the water's edge, down on the dark, still pool below her. The water was black and in it the bright little stars glittered like diamonds scattered over its surface. The warm, rich odor of cattle filled the air, touched by the faint, ghostly perfume of the last white nympheas that bordered the pool.

And while she stood there, bathed in the stillness of the dark solitude, she began to understand a little what had really passed between them in the room smelling of whisky and saddle-soap. She saw how the whole tragedy of John Pentland and his life had been born of the stupidity, the ignorance, the hypocrisy of others, and she saw, too, that he was beyond all doubt the grandson of the Toby Cane who had written those wild passionate letters glorifying the flesh; only John Pentland had found himself caught in the prison of that other terrible thing—the code in which he had been trained, in which he *believed*. She saw now that it was not strange that he sought escape from reality by shutting himself in and drinking himself into a stupor. He had been caught, tragically, between those two powerful forces. He thought himself a Pentland and all the while there burned in him the fire that lay in Toby Cane's letters and in the wanton look that was fixed forever in the portrait of Savina Pentland. She kept seeing him as he said, "I have never been unfaithful to *her*, not once in all the years since our wedding-night. . . I wanted you to know because, you see, you and Mrs. Soames are the only ones who matter to me. . . and she *knows* that it is true."

It seemed to her that this fidelity was a terrible, a wicked, thing.

And she came to understand that through all their talk together, the thought, the idea, of Michael had been always present. It was almost as if they had been speaking all the while about Michael and herself. A dozen times the old man had touched upon it, vaguely but surely. She had no doubts that Aunt Cassie had long since learned all there was to learn from Miss Peavey of the encounter by the catnip-bed, and she was certain that she had taken the information to her brother. Still, there was nothing definite in anything Miss Peavey had seen, very little that was even suspicious. And yet, as she looked back upon her talk with the old man, it seemed to her that in a dozen ways, by words, by intonation, by glances, he had implied that he knew the secret. Even in the end when, cruelly, he had with an uncanny sureness touched the one fear, the one suspicion that marred her love for Michael, by saying in the most casual way, "Still, I think we'd better be careful of him. He's a clever Irishman on the make. . . and such gentlemen need watching. They're usually thinking only of themselves."

And then the most fantastic of all thoughts occurred to her. . . that all their talk together, even the painful, tragic confidence made with such an heroic effort, was directed at herself. He had done all this—he had emerged from his shell of reticence, he had humiliated his fierce pride—all to force her to give up Michael, to force her to sacrifice herself on the altar of that fantastic ideal in which he believed.

And she was afraid because he was so strong; because he had asked her to do nothing that he himself had not done.

She would never know for certain. She saw that, after all, the John Pentland she had left a little while before still remained an illusion, veiled in mystery, unfathomable to her perhaps forever. She had not seen him at all.

STANDING THERE ON THE BRIDGE in the black shadow of the hawthorns, all sense of time or space, of the world about her, faded out of existence, so that she was aware of herself only as a creature who was suffering. She thought, "Perhaps he is right. Perhaps I have become like them, and that is why this struggle goes on and on. Perhaps if I were an ordinary person. . . sane and simple. . . like Higgins. . . there would be no struggle and no doubts, no terror of simply *acting*, without hesitation."

She remembered what the old man had said of a world in which all action had become paralyzed, where one was content simply to watch others act, to live vicariously. The word "sane" had come to her quite naturally and easily as the exact word to describe a state of mind opposed to that which existed perpetually at Pentlands, and the thought terrified her that perhaps this thing which one called "being a Pentland," this state of enchantment, was, after all, only a disease, a kind of madness that paralyzed all power of action. One came to live in the past, to acknowledge debts of honor and duty to people who had been dead for a century and more.

"Once," she thought, "I must have had the power of doing what I wanted to do, what I thought right."

And she thought again of what Sabine had said of New England as "a place where thoughts became higher and fewer," where every action became a problem of moral conduct, an exercise in transcendentalism. It was passing now, even from New England, though it still clung to the world of Pentlands, along with the souvenirs of celebrated "dear friends." Even stowing the souvenirs away in the attic had changed nothing. It was passing all about Pentlands; there was nothing of this sort in the New England that belonged to O'Hara and Higgins and the Polish millworkers of Durham. The village itself had become a new and different place.

In the midst of this rebellion, she became aware, with that strange acuteness which seemed to touch all her senses, that she was no longer alone on the bridge in the midst of empty, mist-veiled meadows. She knew suddenly and with a curious certainty that there were others somewhere near her in the darkness, perhaps watching her, and she had for a moment a wave of the quick, chilling fear which sometimes overtook her at Pentlands at the times when she had a sense of figures surrounding her who could neither be seen nor touched. And almost at once she distinguished, emerging from the mist that blanketed the meadows, the figures of two people, a man and a woman, walking very close to each other, their arms entwined. For a moment she thought, "Am I really mad? Am I seeing ghosts in reality?" The fantastic idea occurred to her that the two figures were perhaps Savina Pentland and Toby Cane risen from their lost grave in the sea to wander across the meadows and marshes of Pentland. Moving through the drifting, starlit mist, they seemed vague and indistinct and watery, like creatures come up out of the water. She fancied them, all dripping and wet, emerging from the waves and crossing the white rim of beach on their way toward the big old house. . .

The sight, strangely enough, filled her with no sense of horror, but only with fascination.

And then, as they drew nearer, she recognized the man—something at first vaguely familiar in the cocky, strutting walk. She knew the bandy legs and was filled suddenly with a desire to laugh wildly and hysterically. It was only the rabbit-like Higgins engaged in some new conquest. Quietly she stepped farther into the shadow of the hawthorns and the pair passed her, so closely that she might have reached out her hand and touched them. It was only then that she recognized the woman. It was no Polish girl from the village, this time. It was Miss Egan—the starched, the efficient Miss Egan, whom Higgins had seduced. She was leaning on him as they walked—a strange, broken, feminine Miss Egan whom Olivia had never seen before.

At once she thought, "Old Mrs. Pentland has been left alone. Anything might happen. I must hurry back to the house." And she had a quick burst of anger at the deceit of the nurse, followed by a flash of intuition which seemed to clarify all that had been happening since the hot night early in the summer when she had seen Higgins leaping the wall like a goat to escape the glare of the motor-lights. The mysterious woman who had disappeared over the wall that night *was* Miss Egan. She had been leaving the old woman alone night after night since then; it explained the sudden impatience and bad temper of these last two days when Higgins had been shut up with the old man.

She saw it all now—all that had happened in the past two months—in an orderly procession of events. The old woman had escaped, leading the way to Savina Pentland's letters, because Miss Egan had deserted her post to wander across the meadows at the call of that mysterious, powerful force which seemed to take possession of the countryside at nightfall. It was in the air again tonight, all about her. . . in the air, in the fields, the sound of the distant sea, the smell of cattle and of ripening seeds. . . as it had been on the night when Michael followed her out into the garden.

In a way, the whole chain of events was the manifestation of the disturbing force which had in the end revealed the secret of Savina's letters. It had mocked them, and now the secret weighed on Olivia as a thing which she must tell someone, which she could no longer keep to herself. It burned her, too, with the sense of possessing a terrible and shameful weapon which she might use if pushed beyond endurance.

Slowly, after the two lovers had disappeared, she made her way back again toward the old house, which loomed square and black against the deep blue of the sky, and as she walked, her anger at Miss Egan's betrayal of trust seemed to melt mysteriously away. She would speak to Miss Egan tomorrow, or the day after; in any case, the affair had been going on all summer and no harm had come of it—no harm save the discovery of Savina Pentland's letters. She felt a sudden sympathy for this starched, efficient woman whom she had always disliked; she saw that Miss Egan's life, after all, was a horrible thing—a procession of days spent in the company of a mad old woman. It was, Olivia thought, something like her own existence. . .

And it occurred to her at the same time that it would be difficult to explain to so sharp-witted a creature as Miss Egan why she herself should have been on the bridge at such an hour of the night. It was as if everything, each little thought and action, became more and more tangled and hopeless, more and more intricate and complicated with the passing of each day. There was no way out save to cut the web boldly and escape.

"No," she thought, "I will not stay. . . I will not sacrifice myself. Tomorrow I shall tell Michael that when Sybil is gone, I will do whatever he wants me to do. . ."

When she reached the house she found it dark save for the light which burned perpetually in the big hall illuminating faintly the rows of portraits; and silent save for the creakings which afflicted it in the stillness of the night.

III

SHE WAS WAKENED EARLY, AFTER having slept badly, with the news that Michael had been kept in Boston the night before and would not be able to ride with her as usual. When the maid had gone away she grew depressed, for she had counted upon seeing him and coming to some definite plan. For a moment she even experienced a vague jealousy, which she put away at once as shameful. It was not, she told herself, that he ever neglected her; it was only that he grew more and more occupied as the autumn approached. It was not that there was any other woman involved; she felt certain of him. And yet there remained that strange, gnawing little suspicion placed in her mind when John Pentland had said, "He's a clever Irishman on the make. . . and such gentlemen need watching."

After all, she knew nothing of him save what he had chosen to tell her. He was a free man, independent, a buccaneer, who could do as he chose in life. Why should he ruin himself for her?

She rose at last, determined to ride alone, in the hope that the fresh morning air and the exercise would put to rout this cloud of morbidity which had kept possession of her from the moment she left John Pentland in the library.

As she dressed, she thought, "Day after tomorrow I shall be forty years old. Perhaps that's the reason why I feel tired and morbid. Perhaps I'm on the borderland of middle-age. But that can't be. I am strong and well and I look young, despite everything. I am tired because of what happened last night." And then it occurred to her that perhaps Mrs. Soames had known these same thoughts again and again during her long devotion to John Pentland. "No," she told herself, "whatever happens I shall never lead the life she has led. Anything is better than that. . . anything."

It seemed strange to her to awaken and find that nothing was changed in all the world about her. After what had happened the night before in the library and on the dark meadows, there should have been some mark left upon the life at Pentlands. The very house, the very landscape, should have kept some record of what had happened; and yet everything was the same. She experienced a faint shock of surprise to find the sun shining brightly, to see Higgins in the stable yard saddling her horse and whistling all the while in an excess of high spirits, to hear the distant barking of the beagles, and to see Sybil crossing the meadow toward the river to meet Jean. Everything was the same, even Higgins, whom she had mistaken for a ghost as he crossed the mist-hung meadows a few hours earlier. It was as if there were two realities at Pentlands—one, it might have been said, of the daylight and the other of the darkness; as if one life—a secret, hidden one—lay beneath the bright, pleasant surface of a world composed of green fields and trees, the sound of barking dogs, the faint odor of coffee arising from the kitchen, and the sound of a groom whistling while he saddled a thoroughbred. It was a misfortune that chance had given her an insight into both the bright, pleasant world and that other dark, nebulous one. The others, save perhaps old John Pentland, saw only this bright, easy life that had begun to stir all about her.

And she reflected that a stranger coming to Pentlands would find it a pleasant, comfortable house, where the life was easy and even luxurious, where all of them were protected by wealth. He would find them all rather pleasant, normal, friendly people of a family respected and even distinguished. He would say, "Here is a world that is solid and comfortable and sound."

Yes, it would appear thus to a stranger, so it might be that the dark, fearful world existed only in her imagination. Perhaps she herself was ill, a little unbalanced and morbid. . . perhaps a little touched like the old woman in the north wing.

Still, she thought, most houses, most families, must have such double lives—one which the world saw and one which remained hidden.

As she pulled on her boots she heard the voice of Higgins, noisy and cheerful, exchanging amorous jests with the new Irish kitchen-maid, marking her already for his own.

SHE RODE LISTLESSLY, ALLOWING THE mare to lead through the birch thicket over the cool dark paths which she and Michael always followed. The morning air did not change her spirits. There was something sad in riding alone through the long green tunnel.

When at last she came out on the opposite side by the patch of catnip where they had encountered Miss Peavey, she saw a Ford drawn up by the side of the road and a man standing beside it, smoking a cigar and regarding the engine as if he were in trouble. She saw no more than that and would have passed him without troubling to look a second time, when she heard herself being addressed.

"You're Mrs. Pentland, aren't you?"

She drew in the mare. "Yes, I'm Mrs. Pentland."

He was a little man, dressed rather too neatly in a suit of checkered stuff, with a high, stiff white collar which appeared to be strangling him. He wore nose-glasses and his face had a look of having been highly polished. As she turned, he took off his straw hat and with a great show of manners came forward, bowing and smiling cordially.

"Well," he said, "I'm glad to hear that I'm right. I hoped I might meet you here. It's a great pleasure to know you, Mrs. Pentland. My name is Gavin. . . I'm by way of being a friend of Michael O'Hara."

"Oh!" said Olivia. "How do you do?"

"You're not in a great hurry, I hope?" he asked. "I'd like to have a word or two with you."

"No, I'm not in a great hurry."

It was impossible to imagine what this fussy little man, standing in the middle of the road, bowing and smiling, could have to say to her.

Still holding his hat in his hand, he tossed away the end of his cigar and said, "It's about a very delicate matter, Mrs. Pentland. It has to do with Mr. O'Hara's campaign. I suppose you know about that. You're a friend of his, I believe?"

"Why, yes," she said coldly. "We ride together."

He coughed and, clearly ill at ease, set off on a tangent from the main subject. "You see, I'm a great friend of his. In fact, we grew up together. . . lived in the same ward and fought together as boys. You mightn't think it to see us together. . . because he's such a clever one. He's made for big things and I'm not. . . I'm. . . I'm just plain John Gavin. But we're friends, all the same, just the same as ever. . . just as if he wasn't a big man. That's one thing about Michael. He never goes back on his old friends, no matter how great he gets to be."

A light of adoration shone in the blue eyes of the little man. It was, Olivia thought, as if he were speaking of God; only clearly he thought of Michael O'Hara as greater than God. If Michael affected men like this, it was easy to see why he was so successful.

The little man kept interrupting himself with apologies. "I shan't keep you long, Mrs. Pentland. . . only a moment. You see I thought it was better if I saw you here instead of coming to the house." Suddenly screwing up his shiny face, he became intensely serious. "It's like this, Mrs. Pentland. . . I know you're a good friend of his and you wish him well. You want to see him get elected. . . even though you people out here don't hold much with the Democratic party."

"Yes," said Olivia. "That's true."

"Well," he continued with a visible effort, "Michael's a good friend of mine. I'm sort of a bodyguard to him. Of course, I never come out here. I don't belong in this world. . . I'd feel sort of funny out here."

(Olivia found herself feeling respect for the little man. He was so simple and so honest and he so obviously worshiped Michael.)

"You see. . . I know all about Michael. I've been through a great deal with him. . . and he's not himself just now. There's something wrong. He ain't interested in his work. He acts as if he'd be willing to chuck his whole career overboard. . . and I can't let him do that. None of his friends. . . can't let him do it. We can't get him to take a proper interest in his affairs. Usually, he manages everything. . . better than anyone else could." He became suddenly confidential, closing one eye. "D'you know what I think is the matter? I've been watching him and I've got an idea."

He waited until Olivia said, "No. . . I haven't the least idea."

Cocking his head on one side and speaking with the air of having made a great discovery, he said, "Well, I think there's a woman mixed up in it."

She felt the blood mounting to her head, in spite of anything she could do. When she was able to speak, she asked, "Yes, and what am I to do?"

He moved a little nearer, still with the same air of confiding in her. "Well, this is my idea. Now, you're a friend of his. . . you'll understand. You see, the trouble is that it's some woman here in Durham. . . some swell, you see, like yourself. That's what makes it hard. He's had women before, but they were women out of the ward and it didn't make much difference. But this is different. He's all upset, and. . ." He hesitated for a moment. "Well, I don't like to say a thing like this about Michael, but I think his head is turned a little. That's a mean thing to say, but then we're all human, aren't we?"

"Yes," said Olivia softly. "Yes. . . in the end, we're all human. . . even swells like me." There was a twinkle of humor in her eye which for a moment disconcerted the little man.

"Well," he went on, "he's all upset about her and he's no good for anything. Now, what I thought was this. . . that you could find out who this woman is and go to her and persuade her to lay off him for a time. . . to go away some place. . . at least until the campaign is over. It'd make a difference. D'you see?"

He looked at her boldly, as if what he had been saying was absolutely honest and direct, as if he really had not the faintest idea who this woman was, and beneath a sense of anger, Olivia was amused at the crude tact which had evolved this trick.

"There's not much that I can do," she said. "It's a preposterous idea. . . but I'll do what I can. I'll try. I can't promise anything. It lies with Mr. O'Hara, after all."

"You see, Mrs. Pentland, if it ever got to be a scandal, it'd be the end of him. A woman out of the ward doesn't matter so much, but a woman out here would be different. She'd get a lot of publicity from the sassiety editors and all. . . That's what's dangerous. He'd have the whole church against him on the grounds of immorality."

While he was speaking, a strange idea occurred to Olivia—that much of what he said sounded like a strange echo of Aunt Cassie's methods of argument.

The horse had grown impatient and was pawing the road and tossing his head; and Olivia was angry now, genuinely angry, so that she waited for a time before speaking, lest she should betray herself and spoil all this little game of pretense which Mr. Gavin had built up to keep himself in countenance. At last she said, "I'll do what I can, but it's a ridiculous thing you're asking of me."

The little man grinned. "I've been a long time in politics, Ma'am, and I've seen funnier things than this. . ." He put on his hat, as if to signal that he had said all he wanted to say. "But there's one thing I'd like to ask. . . and that's that you never let Michael know that I spoke to you about this."

"Why should I promise. . . anything?"

He moved nearer and said in a low voice, "You know Michael very well, Mrs. Pentland. . . You know Michael *very* well, and you know that he's got a bad, quick temper. If he found out that we were meddling in his affairs, he might do anything. He might chuck the whole business and clear out altogether. He's never been like this about a woman before. He'd do it just now. . . That's the way he's feeling. You don't want to see him ruin himself anymore than I do. . . a clever man like Michael. Why, he might be president one of these days. He can do anything he sets his will to, Ma'am, but he is, as they say, temperamental just now."

"I'll not tell him," said Olivia quietly. "And I'll do what I can to help you. And now I must go." She felt suddenly friendly toward Mr. Gavin, perhaps because what he had been telling her was exactly what she wanted most at that moment to hear. She leaned down from her horse and held out her hand, saying, "Good-morning, Mr. Gavin."

Mr. Gavin removed his hat once more, revealing his round, bald, shiny head. "Good-morning, Mrs. Pentland."

As she rode off, the little man remained standing in the middle of the road looking after her until she had disappeared. His eye glowed with the light of admiration, but as Olivia turned from the road into the meadows, he frowned and swore aloud. Until now he hadn't understood how a good politician like Michael could lose his head over any woman. But he had an idea that he could trust this woman to do what she had promised. There was a look about her. . . a look which made her seem different from most women; perhaps it was this look which had made a fool of Michael, who usually kept women in their proper places.

Grinning and shaking his head, he got into the Ford, started it with a great uproar, and set off in the direction of Boston. After he had gone a little way he halted again and got out, for in his agitation he had forgotten to close the hood.

FROM THE MOMENT SHE TURNED and rode away from Mr. Gavin, Olivia gave herself over to action. She saw that there was need of more than mere static truth to bring order out of the hazy chaos at Pentlands; there must be action as well. And she was angry now, really angry, even at Mr. Gavin for his impertinence, and at the unknown person who had been his informant. The strange idea that Aunt Cassie or Anson was somehow responsible still remained; tactics such as these were completely sympathetic to them—to go thus in Machiavellian fashion to a man like Gavin instead of coming to her. By using Mr. Gavin there would be no scene, no definite unpleasantness to disturb the enchantment of Pentlands. They could go on pretending that nothing was wrong, that nothing had happened.

But stronger than her anger was the fear that in some way they might use the same tactics to spoil the happiness of Sybil. They would, she was certain, sacrifice everything to their belief in their own rightness.

She found Jean at the house when she returned, and, closing the door of the drawing room, she said to him, "Jean, I want to talk to you for a moment. . . alone."

He said at once, "I know, Mrs. Pentland. It's about Sybil."

There was a little echo of humor in his voice that touched and disarmed her as it always did. It struck her that he was still young enough to be confident that everything in life would go exactly as he wished it. . .

"Yes," she said, "that was it." They sat on two of Horace Pentland's chairs and she continued. "I don't believe in meddling, Jean, only now there are circumstances. . . reasons. . ." She made a little gesture. "I thought that if really. . . really. . ."

He interrupted her quickly. "I do, Mrs. Pentland. We've talked it all over, Sybil and I. . . and we're agreed. We love each other. We're going to be married."

Watching the young, ardent face, she thought, "It's a nice face in which there is nothing mean or nasty. The lips aren't thin and tight like Anson's, nor the skin sickly and pallid the way Anson's has always been. There's life in it, and force and charm. It's the face of a man who would be good to a woman. . . a man not in the least cold-blooded."

"Do you love her. . . really?" she asked.

"I. . . I. . . It's a thing I can't answer because there aren't words to describe it."

"Because. . . well. . . Jean, it's no ordinary case of a mother and a daughter. It's much more than that. It means more to me than my own happiness, my own life. . . because, well, because Sybil is like a part of myself. I want her to be happy. It's not just a simple case of two young people marrying. It's much more than that." There was a silence, and she asked, "How do you love her?"

He sat forward on the edge of his chair, all eagerness. "Why. . ." he began, stammering a little, "I couldn't think of living without her. It's different from anything I ever imagined. Why. . . we've planned everything. . . all our lives. If ever I lost her, it wouldn't matter what happened to me afterwards." He grinned and added, "But you see. . . people have said all that before. There aren't any words to explain. . . to make it seem as different from anything else as it seems to me."

"But you're going to take her away?"

"Yes. . . she wants to go where I go."

("They are young," thought Olivia. "They've never once thought of anyone else. . . myself or Sybil's grandfather.")

Aloud she said, "That's right, Jean. . . I want you to take her away. . . no matter what happens, you must take her away. . ." ("And then I won't even have Sybil.")

"We're going to my ranch in the Argentine."

"That's right. . . I think Sybil would like that." She sighed, in spite of herself, vaguely envious of these two. "But you're so young. How can you know for certain."

A shadow crossed his face and he said, "I'm twenty-five, Mrs. Pentland. . . but that's not the only thing. . . I was brought up, you see, among the French. . . like a Frenchman. That makes a difference." He hesitated, frowning for a moment. "Perhaps I oughtn't to tell. . . You mightn't understand. I know how things are in this part of the world. . . You see, I was brought up to look upon falling in love as something natural. . . something that was pleasant and natural and amusing. I've been in love before, casually. . . the way young Frenchmen are. . . but in earnest, too, because a Frenchman can't help surrounding a thing like that with sentiment and romance. He can't help it. If it were just. . . just something shameful and nasty, he couldn't endure it. They don't have affairs in cold blood. . . the way I've heard men talk about such things since I've come here. It makes a difference, Mrs. Pentland, if you look at the thing in the light they do. It's different here. . . I see the difference more everyday."

He was talking earnestly, passionately, and when he paused for a moment she remained silent, unwilling to interrupt him until he had finished.

"What I'm trying to say is difficult, Mrs. Pentland. It's simply this. . . that I'm twenty-five, but I've had experience with life. Don't laugh! Don't think I'm just a college boy trying to make you think I'm a roué. Only what I say is true. I know about such things. . . and I'm glad because it makes me all the more certain that Sybil is the only woman in the world for me. . . the one for whom I'd sacrifice everything. And I'll know better how to make her happy, to be gentle with her. . . to understand her. I've learned now, and it's a thing which needs learning. . . the most important thing in all life. The French are right about it. They make a fine, wonderful thing of love." He turned away with a sudden air of sadness. "Perhaps I shouldn't have told you all this. . . I've told Sybil. She understands."

"No," said Olivia, "I think you're right. . . perhaps." She kept thinking of the long tragic story of John Pentland, and of Anson, who had always been ashamed of love and treated it as something distasteful. To them it had been a dark, strange thing always touched by shame. She kept thinking, despite anything she could do, of Anson's clumsy, artificial attempts at love-making, and she was swept suddenly by shame for him. Anson, so proud and supercilious, was a poor thing, inferior even to his own groom.

"But why," she asked, "didn't you tell me about Sybil sooner? Everyone has seen it, but you never spoke to me."

For a moment he did not answer her. An expression of pain clouded the blue eyes, and then, looking at her directly, he said, "It's not easy to explain why. I was afraid to come to you for fear you mightn't understand, and the longer I've been here, the longer I've put it off because. . . well, because here in Durham, ancestors, family, all that, seems to be the beginning and end of everything. It seems always to be a question of who one's family is. There is only the past and no future at all. And, you see, in a way. . . I haven't any family." He shrugged his big shoulders and repeated, "In a way, I haven't any family at all. You see, my mother was never married to my father. . . I've no blood-right to the name of de Cyon. I'm. . . I'm. . . well, just a bastard, and it seemed hopeless for me even to talk to a Pentland about Sybil."

He saw that she was startled, disturbed, but he could not have known that the look in her eyes had very little to do with shock at what he had told her; rather she was thinking what a weapon the knowledge would be in the hands of Anson and Aunt Cassie and even John Pentland himself.

He was talking again with the same passionate earnestness.

"I shan't let it make any difference, so long as Sybil will have me, but, you see, it's very hard to explain, because it isn't the way it seems. I want you to understand that my mother is a wonderful woman. . . I wouldn't bother to explain, to say anything. . . except to Sybil and to you."

"Sabine has told me about her."

"Mrs. Callendar has known her for a long time. . . They're great friends," said Jean. "She understands."

"But she never told me. . . that. You mean that she's known it all along?"

"It's not an easy thing to tell. . . especially here in Durham, and I fancy she thought it might make trouble for me. . . after she saw what had happened to Sybil and me."

He went on quickly, telling her what he had told Sybil of his mother's story, trying to make her understand what he understood, and Sabine and even his stepfather, the distinguished old de Cyon. . .

trying to explain a thing which he himself knew was not to be explained. He told her that his mother had refused to marry her lover, "because in his life outside. . . the life which had nothing to do with her. . . she discovered that there were things she couldn't support. She saw that it was better not to marry him. . . better for herself and for him and, most of all, for me. . . He did things for the sake of success—mean, dishonorable things—which she couldn't forgive. . . and so she wouldn't marry him. And now, looking back, I think she was right. It made no great difference in her life. She lived abroad. . . as a widow, and very few people—not more than two or three—ever knew the truth. *He* never told because, being a politician, he was afraid of such a scandal. She didn't want me to be brought up under such an influence, and I think she was right. He's gone on doing things that were mean and dishonorable. . . He's still doing them today. You see he's a politician. . . a rather cheap one. He's a Senator now and he hasn't changed. I could tell you his name. . . I suppose some people would think him a distinguished man. . . only I promised her never to tell it. He thinks that I'm dead. . . He came to her once and asked to see me, to have a hand in my education and my future. There were things, he said, that he could do for me in America. . . and she told him simply that I was dead. . . that I was killed in the war." He finished in a sudden burst of enthusiasm, his face alight with affection. "But you must know her really to understand what I've been saying. Knowing her, you understand everything, because she's one of the great people. . . the strong people of the world. You see, it's one of the things which it is impossible to explain—to you or even to Sybil—impossible to explain to the others. One must know her."

If she had had any doubts or fears, she knew now that it was too late to act; she saw that it was impossible to change the wills of two such lovers as Jean and Sybil. In a way, she came to understand the story of Jean's mother more from watching him than by listening to his long explanation. There must be in her that same determination and ardor that was in her son. . . a thing in its way irresistible. And yet it was difficult; she was afraid, somehow, of this unexpected thing, perhaps because it seemed vaguely like the taint of Savina Pentland.

She said, "If no one knows this, there is no reason to tell it here. It would only make unhappiness for all concerned. It is your business alone. . . and Sybil's. The others have no right to interfere, even to know; but they will try, Jean. . . unless. . . unless you both do what you want. . . quickly. Sometimes I think they might do anything."

"You mean. . ." he began impatiently.

Olivia fell back upon that vague hint which John Pentland had dropped to her the night before. She said, "There was once an elopement in the Pentland family."

"You wouldn't mind that?" he asked eagerly. "You wouldn't be hurt. . . if we did it that way?"

"I shouldn't know anything about it," said Olivia quietly, "until it was too late to do anything."

"It's funny," he said; "we'd thought of that. We've talked of it, only Sybil was afraid you'd want to have a big wedding and all that. . ."

"No, I think it would be better not to have any wedding at all. . . especially under the circumstances."

"Mrs. Callendar suggested it as the best way out. . . She offered to lend us her motor," he said eagerly.

"You discussed it with her and yet you didn't speak to me?"

"Well, you see, she's different. . . she and Thérèse. . . They don't belong here in Durham. Besides, she spoke of it first. She knew what was going on. She always knows. I almost think that she planned the whole thing long ago."

Olivia, looking out of the window, saw entering the long drive the antiquated motor with Aunt Cassie, Miss Peavey, her flying veils and her Pekinese.

"Mrs. Struthers is coming. . ." she said. "We mustn't make her suspicious. And you'd best tell me nothing of your plans and then. . . I shan't be able to interfere even if I wanted to. I might change my mind. . . one never knows."

He stood up and, coming over to her, took her hand and kissed it. "There's nothing to say, Mrs. Pentland. . . except that you'll be glad for what you've done. You needn't worry about Sybil. . . I shall make her happy. . . I think I know how."

He left her, hurrying away past the ancestors in the long hall to find Sybil, thinking all the while how odd it would seem to have a woman so young and beautiful as Mrs. Pentland for a mother-in-law. She was a charming woman (he thought in his enthusiasm), a great woman, but she was so sad, as if she had never been very happy. There was always a cloud about her.

He did not escape quickly enough, for Aunt Cassie's sharp eyes caught a glimpse of him as he left the house in the direction of the stables. She met Olivia in the doorway, kissing her and saying, "Was that Sybil's young man I saw leaving?"

"Yes," said Olivia. "We've been talking about Sybil. I've been telling him that he mustn't think of her as someone to marry."

The yellow face of Aunt Cassie lighted with a smile of approval. "I'm glad, my dear, that you're being sensible about this. I was afraid you wouldn't be, but I didn't like to interfere. I never believe any good comes of it, unless one is forced to. He's not the person for Sybil... Why, no one knows anything about him. You can't let a girl marry like that... just anyone who comes along. Besides, Mrs. Pulsifer writes me... You remember her, Olivia, the Mannering boy's aunt who used to have a house in Chestnut Street... Well, she lives in Paris now at the Hotel Continental, and she writes me she's discovered there's some mystery about his mother. No one seems to know much about her."

"Why," said Olivia, "should she write you such a thing? What made her think you'd be interested?"

"Well, Kate Pulsifer and I went to school together and we still correspond now and then. I just happened to mention the boy's name when I was writing her about Sabine. She says, by the way, that Sabine has very queer friends in Paris and that Sabine has never so much as called on her or asked her for tea. And there's been some new scandal about Sabine's husband and an Italian woman. It happened in Venice..."

"But he's not her husband any longer."

The old lady seated herself and went on pouring forth the news from Kate Pulsifer's letter; with each word she appeared to grow stronger and stronger, less and less yellow and worn.

("It must be," thought Olivia, "the effect of so many calamities contained in one letter.")

She saw now that she had acted only just in time and she was glad that she had lied, so flatly, so abruptly, without thinking why she had done it. For Mrs. Pulsifer was certain to go to the bottom of the affair, if for no other reason than to do harm to Sabine; she had once lived in a house on Chestnut Street with a bow-window which swept the entrance to every house. She was one of John Pentland's dead, who lived by watching others live.

IV

FROM THE MOMENT SHE ENCOUNTERED Mr. Gavin on the turnpike until the tragedy which occurred two days later, life at Pentlands appeared to lose all reality for Olivia. When she thought of it long afterward, the hours became a sort of nightmare in which the old enchantment snapped and gave way to a strained sense of struggle between forces which, centering about herself, left her in the end bruised and a little broken, but secure.

The breathless heat of the sort which from time to time enveloped that corner of New England, leaving the very leaves of the trees hanging limp and wilted, again settled down over the meadows and marshes, and in the midst of the afternoon appeared the rarest of sights—the indolent Sabine stirring in the burning sun. Olivia watched her coming across the fields, protected from the blazing sun only by the frivolous yellow parasol. She came slowly, indifferently, and until she entered the cool, darkened drawing room she appeared the familiar bored Sabine; only after she greeted Olivia the difference appeared.

She said abruptly, "I'm leaving day after tomorrow," and instead of seating herself to talk, she kept wandering restlessly about the room, examining Horace Pentland's bibelots and turning the pages of books and magazines without seeing them.

"Why?" asked Olivia. "I thought you were staying until October."

"No, I'm going away at once." She turned and murmured, "I've hated Durham always. It's unbearable to me now. I'm bored to death. I only came, in the first place, because I thought Thérèse ought to know her own people. But it's no good. She'll have none of them. I see now how like her father she is. They're not her own people and never will be. . . I don't imagine Durham will ever see either of us again."

Olivia smiled. "I know it's dull here."

"Oh, I don't mean you, Olivia dear, or even Sybil or O'Hara, but there's something in the air. . . I'm going to Newport for two weeks and then to Biarritz for October. Thérèse wants to go to Oxford." She grinned sardonically. "There's a bit of New England in her, after all. . . this education business. I wanted a *femme du monde* for a daughter and God and New England sent me a scientist who would rather wear flat heels and look through a microscope. It's funny how children turn out."

("Even Thérèse and Sabine," thought Olivia. "Even they belong to it.")

She watched Sabine, so worldly, so superbly dressed, so hard—such a restless nomad; and as she watched her it occurred to her again that she was very like Aunt Cassie—an Aunt Cassie in revolt against Aunt Cassie's gods, an Aunt Cassie, as John Pentland had said, "turned inside out."

Without looking up from the pages of the *Nouvelle Revue*, Sabine said, "I'm glad this thing about Sybil is settled."

"Yes."

"He told you about his mother?"

"Yes."

"You didn't let that make any difference? You didn't tell the others?"

"No. . . Anything I had to say would have made no difference."

"You were wise. . . I think Thérèse is right, perhaps. . . righter than any of us. She says that nature has a contempt for marriage certificates. Respectability can't turn decay into life. . . and Jean is alive. . . So is his mother."

"I know what you are driving at."

"Certainly, my dear, you ought to know. You've suffered enough from it. And knowing his mother makes a difference. She's no ordinary light woman, or even one who was weak enough to allow herself to be seduced. Once in fifty years there occurs a woman who can. . . how shall I say it? . . . get away with a thing like that. You have to be a great woman to do it. I don't think it's made much difference in her life, chiefly because she's a woman of discretion and excellent taste. But it might have made a difference in Jean's life if he had encountered a mother less wise than yourself."

"I don't know whether I'm being wise or not. I believe in him and I want Sybil to escape."

Olivia understood that for the first time they were discussing the thing which none of them ever mentioned the thing which up to now Sabine had only touched upon by insinuation. Sabine had turned away and stood looking out of the window across the meadows where the distant trees danced in waves of heat.

"You spoiled my summer a bit, Olivia dear, by taking away my Irish friend from me."

Suddenly Olivia was angry as she was angry sometimes at the meddling of Aunt Cassie. "I didn't take him away. I did everything possible to avoid him. . . until you came. It was you who threw us together. That's why we're all in a tangle now." And she kept thinking what a strange woman Sabine Callendar really was, how intricate and unfathomable. She knew of no other woman in the world who could talk thus so dispassionately, so without emotion.

"I thought I'd have him to amuse," she was saying, "and instead of that he only uses me as a confidante. He comes to me for advice about another woman. And that, as you know, isn't very interesting. . ."

Olivia sat suddenly erect. "What does he say? What right has he to do such a thing?"

"Because I've asked him to. When I first came here, I promised to help him. You see, I'm very friendly with you both. I want you both to be happy and. . . besides I can think of nothing happening which could give me greater pleasure."

When Olivia did not answer her, she turned from the window and asked abruptly, "What are you going to do about him?"

Again Olivia thought it best not to answer, but Sabine went on pushing home her point relentlessly, "You must forgive me for speaking plainly, but I have a great affection for you both. . . and I. . . well, I have a sense of conscience in the affair."

"You needn't have. There's nothing to have a conscience about."

"You're not being very honest."

Suddenly Olivia burst out angrily, "And why should it concern you, Sabine. . . in the least? Why should I not do as I please, without interference?"

"Because, here. . . and you know this as well as I do. . . here such a thing is impossible."

In a strange fashion she was suddenly afraid of Sabine, perhaps because she was so bent upon pushing things to a definite solution. It seemed to Olivia that she herself was losing all power of action, all capacity for anything save waiting, pretending, doing nothing.

"And I'm interested," continued Sabine slowly, "because I can't bear the tragic spectacle of another John Pentland and Mrs. Soames."

"There won't be," said Olivia desperately. "My father-in-law is different from Michael."

"That's true. . ."

"In a way. . . a finer man." She found herself suddenly in the amazing position of actually defending Pentlands.

"But not," said Sabine with a terrifying reasonableness, "so wise a one. . . or one so intelligent."

"No. It's impossible to say. . ."

"A thing like this is likely to come only once to a woman."

("Why does she keep repeating the very things that I've been fighting all along," thought Olivia.) Aloud she said, "Sabine, you must leave me in peace. It's for me alone to settle."

"I don't want you to do a thing you will regret the rest of your life. . . bitterly."

"You mean. . ."

"Oh, I mean simply to give him up."

Again Olivia was silent, and Sabine asked suddenly. "Have you had a call from a Mr. Gavin? A gentleman with a bald head and a polished face?"

Olivia looked at her sharply. "How could you know that?"

"Because I sent him, my dear. . . for the same reason that I'm here now. . . because I wanted you to do something. . . to act. And I'm confessing now because I thought you ought to know the truth, since I'm going away. Otherwise you might think Aunt Cassie or Anson had done it. . . and trouble might come of that."

Again Olivia said nothing; she was lost in a sadness over the thought that, after all, Sabine was no better than the others.

"It's not easy to act in this house," Sabine was saying. "It's not easy to do anything but pretend and go on and on until at last you are an old woman and die. I did it to help you. . . for your own good."

"That's what Aunt Cassie always says."

The shaft went home, for it silenced Sabine, and in the moment's pause Sabine seemed less a woman than an amazing, disembodied, almost malevolent force. When she answered, it was with a shrug of the shoulders and a bitter smile which seemed doubly bitter on the frankly painted lips. "I suppose I *am* like Aunt Cassie. I mightn't have been, though. . . I might have been just a pleasant normal person. . . like Higgins or one of the servants."

The strange speech found an echo in Olivia's heart. Lately the same thought had come to her again and again—if only she could be simple like Higgins or the kitchen-maid. Such a state seemed to her at the moment the most desirable thing in the world. It was perhaps this strange desire which led Sabine to surround herself with what Durham called "queer people," who were, after all, simply people like Higgins and the kitchen-maid who happened to occupy a higher place in society.

"The air here needs clearing," Sabine was saying. "It needs a thunderstorm, and it can be cleared only by acting. . . This affair of Jean and Sybil will help. We are all caught up in a tangle of thoughts and ideas. . . which don't matter. . . You can do it, Olivia. You can clear the air once and for all."

Then for the first time Olivia thought she saw what lay behind all this intriguing of Sabine; for a moment she fancied that she saw what it was Sabine wanted more passionately than anything else in the world.

Aloud she said it, "I could clear the air, but it would also be the destruction of everything."

Sabine looked at her directly. "Well? . . . and would you be sorry? Would you count it a loss? Would it make any difference?"

Impulsively she touched Sabine's hand. "Sabine," she said, without looking at her, "I'm fond of you. You know that. Please don't talk anymore about this. . . please, because I want to go on being fond of you. . . and I can't otherwise. It's our affair, mine and Michael's. . . and I'm going to settle it, tonight perhaps, as soon as I can have a talk with him. . . I can't go on any longer."

Taking up the yellow parasol, Sabine asked, "Do you expect me for dinner tonight?"

"Of course, more than ever tonight. . . I'm sorry you've decided to go so soon. . . It'll be dreary without you or Sybil."

"You can go, too," said Sabine quickly. "There is a way. He'd give up everything for you. . . everything. I know that." Suddenly she gave Olivia a sharp look. "You're thirty-eight, aren't you?"

"Day after tomorrow I shall be forty!"

Sabine was tracing the design of roses on Horace Pentland's Savonnerie carpet with the tip of her parasol. "Gather them while you may," she said and went out into the blazing heat to cross the meadows to Brook Cottage.

Left alone, Olivia knew she was glad that day after tomorrow Sabine would no longer be here. She saw now what John Pentland meant when he said, "Sabine ought never to have come back here."

V

THE HEAT CLUNG ON FAR into the evening, penetrating with the darkness even the drawing room where they sat—Sabine and John Pentland and old Mrs. Soames and Olivia—playing bridge for the last time, and as the evening wore on the game went more and more badly, with the old lady forgetting her cards and John Pentland being patient and Sabine sitting in a controlled and sardonic silence, with an expression on her face which said clearly, "I can endure this for tonight because tomorrow I shall escape again into the lively world."

Jean and Sybil sat for a time at the piano, and then fell to watching the bridge. No one spoke save to bid or to remind Mrs. Soames that it was time for her shaking hands to distribute the cards about the table. Even Olivia's low, quiet voice sounded loud in the hot stillness of the old room.

At nine o'clock Higgins appeared with a message for Olivia—that Mr. O'Hara was being detained in town and that if he could get away before ten he would come down and stop at Pentlands if the lights were still burning in the drawing room. Otherwise he would not be down to ride in the morning.

Once during a pause in the game Sabine stirred herself to say, "I haven't asked about Anson's book. He must be near to the end."

"Very near," said Olivia. "There's very little more to be done. Men are coming tomorrow to photograph the portraits. He's using them to illustrate the book."

At eleven, when they came to the end of a rubber, Sabine said, "I'm sorry, but I must stop. I must get up early tomorrow to see about the packing." And turning to Jean she said, "Will you drive me home? Perhaps Sybil will ride over with us for the air. You can bring her back."

At the sound of her voice, Olivia wanted to cry out, "No, don't go. You mustn't leave me now. . . alone. You mustn't go away like this!" But she managed to say quietly, in a voice which sounded far away, "Don't stay too late, Sybil," and mechanically, without knowing what she was doing, she began to put the cards back again in their boxes.

She saw that Sabine went out first, and then John Pentland and old Mrs. Soames, and that Jean and Sybil remained behind until the others had gone, until John Pentland had helped the old lady gently into his motor and driven off with her. Then, looking up with a smile which somehow seemed to give her pain she said, "Well?"

And Sybil, coming to her side, kissed her and said in a low voice, "Goodbye, darling, for a little while. . . I love you. . ." And Jean kissed her in a shy fashion on both cheeks.

She could find nothing to say. She knew Sybil would come back, but she would be a different Sybil, a Sybil who was a woman, no longer the child who even at eighteen sometimes had the absurd trick of sitting on her mother's knee. And she was taking away with her something that until now had belonged to Olivia, something which she could never again claim. She could find nothing to say. She could only follow them to the door, from where she saw Sabine already sitting in the motor as if nothing in the least unusual were happening; and all the while she wanted to go with them, to run away anywhere at all.

Through a mist she saw them turning to wave to her as the motor drove off, to wave gaily and happily because they were at the beginning of life. . . She stood in the doorway to watch the motor-lights slipping away in silence down the lane and over the bridge through the blackness to the door of Brook Cottage. There was something about Brook Cottage. . . something that was lacking from the air of Pentlands: it was where Toby Cane and Savina Pentland had had their wanton meetings.

In the still heat the sound of the distant surf came to her dimly across the marshes, and into her mind came absurdly words she had forgotten for years. . . "The breaking waves dashed high on the stern and rockbound coast." Against the accompaniment of the surf, the crickets and katydids (harbingers of autumn) kept up a fiddling and singing; and far away in the direction of Marblehead she watched the eye of a lighthouse winking and winking. She was aware of every sight and sound and odor of the breathless night. It might storm, she thought, before they got into Connecticut. They would be motoring all the night. . .

The lights of Sabine's motor were moving again now, away from Brook Cottage, through O'Hara's land, on and on in the direction of the turnpike. In the deep hollow by the river they disappeared for a moment and then were to be seen once more against the black mass of the hill crowned by the town burial-ground. And then abruptly they were gone, leaving only the sound of the surf and the music of the crickets and the distant, ironically winking lighthouse.

She kept seeing them side by side in the motor racing through the darkness, oblivious to all else in the world save their own happiness. Yes, something had gone away from her forever. . . She felt a terrible, passionate envy that was like a physical pain, and all at once she knew that she was terribly alone standing in the darkness before the door of the old house.

SHE WAS ROUSED BY THE sound of Anson's voice asking, "Is that you, Olivia?"

"Yes."

"What are you doing out there?"

"I came out for some air."

"Where's Sybil?"

For a moment she did not answer, and then quite boldly she said, "She's ridden over with Jean to take Sabine home."

"You know I don't approve of that." He had come through the hall now and was standing near her.

"It can't do any harm."

"That's been said before. . ."

"Why are you so suspicious, Anson, of your own child?" She had no desire to argue with him. She wanted only to be left in peace, to go away to her room and lie there alone in the darkness, for she knew now that Michael was not coming.

"Olivia," Anson was saying, "come inside for a moment. I want to talk to you."

"Very well. . . but please don't be disagreeable. I'm very tired."

"I shan't be disagreeable. . . I only want to settle something."

She knew then that he meant to be very disagreeable, and she told herself that she would not listen to him; she would think of something else while he was speaking—a trick she had learned long ago. In the drawing room she sat quietly and waited for him to begin. Standing by the mantelpiece, he appeared more tired and yellow than usual. She knew that he had worked on his book; she knew that he had poured all his vitality, all his being, into it; but as she watched him her imagination again played her the old trick of showing her Michael standing there in his place. . . defiant, a little sulky, and filled with a slow, steady, inexhaustible force.

"It's chiefly about Sybil," he said. "I want her to give up seeing this boy."

"Don't be a martinet, Anson. Nothing was ever gained by it."

(She thought, "They must be almost to Salem by now.") And aloud she added, "You're her father, Anson; why don't you speak?"

"It's better for you. I've no influence with her."

"I have spoken," she said, thinking bitterly that he could never guess what she meant.

"And what's the result? Look at her, going off at this hour of the night. . ."

She shrugged her shoulders, filled with a warm sense of having outwitted the enemy, for at the moment Anson seemed to her an enemy not only of herself, but of Jean and Sybil, of all that was young and alive in the world.

LOUIS BROMFIELD

"Besides," he was saying, "she hasn't proper respect for me. . . her father. Sometimes I think it's the ideas she got from you and from going abroad to school."

"What a nasty thing to say! But if you want the truth, I think it's because you've never been a very good father. Sometimes I've thought you never wanted children. You've never paid much attention to them. . . not even to Jack. . . while he was alive. It wasn't ever as if they were our children. You've always left them to me. . . alone."

The thin neck stiffened a little and he said, "There are reasons for that. I'm a busy man. . . I've given most of my time, not to making money, but to doing things to better the world in some way. If I've neglected my children it's been for a good reason. . . few men have as much on their minds. And there's been the book to take all my energies. You're being unjust, Olivia. You never could see me as I am."

"Perhaps," said Olivia. (She wanted to say, "What difference does the book make to anyone in the world? Who cares whether it is written or not?") She knew that she must keep up her deceit, so she said, "You needn't worry, because Sabine is going away tomorrow and Jean will go with her." She sighed. "After that your life won't be disturbed any longer. Nothing in the least unusual is likely to happen."

"And there's this other thing," he said, "this disloyalty of yours to me and to all the family."

Stiffening slightly, she asked, "What can you mean by that?"

"You know what I mean."

She saw that he was putting himself in the position of a wronged husband, assuming a martyrdom of the sort which Aunt Cassie practised so effectively. He meant to be a patient, well-meaning husband and to place her in the position of a shameful woman; and slowly, with a slow, heavy anger she resolved to circumvent his trick.

"I think, Anson, that you're talking nonsense. I haven't been disloyal to anyone. Your father will tell you that."

"My father was always weak where women are concerned and now he's beginning to grow childish. He's so old that he's beginning to forgive and condone anything." And then after a silence he said, "This O'Hara. I'm not such a fool as you think, Olivia."

For a long time neither of them said anything, and in the end it was Olivia who spoke, striking straight into the heart of the question. She said, "Anson, would you consider letting me divorce you?"

The effect upon him was alarming. His face turned gray, and the long, thin, oversensitive hands began to tremble. She saw that she had touched him on the rawest of places, upon his immense sense of pride and dignity. It would be unbearable for him to believe that she would want to be rid of him in order to go to another man, especially to a man whom he professed to hold in contempt, a man who had the qualities which he himself did not possess. He could only see the request as a humiliation of his own precious dignity.

He managed to grin, trying to turn the request to mockery, and said, "Have you lost your mind?"

"No, Anson, not for a moment. What I ask is a simple thing. It has been done before."

He did not answer her at once, and began to move about the room in the deepest agitation, a strange figure curiously out of place in the midst of Horace Pentland's exotic, beautiful pictures and chairs and bibelots—as wrong in such a setting as he had been right a month or two earlier among the museum of Pentland family relics.

"No," he said again and again. "What you ask is preposterous! Tomorrow when you are less tired you will see how ridiculous it is. No. . . I couldn't think of such a thing!"

She made an effort to speak quietly. "Is it because you don't want to put yourself in such a position?"

"It has nothing to do with that. Why should you want a divorce? We are well off, content, comfortable, happy. . ."

She interrupted him, asking, "Are we?"

"What is it you expect, Olivia. . . to live always in a sort of romantic glow? We're happier than most."

"No," she said slowly. "I don't think happiness has ever meant much to you, Anson. Perhaps you're above such things as happiness and unhappiness. Perhaps you're more fortunate than most of us. I doubt if you have ever known happiness or unhappiness, for that matter. You've been uncomfortable when people annoyed you and got in your way, but. . . that's all. Nothing more than that. Happiness. . . I mean it in the sensible way. . . has sometimes to do with delight in living, and I don't think you've ever known that, even for a moment."

He turned toward her saying, "I've been an honest, God-fearing, conscientious man, and I think you're talking nonsense!"

"No, not for a moment. . . Heaven knows I ought to know the truth of what I've been saying."

Again they reached an impasse in the conversation and again they both remained silent, disturbed perhaps and uneasy in the consciousness that between them they had destroyed something which could never be restored; and yet with Olivia there was a cold, sustained sense of balance which came to her miraculously at such times. She felt, too, that she stood with her back against a wall, fighting. At last she said, "I would even let you divorce me—if that would be easier for you. I don't mind putting myself in the wrong."

Again he began to tremble. "Are you trying to tell me that. . ."

"I'm not telling you anything. There hasn't been anything at all. . . but. . . but I would give you grounds if you would agree."

He turned away from her in disgust. "That is even more impossible. . . A gentleman never divorces his wife."

"Let's leave the gentlemen out of it, Anson," she said. "I'm weary of hearing what gentlemen do and do not do. I want you to act as yourself, as Anson Pentland, and not as you think you ought to act. Let's be honest. You know you married me only because you had to marry someone. . . and I. . . I wasn't actually disreputable, even, as you remind me, if my father was shanty Irish. And. . . let's be just too. I married you because I was alone and frightened and wanted to escape a horrible life with Aunt Alice. . . I wanted a home. That was it, wasn't it? We are both guilty, but that doesn't change the reality in the least. No, I fancy you practised loving me through a sense of duty. You tried it as long as you could and you hated it always. Oh, I've known what was going on. I've been learning ever since I came to Pentlands for the first time."

He was regarding her now with a fixed expression of horrid fascination; he was perhaps even dazed at the sound of her voice, slowly, resolutely, tearing aside all the veils of pretense which had made their life possible for so long. He kept mumbling, "How can you talk this way? How can you say such things?"

Slowly, terribly, she went on and on: "We're both guilty. . . and it's been a failure, from the very start. I've tried to do my best and perhaps sometimes I've failed. I've tried to be a good mother. . . and now that Sybil is grown and Jack. . . is dead, I want a chance at freedom. I'm still young enough to want to live a little before it is too late."

Between his teeth he said, "Don't be a fool, Olivia. . . You're forty years old. . ."

"You needn't remind me of that. Tomorrow I shall be forty. I know it. . . bitterly. But my being forty makes no difference to you. To you it would be all the same if I were seventy. But to me it makes a difference . . . a great difference." She waited a moment, and then said, "That's the truth, Anson; and it's the truth that interests me tonight. Let me be free, Anson. . . Let me go while being free still means something."

Perhaps if she had thrown herself at his feet in the attitude of a wretched, shameful woman, if she had made him feel strong and noble and heroic, she would have won; but it was a thing she could not do. She could only go on being coldly reasonable.

"And you would give up all this?" he was saying. "You'd leave Pentlands and all it stands for to marry this cheap Irishman. . . a nobody, the son perhaps of an immigrant dock-laborer."

"He *is* the son of a dock-laborer," she answered quietly. "And his mother was a housemaid. He's told me so himself. And as to all this. . . Why, Anson, it doesn't mean anything to me. . . nothing at all that I can't give up, nothing which means very much. I'm fond of your father, Anson, and I'm fond of you when you are yourself and not talking about what a gentleman would do. But I'd give it all up. . . everything. . . for the sake of this other thing."

For a moment his lips moved silently and in agitation, as if it were impossible for him to answer things so preposterous as those his wife had just spoken. At last he was able to say, "I think you must have lost your mind, Olivia. . . to even think of asking such a thing of me. You've lived here long enough to know how impossible it is. Some of us must make a stand in a community. There has never been a scandal, or even a divorce, in the Pentland family. . . never. We've come to stand for something. Three hundred years of clean, moral living can't be dashed aside so easily. . . We're in a position where others look up to us. Can't you see that? Can't you understand such a responsibility?"

For a moment she had a terrible, dizzy, intoxicating sense of power, of knowing that she held the means of destroying him and all this whited structure of pride and respectability. She had only to begin by saying, "There was Savina Pentland and her lover. . ." The moment passed quickly and at once she knew that it was a thing she could not do. Instead, she murmured, "Ah, Anson, do you think the world really looks at us at all? Do you think it really cares what we do or don't do? You can't be as blind as that."

"I'm not blind. . . only there's such a thing as honor and tradition. We stand for something. . ."

She interrupted him. "For what?"

"For decency, for a glorious past, for stability. . . for endless things. . . all the things which count in a civilized community."

He really believed what he was saying; she knew that he must have believed it to have written all those thousands of dull, laborious words in glorification of the past.

He went on. "No, what you ask is impossible. You knew it before you asked. . . And it would be a kindness to me if you never mentioned it again."

He was still pale, but he had gained control of himself and his hands no longer trembled; as he talked, as his sense of virtue mounted, he even grew eloquent, and his voice took on a shade of that unction which had always colored the voice of the Apostle to the Genteel and made of him a celebrated and fashionable cleric. Perhaps for the first time since his childhood, since the days when the red-haired little Sabine had mocked his curls and velvet suits, he felt himself a strong and powerful person. There was a kind of fierce intoxication in the knowledge of his power over Olivia. In his virtuous ardor he seemed for a moment to become a positive, almost admirable person.

At length she said quietly, "And what if I should simply go away. . . without bothering about a divorce?"

The remark shattered all his confidence once more; and she knew that she had struck at the weakest point in all his defense—the fear of a scandal. "You wouldn't do that!" he cried. "You couldn't—you couldn't behave like a common prostitute!"

"Loving one man is not behaving like a common prostitute. . . I never loved any other."

"You couldn't bring such a disgrace on Sybil, even if you don't care for the rest of us."

("He knew, then, that I couldn't do such a thing, that I haven't the courage. He knows that I've lived too long in this world.") Aloud she said, "You don't know me, Anson. . . In all these years you've never known me at all."

"Besides," he added quickly, "he wouldn't do such a thing. Such a climber isn't likely to throw over his whole career by running away with a woman. You'd find out if you asked him."

"But he *is* willing. He's already told me so. Perhaps you can't understand such a thing." When he did not answer, she said ironically, "Besides, I don't think a gentleman would talk as you are talking. No,

Anson. . . I don't think you know what the world is. You've lived here always, shut up in your own little corner." Rising, she sighed and murmured, "But there's no use in talk. I am going to bed. . . I suppose we must struggle on as best we can. . . but there are times. . . times like tonight when you make it hard for me to bear it. Someday. . . who knows. . . there's nothing any longer to keep me. . ."

She went away without troubling to finish what she had meant to say, lost again in an overwhelming sense of the futility of everything. She felt, she thought, like an idiot standing in the middle of an empty field, making gestures.

Chapter X

I

Toward morning the still, breathless heat broke without warning into a fantastic storm which filled all the sky with blinding light and enveloped the whole countryside in a wild uproar of wind and thunder, leaving the dawn to reveal fields torn and ravaged and strewn with broken branches, and the bright garden bruised and battered by hail.

At breakfast Anson appeared neat and shaven and smooth, as though there had been no struggle a few hours before in the drawing room, as if the thing had made no impression upon the smooth surface which he turned toward the world. Olivia poured his coffee quietly and permitted him to kiss her as he had done everyday for twenty years—a strange, cold, absent-minded kiss—and stood in the doorway to watch him drive off to the train. Nothing had changed; it seemed to her that life at Pentlands had become incapable of any change.

And as she turned from the door Peters summoned her to the telephone to receive the telegram from Jean and Sybil; they had been married at seven in Hartford.

She set out at once to find John Pentland and after a search she came upon him in the stable yard talking with Higgins. The strange pair stood by the side of the red mare, who watched them with her small, vicious red eyes; they were talking in that curious intimate way which descended upon them at the mention of horses, and as she approached she was struck, as she always was, by the fiery beauty of the animal, the pride of her lean head, the trembling of the fine nostrils as she breathed, the savagery of her eye. She was a strange, half-evil, beautiful beast. Olivia heard Higgins saying that it was no use trying to breed her. . . an animal like that, who kicked and screamed and bit at the very sight of another horse. . .

Higgins saw her first and, touching his cap, bade her good-morning, and as the old man turned, she said, "I've news for you, Mr. Pentland."

A shrewd, queer look came into his eyes and he asked, "Is it about Sybil?"

"Yes. . . It's done."

She saw that Higgins was mystified, and she was moved by a desire to tell him. Higgins ought to know certainly among the first. And she added, "It's about Miss Sybil. She married young Mr. de Cyon this morning in Hartford."

The news had a magical effect on the little groom; his ugly, shriveled face expanded into a broad grin and he slapped his thigh in his enthusiasm. "That's grand, Ma'am. . . I don't mind telling you I was for it all along. She couldn't have done better. . . nor him either."

Again moved by impulse, she said, "So you think it's a good thing?"

"It's grand, Ma'am. He's one in a million. He's the only one I know who was good enough. I was afraid she was going to throw herself away on Mr. O'Hara. . . But she ought to have a younger man."

She turned away from him, pleased and relieved from the anxiety which had never really left her since the moment they drove off into the darkness. She kept thinking, "Higgins is always right about people. He has a second sight." Somehow, of them all, she trusted him most as a judge.

John Pentland led her away, out of range of Higgins' curiosity, along the hedge that bordered the gardens. The news seemed to affect him strangely, for he had turned pale, and for a long time he simply stood looking over the hedge in silence. At last he asked, "When did they do it?"

"Last night. . . She went for a drive with him and they didn't come back."

"I hope we've been right. . ." he said. "I hope we haven't connived at a foolish thing."

"No. . . I'm sure we haven't."

Something in the brilliance of the sunlight, in the certainty of Sybil's escape and happiness, in the freshness of the air touched after the storm by the first faint feel of autumn, filled her with a sense of giddiness, so that she forgot her own troubles; she forgot, even, that this was her fortieth birthday.

"Did they go in Sabine's motor?" he asked.

"Yes."

Grinning suddenly, he said, "She thought perhaps that she was doing us a bad turn."

"No, she knew that I approved. She did think of it first. She did propose it. . ."

When he spoke again there was a faint hint of bitterness in his voice. "I'm sure she did. I only hope she'll stop her mischief with this. In any case, she's had a victory over Cassie. . . and that's what she wanted, more than anything. . ." He turned toward her sharply, with an air of anxiety. "I suppose he'll take her away with him?"

"Yes. They're going to Paris first and then to the Argentine."

Suddenly he touched her shoulder with the odd, shy gesture of affection. "It'll be hard for you, Olivia dear. . . without her."

The sudden action brought a lump into her throat, and yet she did not want to be pitied. She hated pity, because it implied weakness on her part.

"Oh," she said quickly, "they'll come back from time to time. . . I think that someday they may come back here to live."

"Yes. . . Pentlands will belong to them one day."

And then for the first time she remembered that there was something which she had to tell him, something which had come to seem almost a confession. She must tell him now, especially since Jean would one day own all of Pentlands and all the fortune.

"There's something I didn't tell you before," she began. "It's something which I kept to myself because I wanted Sybil to have her happiness. . . in spite of everything."

He interrupted her, saying, "I know what it is."

"You couldn't know what I mean."

"Yes; the boy told me himself. I went to him to talk about Sybil because I wanted to make sure of him. . . and after a time he told me. It was an honorable thing for him to have done. He needn't have told. Sabine would never have told us. . . never until it was too late."

The speech left her feeling weak and disconcerted, for she had expected anger from him and disapproval. She had been fearful that he might treat her silence as a disloyalty to him, that it might in the end shatter the long, trusting relationship between them.

"The boy couldn't help it," he was saying. "It's a thing one can't properly explain. But he's a nice boy. . . and Sybil was so set on him. I think she has a good, sensible head on her young shoulders." Sighing and turning toward her again, he added, "I wouldn't speak of it to the others. . . not even to Anson. They may never know, and if they don't what they don't know won't hurt them."

The mystery of him, it seemed, grew deeper and deeper each time they talked thus, intimately, perhaps because there were in the old man depths which she had never believed possible. Perhaps, deep down beneath all the fierce reticence of his nature, there lay a humanity far greater than any she had ever encountered. She thought, "And I have always believed him hard and cold and disapproving." She was beginning to fathom the great strength that lay in his fierce isolation, the strength of a man who had always been alone.

"And you, Olivia?" he asked presently. "Are you happy?"

"Yes. . . At least, I'm happy this morning. . . on account of Sybil and Jean."

"That's right," he said with a gentle sadness. "That's right. They've done what you and I were never able to do, Olivia. They'll have what we've never had and never can have because it's too late. And we've helped them to gain it. . . That's something. I merely wanted you to know that I understood." And then, "We'd better go and tell the others. The devil will be to pay when they hear."

She would have gone away then, but an odd thought occurred to her, a hope, feeble enough, but one which might give him a little pleasure. She was struck again by his way of speaking, as if he were very near to death or already dead. He had the air of a very old and weary man.

She said, "There's one thing I've wanted to ask you for a long time." She hesitated and then plunged. "It was about Savina Pentland. Did she ever have more than one child?"

He looked at her sharply out of the bright black eyes and asked, "Why do you want to know that?"

She tried to deceive him by shrugging her shoulders and saying casually, "I don't know. . . I've become interested lately, perhaps on account of Anson's book."

"You. . . interested in the past, Olivia?"

"Yes."

"Yes, she only had one child. . . and then she was drowned when he was only a year old. He was my grandfather." Again he looked at her sharply. "Olivia, you must tell me the truth. Why did you ask me that question?"

Again she hesitated, saying, "I don't know. . . it seemed to me. . ."

"Did you find something? Did *she*," he asked, making the gesture toward the north wing, "did *she* tell you anything?"

She understood then that he, marvelous old man, must even know about the letters. "Yes," she said in a low voice, "I found something. . . in the attic."

He sighed and looked away again, across the wet meadows. "So you know, too. . . *She* found them first, and hid them away again. She wouldn't give them to me because she hated me. . . from our wedding-night. I've told you about that. And then she couldn't remember where she'd hid them. . . poor thing. But she told me about them. At times she used to taunt me by saying that I wasn't a Pentland at all. I think the thing made her mind darker than it was before. She had some terrible idea about the sin in my family for which she must atone. . ."

"It's true," said Olivia softly. "There's no doubt of it. It was written by Toby Cane himself. . . in his own handwriting. I've compared it with the letters Anson has of his." After a moment she asked, "And you. . . you've known it always?"

"Always," he said sadly. "It explains many things. . . Sometimes I think that those of us who have lived since have had to atone for their sin. It's all worked out in a harsh way, when you come to think of it. . ."

She guessed what it was he meant. She saw again that he believed in such a thing as sin, that the belief in it was rooted deeply in his whole being.

"Have you got the letters, Olivia?" he asked.

"No. . . I burned them. . . last night. . . because I was afraid of them. I was afraid that I might do something shameful with them. And if they were burned, no one would believe such a preposterous story and there wouldn't be any proof. I was afraid, too," she added softly, "of what was in them. . . not what was written there, so much as the way it was written."

He took her hand and with the oddest, most awkward gesture, kissed it gently. "You were right, Olivia dear," he said. "It's all they have. . . the others. . . that belief in the past. We daren't take that from them. The strong daren't oppress the weak. It would have been too cruel. It would have destroyed the one thing into which Anson poured his whole life. You see, Olivia, there are people. . . people like you. . . who have to be strong enough to look out for the others. It's a hard task. . . and sometimes a cruel one. If it weren't for such people the world would fall apart and we'd see it for the cruel, unbearable place it is. That's why I've trusted everything to you. That's what I was trying to tell you the other night. You see, Olivia, I know you. . . I know there are things which people like us can't do. . . Perhaps it's because we're weak or foolish— who knows? But it's true. I knew that you were the sort who would do just such a thing."

Listening to him, she again felt all her determination slipping from her. It was a strange sensation, as if he took possession of her, leaving her powerless to act, prisoning her again in that terrible wall of rightness in which he believed. The familiar sense of his strength frightened her, because it seemed a force so irresistible. It was the strength of one who was more than right; it was the strength of one who *believed*.

She had a fierce impulse to turn from him and to run swiftly, recklessly, across the wet meadows toward Michael, leaving forever behind her the placid, beautiful old house beneath the elms.

"There are some things," he was saying, "which it is impossible to do. . . for people like us, Olivia. They are impossible because the mere act of doing them would ruin us forever. They aren't things which we can do gracefully."

And she knew again what it was that he meant, as she had known vaguely while she stood alone in the darkness before the figures of Higgins and Miss Egan emerged from the mist of the marshes.

"You had better go now and telephone to Anson. I fancy he'll be badly upset, but I shall put an end to that. . . and Cassie, too. She had it all planned for the Mannering boy."

II

ANSON WAS NOT TO BE reached all the morning at the office; he had gone, so his secretary said, to a meeting of the Society of Guardians of Young Working Girls without Homes and left express word that he was not to be disturbed. But Aunt Cassie heard the news when she arrived on her morning call at Pentlands. Olivia broke it to her as gently as possible, but as soon as the old lady understood what had happened, she went to pieces badly. Her eyes grew wild; she wept, and her hair became all disheveled. She took the attitude that Sybil had been seduced and was now a woman lost beyond all hope. She kept repeating between punctuations of profound sympathy for Olivia in the hour of her trial, that such a thing had never happened in the Pentland family; until Olivia, enveloped in the old, perilous calm, reminded her of the elopement of Jared Pentland and Savina Dalgedo and bade her abruptly to stop talking nonsense.

And then Aunt Cassie was deeply hurt by her tone, and Peters had to be sent away for smelling-salts at the very moment that Sabine arrived, grinning and triumphant. It was Sabine who helped administer the smelling-salts with the grim air of administering burning coals. When the old lady grew a little more calm she fell again to saying over

　　　　　　　　　　　　　　　　　　　LOUIS BROMFIELD

and over again, "Poor Sybil. . . My poor, innocent little Sybil. . . that this should have happened to her!"

To which Olivia replied at last, "Jean is a fine young man. I'm sure she couldn't have done better." And then, to soften a little Aunt Cassie's anguish, she said, "And he's very rich, Aunt Cassie. . . a great deal richer than many a husband she might have found here."

The information had an even better effect than the smelling-salts, so that the old lady became calm enough to take an interest in the details and asked where they had found a motor to go away in.

"It was mine," said Sabine dryly. "I loaned it to them."

The result of this statement was all that Sabine could have desired. The old lady sat bolt upright, all bristling, and cried, with an air of suffocation, "Oh, you viper! Why God should have sent me such a trial, I don't know. You've always wished us evil and now I suppose you're content! May God have mercy on your malicious soul!" And breaking into fresh sobs, she began all over again, "My poor, innocent little Sybil. . . What will people say? What will they think has been going on!"

"Don't be evil-minded, Aunt Cassie," said Sabine sharply; and then in a calmer voice, "It will be hard on me. . . I won't be able to go to Newport until they come back with the motor."

"You! . . . You! . . ." began Aunt Cassie, and then fell back, a broken woman.

"I suppose," continued Sabine ruthlessly, "that we ought to tell the Mannering boy."

"Yes," cried Aunt Cassie, reviving again. "Yes! There's the boy she ought to have married. . ."

"And Mrs. Soames," said Sabine. "She'll be pleased at the news."

Olivia spoke for the first time in nearly half an hour. "It's no use. Mr. Pentland has been over to see her, but she didn't understand what it was he wanted to tell her. She was in a daze. . . only half-conscious. . . and they think she may not recover this time."

In a whisper, lost in the greater agitation of Aunt Cassie's sobs, she said to Sabine, "It's like the end of everything for him. I don't know what he'll do."

THE CONFUSION OF THE DAY seemed to increase rather than to die away. Aunt Cassie was asked to stay to lunch, but she said it was impossible to consider swallowing even a crust of bread. "It would choke me!" she cried melodramatically.

"It is an excellent lunch," urged Olivia.

"No. . . no. . . don't ask me!"

But, unwilling to quit the scene of action, she lay on Horace Pentland's Regence sofa and regained her strength a little by taking a nap while the others ate.

At last Anson called, and when the news was told him, the telephone echoed with his threats. He would, he said, hire a motor (an extravagance by which to guage the profundity of his agitation) and come down at once.

And then, almost immediately, Michael telephoned. "I have just come down," he said, and asked Olivia to come riding with him. "I must talk to you at once."

She refused to ride, but consented to meet him halfway, at the pine thicket where Higgins had discovered the foxcubs. "I can't leave just now," she told him, "and I don't think it's best for you to come here at the moment."

For some reason, perhaps vaguely because she thought he might use the knowledge as a weapon to break down her will, she said nothing of the elopement. For in the confusion of the day, beneath all the uproar of scenes, emotions and telephone-calls, she had been thinking, thinking, thinking, so that in the end the uproar had made little impression upon her. She had come to understand that John Pentland must have lived thus, year after year, moving always in a secret life of his own, and presently she had come to the conclusion that she must send Michael away once and for all.

As she moved across the meadow she noticed that the birches had begun to turn yellow and that in the low ground along the river the meadows were already painted gold and purple by masses of goldenrod and ironweed. With each step she seemed to grow weaker and weaker, and as she drew near the blue-black wall of pines she was seized by a violent trembling, as if the sense of his presence were able somehow to reach out and engulf her even before she saw him. She kept trying to think of the old man as he stood beside her at the hedge, but something stronger than her will made her see only Michael's curly black head and blue eyes. She began even to pray. . . she (Olivia) who never prayed because the piety of Aunt Cassie and Anson and the Apostle to the Genteel stood always in her way.

And then, looking up, she saw him standing half-hidden among the lower pines, watching her. She began to run toward him, in terror lest her knees should give way and let her fall before she reached the shelter of the trees.

In the darkness of the thicket where the sun seldom penetrated, he put his arms about her and kissed her in a way he had never done before, and the action only increased her terror. She said nothing; she only wept quietly; and at last, when she had gained control of herself, she struggled free and said, "Don't, Michael. . . please don't. . . please."

They sat on a fallen log and, still holding her hand, he asked, "What is it? What has happened?"

"Nothing. . . I'm just tired."

"Are you willing to come away with me? Now?" And in a low, warm voice, he added, "I'll never let you be tired again. . . never."

She did not answer him, because it seemed to her that what she had to tell him made all her actions in the past seem inexplicable and cheap. She was filled with shame, and tried to put off the moment when she must speak.

"I haven't been down in three days," he was saying, "because there's been trouble in Boston which made it impossible. I've only slept an hour or two a night. They've been trying to do me in. . . some of the men I always trusted. They've been double-crossing me all along and I had to stay to fight them."

He told her a long and complicated story of treachery, of money having been passed among men whom he had known and trusted always. He was sad and yet defiant, too, and filled with a desire to fight the thing to an end. She failed to understand the story; indeed she did not even hear much of it: she only knew that he was telling her everything, pouring out all his sadness and trouble to her as if she were the one person in all the world to whom he could tell such things.

And when he had finished he waited for a moment and then said, "And now I'm willing to chuck the whole dirty business and quit. . . to tell them all to go to hell."

Quickly she answered, "No, you mustn't do that. You can't do that. A man like you, Michael, daren't do such a thing. . ." For she knew that without a battle life would mean nothing to him.

"No. . . I mean it. I'm ready to quit. I want you to go with me."

She thought, "He says this. . . and yet he stayed three days and nights in Boston to fight!" She saw that he was not looking at her, but sitting with his head in his hands; there was something broken, almost pitiful, in his manner, and it occurred to her that perhaps for the first time he found all his life in a hopeless tangle. She thought, "If I had never known him, this might not have happened. He would have been able to fight without even thinking of me."

Aloud she said, "I can't do it, Michael. . . It's no use. I can't."

He looked up quickly, but before he could speak she placed her hand over his lips, saying, "Wait, Michael, let me talk first. Let me say what I've wanted to say for so long. . . I've thought. . . I've done nothing else but think day and night for the past three days. And it's no good, Michael. . . It's no good. I'm forty years old today, and what can I give you that will make up for all you will lose? Why should you give up everything for me? No, I've nothing to offer. You can go back and fight and win. It's what you like more than anything in the world. . . more than any woman. . . even me."

Again he tried to speak, but she silenced him. "Oh, I know it's true. . . what I say. And if I had you at such a price, you'd only hate me in the end. I couldn't do it, Michael, because. . . because in the end, with men like you it's work, it's a career, which is first. . . You couldn't bear giving up. You couldn't bear failure. . . And in the end that's right, as it should be. It's what keeps the world going."

He was watching her with a look of fascination in his eyes, and she knew—she was certain of it—that he had never been so much in love with her before; but she knew, too, from the shadow which crossed his face (it seemed to her that he almost winced) and because she knew him so well, that he recognized the truth of what she had said.

"It's not true, Olivia. . . You can't go back on me now. . . just when I need you most."

"I'd be betraying you, Michael, if I did the other thing. It's not me you need half so much as the other thing. Oh, I know that I'm right. What you should have in the end is a young woman. . . a woman who will help you. It doesn't matter very much whether you're terribly in love with her or not. . . but a woman who can be your wife and bear your children and give dinner parties and help make of you the famous man you've always meant to be. You need someone who will help you to found a family, to fill your new house with children. . . someone who'll help you and your children to take the place of families like ours who are at the end of things. No, Michael. . . I'm right. . . Look at me," she commanded suddenly. "Look at me and you'll know that it's not because I don't love you."

LOUIS BROMFIELD

He was on his knees now, on the carpet of scented pine-needles, his arms about her while she stroked the thick black hair with a kind of hysterical intensity.

"You don't know what you're saying, Olivia. It's not true! It's not true! I'd give up everything. . . I don't want the other thing. I'll sell my farm and go away from here forever with you."

"Yes, Michael, you think that today, just now. . . and tomorrow everything will be changed. That's one of the mean tricks Nature plays us. It's not so simple as that. We're not like Higgins and. . . the kitchen-maid. . . at least not in some ways."

"Olivia. . . Olivia, do you love me enough to. . ."

She knew what he meant to ask. She thought, "What does it matter? Why should I not, when I love him so? I should be harming no one. . . no one but myself."

And then, abruptly, through the mist of tears she saw through an opening in the thicket a little procession crossing the meadows toward the big house at Pentlands. She saw it with a terrible, intense clarity. . . a little procession of the gardener and his helper carrying between them on a shutter a figure that lay limp and still, and following them came Higgins on foot, leading his horse and moving with the awkward rolling gait which afflicted him when his feet were on the ground. She knew who the still figure was. It was John Pentland. The red mare had killed him at last. And she heard him saying, "There are some things which people like us, Olivia, can't do."

WHAT HAPPENED IMMEDIATELY AFTERWARD SHE was never able to remember very clearly. She found herself joining the little procession; she knew that Michael was with her, and that there could be no doubt of the tragedy. . . John Pentland was dead, with his neck broken. He lay on the shutter, still and peaceful, the bitter lines all melted from the grim, stern face, as he had been when she came upon him in the library smelling of dogs and woodsmoke and whisky. Only this time he had escaped for good. . .

And afterward she remembered telling Michael, as they stood alone in the big white hall, that Sybil and Jean were married, and dismissing him by saying, "*Now*, Michael, it is impossible. While he was living I might have done it. . . I might have gone away. But now it's impossible. Don't ask me. Please leave me in peace."

Standing there under the wanton gaze of Savina Pentland, she watched him go away, quietly, perhaps because he understood that all she had said was true.

III

IN THE TRAGEDY THE ELOPEMENT became lost and forgotten. Doctors came and went; even reporters put in an awkward appearance, eager for details of the death and the marriage in the Pentland family, and somehow the confusion brought peace to Olivia. They forgot her, save as one who managed everything quietly; for they had need just then of someone who did not break into wild spasms of grief or wander about helplessly. In the presence of death, Anson forgot even his anger over the elopement, and late in the afternoon Olivia saw him for the first time when he came to her helplessly to ask, "The men have come to photograph the portraits. What shall we do?"

And she answered, "Send them away. We can photograph ancestors anytime. They'll always be with us."

Sabine volunteered to send word to Sybil and Jean. At such times all her cold-blooded detachment made of her a person of great value, and Olivia knew that she could be trusted to find them because she wanted her motor again desperately. Remembering her promise to the old man, she went across to see Mrs. Soames, but nothing came of it, for the old lady had fallen into a state of complete unconsciousness. She would, they told Olivia, probably die without ever knowing that John Pentland had gone before her.

Aunt Cassie took up her throne in the darkened drawing room and there, amid the acrid smell of the first chrysanthemums of the autumn, she held a red-eyed, snuffling court to receive the calls of all the countryside. Again she seemed to rise for a time triumphant and strong, even overcoming her weakness enough to go and come from the gazeboed house on foot, arriving early and returning late. She insisted upon summoning Bishop Smallwood to conduct the services, and discovered after much trouble that he was attending a church conference in the West. In reply to her telegram she received only an answer that it was impossible for him to return, even if they delayed the funeral. . . that in the role of prominent defender of the Virgin Birth he could not leave the field at a moment when the power of his party was threatened.

It seemed for a time that, as Sabine had hoped, the whole structure of the family was falling about them in ruins.

As for Olivia, she would have been at peace save that three times within two days notes came to her from Michael—notes which she sent back unopened because she was afraid to read them; until at last she wrote on the back of one, "There is nothing more to say. Leave me in peace." And after that there was only silence, which in a strange way seemed to her more unbearable than the sight of his writing. She discovered that two persons had witnessed the tragedy—Higgins, who had been riding with the old man, and Sabine, who had been walking the river path—walking only because Jean and Sybil had her motor. Higgins knew only that the mare had run off and killed his master; but Sabine had a strangely different version, which she recounted to Olivia as they sat in her room, the day after.

"I saw them," she said, "coming across the meadow. . . Cousin John, with Higgins following. And then, all at once, the mare seemed to be frightened by something and began to run. . . straight in a line for the gravel-pit. It was a fascinating sight. . . a horrible sight. . . because I knew—I was certain—what was going to happen. For a moment Cousin John seemed to fight with her, and then all at once he leaned forward on her neck and let her go. Higgins went after him; but it was no use trying to catch her. . . One might as well have tried to overtake a whirlwind. They seemed to fly across the fields straight for the line of elders that hid the pit, and I knew all the while that there was no saving them unless the mare turned. At the bushes the mare jumped. . . the prettiest jump I've ever seen a horse make, straight above the bushes into the open air. . ."

For a moment Sabine's face was lighted by a macabre enthusiasm. Her voice wavered a little. "It was a horrible, beautiful sight. For a moment they seemed almost to rise in the air as if the mare were flying, and then all at once they fell. . . into the bottom of the pit."

Olivia was silent, and presently, as if she had been waiting for the courage, Sabine continued in a low voice, "But there's one thing I saw beyond any doubt. At the edge of the pit the mare tried to turn. She would have turned away, but Cousin John raised his crop and struck her savagely. There was no doubt of it. He forced her over the elders. . ." Again after a pause, "Higgins must have seen it, too. He followed them to the very edge of the pit. I shall always see him there, sitting on his horse outlined against the sky. He was looking down into the pit and for a moment the horse and man together looked exactly like a centaur. . . It was an extraordinary impression."

She remembered him thus, but she remembered him, too, as she had seen him on the night of the ball, slipping away through the lilacs like a shadow. Rising, she said, "Jean and Sybil will be back tomorrow, and then I'll be off for Newport. I thought you might want to know what Higgins and I knew, Olivia." For a moment she hesitated, looking out of the window toward the sea. And at last she said, "He was a queer man. He was the last of the great Puritans. There aren't anymore. None of the rest of us believe anything. We only pretend. . ."

But Olivia scarcely heard her. She understood now why it was that the old man had talked to her as if he were very near to death, and she thought, "He did it in a way that none would ever discover. He trusted Higgins, and Sabine was an accident. Perhaps. . . perhaps. . . he did it to keep me here. . . to save the thing he believed in all his life."

It was a horrible thought which she tried to kill, but it lingered, together with the regret that she had never finished what she had begun to tell him as they stood by the hedge talking of the letters—that one day Jean might take the name of John Pentland. He had, after all, as much right to it as he had to the name of de Cyon; it would be only a little change, but it would allow the name of Pentland to go on and on. All the land, all the money, all the tradition, would go down to Pentland children, and so make a reason for their existence; and in the end the name would be something more then than a thing embalmed in "The Pentland Family and the Massachusetts Bay Colony." The descendants would be, after all, of Pentland blood, or at least of the blood of Savina Dalgedo and Toby Cane, which had come long ago to be Pentland blood.

And she thought grimly, "He was right, after all. I am one of them at last. . . in spite of everything. It's I who am carrying on now."

ON THE MORNING OF THE funeral, as she stood on the terrace expecting Jean and Sybil, Higgins, dressed in his best black suit and looking horribly awkward and ill at ease, came toward her to say, looking away from her, "Mr. O'Hara is going away. They're putting up a 'For Sale' sign on his gate. He isn't coming back." And then looking at her boldly he added, "I thought you might want to know, Mrs. Pentland."

　　　　　　　　　　　　　　　　　　LOUIS BROMFIELD

For a moment she had a sudden, fierce desire to cry out, "No, he mustn't go! You must tell him to stay. I can't let him go away like that!" She wanted suddenly to run across the fields to the bright, vulgar, new house, to tell him herself. She thought, "He meant, then, what he said. He's given up everything here."

But she knew, too, that he had gone away to fight, freed now and moved only by his passion for success, for victory.

And before she could answer Higgins, who stood there wanting her to send him to Michael, Miss Egan appeared, starched and rigid and wearing the professional expression of solemnity which she adopted in the presence of bereaved families. She said, "It's about *her*, Mrs. Pentland. She seems very bright this morning and quite in her right mind. She wants to know why he hasn't been to see her for two whole days. I thought. . ."

Olivia interrupted her quietly. "It's all right," she said. "I'll go and tell her. I'll explain. It's better for me to do it."

She went away into the house, knowing bitterly that she left Miss Egan and Higgins thinking of her with pity.

As she climbed the worn stair carpet to the north wing, she knew suddenly a profound sense of peace such as she had not known for years. It was over and done now, and life would go on the same as it had always done, filled with trickiness and boredom and deceits, but pleasant, too, in spite of everything, perhaps because, as John Pentland had said, "One had sometimes to pretend." And, after all, Sybil had escaped and was happy.

She knew now that she herself would never escape; she had been too long a part of Pentlands, and she knew that what the old man had said was the truth. She had acted thus not because of duty, or promises, or nobility, or pride, or even out of virtue. . . Perhaps it was even because she was not strong enough to do otherwise. But she knew that she had acted thus because, as he said, "There are things, Olivia, which people like us can't do."

And as she moved along the narrow hall, she saw from one of the deep-set windows the figure of Sabine moving along the lane in a faint cloud of dust, and nearer at hand, at the entrance of the elm-bordered drive, Aunt Cassie in deep black, coming along briskly in a cloud of crape. No, nothing had changed. It would go on and on. . .

The door opened and the sickly odor of medicines flooded the hallway. Out of the darkness came the sound of a feeble, reed-like voice, terrible in its sanity, saying, "Oh, it's you, Olivia. I knew you'd come. I've been waiting for you. . ."

THE END

Cold Spring Harbor, Long Island
June 4, 1925
St. Jean-de-Luz, B. P., France
July 21, 1926

A Note About the Author

At one point considered to be, "the most promising of all the young American authors writing today," Louis Bromfield (1896–1956) was a bestselling author and dedicated conservationist. Beginning with his first novel, *The Green Bay Tree* (1924) Bromfield would consistently produce books that were both critical and commercial darlings such as *Possession* (1925), *Early Autumn* (1926), and *A Good Woman* (1927) with *Early Autumn* securing him a Pulitzer in 1927. Later in life, his books would see a shift from themes of family and tradition to those of agriculture and sustainability as he became more involved with the environmental movement and brought his focus to the creation of the experimental Malabar Farm in Ohio.

A Note from the Publisher

Spanning many genres, from non-fiction essays to literature classics to children's books and lyric poetry, Mint Edition books showcase the master works of our time in a modern new package. The text is freshly typeset, is clean and easy to read, and features a new note about the author in each volume. Many books also include exclusive new introductory material. Every book boasts a striking new cover, which makes it as appropriate for collecting as it is for gift giving. Mint Edition books are only printed when a reader orders them, so natural resources are not wasted. We're proud that our books are never manufactured in excess and exist only in the exact quantity they need to be read and enjoyed.

bookfinity™

Discover more of your favorite classics with Bookfinity™.

- Track your reading with custom book lists.
- Get great book recommendations for your personalized Reader Type.
- Add reviews for your favorite books.
- AND MUCH MORE!

Visit **bookfinity.com** and take the fun Reader Type quiz to get started.

Enjoy our classic and modern companion pairings!

Classic & Modern

Printed in the USA
CPSIA information can be obtained
at www.ICGtesting.com
JSHW021512091023
49904JS00009B/55